A Tale
of Two
Tweeps

Andrew Voller
@NatureandRobots

A. Vohwer

Thank you very much to all of my **Twitter followers** for their many kind words of encouragement and outrageous laughter which takes the edge off life. I really appreciate everyone's friendship and support.

Many thanks to BFF **Mimi the Bug** who has tried to gaslight me on multiple occasions and failed. Thank you to the following **cool tweeps** for being there for me at the right time: **Maribeth** who is layered like nachos; decent guy and songwriter **BardsAntiquity**; and truehearted smartass **Alice** from California. And a special thanks to my **mum** who really has been the best mum anyone could hope for.

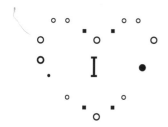

Contents

Preface

What's up with Twitter? I thought I would become famous in a week or two.

My twitter book was primarily **written to entertain** social media enthusiasts, yet please feel free to read into the deeper levels and thought-provoking concepts as well. I wrote the novel hoping one day it would be turned into one of those highly entertaining and ludicrous action movies just within the realms of possibility. Scarlett Johansson would play Juliet, Brad Pitt as Ryan and Jason Momoa, Flynn.

I've got some silly dreams but they're all mine.

This black comedy also shows you some of the **perils of technology** in your life. Millions of people are addicted to the escapism mobile phones and game consoles give you. Electronic simulations of life can create multiple personalities, splitting your life in two. Generally speaking, technology takes jobs away and makes people unhappy, whereas being in nature makes you very content. Be aware that technology is your aide and entertainment, not your master.

Twitter is not your life; it's entertainment. If that entertainment turns to upsetting you, it's time to take a break and walk with nature instead.

I don't want my daughters or anyone's children to live in an emotionally cold dystopia where robots or clones have removed everyone's purpose in life. Our sinister billionaire global rulers are working towards AI removing the need for the masses to even exist. I believe their evil plan will fail because us everyday folk who do all the real work are far more intelligent, creative and resourceful than greedy individuals who inherit their power. Technology is a **battle against love**.

You can follow the crowd or follow your heart.

This novel is loosely inspired by **a true story** I came across on Twitter of a woman being stalked. Her creepy pursuer initially manipulated her with lies and fake friendship to find out a few personal facts, and then began an unprovoked campaign of hatred and harassment. After blocking and complaining to the police about him, she moved house and shortly after received a message from her stalker saying, "Watch out because your new house is built on a flood plain," sending a Google Street View picture of her home with the correct address attached, promising to visit her.

Is it normal for men to DM you without having established any rapport? It feels wrong.

So there's no confusion, I have written 100% of the tweets interjected throughout this work of fiction, as well as the novel itself obviously. I want **'thinking for yourself'** to be the new fashion and fashion to become extinct because it puts too much pressure on everyone to conform. Don't listen to me though because I got blocked by someone with only three followers, including me, and see that as an achievement. Anyway, the most popular tweets don't have any real point to them, like this one:

Is that guy still alive? You know, the one who said no women over 35 are attractive.

In a few fragmented parts of this novel you explore a magnificent painting called the 'Metamorphosis of Narcissus' (1937) by the famous eccentric Spanish artist **Salvador Dali**. Its subconscious themes and alternative interpretations lead you into a criminal riddle which needs solving. To make life easy for you, a picture of Dali's interesting surrealist painting is on the back cover.

You will only start your creative journey when you realize our system is built on lies.

There's definitely something magical about making someone thousands of miles away laugh. So now you are about to enter one controlled cube of chaos in our galaxy: the Twittersphere! Hang out with me because I'm not cool but at least I know it. **Beware**: some extreme swear words or fictional situations in this novel could cause offence.

I will never forget my first followers on Twitter who helped me lose my nerves, become comfortable on the Twitter sofa and then spiked my expectations before abusing my virginity. Thank you for taking my good intentions and suffocating them face down in a rough pillow. Love me. ♥

Main Characters
(in order of appearance)

Juliet J. Green (the heroine)
Ryan Moore (love interest)
God (in the sky)
Shirley (one of a kind)
Caesar (serpent and maniac)
Bagel (a cat with covert narcissism)
Flynn O'Connell (mystery man)
Justine (black orchid)
Abigail (survivor of man-made lies)
Dr. Sheink (sinister psychologist)
Professor Zinkel (mad scientist)
Apollo (a wolfdog with samurai skills)

1

Hope of Love

Have faith in humanity and nature, not society. Society is a rusty tin can floating in stagnant water. The air and politics are poisonous. Your emotions need to absorb sunshine, rivers and trees instead. Take your feelings for a nice walk in the woods to remember who you are otherwise you'll be stuck indoors playing the evil fiddle of social media.

Nevertheless, in one such fucked up fantasy world called TWITTER was a beautiful story of true love that will reignite your faith in humanity. If you have the courage to walk into your own darkness to find yourself, you will discover that evil hasn't the stamina and integrity of the light of goodness which love provides.

Save nearly all your love for those who deserve it. Just now and then hide a little love in a safe place for a stranger to find.

One warm summer nighttime, two future lovers looked at The Big Dipper from neighbouring US States wondering if their true love was out there in the expanding universe. Without question *the* one exists. Finding that special person though is the biggest problem you are likely to face in your life apart from the sombre curtain of death whom no-one can out perform. Love is a field of wild flowers which sway to your dreams.

The heroes in this real-life tale are extraordinary people with average lives; which could easily describe virtually all of us. **JULIET** was a modest hairdresser who lived in Manhattan, New York: @911Nightingale. And **RYAN** was a sturdy park ranger who lived in Pawtucket, Rhode Island: @KingKong6393. Both were single and decent people destined to meet along the precarious path of life filled with good graces and wickedness.

When life hands you an empty sandwich, roll your sleeves up and fill it with your own homemade destiny.

The real world was a fickle place to our star Juliet because she was unique. She felt it was full of fake personalities and too many people with the attention span of a goldfish. Juliet wanted romance, travelling and simply just more from a society that offers normal people very little hope or money. She had always seen the moon as a symbol of hope and had no idea why. Juliet was a smart cookie with a heart of gold and deserved much better.

Ryan also felt the same way about our shocking lack of community and he travelled deeper into his soul to find a valid reason to keep going. His sanctuary was nature and Juliet's was poetry. She loved words and when a moment of tranquillity fell into her mind like snow on white fields, Juliet could write elegant verse to rival keen poets:

A silky white angel ready to marry the world's
hope,

Stands at a doorway all soapy and clean
Like every man's dream.

She's only young but believes in Karma
And is already a farmer

17

Of good ideas beyond her years.
Her signature is no dilemma,
Now as a glorious white swan forever.

And Ryan the naturalist thought that life is about the sky and seas, and he was happiest among tress. Ryan believed if you love nature and it will love you back. Both Juliet and Ryan were outdoors people who lived their lives with eternal values, adding positivity and charisma to an indoor society.

I've only ever been disappointed by people. Animals and nature have been a true pleasure.

It was late June and warm raindrops gave the promise of a hot summer as Ryan sat under a tree to let the passing shower be. He munched into a crisp red apple overseeing a green hilltop view and looked down in mock despair as he randomly signed up for Twitter on his iPhone. It felt surreal, like a dream or another world. To him this was a sorrowful defeat of some kind; technology beating nature.

Ryan was a philosophical rock but couldn't take away an uncomfortable lonely and lingering feeling he'd felt for a few months now. Joining Twitter was an attempt to reach out to the world he was no longer looking at. Ryan Moore was more divorced from the world than a lonely soul, if you catch the meaning to his melancholy. Being a hard worker and lover of nature he had sternly resisted the evil pull of social media for years, but a biological urge to find a mate broke his stoical principles. Principles are only for people who can afford them and despite being a handsome man, Ryan was a weathered forty seven years old and unlucky in love. He was a kind man but no pushover who made you feel like sunshine behind curtains every morning where momma had just made fresh syrupy pancakes downstairs.

About 4 hours drive away in The Big Apple, Juliet had just opened a brand new Twitter account to shake off all the perverts following her very successful previous 3 year account. She uploaded a new avi at exactly the same time Ryan did because God in the sky had ordained it so. God is often a perfectly reasonable explanation for strange coincidences, including alien abductions.

Juliet's original motivation for signing up was loneliness too and her reason for believing in God was the same. She was bored cutting hair off people's heads which grows about 1mm a day. Life seemed never-ending, but not in a romantic way. Juliet wondered if perhaps Twitter could spice up her mundane lifestyle full of insincere men just wanting to hump her cootie.

Juliet

@911Nightingale

Run your fingers through my hair and tell me you love cult movies. Your penis is fine in your pants, thanx.

⊚ Manhattan, NY

The problem Juliet and Ryan now both faced though were the flocks of angry victims on Twitter venting their personal frustrations to total strangers. Honour and integrity is dead these days, replaced by the biggest killer of souls; Materialism. Thankfully, some special souls carrying kindness shine through. In this shitheap society the only thing that really matters is finding people who will be kind to you.

If Juliet and Ryan could wade through the black Twitter treacle of confused liberalism without hanging themselves, they would certainly deserve to meet and fall happily in love forever. But first they had to be hazed by insanely popular groups of vain twits blocking real, sincere tweeps from being heard.

You're not uncool, you just don't want to spend your whole waking life pretending to be cool like superficial people do.

Twitter is honestly like nothing you will ever encounter. It can become more acidic and hurtful than your 'real life' because people talk truthfully on there, just like children do. In fact, some people feel the whole point of Twitter is to be a tad childish, completely fuck up your arguments and still hold your head up high. Basically, you create a persona which is a thousand times better than you are which slowly erodes your real life. Using Twitter is like talking to yourself with purpose.

Everyone who joins Twitter is at some point forced to question that decision. It would however be super easy to leave this egotistical venting machine, were it not for the large handful of excellent humans you get to know. Your only hope of escape is to have your family secretly arrange a Twitter obsession intervention, or by melodramatically throwing your phone into a lake like it's Excalibur.

When tweeting away all day, you'll suffocate as many bad replies with lols as you drown misery with emojis. If you get dragged into a Twitter argument, always approach with loose shoulders, a pinch of salt and wry sense of humour. In brief, Twitter is an open notepad for your life and thoughts, and may be one of the few places on planet Earth where you can joke around with people who would like to murder you.

Twitter can be your vice or inspiration. You choose.

So what is this crazy loony bin of an electronic environment preventing everyone from going outside for nice walks in the sunshine? A few mad tweeps believe it is a secret recruitment agency for the Borg. Other people believe its main appeal is that unattractive people can flirt with the beautiful people, which would never happen in real life. It breaks down social boundaries. Many peeps like to talk politics and can't wait to call President Trump a cunt. There are as many reasons for joining as there are people, but the truth is that tits are definitely more popular than brains on Twitter. If they banned cleavage, really clever women would finally be heard.

Whatever high-tech animal Twitter is, Juliet and Ryan would soon find out and have their personalities tested to the absolute limit. **GOD** was overseeing proceedings somewhere out there in the ether, but He was the old fashioned type who himself struggled to fathom what Twitter was all about and also felt a little depressed that humans had turned out so fucking disappointingly. God originally created a fixed plan, but now wished he'd been much more mentally flexible.

There is every good reason in the world to run your whole life on your instincts because they never let you down.

2

Humans Should Be Meerkats

To communicate his good intentions, God had the ignominy of having to buy the latest smartphone from a greed-based consumerist society *he* himself opposed. The Almighty suddenly felt claustrophobic and questioned the good of creating a species which trapped itself in a zoo it made.

God scrolled through reams and reams of people complaining about nothing and frustratingly shouted, "Damn it!" blaspheming himself, "I've created a monster! They were originally supposed to be like meerkats. And what's this stuff about dozens of genders? That wasn't part of the grand plan." He worried that Twitter was turning people into the most fake versions of themselves. Then God's deeply concerned mood rapidly changed as thunderous laughter boomed across the universe when he came across a few amusing tweets:

A woman said, "I don't need men to handle my shit!"

And I replied, "You do know they've invented toilet paper."

Then she blocked me. Good luck in the big bad world dear lady.

"Ha, ha, haaa!" bellowed God as he came across another good one:

What's your most used chat up line?

Reply: I'm taking you home. Please don't make me use the hammer.

God flicked his finger frantically across the screen for another joke. He was tired of being criticized all the time and just wanted a good laugh like everyone else:

When a doctor checks your mouth for tonsillitis, where exactly are you meant to look?

Reply: Deep into their eyes to see if there's a love connection.

He was booming out bursts of sunshine until the rally of stress-relieving humour was soon cut short when a party pooper posted this:

I'm beginning to question the overall sanity levels displayed on Twitter. Some people are actually normal on here. And some lunatics even believe God is going to help them.

God then returned to his Twitter account and was truly flabbergasted by the negativity it was attracting. Calling himself **The Last Word** to act incognito was not a great move. His Holiness had been away from Earth for a long time sorting out shit he screwed up in other galaxies too. His conscience finally decided to dust itself down and sort out this mess of humanity once and for all! But after just 10 minutes on Twitter, God realised this would be impossible. Sometimes what you start can't be finished or even fixed by you. So in a panic, God then decided to repeat his mistakes and lower his expectations by picking another hopeful couple again. He would obviously not be able to organise the shit storm that human greed had caused. Second best is better than nothing, thought God lying to himself, "I shall create a perfect world of love for two deserving contestants this time." But first he had to understand and research the nature of the Twitter beast, turned slippery leviathan.

You can learn a lot from Twitter. Only joking. All you'll learn is that an embarrassing amount of people think Psychology is a Hitchcock film.

On Twatter, 321 million international users hide behind the cowardly shield of their smartphones with no chance of retribution. That is originally why they are called smart phones. Welcome to the largest collection of confused sound bites and the most poetic bullshit you will *ever* hear in your entire life!

Whereas Instagram is for vain people who can't string a sentence together and Facebook is there to pretend your life is much better than it is, the whole point of Twitter is to list every last problem you have so total strangers can discuss it for hours on end. This psychologically warped social media game was perfectly designed to stamp adverts into lonely people's heads and promote rich people whilst you think you are making friends. You can put a lot of effort into social media and get very little back. And going through Twitter notifications can feel like homework. The main thing is great ideas are ignored in favour of smut.

I've worked out a practical formula based on the Fibonacci sequence for curing mental illness. (2 likes)

I've got a vagina like a ham sandwich which I call my cheese cellar! (92,156 likes)

God perused this antagonistic platform with astonishment and prayed that he could go back in time and support his son more. This was a place where its own users voted in a poll they thought elephants and dolphins were over three times more mentally stable than people. And the way some random men spoke to women on Twitter was nothing short of disgusting.

Twitter poll: What do you think women most like to be called?

Intelligent & thoughtful	45%
Beautiful and elegant	18%
A leader and inspiration	17%
Sexy and desirable	20%
296 votes • Final results	

Honestly, some people on Twitter are unbelievable. You can't say boo to a goose these days without offending someone's sensibilities. Do we all really want a society where everyone is repressed and free thoughts go underground, becoming more dangerous?

Twitter is where many twats start invisible fights over absolutely nothing and random pictures of penises wave around women's faces. In the space of just 24 hours, strangers can meet for the first time, become best friends or even lovers and then hate each other's guts, ending with threats of violence or death.

For example, one very, very ordinary man called **NEVILLE** fancied himself as a bit of a smooth flowing poet and Casanova in his spare time. In real life he was a routine tax inspector from Scotland. But on Twitter Neville called himself Don Juan and late one night came across a Sultry Sultana (her handle on life) who was home-grown in Carolina, USA. On Twitter you're either a comedian, a healer, a moaner, a pervert or prophet, boring, own a snake or tattoo, or you're a miserable man called Jack from Wales. Neville was a pervert and this was his untruthful bio:

Don Juan DeMarco
@LoverOfFemales

'Every woman is a mystery to be solved.' 'Have you ever met a woman who inspires you to love?' I have & I'm here to take you to sandy shores & wet your appetite! 😄

⊙ Wherever your heart is!

4,369 Following   **103** Followers

So Neville followed his imaginary online mistress very closely and the Sultana lady followed him back with real apathy. Later that week Neville went for the kill by sending the hot honey a DM and he waited with baited breath for her response.

When first joining Twitter, Neville genuinely thought a DM stood for Dirty Messages which caused him some problems when he messaged 'Open for DMs' women the same tired joke about opened legs inviting a lover. The following week a picture of his small stung pride and penis was circulated around the whole world and Neville did his best to not feel humiliated. That was a busy damage limitation and account blocking week for him. In the end though Neville got the hang of not sexually harassing or flashing loads of women on the internet behind his wife's back and messaged the sexy looking Sultana a normal response instead:

Brilliant! I really hoped you would follow me. I really love your messages of happiness and your pretty face too :)

...said a hopeful Neville trying to pretend he's not an asshole and lying about having read any of her timeline. Last Wednesday, pervert Neville went straight for her media content and scanned through the images with his trousers around his ankles – very frustrated with all the Gifs that weren't her looking like a tribal tattooed slut. He was very taken by her profile too: a heavy on the cleavage avi underneath a header picture saying the word CUNT made from daisy flowers, plus an alluring and sexy bio. Twitter represents freedom and allows normal, restrained people an outlet to have absolutely no shame, morals or self-respect whatsoever:

Sultry Sultana

@ClockHungryHo

Lover of all things purple | Cock enthusiast | Fake fuck love and half ass friends | A proud bitch | Unhappy and doesn't give a shit | Fuck you meat head! 🐌 in disguise

⊚ On a man's dildo

1,500 Following   **24,358** Followers

Now what self-respecting gentleman wouldn't be attracted to such a charming introduction? Anyway, the two flimsy characters chatted for a while and then the following morning (GMT), Neville began his one day love affair with the dark olive-skinned Sultana before real life kicked him in the bollocks!

If you get over 25 likes without using your tits, you're a natural born winner.

3

Twitter Rocks

DAY ONE OF THE LOVE DANCE (morning):

Neville stayed up very late last night to write a poem to **MAISIE** (the ripe Sultana's real name). He put some real effort into writing it, like homework or something. The tiredness made him moody the following morning and all he could say to his actual wife was, "I don't really like eggs that runny. I've said that many times now."

The eggs suddenly found the bin in silence and Neville went hungry, but he couldn't wait to re-read the gloriously tacky poem he sent his online mistress in the early hours and to message voluptuous Maisie again:

The Highlight of Missouri

Somewhere deep in Missouri,
Lies a lonely coat hanger,
On silken bed sheets missing,
The beauty we're reminiscing.

Lady wears a lacy top with grace,
And her saucer eyes hypnotise.
A goddess of natural law,
Casting men in mortal awe.

Missouri is heavenly glory,
A glowing elf beyond wealth.
To gaze on such beauty with brains,
My dream's heart entertains.

OK, it wasn't *extremely* bad. The poem was certainly better than most of the cheesy rhyming crap on Twitter and she liked it too:

That's beautiful. Thank you. I look forward to more poetry.

…typed back Maisie feeling flattered, followed by three red heart emojis. When Neville finally turned up at work he found himself developing a BS stomach problem and then DMed Maisie this long creepy shit on the toilet:

I spent many an hour looking at a photo and zooming in on her stunning eyes to understand who the mystery lady is. Can we see through a screen and look into the soul of an American beauty from across an ocean? Who was she? What does she love? Is she alone?

I see beautiful and tender lips to kiss, a cute chin to tickle, a pretty nose to adore and sharp arrow eyebrows to set off the jewel in her crown which are those galactic eyes from which no man can return. They are two worlds of unparalleled desires which beg to be explored and resist being conquered.

Fucking fingers down your throat sickening! However, married Maisie really liked it.

LOVER'S TWITTER ROMANCE (the evening):

Neville woke up in a another bad mood after a nap in his car and foolishly decided to continue the loving rapport instead of focusing on his own wife he once loved. So he stalked the Sultry Sultana's ongoing conversations with many other men and jumped in the middle of her #hashtag:

#TheTinyVoiceInMyHead promises me that the happiest day of my life is yet to come!

…said the soon to be pressed sultana.

Waiting for happiness is like waiting for the lottery. Your best bet is to make today a happy enterprise – assuming you haven't planned to clean the grey gunk out of the washing machine rim, lol.

…interjected Neville, thinking he was being funny when he clearly wasn't. Neville had a PhD in dad jokes.

How do you know about my OCD?

…replied Maisie, the juicy sultana.

I don't know. You just seem like the kind of person who would dedicate unreasonable amounts of time to cleaning kitchen surfaces, fridge draws, washing machine rims and lime scale erosion, etc.

…wrote Neville sinking himself fast in the submarine eyes of Maisie who was beginning to get annoyed. She was having a bad day and just needed no jerks for once.

Oh yeah, you've got me pegged correctly. Not! To be honest, I was bored rigid by the time I reached 'fridge drawers', so a shorter, more tailored reply would be welcome. Or feel free to document whatever you like and email me a PDF so I can save it for bedtime reading. Won't!

…said a now angry Maisie questioning her new lover's character for the first time since they met way back last week. Twitter always makes you ask WHY.

Are you throwing a temper tantrum because I spelt 'drawers' wrong?

…asked a nervous Neville, feeling like he was losing her because he was.

If you choose incorrect words, that's on you Don Juan. Ha! As for moods. Not Applicable, well, not here at least.

…piped up Maisie with defiance.

I guessed yesterday was a tough day for you that dragged into today? Would you like to help me remove the smelly dead cat with its tail tied around your ankle? Poor cat probably got its tail caught in a drawer and then jumped into the nearest person who is used to taking abuse.

…said Neville knowing he'd already fucked everything up.

Yet again, very astute (you're not). Nothing has been dragged into today, as I'm currently continuing yesterday. No dead cats, no trapped tails. Unless they're possible code words for exhaustion, apathy, disappointment. I feel 2 out of 10 and you're not helping.

…said Maisie getting really pissed off. After his poetry she mistakenly thought he might be different from all the other jackass players on Twitter.

I see, so you don't live your life by the sun cycle? Everything just blends in together like minestrone soup. I'm sorry you're feeling so drained number two. Maybe happiness is a bus coming around the corner with me upstairs in your head smoking below a No Smoking sign? Am I helping?

…typed a sarcy Neville, not quite knowing what he was going on about.

I'm always on the bus to happiness. I'm the conductor, after all. Just not particularly happy that my pre-booked passenger(s) are a no show.

…said the clearly unhappy woman talking about her friends IRL who had blown her out again. Neville was so annoyed that another Twitter romance had gone so rapidly wrong again, he foolishly chose to crash and burn in style by saying…

That's why I sneaked on the bus without paying. Happy to help out. The bus says HAPPINESS on the front, but I think it's actually going to MOODINESS CENTRAL just after Tampon Street!

Maisie was not impressed with Neville turning from lovey-dovey to troll in just one hour.

Erm, heads up, without knowing me you have no fucking clue rude asshole! I can't be measured by rides, theories or algorithms. I refuse to accept any judgment on your cursory glances. I CAN have a high level of positivity yet be unhappy with my situation. My misery scores don't lie.

...said the upset lady all confused with Neville's plain idiocy.

Oxymoron alert: 'I CAN have a high level of positivity yet be unhappy with the situation.' Do your hips lie as well? You won't hear from me again today because I'm concerned your extreme anger may actually pop your head off like a Lego figure, or just give you a stroke.

...exploded Neville with bitter comedy.

I don't care who you are, or even, who you 'think' you are. Don't ever dare speak to me like that, question, judge or score me. God bless X.

...finalised Maisie, hovering over the block button.

Automatic robot response: You have a lovely heart even if some of it has been dipped in man-hating tar.

...burned up Neville on re-entry, despite having already been dumped a few replies ago.

Have you got rocks in your head instead of grey matter? I love men. I only loathe and detest one man! YOU!

...shouted Maisie at her phone and then she finally typed the words in with seething anger to the man she thought only yesterday might be able to love her.

Your hysteria stops you from being honest with yourself.

...concluded Neville, who had totally lost the plot and insisted on having the evil last word like all unhappy people do.

And that was the complete and utter end of that short-lived Twitter romance! Neville was such a fucking loser it was unbelievable. Three months later those nasty old tweets came back to haunt him as vengeful screenshots. His wife saw them via an eagle-eyed Twitter loving friend and asked him to pack his bags for good. Their marriage was tittering on the edge before his twittering anyway and they were better off without each other.

God was glued to Neville and Maisie's online feud and consequently promised to help more people find real face-to-face friendships in real life. *The* creator of all life then left planet Earth indefinitely because another Holocaust had begun on an unknown, dark planet hiding behind the sun. He vowed to never let that happen again, raising his finger and shouting, "Not on my watch!" about 80 years too late for the human race though. In the meantime, God left the stewardship of his good intentions in the hands of a well meaning soul called **MARTIN WIMBLE** who was far from normal.

Don't ever give evil people the benefit of the doubt.

4

Martini For One Please

Good morning tweeps and dic pic creeps! Let's hope you all have a great day under the oppression of a deeply controlling and restricting financial subjugation. Oh dear, that wasn't as uplifting as hoped. Love Martin.

Martin Wimble from England was unaware he had been touched by God. As far as he was concerned his frequent goose bumps and shivers were caused by ghosts walking through him. There's a fine line between superstition and extreme stupidity.

In spite of everything, Martin had a great sense of humour and people without laughter were toxic to him. He teased that men must be smarter than women because they can think with two heads. Martin also muted vain people for fun, only chatted with sincere folk and believed the problem with snowflakes is they never build a snowman.

Mr. Wimble was strangely very much like God but without all the omnipotent powers. He was sort-of an atheist who followed and believed in all of the Christian values and teachings of Jesus Christ superstar, but not the resurrection and burning bushes malarkey.

Humans do very few things without the approval of the mass group, so God picked Martin for being a former over-thinker who'd learnt to unthink and unpick life all by himself. Martin was generally an Un person, including *un*popular. But he was mainly chosen by God out of convenience because Martin was one of the few people on Twitter who didn't need regular doses of coffee or cannabis to keep going. Money was not his god either, which made Martin quite powerful, just like God.

41

In the outside world, Martin was a therapist with a strong moral compass, AKA as stubborn as a mule. He always knew he was right because he *was* virtually always right – which was his only real fault. Sometimes pretending to be wrong is right. And Martin wasn't prepared to lie to make people happy either: truth was his king and queen, and that was his safe place and peace of mind. We only hear what we want to and only see the truth if it doesn't stand in our way.

People will respect you for telling the truth even if they hate you for doing so.

Over many years, Martin had amassed a vast wealth of enthusiastic knowledge about mental health issues born from thinking things through from scratch. Regardless, like all eccentric thinkers he eventually woke up from the sterility of theories and thought, 'Shit! I better tell someone else about all these pages of writing hidden under my bed.' Consequently, Martin joined Twitter to educate the survivors, empaths, INFJ's, sex tweeters, dumbfucks, pansexuals, exhibitionists, blue wave resistors, liberals and lefties, dad joke comedians, budding poets, nutty pet lovers and dick pic senders who make up the bulk of the forum. And let's not forget the hordes of trolls who are not monsters, they're just bitter and twisted loners who can't stand to see you happy. Unfortunately, at first Martin chose to edify his fellow tweeps in a very condescending way:

If everyone was like you, Twitter would run out of violin emojis.

Martin got much better and less offensive over time after rapidly discovering nobody gave a rat's arse about his moral judgments. Judgments are totally off the Twitter menu unless you want to get insulted and blocked by mob rule. It seemed that positively and constructively criticising anyone for their real-life atrocious behaviour was not the done thing. Twitter acts as a sanctuary for some buffoons, baboons and loons.

Shallow people hate being criticised. Great people welcome criticism.

Martin had knocked out hundreds of tweets, yet the tumbleweed still rolled. However, brainbox Martin was not the defeatist type. Unpopularity to him was a badge of uniqueness. So he came up with a cunning plan most Twitter users were already doing: use an alias and more importantly don't ever criticise Feminists because they basically run Twitter. People become as superficial as society wants them to be.

Don't bother carrying messages of wisdom to ignorant people because they'd rather shoot you than change their behaviour.

Most people nowadays have conveniences, not principles. Nonetheless Martin, who was sometimes agnostic, felt a tad desperate to tell people about his psychology ideas so naturally adopted religion as a good business strategy. As a corrupt soul once said, 'God is a good closer.'

Religion is a great way to spread your kind words and connect with many more people because most people are naive, believed Martin. Therefore, he donned his cape of disguise and became God on Twitter because the real God had planned it so. What God had not planned though was Martin's inability to listen to an effing word anyone says! This was a man who found trees generally much easier to talk to than people.

Nonetheless, Martin's god account soon become a real triumph, reaching over 97,000 followers in just 3 months. Then, in a strange midlife crisis kind of way, Martin Wimble started to sabotage his own success by questioning the truth behind his God allusion. He decided he didn't want to live a lie to succeed. He would rather fail and keep his integrity. Consequently, he first questioned God's existence on podcasts, which immediately lost him thousands of followers and then he put the nail in the coffin by turning God into a woman. Why, thought Martin, did God have to be a man: because a load of powerful men in the past wrote it that way? "Screw that, I'm going to get my message across even if it means being cross gender," he said under his breath at home looking at his laptop with a concerned wife listening to his mutterings behind him.

In brief, Martin's Twitter God account rapidly crashed after being reported hundreds of times for blaspheming. He was pretty fucked-off his truth was trampled on. "And where the hell is Wesley Snipes when you need him to kick some ass!?" exclaimed Martin, bitter that Wesley liked and then unliked one of his recent replies.

Unperturbed, a dogged Martin had to start all over again, this time as **PRACTICAL PSYCHOLOGY** which he opened with a heart-warming tweet which grabbed our heroine Juliet's attention.

Juliet had experienced a rough day and was dog tired. She felt like everyone was taking little chucks of her goodness out of her creamy yoghurt pot soul. Yes, she had a flare for dramatics but was also a seeker of truth and justice. Her tired sofa eyes caught sight of the picture below Martin's tweet of two lovers kissing underneath a yellow leafed tree:

In warm autumn showers
your mind expunges
highs and lows
of rainbow glows to
a bright future of
colourful shows.

Life is a series of helpful coincidences. When one door closes, a revolving door spins you round until you find something good to focus your pain on. Juliet was intrigued by Practical Psychology, clicked on Martin's timeline and read more words bolstering her hopeful vibe. Good vibes are like oxygen for your soul:

Show love for yourself and
the world, otherwise you
will attract the wrong
kind of people.
Love has a great way
of protecting you from harm.

And Martin also did armchair philosophy:

The problem with life is it's long enough to make big mistakes
and too short to get it just right.

Juliet really liked what she read and wanted more from a world which offers poor people so little, so she followed Practical Psychology. Martin saw the follow and followed her back. He always followed everyone back because that's the right thing to do. Anyway, self-righteous Martin had played his little part in Juliet and Ryan's journey and now in traditional Twitter style he can fuck off, thankfully never to be heard of again.

Has anyone seen my keys?

However, before leaving our scene, Martin did notice when Juliet followed him, he picked up a simultaneous shadow follower too, who followed everyone Juliet followed. Juliet was way too tired to notice petty things like that and her defences were dangerously low.

An account named **Caesar Or Nothing** had been following her for months without pressing Like once. Juliet was blissfully unaware she had picked up a crazy. We're not talking your average Twitter nutcase or radical obsessive; we're talking about someone who printed out pictures of her and masturbated over them whilst reading her live tweets as he imagined suffocating her when cumming. Each to their own as they say. But that's the fundamental problem with lunatics: they rarely keep it to themselves.

Why is there no emoji for Hope? Surely that's the most important one. Hope is the only thing that will never abandon you or let you down.

5

The Dark Mask

Experience teaches you that beauty isn't skin deep, it travels to the furthest reaches of your imagination and hugs you tight.

One would think that being a beautiful woman should be a major lifestyle advantage. Well it is. Nevertheless, being a top notch stunner, as Juliet was, is unknowingly entering a lottery to see who gets the sexually harassing boss, the persistent stalker or least likely a deranged wannabe serial killer.

Most unfortunately, for a number of reasons Juliet's aura was at such a low ebb she drew the last two short straws from her lot. The dark mask of destiny now needed to save her.

When you connect with someone on a deep level, it goes way beyond appearances. It's the look of destiny explored.

Juliet was pretty much the antithesis of the aberrant man who had decided he wanted to rape and kill her soon. As a hairdresser, make-up artist and part-time singer she had become accustomed to insouciant chat and putting customers at ease. Juliet dreamed of coffee and donuts and every other doable pleasure in the world, but was not a hopeless romantic. She knew exactly what kind of man she wanted and just wasn't prepared to settle down with anyone but the right man who could touch her soul. Juliet wanted a man who opened the door for her and let her open the door for him. She wanted a strong willed man who wasn't a bully. Her man had to make her glow warmly inside with sincere compliments and make love to her with perpetual motion and passion.

She was a woman who lit up the sky with fireworks, melting his heart & blazing his mind with limitless passion for her quirks & elegant grace. She felt weak in his presence and he knew it. Yet

he waited to pluck this white mountain orchid to the tune of
Spring.

Ryan, her potential knight in shining armour was
only a happy dream away. Juliet had just woken at
6:37am to the melodic sound of traffic when she
made the mistake of checking her Twitter messages
only to receive a random picture of a 9 ½ inch erect
penis from a man in Turkey.

The worst bit about the vile phallic shock was
actually taking a second to wonder if that was a
normal cultural thing for men to do in his country.
That's what political correctness does to you. The
problem with a politically correct society is everyone
ends up feeling sorry for the criminal who mugs
your grandma. Juliet showered the man's sins away
and cracked open some eggs for breakfast. She was
a beautiful blonde with a sadness in her eyes that
reflected in her light pink egg bathed in oil. Juliet
soaked-up the lovely dawn sun with some
wholesome bread and thought no more of it.

Despite being a modest earning hairdresser, Juliet
was living in a small apartment in a wealthy suburb
of Manhattan because her father had recently passed
away from prostate cancer and surprisingly left it to
his ex in guilt, Juliet's mother, who let Juliet live
there for free. Dad was a successful biochemist by
profession and despite being very disappointed
Juliet 'never used her brains enough', daddy always
loved his youngest princess very much.

However, Juliet never really gelled with her mother and as her beauty grew, mommy's jealousy grew in tandem. Instead of admiring her daughter developing into an intelligent and desired woman, mother **SHIRLEY** felt threatened because the men weren't looking at her anymore. To give her some credit though, Shirley knew she was being pathetic but simply couldn't control how she felt. Mental illness ran in her side of the family.

As a result, Juliet didn't receive the balance of love she craved, yet her naturally open-minded and optimistic demeanour always left space for all positive outcomes. Juliet was very clever and academic, yet declined university because her creative mind just couldn't stand being boxed-up by boring old-fashioned dogma. She was an avant-guard lady with class, having a beguiling presence and an Audrey Hepburn elegance which illuminated her as special. Juliet's life was full of bluebell promise carpeting the streets with optimism as she sauntered along happily. She soon became a beacon of hope for all women on Twitter looking for a contemporary way of thinking about a fucked-up world that doesn't know where it is going.

Really nice people are like butterflies; you only see them now and again, and they remind you there is hope in this world. Butterflies are so unique we've forgotten to learn from them.

In stark contrast, the dangerous Twitter user Caesar Or Nothing was a depth charge of anguish. He had delusions of grandeur because he was physically abused by his step-dad throughout his childhood until running away at seventeen. This was his main reason for being mentally disturbed. At what point does a reason for nastiness become a valid excuse or opportunity to bring balance to the universe?

After his escape from sexual tyranny, for 12 years he had been in and out of jail for petty offences and one case of attempted rape. It's safe to say **CAESAR** was not the kind of man you'd take home to meet the parents. Being constantly rejected by women was his biggest problem which soon became their problem. Caesar's real name is unimportant because he had chosen to walk into the limitless arms of Satan to reach for immortality and the freedom of blankness.

Evil is always circling around waiting for its chance to get you when you're weak and vulnerable. So always stay in the light of kindness behind the solid shield of experience and your instincts.

American based Caesar spent many a night totally obsessing about beautiful Juliet. It took him less than a minute to follow her new account because he kept close tabs on her best friends. He'd saved every last picture she posted and anything which could lead him to her in real life.

Through some very calculated pieces of puzzle connecting background images from her selfies and fragments of descriptions, Caesar had managed to find out the street and salon Juliet worked in. Computers are a sin to control the people. It didn't take much effort to track her down, just a little determination – of which Caesar had plenty. Hatred and anger were his primary driving forces. All he needed now to trigger and project his evil at Juliet was an excuse to hate her which he hastily engineered:

Juliet: Dear Weird Men,

Please carry on calling me a worthless whore, demean and try to upset me because I don't sleep with you after seeing an unsolicited pic of your penis in my private DMs.

Good chat, Juliet.

Caesar's reply: If u dress like a hoe in selfies u wouldnt get dics slapping u in the face. I wanna tie u up slap yo ass bitch! You are mine fuck slut!!! 👿👿👿

That was the first and only time Caesar ever interacted with Juliet via Twitter: not true of course. He was more a vile watcher than a poet. After receiving a serious tongue lashing from Juliet and about twenty of her best Twitter friends, his intense misogyny was blocked tons, reported and shut down by Twitter immediately. It made no difference anyway. Caesar already followed her on two other

53

accounts and was laughing at the chaos his nastiness had provoked. When we say 'laughing' we mean jerking off like a demonic baboon on crack.

Juliet had encountered thousands of nasty comments on Twitter and had become an expert at rebuffing them without seeming upset. But Caesar's reply felt different, vicious and extremely concerning. Her friends said report it to the cops, but her lingering tiredness stupidly let it slide now he was apparently gone for good – in her mind. You are always being watched on Twitter by your enemies. Toxic people are like swamps; as soon as you walk into one you want to go home and dry out. Caesar spat on God and God just wiped it off with dignity.

Do you love yourself enough to never hate people?

Twitter doesn't feel like real life. If feels more like being drunk at a swingers party where everyone's morals are extremely lax. It is as deceptive as a circus hall of mirrors and turns you into something you're not. The only thing Twitter has in common with nature is that only the strong survive.

Caesar was inarticulate, but when a human wants something badly they suddenly up their game considerably. On another account following Juliet he pretended to be a nice guy and got her to leak a few golden nuggets of stalking information. Ironically this was just after his Caesar Or Nothing account upset her and he played the part of a white knight for which he received a heartfelt thanks.

Even more deceptively, on his third account he transformed himself into a catfish in sympathy and lifestyle similarity to Juliet, which gave him the crucial link to her salon's whereabouts. Who knows how many accounts he had, what costume he would wear today or even how many people he was? Caesar was ignorant and congenitally mentally unbalanced. He was also a closet transvestite who deep down in his toxic mind just wanted to be one of the popular girls shopping for labels all day.

That night, Juliet lay her head quietly down on an eider duck feather pillow and felt the fuck of life. Caesar's venomous hatred had touched her like the black spot and she considered deleting her new account and running away from Twitter for good. He was a frightening man to meet and his acidic words hit home as planned. But she couldn't and wouldn't let some lonely jerk on Twitter dictate her destiny!

As a young child, Juliet genuinely thought stars were humongous diamonds in the night's sky. She also believed adulthood only seems disappointing if you lose your imagination. Juliet lay snugly under her duvet and thought of the stars and all the good things she'd ever done for anyone. This filled her heart with restful optimism and despite everything, she slept like a baby.

To be happy you must believe that your dreams can come true otherwise the stars in the night's sky are just crystal lies and the moon a broken plate of hope.

6

Love at Third Tweet

What is darkness? What makes someone deadly unlucky? 'Why me' we all think from time to time without perspective. The older you get the more you entertain the idea that everything happens for a reason and it does. We experience the universe as a strange cause-and-effect organism shaped by energy.

The planets are vast and unfathomable, as is your brain. So never get bored with being you and always explore your mind.

57

The disturbed man Caesar felt murderous because he was in chaos and pain, and had lost all hope. Nothing pinned him to sanity or reality. He had no job or money to enter the matrix and nobody to love or love him in return. His flawed conscience figured that if the flock look down on the wolf then it was time to make a slaughter to be counted. The idea of being loved by a woman had turned into poison ivy. Caesar was so lonely he'd forgotten what loneliness felt like.

Depression is a blood clot
in a knackered mind
stopping work or drive,
struggling to survive.
It's like a disease
that rots your will
until a tear of hope
drops new light,
tearing black from white.

His prison release flat was dirty and unfriendly looking. It suited him well. Instead of making any attempt to tidy up and become normal, Caesar could be himself because the State paid for this holding cell of an apartment. His mind was in hell and had been for about the last two years of doing drugs and crime. He was only 32 years old but looked a lot older. Prostitutes were his only human contact when he could be bothered to sell enough weed.

From the outside, Caesar was a short man with a menacing appearance. But it was his fish dead eyes that gave away his evil intent. In his late teens he used to justify his nastiness with implausible excuses. But now, Caesar's brain was a Hammer Horror swamp full of terror. Nothing connected or made any sense and he had given up trying to understand a society that gave him nothing but abuse and rejection from his point of understanding.

Inside though, Caesar was suicidal and wanted to make his mark on this cruel world by raping or ending the life of someone who was happy and very beautiful. The unfairness of life had made Caesar monstrously jealous. To him everyone seemed privileged. "Fuck you!" he said just now to a black man in the street for being black. All Caesar did was cause trouble because he knew no other way. His common mantra was, 'Why be friendly when you can be a cunt.' He ate niceness like crisps and shit out vile behaviour as regular as clockwork.

Caesar may have fantasised about playing the part of a concerned hero to impress himself, not Juliet, but her real champion knight *was* a man to be admired. For a start, Ryan genuinely thought of other people before himself. Working as a park ranger in Blackstone River Valley National Park, Rhode Island, he had become at one with nature which gave him an earthly character, transcending pettiness. Women just liked Ryan. He was tall, athletic, more handsome than most, humorous and gave people the space to be themselves. This protective kindness resonated throughout his bio and timeline. Nearly every single one of his tweets echoed a solid oak life experience:

Gentleman Beast

@KingKong6393

Forgive yourself for mistakes made this year otherwise you can't move on. 🙏

◎ Rhode Island, USA

📌 Pinned Tweet

Only old-fashioned souls cross their 7s.

....

Intelligent women are far more sexy than sexy women.

You're a beautiful person. Blame society for not noticing.

If you love someone then make sure they feel your love daily.

Crack the hard seed of potential inside your mind by believing in yourself.

Genuine love is the greatest healer of mental health problems.

Don't give someone who has wrecked your mind a second chance.

Imagine every road in your country without trees: no insects, no birds, no photosynthesis, no life. We take nature for granted. Save our planet to help all the creatures that have no say in their future.

Don't ask yourself what the point of life is. Ask yourself what relevant point you are going to have in life.

A small thoughtfulness from you can become like lifeline for others.

Ryan was a contemporary philosopher with his hand on the axe. He loved skimming flat pebbles on ponds and seeing the sun's reflection glisten on still water. In a short space of time he had gained a lot of keen female interest. Some big Twitter hitters had signed up for his charm and wisdom, and word travelled fast a decent guy was in town. A few of Juliet's friends had parleyed with him too and were hooked. But 39 year old Juliet was the old fashioned type who believed in destiny and being chased by the man.

Over a month or so, Juliet's beautiful avi face began to pop up more frequently on the main feed. Ryan was very interested in her and made his move because every real man has to make The Move. He opened with a comedy one liner, then a second realist reply and finally grabbed Juliet's heart with a comment of kindness:

Juliet: Kisses should spark sex

Ryan: Hopefully you won't suggest that to my grandma who loves a goodbye kiss?

It was a great joke. Juliet and everyone loved it! But this was Twitter, so some envious knob-head out there in the randomness of space decided to turn a joke into an actual point:

Knobhead interferer: You're reading too far into this.

Juliet was waiting for Ryan's response and hoped he would not disappoint. He did not:

Gentleman Beast: To be a good lover one must read as far as kisses can go.

It's embarrassing but true that Juliet's pussy went a little wet because she felt like Ryan could be a contender for The One! She just felt it. It was mostly her consciousness egging her on, having heard so much gossip about the Gentleman Beast. Now she flicked through her notifications looking for anymore @KingKong6393 replies:

Juliet: One of the best ways to get laid is to put your phone down.

Gentleman Beast: You seem to have missed the 19 other ritualistic steps men have to go through to achieve their sexual goal. Women could keep texting, never put their phone down and still guarantee sex.

Interesting, thought Juliet, he put that in its place.

Juliet: Everybody has been hurt at some time, so please be nice.

Gentleman Beast: As far as I can tell, you're doing a great job of being kind and inspiring a sense of niceness to fellow tweeps. Pat yourself on the back; actually do that now for comedic effect.

Juliet was at work and pretended to flick her hair as she patted her own back with fingertip enthusiasm and her customer saw in the mirror saying, "Yes, I'm very pleased with my hair too," and they laughed. "Does he live close by?" teased her client. Juliet just smiled and then sneaked a look at his location: Rhode Island, Bingo! He's within range of my claws, she joked to herself.

Ryan was pleased with himself too. Not bad for 5 minutes effort, he thought. This morning he had to cull a stag which was necessary for conservation but not a pleasant task. He loved animals, liked people and best of all loved everything that nature had to offer. When he executed a shot into the stag's high shoulder, killing the great beast instantly, Ryan's red heart sank because feelings are greater than precision logic. The stag kill was the catalyst for engaging with Juliet later that day.

Juliet was taken by him and a queue of attractive ladies were lining up to catch Ryan's attention too. He'd never done speed dating, online dating or anything stupid before because he believed in the rawness of first contact and chemical vibes dictating the outcome. Suddenly though, this tittle-tattle Twitter crap didn't seem so bad after all. It was certainly increasing his chances, if one is permitted to think of women in a statistical capacity in these politically sensitive days. One skanky woman even DMed Ryan some flattering words full of decorum and self-respect:

Crazy bitch: I'll let you turn my asshole inside out before I cradle our babies.

Gentleman Beast: That's very kind of you but I'm only here for the fun, not bum.

It was a close evening now as Juliet cuddled into her settee with a frothy hot chocolate and thought of this enigmatic Gentleman Beast who had entered her dreams. Rain was falling on Manhattan rooftops and it helped reflect her mind towards positive changes.

Juliet felt the pressure of a 'good one' escaping her clutch so did something she'd never done before by making the first ever romantic move on a man. She also did the unthinkable for a woman who preached respect, dignity and prearranged rapport regarding DMs: she only DMed him! Fuckin' bitch gone cock crazy, her mind echoed in humour but her fingers were doing the dirty work, not her. Juliet was easily beautiful enough to earn herself a free cool badge. Now suddenly she felt like an awkward, sweaty sci-fi nerd:

Juliet: Hey, thanks for following Gentleman Beast. Can't imagine from your great tweets you'd ever be beastly to anyone, lol. Juliet :)

Direct Messages are the forbidden zone. They are make-or-break time! The DM is a shortcut to glory but mostly for making a tit out of yourself and getting blocked. Ryan played it cool and made her wait until the following morning. This wasn't because he was cool, even though he was. Driving home from work last night he made a road kill pie out of a raccoon. This to Ryan was the very pits of existence; killing an innocent creature using a man-made machine. It was no different to shooting the stag though, if he thought about it for a second. After pretending to feel guilt for a while whilst he shovelled a full English breakfast down his gullet, Ryan finally got round to responding:

The Beast: Hey, ditto on the follow. Beast? Wouldn't you like to know. I see you live in New York. That's in red roses sending range for me, lol. My real name's Ryan. Hopefully that's a secret between you and I? ;)

That was the start of something beautiful. Many days of messages to-and-fro went by until rapport turned to flirting, flirting to romance, romance to questions and questions to feelings.

Juliet had been won over by a rally of words and photos without even meeting the man yet. But as Ryan planned to drive to Manhattan next Saturday and take Juliet to an embarrassingly expensive restaurant on their first ever date, which his moderate wage couldn't regularly afford, Juliet decided to tweet the world she'd met a great guy. She couldn't hold back her excitement:

Being escorted to a little Loeb Boathouse restaurant in Central Park this weekend. Don't wait up for me losers ;)

The nasty creature Caesar saw it and was seething! Somewhere in his pumpkin brain he felt a sense of ownership over Juliet and couldn't hold back his rage at discovering she was dating other men. His mister nice guy account slipped the fury:

Caesar (aka @ShoeStringJoey):   You mean you're jacking in the singing for escorting, lol. New it was only a matter of time 🌀

Juliet just ignored it, blocked him and moved on. Another fake creep, she thought. The world is full of them. He couldn't even spell 'knew' right anyway. Twitter produces a despondence and depression of the mind only real mental illness can outdo. Who cares anyway, the princess shall go to the ball!

Do creepy people know they are creepy?

7

Best Knickers On

Juliet had outstanding charisma, but hot honey attracts wasps. Gossip about who the lucky guy was spread across Twitter like rabbit poo pellets in sodden fields. Basically, a lot of people had nothing better to do than meddle in someone else's affairs because Juliet wanted them to otherwise don't sign up for Twitter.

You inhale more bullshit on Twitter than from the House of Commons on Brexit. But Juliet didn't care about all the background talk. What was most important is she had secured herself a hot date with a great guy, despite having told the world where she was going next Friday, Saturday or Sunday night. Caesar correctly assumed Saturday, but prepared himself for three nights in Central Park anyway.

Central Park at night is statistically nowhere near as bad as it used to be crime wise, but no-one wants to be *the* statistic. During the day it is as safe as a fun park, but with Caesar there anything could happen to anyone. Mad people are predictably unpredictable. He'd made it to New York from god knows where the devil lives and oddly found watching the outdoor chess players very relaxing. There was a monotony to the play his chaotic mind found calming. Caesar didn't even know how to play chess properly either. He just stood in the middle of everything – even on a chair at one point to gain a better view – and made everyone feel uncomfortable. No-one volunteered to ask him to leave. Chess is something you do when you struggle to get laid.

There's always someone out there who will truly understand you, even without you speaking. Keep searching until you find that peaceful person.

It was Friday night and Caesar had time to kill, as well as Juliet, so he did what many misogynistic nutcases do when bored; enjoyed a Chicken Caesar Sandwich with a large banana milkshake (there is no scientific evidence to corroborate that spurious fact. Fuck you McDonalds, thought Caesar). He bought an apple pie too and nearly had a brain seizure over it taking ten minutes to prepare. Caesar guessed his prey, Juliet, meant Saturday because he knew she didn't work on Saturdays and would like to make as much of a meal out of it as possible. This was a weekend affair – maybe a fling if lucky.

Whilst licking-out his now cold pie within the vicinity of the Boathouse restaurant, Caesar looked up to the cold sky, thought nothing and felt no wonder. He then fell asleep leaning up against a tree behind a bush. He was used to an uncomfortable life with sticks up his bum. Everywhere you go crow darkness tries to pick away at your spirits. Stay clear of the temptation to fight evil or risk entering its never-ending spiral.

Good feelings are like garden fairies that only come to light when you open up your conscience and explore the world with creative eyes.

After pissing off lots of fit joggers and lonely lunchtime women, soon the big night arrived for Caesar! Juliet spent approximately 5 hours getting ready which was quite reasonable really. She was born with beautiful blonde locks, so naturally she decided to straighten them into the fashion of the day.

Because Ryan was getting the train all the way from Rhode Island, she suggested they just meet at 8pm at the restaurant to make life easier for him. Juliet was very excited and nervous. This was the first time she'd met with a man from the internet, so memorized his face like Rainman would to make sure it was the dashing chap he advertised himself to be. Better safe than sorry.

Finally Juliet arrived fashionably late wearing a fabulous red evening dress. As soon as her shapely legs glided out of the cab a gentleman offered his hand to help her out, presenting himself with one dozen red roses. Ryan himself couldn't believe how beautiful she was and also how lucky he'd been to choose flowers to match her dress. He was off to a very good start and made great eye contact too. Yes, this is a man I can trust, thought Juliet, and also a man I could ride all night long if he flicks my cortex clit. 😬

"Great to meet you," introduced Ryan warmly, "At last I get to meet the famous @911nightingale," and he kissed her on both cheeks lightly before giving Juliet the flowers.

She smelt quality aftershave and then a rose too, saying, "Perfect," smiling at him. Ryan offered her his arm in a reassuring and manly way, saying, "Shall we dine then my lady?" Juliet liked that a lot and took his arm.

Ryan certainly was nearly as handsome as Juliet was beautiful. They made a fine couple who caught the attention of many diners when they walked into an arena of New York's wealthy elite.

Juliet felt like she could get used to this kind of special treatment as the maître d' seated her. And Ryan thought, shit this is going to cost me an arm and a leg! But Juliet was worth it. She looked radiant like a red rose plucked for exhibition. Juliet was the opposite of a gold-digger, but did like a man to dig deeply into his pocket on the first date because a modern woman should be taken seriously. You either wine and dine a lady or stay hidden in golem's shadows.

The first flutter of love is like a single drop of rain that promises oceans of warm feelings to follow.

The way too hot looking for Juliet's comfort waitress seated them both and conversation tasted the wine.

"She's pretty," observed Juliet.
"Was she? I suppose so but I choose beauty over prettiness any day," replied Ryan looking straight into Juliet's sea-foam green eyes and doing his damndest not to check out the blonde waitresses

most pert of bubble butts after she took their sirloin and bass orders.

Juliet smiled and said, "Smooth talk to match the serene lake. I know it's a cliché but I think beauty is in the eye of the beholder."

"Then my eyes are a cliché," said Ryan. It didn't really make any sense but Juliet made up a meaning and smiled.

"This is nice here isn't it?" commented Juliet, trying to make out this was her regular crowd. It was nice for once to be seated with high society, rather than cutting their hair or singing to the ungrateful swine.

"It's very nice. Well worth the journey and especially to meet you in person. You have skin and everything!" japed Ryan as he leant forward to touch her wrist. "I love your dress and hair. Amazing!"

"Thank you Ryan. I'm happy my skin pleases you." Juliet was loving the attention and possibly hoped her sarcasm would turn into orgasm later.

"I didn't mean it like that, sorry; it's just funny seeing the real version of the mind construct," he explained.

"At least you didn't say, 'She rubs the lotion on the skin' whilst pouring my wine. LOL," mocked Juliet. They both laughed too loud for etiquette's refined palette and a few stiff heads hinged with an old oak creak. "So, do you like the real life product – warts and all?" asked Juliet looking for more compliments.

"I see no warts just good retorts and beautiful lines to accompany the fine wines," fluently replied Ryan. God he was a smooth talker.

"Okay, we're not on Twitter now," laughed Juliet. "I want to see the real you beyond the smooth phone talk," she said rather bluntly, testing his depth of soul because the real life Ryan didn't seem to have the depth his Twitter character suggested. But Ryan was good at chatting to women and knew how to divert his lack of profundity to humour or hubris. Many of his tweets were borrowed and he knew that encouragement and compliments go a long way with the ladies. He had a few clever set speeches planned for those 'tell me who you are' moments and he soon pulled out the betrayal of Mother Nature one.

"Fair enough. I like straight talk because that's who I am and that's why I work with nature. Sometimes when I'm on the hills I..." began Ryan as their starters of pigeon breast and brie, and spicy shrimp and pineapple with a sweet chilli glaze arrived and he caught a sneak peak at the bird's arse, "Sometimes…"

"Wow! This looks lovely," said Juliet romanced by the food, "Yes, sometimes… I want to hear."

"It's like this," exclaimed Ryan, looking Juliet straight in her diluting pupils whilst drawing some passionate animation into his voice, "Nature is everything to me and I'm very grateful God has turned it into my living." Juliet nodded on the word God like a penguin. "We came from nature, not concrete tower blocks. Throughout my life's ups and downs since childhood, nature has been the only one that has always been there for me and she asks for nothing in return. Sometimes I feel life has too much meaning and we just need to trust the wind and breathe in the fresh air. When I'm on the hills looking down at everything, it not only gives my life perspective but I feel connected to a higher plain of existence. Everything connects above the tree roots and grows flowers from eggs of desire. I believe trees are the foundation of life. They support all kinds of wildlife and birds and give us oxygen too. It's like when I'm under my favourite oak tree, I'm sheltered by something special and this gives me the confidence to walk down the mountain with fresh eyes on the world's problems and face them head on. Nature gives me energy and helps me see the true beauty in people – like I see in you Juliet."

Juliet was won over by his short speech and wanted to swing on his tree trunk. The main was satisfying and some creamy Irish coffee concluded a fine dining experience and date. It would be fair to say the night's entertainment was a major success. Juliet never put out on the first night but was considering changing her date night rules which hadn't been upgraded for a whole decade.

Ryan paid the hefty bill, had an internal bilious attack and escorted Juliet outside. The New York air felt simultaneously stifling and a touch chilly, so Ryan offered his jacket.

"Perhaps you would like a horse and carriage ride to take in the sights?" said Ryan hopefully.

Juliet was thinking, I fucking live here and see this same shit every day but hell why not, saying, "That would be lovely, thank you," wearing a sarcastic smile.

Ryan knew he was doing great so pushed his overt confidence as they approached the carriage by trying to stroke the dappled grey horse, which then bit him. Who did he think he was, Crocodile Dundee in New York? Juliet laughed loudly and Ryan seemed annoyed his cool had been crushed. Shit happens and so did the horse, just on cue. Juliet laughed again as the romantic vibe was steaming on the tarmac.

Anyway, Ryan got over his tiny temper tantrum like all men do if given guidance by a woman. He paid the driver a hefty tip, asking him to pull over in front of an old tree for guidance from the Lord. The tree had character which he hoped would to cement his character. That was the pseudo-autistic plan anyway.

"I love maple trees, they're kind of kingly," said Ryan in a mock documentary way.

"Isn't it a London planetree?" clarified Juliet laughing again in a queen-like way.

"Oh yeah," said Ryan, "I was too focused on you," bullshitting his way out of a stupid mistake.

Regardless, the tree offered them a canopy of love to kiss and just as they were about to a small cider drunk crowd of teenagers gathered and started taunting them, but Juliet felt safe in Ryan's solid branches.

One of the boys who couldn't have been more than 13 shouted out, "Fucking pervert!" and they jeered at the love struck couple as another teen strangely threw a half finished packet of crisps towards them and his mates just took the piss out of him for the pathetic effort of intimidation, so started to bully him instead.

Juliet laughed, turned back to Ryan and said, "Are you a fucking pervert then?" They both laughed their heads off, then briefly kissed.

"Hey, I changed my plans earlier and decided to drive here instead in the work van," said Ryan.

"Oh really," said Juliet wondering why he hadn't mentioned that but was actually relieved he hadn't been at all boring during dinner.

"Yes, thought it would be better to have my own space and music out loud and the firm pay for the petrol anyway," he explained. "It's just round the block if you'd like to come and see who I am and what tunes I love? I'm not made of money, but I am me and I like you a lot," explained Ryan in a nervous looking way.

"I know you're not wealthy. I'd be happy to chill out with you for a short time," replied Juliet with a positive vibe.

"I can give you a lift home after as well if you like?" he pushed.

"One step at a time Ryan," Juliet insisted upon saying to let him know the score.

He nodded, smiled and asked, "Do you love Ariana Grande?"

"Oh I love her!" exclaimed Juliet as they walked and chatted away to his slightly dirty and industrial looking white van. The romantic scene was perfect and she'd left her flowers in the horse carriage as well. Love is the least perfect thing anyway.

Save your love for the people who deserve it.

Ryan opened the passenger door for Juliet and then jumped into the driver's seat. It smelt funny and stale inside. She felt a little awkward after having just been in a plush restaurant surrounded by actors and architects of the world, and now she was in a manky van surrounded by used sweet wrappers, dead leaves and cracked CDs on the floor, but hey, life is never perfect.

Ryan dug out Ziggy Stardust whom she also loved and fired up the cramped atmosphere. Playing a bisexual alien's glam rock was hardly the signal for love but unluckily for Juliet it was actually the sign for Caesar, who was hiding in the back of the van behind some curtains ready to grab Juliet by the neck and arm, pulling her into the rear with considerable force and violence.

"I'm gonna fuck the fucking bitch whore like a raped rag doll!" shouted Caesar. For a micro second all three people's subconscious minds laughed at the ludicrous repetitive use of uncreative alliteration. However, 99.9% of Juliet's shocked mind was now fighting for her life! "Hit the fucking gas!" hollered animal Caesar to his partner in crime, Ryan.

As Ryan started her up, he caught the attention of another romantic couple passing by who could hear Juliet's screams reverberating from inside the van. The female pedestrian prodded her boyfriend to go and investigate and her boyfriend actually pointed at himself as if to say, 'what me.' Their pontification was left in the dust as the van's tires screeched away.

Understand and own who you are to prevent others from stealing you away.

Juliet screamed at full volume and got a punch in the face for her alarm. She obviously knew she was heading for a serious gangbang at best, so managed to summon up all of her wits and fighting spirit, and caught Caesar right in the eye with her left high heel connected to her furious hand. He screamed too, like a big girl's blouse, which gave Juliet just enough time to scramble open her handbag and pepper spray him in the face for his pains. She gave Ryan a rapid dose too for good measure.

As she clambered past a blinded Caesar to escape out the back door, Ryan wiped his burning eyes and pulled dangerously across the traffic catching more witness's attention. He banged to a halt with the idea of squeezing through the seat gap to grab her, but Juliet managed to pull the back door handle to jump out so he flawed the accelerator again as Caesar was now heading to stop her escaping, but the acceleration helped her fly out headfirst.

Juliet hit the ground hard, breaking her right arm. Caesar leaped out too but was totally disorientated and banged his head on the road. The van had built up more speed by now, leaving Caesar way behind with blurred vision. Juliet was crying out for help! Caesar was about 5 metres behind her, looking like a dazed and rabid dog. Ryan was a further 10 metres ahead now, stopping and shouting out, "Get in the fucking van!" presumably to Caesar.

A few cars had stopped and a small cowardly crowd just stood by and watched a women in peril without doing a fucking thing. However, the witnesses were amassing around the evil street performance as Ryan ran to Caesar and yanked him towards the getaway vehicle. They were off into a dark red sky as the boyfriend from back yonder finally built up the balls to help and came running to Juliet's aide. The attack was over but the nightmares had just begun.

Juliet was lucky, even though she didn't feel it at the time. She had unknowingly escaped the nefarious clutches of an organised gang of two rapists using Twitter as a meat market. Ryan and Caesar had already battered, raped and dumped alive twelve other women over a 3 year period across four States and had managed to keep their crimes unconnected so far, until tonight's serious blunders.

"Have you *actually* ever fucked a rag doll?" Ryan sincerely asked Caesar a safe distance from their treachery.

"No, but I've fucked a blow-up doll called Britney while my step mom watched." The evil guys both laughed like something from Coming to America (1988) meets The Invisible Man (1933).

The world is full of evil and it's hard to tell what motives anyone has, beyond sex and money. However, it's easy to spot self-obsessed liars because they never ask you how you are feeling.

Why do scammers from Namibia think calling you "my dear" is going to work? It's like they're in the wrong century.

When the ambulance took Juliet away with a heavy police presence taking witness statements, she sobbed into her left hand and felt like she would never recover from the cuntish assault ever again, or trust a single soul, especially men. But she eventually did. Time heals everything if you can stay alive long enough.

You get from life what you put in. But you also get to keep what you don't take from others.

8

Hiding and Healing

Just three words
Need a hug
I love you
You are safe.

Eight weeks later, Juliet's arm had finally healed and the plaster cast covered in well-wisher's love and support came off, but her mind was still cocooned in fear. After the horrendous attack, Juliet felt like she had no choice but to question her own species, or at least her rationality.

The truth comes out when you're really tired and you know who you really love.

The idea of forgiving her assailants was hiding somewhere on Neptune. Beyond the obvious shock and nihilism caused, more than anything Juliet felt ashamed and embarrassed she'd been so stupid to trust a male stranger on Twitter.

All of her self-righteous and confident strong woman tweets came back to haunt her. Juliet simply felt crushed by the whole painful and insane episode, and had many questions convoluting her mind with vice like pressure. Her self-esteem and confidence were nil and rock bottom. And confidence is the chocolate cookie which completes your coffee. Coffee was all she could stomach. At least Juliet had that.

It was now August and the sun was punishing. Juliet couldn't face living alone in her apartment so close to the assault. Not only did the loneliness whilst living in fear feel like a monster lurking, but she understandably also feared her attackers might know her home address. The police didn't help either by suggesting this was a possibility. So it was agreed by all that Juliet was safest at her mom Shirley's house in Crown Heights, Brooklyn, despite not getting on very well with mother because of Juliet's voracious support of Palestine and many other sore family points. The last thing Juliet needed now was a political struggle and accountability with her family who she couldn't just mute. She felt like the world had nothing to offer.

The biggest psychological trap to fall into is believing the world doesn't need you.

The failed sex attack itself lasted no more than a minute. But 1 minute of pure evil can change your life forever. Perspective is a lion that needs taming to enjoy a full life. Madly so, why did Juliet feel guilty when she was innocent? This dirty, chaotic thought kept scampering through her mind like logic resistant rats.

To go from being in the throws of passion to molested and attacked in a split personality second would need deep psychological deciphering to calm a heavily rocked brain. She kept reliving the experience over-and-over until anxiety erased all common sense.

Endorphins changed to cortisol as Caesar spooked her from behind ripping at her breasts. Fear turned to courage as Juliet went into automatic survival mode having the whereabouts and gumption to spray his eyes with chemical pain like a snake. That one horrific minute did feel like a lifetime which Juliet now foolishly trawled through her head repeatedly until she netted the inevitable consequences of negative over-thinking: a former mental illness, which had been under control for years, had resurfaced like a giant octopus trying to take her mythical ship down.

Juliet feared for her broken mirror feelings, reflecting around in so many angles she'd totally lost who she was, her self-respect and most importantly her dreams which were shattered shards, darted into her conscience. She had not tweeted once since the sex attack and hoped to gain support staying at her mothers, but mother Shirley was unfortunately still mother.

Telling someone who is stressed or angry to calm down is like asking a fish to start hopping like a frog.

"It won't do you any good standing there moping around will it?" said the dragon lord Shirley, whilst Juliet was cleaning the kitchen floor with a mop.

"Very good mother. Doesn't do you any good either swanning around criticising me all the time, does it?" defended Juliet, still with a shaken nervous system.

"*Criticising*, here we go, that old chestnut. Since when did good advice and highly amusing jokes become criticism? I'll tell you when…"

"Please don't, I'm not in the mood," interrupted Juliet.

"That's right; hear what you want to hear just when it suits you. That's so-called independent woman Feminism for you! You haven't changed since a little girl. If you just settled down and had a child we'd all be a lot happier," dug in mother with her big mouth and big boots. Two digs in one hit was too much for Juliet to take.

"I don't want a child, *as you know!* I've got a good career and don't need a man to support me!" insisted Juliet for the thousandth time.

"Hairdressing! A career? And who paid for you to train for that and all those years of flicking from one *career* to another; ME! Where's the independence there? You wouldn't be where you are now if you'd just been a bit more… more normal like Ruth."

RUTH was Juliet's eldest sister who had already provided the serpentine with two lovely grandchildren. They were the pride and joy of the family and Ruth was the favourite child. To kick your daughter when she was down was low, but Shirley saw the attack as symbolic of Juliet's lack of direction in life. If she was married that wouldn't have happened, was her asinine thinking.

The kitchen went stone floor quiet and cold with tension. Juliet looked around and saw mother had put her boring diamond egg collection in a locked cabinet in the hallway. The atmosphere was glass cold.

"You like Ruth more because she does as she's told and has given you grandchildren. Bully for her. Whoopee. You just won't accept that many women – like me – don't have a dying need to reproduce," piqued Juliet.

"Yes, because you're not listening to your biology clock ticking away. That's what's making you unhappy all the time and you don't even realise it!" pressed Shirley.

"Biological. You're infuriating me you know that," stressed Juliet.

"More evidence of you going against your maternal instincts!" stated Shirley like she was an expert doctor.

"Don't push it mom, you're out of touch," warned Juliet.

"Oh listen to her. What are you, in the Mafia or something? Ha!" derided Shirley.

"The whole point about being happy is NOT having people force their ways and will upon you, like you're doing now. I chose *not* to have children because I didn't want to bring a living creature into a fucked-up patriarchal society with more unfair and biased rules and regulations than Sharia Law. We're like headless chickens running around aimlessly looking for golden grains with no beaks to peck it up. I wouldn't want my child to experience the chaos and hatred out there I've experienced," explained Juliet with intelligent concern for humanity.

"You've experienced? Chickens? What are you talking about? You've led a charmed life compared to me. I had to work three jobs when your father and I first got married to make ends meet. You're just immature that's all – need to grow up," parried Shirley in her usual stubborn way.

"That's just not true on both counts. I can't be bothered arguing with you anymore to be honest. Taking a detour from the expected norm doesn't make me immature, it makes me a free thinker," justified Juliet.

"All your thinking's got you is headaches," cracked Shirley with aspirin intentions.

"No mother, the headaches are caused by you half the time. Anyway, I don't want to listen to you putting me down anymore. I'm going to pack my bags and look for a new apartment. You're supposed to be helping, not hurting," stated Juliet with candid force.

"I'm not putting you down and I *am* helping you. You're staying here aren't you and who's cooking you healthy meals every day – not all those contemporary salt and sugar takeaways you like?" said Shirley with a fair point.

"Okay, thanks for that but I don't want to hear your constant criticisms all the time – like you're any better. Dad couldn't stand your interfering either. That's why he left," prodded Juliet.

"Oh I suppose having two children was 'interfering' as well?" replied a bitter looking Shirley.

Do you know what's tasty? Eating humble pie.

Neither Juliet or Shirley knew how this argument was going to turn out now but the less intelligent Shirley had more life experience and knew how to push buttons to win debates.

In addition, Shirley had the support of her seriously arrogant bitch Siamese cat who suffered from Covert Narcissistic Personality Disorder and mainly rudeness. Mother was equally well backed-up by her beloved umbrella cockatoo who was actually one year older than Juliet in human years and liked to dish out monosyllabic advice. Shirley also had an anarchist tortoise and three snowflake angelfish. The crafty cat looked at Shirley as if to say, you're not going to take that are you and Shirley reacted.

People don't listen to advice, they hear wisdom.

"I want, I want! That's your way of life isn't it? And your father left because of that trollop secretary, not me!" shouted Shirley.

"You keep telling yourself that," said Juliet in the lippiest way possible as she returned to childhood.

"And you keep telling yourself you're happy the way you are," sarcastically put Shirley, concluding with, "You live in the clouds whilst the rest of us sort everything out."

"And you stole a cat to find happiness, so what does that make you?" stomped home Juliet.

"That was an accidental kidnapping and you know that," justified Shirley with a guilty look on her face.

"What, like the accidental kidnapping of Palestine?" shot home Juliet with her favourite sore point which she knew guaranteed causing mom stress.

Shirley had to do a lot of background damage limitation in her community after her own daughter went on #FreePalestine rallies to deliberately embarrass her, she believed.

"They invaded us first, as you know Juliet! I won't have another word said about that in my own house," insisted Shirley making stern eye contact and meaning it.

"Are you trying to ethnically cleanse my mind too?" said Juliet trying to put a nail in the coffin of that conversation. The taut atmosphere could only be cut with a chainsaw.

"Let me tell you something! I've lost countless good friends over the years defending you," said Shirley getting very upset.

"They weren't good friends then were they?" sarcastically said Juliet.

"They were *my* friends, good or not and they ostrich-necked me out because you couldn't show some appreciation to your community. Sometimes you have to bite the bullet to find peace," said Shirley feeling very perturbed.

"Tell that to the Palestinians who eat bullets every day," retorted Juliet.

"Don't be stupid! Nothing worse than a thankless child, but you wouldn't know that would you?" stabbed home mom knowing she'd gone too far.

"It's *ostracised* anyway mom, not ostrich. Crazy old bird," sighed Juliet with despondency.

Shirley couldn't take the mental tension anymore, so stood up and started doing some kind of improvisational chicken and ostrich tribal dance.

Juliet just shook her head and looked away trying to remain angry. But when mom pretended to lay an egg on the coffee table using an orange from the fruit bowl, Juliet could not withhold anymore and they both cracked-up laughing! It was a stalemate as usual. Mother and daughter always argued and there was a familiarity with that which was weirdly comforting.

The highly intelligent cat who understood English wasn't laughing though. Truth has a way of balancing life. Shirley had secretly always respected her smarter daughter Juliet more than Ruth because they were two peas in a pod. Mom then sat next to her youngest and hugged her, and they began a nice conversation about her mental illness and future plans now the same old battles were over.

Having a family is the most comforting and pleasant torture you will ever experience.

Juliet knew her mother meant well in a warped way, but was wondering if staying at her place was some kind of purgatory or divine trial from the heavens. Mommy was right in many respects. She had been there for Juliet during her mentally unstable years, which in all honesty were largely caused by her mother's dominance. The more you take control away from people, the less they can cope and survive on their own. Regardless, mom Shirley could see Juliet slipping into her inner worldly state again and – just like 20 years previously – still had no idea how to deal with the problem. Shouting didn't help then and it wasn't helping now either! This leopard only changed her spots with a shopping spree.

Juliet was feeling the lurking shadow of mental illness merging into her consciousness and daily life. She had never really known what mental illness was about. Juliet sometimes thought it was like when children put small toys all over the house in random places: move house to mind and that messiness is similar to mental illness.

Mental illness is a strange beast that hunts you from inside. The worst part is the animal is born by you to devour your own weaknesses. It's like an evil pet you have to feed with anxiety every day or it grows bigger as you turn into a carcass of a person. This sometimes self-imposed trap falsely imprisons its own creator. To find the key to escape you must first discover what has to be escaped. Many illnesses are invisible, but few devastate your mind and body like mental illness does.

Experiencing a mental breakdown is like having a skull full of smashed quail's eggs whisking your emotions into raw fear.

Juliet thought mental illness was like having a negative person inside of you always sabotaging your talent and confidence. Half the time it's a by-product of having a personality and rejecting an oppressive society. A good society which treats people fairly is the very best cure for most mental illnesses. And it's very important to remember that mental illness is not your fault. Mental illness is the worst illness in the world because it's the most prolific illness. It kills through suicide, tortures minds and the patient's suffering is often unseen, therefore unappreciated and uncared for.

Mental illness isn't yet accepted like any other illness because there is this perception that anything in the mind can be fixed by a change of lifestyle or attitude, giving it an underrated status. But people don't appreciate that you need a healthy mind to fix a broken mind.

Juliet had suffered with BPD since her late teens. She often wondered if it was borderline personality disorder or just reacting normally to the shit state of the world. Her doctors didn't have a clue anyway. Knowing that very few *so-called* experts knew what to do about her condition somehow made it a lot worse at first.

After trying many different, failed medical techniques, Juliet finally decided just to do her best to ignore it and move forward with her life. And ignorance had been sort of bliss for well over a decade until her nervous system was jarred by the Caesar sandwich, returning her mind to the past.

Now, Juliet faced the nightmare of not knowing how stable her mind would be from day to day. She had also totally given up work to recover and couldn't face press coverage bombardment to catch the dirty duo. The Daily News newspaper nicknamed the criminals The Romance Rapists which seemed to catch on because all serious crime should be mocked by sycophantic journalists who rarely write the truth.

The time turned back to madness because that's what humans are best at. Juliet's mind had been scrambled by recent events and changes. Truthfully, she was worried sick about everything. What was to become of her illness? Where was she going to go now? What was her reason for living? Would she ever trust men again? Who the hell was Ryan to mix such smoothness with horror? As she pondered a million uncertainties, God was back just to pick up his glasses he left behind again, so he rung the doorbell to help her out.

Thus far, Juliet had not wanted to open the door to anyone. She was slowly becoming a recluse and going a bit jittery. But this time round mommy was having trouble doing a poop. Shirley had a strange relationship with shit. Virtually every time Juliet called her up, mom would ask if she had done her daily stool. Shirley was a regular and Juliet was irregular.

"You'll have to get that bunny!" came a muffled shout from the crapper. "Use the eye thing!"

Juliet ignored the bell, but it sounded repeatedly so she reluctantly approached the door and spied on two figures facing. It was the police, again. She'd kinda had enough of them and just wanted to forget the whole attack ever happened, but they looked hot so she opened the door immediately and proved she had learned absolutely nothing. Instincts are more powerful than thoughts.

A strapping man and fit woman presented themselves to Juliet and put her at ease straight away by identifying themselves as police detective and officer. They both remained professional despite inside both thinking, fucking hell I want a piece of that! The controlling and surly cat called **BAGEL** was not impressed with their machismo upsetting her chi and **EMMENTAL** the parrot called out, "Cock!" very loudly.

We know nothing about each other but our souls seem to know everything.

"The department would like to apologize Ms. Green for the lack of closure on your case so far. So far we've had less leads than hoped for, so Deputy Inspector Maddox has reassigned a fresh pair of faces to re-examine all possibilities again," said the handsome chap.

Fresh face, she thought, I like freshness! Juliet's sexy thought made her immediately question how ill she really was. It's amazing what a beautiful face can do to raise one's spirits. "May we come in please?" asked Detective **FLYNN O'CONNELL** in his usual calm manner.

Flynn was a tall, handsome man, very strong and rugged looking. He also had a determined look in his eyes which said, I don't give up easily on anything, ever. Flynn made his way up through the ranks, coming from Irish American poverty in Bay Ridge, Brooklyn after his Hawaiian mother eloped with his Irish dad on military leave.

Flynn had drive and integrity, and was exactly what Juliet needed in her life. However, going over the same facts all over again for an hour, kind of quashed a lot of life sparkle. Nevertheless, their time together was productive. Not only had Flynn spontaneously made up his mind that Juliet was love at first sight, but he'd uncovered a significant piece of information the other detectives nicknamed Bummer & Jackass had missed.

The anticipated CCTV footage of Ryan at the restaurant with Juliet was botched because the acting manager called **PIERRE** simply forgot to wipe the previous month's video and reset it for that whole week. He was too busy juggling surly staff and flambéed crêpe suzettes to remember security protocol, and was fired for causing the Boatman owners some embarrassment. And all footage of Ryan and Juliet outside – from multiple angles – was more silhouette than recognisable. It was apparent to Flynn that some more inventive detective work would be required to catch the filthy scumbags.

Juliet had already described in detail to a police sketch artist the odd fragmented tattoo going across

Ryan's palm, side fingers and outer thumb of his right hand, which looked like skin wrinkled half moons with divots in them. Detectives B & J just did the obvious routine line of enquiries asking around at tattoo places if any of the artists recognised the finger-jumping design, which no-one did. But the dumb detectives failed to appreciate the significance of every last detail of seemingly irrelevant evidence.

A man's vehicle is often his pride and machinery status to show off. Real men like the roar of a powerful engine which promises so much more piston bang than they can offer. A car is god's gift to men as they are to women in their fantasies; it's their aesthetic, metallic reference and revved up mark on the world. Logically then, the inside of a man's car reflects a his inner mind, so Flynn took some uncomfortable questioning time gaining a feel for the driver's cockpit.

Among a bedrock of fast food plastic and a hanging skull and cross bones air freshener, Juliet recalled a number of small dashboard stickers with pop culture references. And when she came to think about it more this cross referenced with multiple other snippets of comments from Ryan and Pulp Fiction type, cult patronisations she didn't really get at dinner.

The man who obviously wasn't called Ryan was a pop culture snob and secret geek whose passion for tattoos was equal to his lust for the grape and rape. Beneath the predictable aftershave, he was hiding a cigarette and alcohol addiction which stemmed from an abusive and insecure childhood. Ryan was an arrogant piece of work with a cocky swagger to his walk and an underground asshole who belittled anyone who didn't catch his cult references. He spoke in riddles so he could feel superior to people who didn't have time to be a man-child.

Ryan wasn't as cunning as he thought though. Much of what he said during the dinner scattered many random breadcrumbs he knew Juliet wouldn't grasp, but after some thinking away from Juliet's beauty, professional detective Flynn had a few good hunches. Until him and officer González left, Flynn was mesmerized by Juliet as though he were spellbound. He certainly wanted to see her again and was already looking forward to gathering enough breadcrumb evidence to put a bun in the oven.

Yeah sex is sex, but have you ever fallen asleep in someone's arms and felt totally safe and secure?

That star filled night, Juliet felt the first real wave of optimism since her traumatic ordeal. Detective Flynn O'Connell had done the greatest thing anyone can do for anybody who is depressed: he gave Juliet the gift of hope!

Her pillow suddenly looked whiter than normal. Her thoughts also picked themselves up and started to dust themselves down. Then her mind began to fill up with many options thanks to this dashing prince who parted with the words, "I feel confident Ms. Green the NYPD will find and arrest these men after the help you have provided today, thank you ma'am."

Of course he got caught up with chivalry to impress because the chances of catching the thugs were more paper thin than slim, but Flynn now had the greatest motivation any red-blooded man needs; a shot at a beautiful woman without using a bullet.

I didn't think I could get any happier until I met you. You are my light, my moon and stars, and every breath I take.

Juliet had been reinvigorated by Flynn's optimistic outlook. He was just the injection of positive energy she needed. As the evening drew to a quiet close, her mind and soul began to return to a natural shape, like a tulip. Despair and fear seemed a lot less as Juliet lay down in bed and gazed through the window, unfortunately facing the neighbour's brick wall, which strangely tonight seemed to be full of beautiful reds, purples and oranges not noticed before.

Flynn had clearly made her day lighter and happier because he believed in living every day to the fullest without worrying. Suddenly, Juliet sprung from her bed mattress with some bounce and said out loud, "Fuck it!" as she went for her mobile which had been hidden in a drawer for the last two weeks; the longest period of technological isolation in her entire life. It was almost revolutionary.

She then fired the phone up like starship Enterprise to explore the world again, after plugging the charger in which took about 6 minutes to reboot. Twitter was Juliet's former home where she had a large fan base waiting to follow their leader's lifestyle again. They needed her as much as she needed them now.

After a further 9 minutes sorting out a new password, Juliet was free again to air her most inner thoughts to total strangers; that is, after spending 7 ½ hours filtering through and politely responding to 6,729 missed replies and well wishers.

It was now about 5am and a pink sun rose from happy house lines. Juliet was exhausted but relieved to read her internet pal's jokes and thoughts again. Now felt like the right time to rise with the sun and deliver the thread of a lifetime:

Hi, The Twitter bitch is back! Thanks for all your kind words of support which mean the world to me. Why was I missing? It's very hard for me to say this but you all deserve to know the truth. In short, a fake man took me out to dinner, offered to drop me off home and then tried to...

...rape me. Oh, I forgot the best part. The rapist had a rapist buddy hiding in his van too who thought he'd join in the party. Fortunately for me I had somewhere else to be so stabbed one in the eye with my heel and pepper sprayed all available male eyes before escaping. Broke my...

100

...arm in the high jinks, better now. The worst part was returning to the dragon lord's home again for a respite to be fed boiled marrow, stewed liver & other wives' tale recipes. And yes, mother still believes that a coffee & donut lifestyle is evil, lol. Thanx again u guys 4 your 🖤 💋

Juliet pressed send to this triple tweet, but the words sounded upsettingly hollow to her. Making a joke out of the frightful ordeal was the popular Twitter Juliet of her recent past. She had changed a lot and lost her confidence in buckets and spades, like being helplessly trapped under sand.

Juliet's Twitter friends bounced love back into her but the magic and charisma was washing away with the flotsam and jetsam of uncertainty. She was confused, in the shadows and dreamt of a reviving sun kissing her skin. A heavy heart smudged words in her sunken mind.

Ever read a word definition and understood it less than before?

9

Crackerjack Catch

One week after Juliet dealt with all the many thousands of kind replies to her confessional thread, she remembered the real world existed. She was obviously very moved by everyone's phenomenal support. Each day Juliet had a good cry into a pillow before bedtime which helped release her anxiety. Her Twitter account octodecupled since her heroine fame went viral. Being a victim on social media is top currency.

The truth is less popular than burnt toast.

Early September rain soaked into dry cracks. Juliet's mind was healing well. Detective Flynn had kick-started a psychological revival which felt like listening to Mozart's Eine Kleine Nachtmusik. Waking up from the dark spell of depression, Juliet obviously realized the importance of catching the Romance Rapists because she didn't want other women suffering the full romantic experience. But if she was totally honest with herself, her newfound desire to punish the perpetrators was also a convenient chance to interact with Flynn again, a lot more and many more times hopefully. She dreamed with frivolity like a schoolgirl crush. He was also five years younger than her, which would be a first in her bf history. Juliet now felt ready for some change! Change is good.

You won't make any major positive changes until you turn your mind the whole way towards the grim face of reality and say hello.

Making a beeline for her handbag, Juliet sifted through a lifetime of memories and eventually found detective Flynn's neat looking business card. Her mind raced through the attack again, but this time in a slightly detached way. She too was looking to impress him with her determination to nab the duo. A distanced calm came over Juliet and she recalled a few more tiny fragments of evidence which could help. Her mind logically started from the beginning to the broken end of the fateful night: Ryan may have hired his suit and he also had a tiny lisp she was previously prepared to overlook; his beautiful blue eyes seemed very blue too, maybe contacts; he was a bit too aggressive with the youths who threw a piece of featherweight plastic at them and with the horse; one of the van stickers was a hand holding a walnut and another had a single pawn on a chessboard; she tripped over a toolbox in the back; Caesar was abnormally muscular and smelt of rank rotting dog BO.

Perhaps these tidbits of extra clues could help handsome Flynn become her daddy protector? She texted him all the points and other ones like an obsessive throughout the evening. Obviously being very busy Flynn didn't even look at his phone until his shift was over at 11pm. He was tired, hungry and just thinking about bed. However, like most men, Flynn was a slave to his penis which made him trawl through tons of mental Juliet messages against the grain until tiredness drowned some professionalism and he texted her back:

Flynn: Hi, thanks for all the information. That's great work Juliet! I appreciate your help. Just knowing you exist is a great source of inspiration to me.

Juliet: That's really nice. Thank you. Inspiration for what? X

Flynn: I like to write about the beauty of the world in the little spare time I have. It helps me counter the nastiness I frequently see as a cop. I wrote a short poem for you in the evening after we first met. Would you like to see it?

Juliet: Yes please! 👍

Flynn: When I gaze into her beautiful eyes,
And listen to her alone song,
I feel passionate skies
Calling me to belong
To a higher plain beyond.

Juliet: Beautiful! I'd love to read more of your writing sometime 💕

Flynn: Alas, tonight's clouds shield the star's beauty from my delight, so I say goodnight xx

Juliet: Goodnight xx

Flynn had to cut Juliet off because he had nothing left in the tank. He was knackered and his best friend sleep called to him. Juliet liked the fact he didn't seem desperate anyway and had a full life. However, Flynn was as desperate as every eligible bachelor out there who'd ploughed the field and now wanted a farmstead family of his own. Every genuine man's dream is to be loved and respected for being a good dad. The day eventually comes when you want the truth, not convenient interpretations of life.

She came in pretty
with a light breeze
taking my heart
and troubles away.

The following lemon sunshine morning Flynn was annoyed with himself for mixing business with pleasure. Smartphones make that easy to happen and shuffle your thoughts up too. Flynn had always remained professional in his career and had seen many officers fired for conduct unbecoming. He was also tipped as a contender for the upcoming rank of Sergeant; one great jump up the ladder. Unbeknown to him, Deputy **INSPECTOR MADDOX** had earmarked him for the esteemed position if he were to solve this feather in his cap Romance Rapists case. So Flynn called Juliet up to apologise but her sultry voice melted his heart and they chatted for over an hour about life. As they emotionally connected, the evidence did too and Flynn now had an educated guess the rapists were into tattoos possibly beyond just wearing them.

A few drop-ins and stop-bys to Shirley's house for lunch throughout that week and the well matched couple really were getting on well. Juliet was moulding him into The One in her mind; Flynn was keen for her beauty and a serious relationship; and Shirley wished they would both just fuck off out so she could watch The Golden Girls in peace! She was of course pleased for her daughter looking a lot happier and laughing, but TV is the new God. God did not agree.

If you don't own a television chances are you've got a life.

The only creature genuinely unhappy with a *man* frequenting their house was Bagel the crackerjack cat. Emmental the parrot was much more easy going and had got used to the shift in hormones, evidenced by croaking, "Pussy!" whenever Flynn entered the lounge.

Emmental was actually mocking Bagel who'd had the whip hand over everyone, especially Shirley, for years on end until Juliet upset the balance by moving in and now Flynn's presence ruined everything. Bagel's manipulative powers had been shrunk by handsome Flynn because Shirley was now spending a fair portion of her usual Bagel stroking, fresh food preparing and cat worshiping time flirting with the younger man instead.

Bagel was understandably upset though with the demise of her lifestyle. The embittered Siamese cat once had a glorious family life full of love and children until Juliet's father, Eric, reached maximum overload with Shirley's nagging and controlling ways which led him to having an affair. After their rapid divorce, Shirley couldn't go to her favourite Long Island hotels anymore with her rich friends because

107

she was the laughing stock of Brooklyn, in her mind. Instead she took a long Block Island, Rhode Island vacation to recover from the trauma and neighbourhood embarrassment, and found herself a stray cat lingering around the hotel seeming very hungry.

Formerly called Suzie, Bagel wasn't a stray or remotely hungry though. She lived a lovely life a few doors down and was fuck buddy's with the hotel concierges' American bobtail cat, **ROMEO**, who used to shag any cat in sight, but always left his conquests feeling individually special.

Romeo was such a stud cat he even humped a poodle once for sport. The guy had moves and Bagel missed him enormously after Shirley lured her back to her hotel room and callously imprisoned her against hotel regulations. Romeo even scratched out a poem for her once:

I've got the hots for Suzie fur.
I listen to her beautiful purr,
And have no choice, falling into trance
Dancing my heart away it's true,
I can't get enough of you.

Shirley couldn't quite recall if Bagel had a collar and identity tag. Suzie the cat *did* and Shirley cut it off and threw it in the bin to be reborn as Bagel.

Shirley's humiliating divorce confused lots of things and she felt incredibly attached to her newfound friend whom she'd saved from certain disaster and starvation on the mean streets – her mind imagined for its own convenience. Her deep depression turned cat kidnapping into an act of charity and that was the story Shirley had been telling everyone since. 'It was an act of compassion,' she told one vague friend and, 'I lost a husband and God gave me a cat,' she explained to a stranger in Walmart too.

Shirley was not good at making friends and now she had one who couldn't argue back or needed to be caged like Emmental. It takes a big person to admit they were wrong and an even bigger one to find out why.

The darkest nights of depression will make you rise like a phoenix one day. So do not despair.

On her first day in Brooklyn, Bagel recognised straight away that all of Shirley's pets were locked up in some way or another. **TONY CURTIS** the tortoise had been trying for years to break out of the garden to escape Shirley's dietary tyranny and nearly made it one day through a fence panel he'd been working loose for over 6 months of hard toil for a tortoise (a 1 minute task for any human). But alas the neighbour caught Tony in their garden munching on petunia petals and returned him within 7 minutes of going AWOL.

I'd rather fight for what I believe in and fail, than be rewarded for turning blind eye to the truth.

Bagel was very smart though and knew she could exploit her pet role and conventional freedoms given to a cat. It didn't take long before the more intelligent cat used Shirley's divorce and emotional pain to her advantage, making Shirley dependent upon Bagel's company.

To summarize her guile, using a series of established psychological tools developed by psychologists Pavlov and Skinner, Bagel had managed to wrap Shirley around her little claws and soon all Bagel's pets had to tow Bagel's line. Bagel did what she had to do to survive at first, but just like with human frailties, excessive comfort turned to abusive demands not before long. Tony wasn't allowed to chew anything when Bagel was relaxing in the garden and Emmental lost his daily fruit rations if he ever made a peep when Bagel was watching television. Bagel had become a worse dictator than her captor and even punished Shirley by running away for a night or two if her menu or something didn't suit. Once Bagel saw loads of missing posters Shirley pinned up on lampposts and tress just hours after absconding – showing how much she cared – Bagel knew she had her human owner well and truly whipped. Slave had become master.

Recently though, Flynn and Juliet's newfound happiness had tipped Bagel over the edge. Not only was her routine completely kaput, but it triggered memories of happy days with Romeo. Most cats have a pencil penis, yet Romeo's prick was like a thick black marker pen which vandalised her pussy passions. Suzie really missed his graffiti play and signature moves.

We don't give pets enough credit. Pets are amazing! They comfort you in troubled times and save many lives.

Bagel was determined that one way or another, Shirley, Juliet and/or Flynn would suffer for their crimes against animal rights! Confusing things, Bagel was also a Communist who believed working American Capitalism no longer practiced free trade and was therefore Communist in style. Furthermore, Bagel the Chinese cat by origin and look was paranoid everyone around her was always being racist. She once lashed out at Emmental for merely asking if she'd like a Chinese takeaway from the local restaurant bins. It would be fair to say Bagel was hard to live with.

The human trio had all gone out for lunch today and again the pets suffered for their absence. However, it was the perfect opportunity for Bagel to rally support for her righteous animal rights cause. Obviously all of the pets could communicate in English with each other because this is America and anything can happen, including mass shootings occurring on a daily basis (434 in 2019, killing 517 people and injuring a further 1,643).

"Pets are not entertainment! Pets shouldn't even be called *pets*. It's degrading," meowed Bagel to Emmental.

"Are you saying I'm not entertaining?" mocked Emmental, who knew that would cost him tonight's dinner. "What are we then?" he said with a sarcastic drawl.

"We feel, we sense, we know so much more about plains of intuition than people, yet we are their possessions – like trophy wives," objected Bagel.

"Well yes, but they do all the hard work and we do fuck all every day. *La dolce vita mon amie*. Plus, what do you know of flying?" Emmental only spoke tourist Italian or French and it showed.

"I'll ignore your *plane* attempts at humour caged cockatoo. Don't you want to fly free with the other birds?" asked Bagel, trying to win him over with violence.

"No. The wild birds would beat me to a pulp in minutes and peck my eyes out. I loved it here until you changed everything. This cage keeps *you* away from *me* thank God," rudely explained Emmental.

"Yes, you're a bully Bagel!" muttered the brave tortoise who finally made it to the meeting. "The fish live in fear of you too!" concluded Tony Curtis who was just ready to sneak into his shell when he hesitated after seeing a contrite looking Bagel with downturned whiskers. She looked shocked. The pets had spoken and they were not united as Bagel assumed. Assumptions are for gaslighters, gamblers and fools.

This was kinda upsetting for Bagel. Realising she had become the living embodiment of everything she stood against wasn't easy to hear. Bagel knew it was now time to gather the courage to make the very long journey back home to Block Island on paw, even though it meant certain failure, doom and drowning. She'd been cowardly and taken the easy route, like most creatures naturally do.

You become a worthwhile person once you believe other people are worthwhile too.

Bagel once attempted the nearly 190 mile journey, only to be stopped dead after just 9 miles by a mob of nasty rats called Fresh Meat, known for abducting and cannibalising stray pets like gerbils, hamsters and even cats. Their motto was, 'Roses are red, Violets are blue, Please stop dead, Or I'll cut you in two,' which they did anyway. If it wasn't for promising to put out to a local alley cat who defended her, Bagel never would have survived.

The humans have created a society which is like a polite prison and without money you literally get fucked. Having to prostitute herself to stay alive was truly degrading and totally knocked Suzie's confidence for six. She returned to being called

Bagel and never made another attempt back to her real human family who were so heartbroken when she disappeared they got a kitten just one week later to console the children.

Bagel looked at her fellow pets, said sorry for her behaviour and finally explained everything that happened as the floodgates of her heart opened. Emmental, Tony and the angelfish called **THREE WISE MEN** – albeit females – accepted her apology after seeing her pain. They vowed to help Bagel return to her former home and in order to do so without dying, she would need a car and a driver willing to chauffeur a cat across US States. Easier said than done.

Despite the difficult challenge ahead, the moon seemed much more whole that night to Bagel and her faith in God restored. And a good job too because God was now on his final attempt to do some good for humanity after failing so miserably by putting Juliet and Ryan together. God's whole attention now focused on returning Bagel to her former owners, which could cause some major confusion because the children had already buried her in a pretend shoebox ceremony.

When I hug you, you will know you are loved and protected.

10

Snoop Dogs

Back in a sincere human mind, Flynn told Juliet not to mention any of the thoughts about his investigation to anyone. Therefore, she obviously went straight on Twitter and told her best friends everything in confidence. Soon, ideas and conjectures started bouncing off Twitter walls everywhere. Twitter is like the world's largest pick-

'n'-mix of thoughts. Choose wisely which ones you scoop up.

A handful of Juliet's absolute finest BFF tweepz continued to offer support and sent loving messages throughout her distressed absence. They were genuinely worried about Juliet and no-one had her real-life phone number or email either.

Juliet got mental strength from her best Twitter buddies who now formed a United Nation's conglomerate of bored amateur sleuths keenly looking to solve her case. They called themselves the **Bird-Dogs**, opening up a secure chat room to delegate lines of gumshoe enquiry and also to have a shot at 15 minutes of fame. Juliet was concerned her attack was being turned into a game show hunt, but Twitter is just a game so what did she expect. Twitter would be so much better if only pigeons were allowed to use it. Anyway, you're not doing Twitter right unless it slightly ruins your real life.

Ever felt the beauty of a generous spirit touch your heart? Magical!

Apart from a fucking waste of time and avoidance of work, Twitter chat rooms are the nerve centre of the pointlessness and apathy surrounding Twitter. They are the ultimate bubble distraction and avoidance of life, perfect for very unproductive artists. Chat rooms are like secret societies for low earners. When you enter a chat room, time stands still and the bitching begins!

Ever get tired of the sound of your own voice and wish you'd just shut the fuck up a bit more and listen?

On their virgin session, the Bird-Dog bloodhounds chatted into the early hours of the night whilst their real life partners did all the hard work. The group's names in order of intellect were **PHILIPPA**, **BUBBLES**, **BLACK ORCHID**, **JULIET**, **FUNKIN' DUDE** and **MISERY LOWLIFE**.

It was evident things may become problematic because Juliet had especially handpicked an A-Team from hundreds of Twitter friends in order to get the greatest minds at work. Unfortunately, half of them hated one another, or just didn't gel well at least, having experienced multiple bitter skirmishes in their Twitter past. And two of them, Misery and Philippa, even had to hold up the white flags and unblock each other for Juliet's sake. Not before long, Juliet rapidly became UN Peacekeeper to half a dirty dozen great Twitter characters adored by thousands of pretend fans.

As the heartbeat, victim and bureau chief of Operation BIRDBATH, Juliet was unsure where these private investigations were going to lead but was a coddiwomple by nature.

It was 2:32am (EST) and the Bird-Dogs had only wasted about 3 hours chatting – more like arguing –

mainly about Feminism and Ecology. Once Philippa said she didn't believe global warming actually exists and this was not a belief but *fact*, their precious time was going to be limited. Eventually things settled down a bit:

Juliet: I don't think we should talk about my mom's cat's covert narcissistic personality disorder anymore guys. Bagel already controls every aspect of my mom's confidence. She IS my mom, lol. 🐌

Misery Lowlife: You sure you've not been brainwashed by the evil cat too, LMFAO!

Misery Lowlife
@BeautifulMoths

Unapologetic Feminist who don't take no shit from any man, woman or alien. Fuck you, I do what I want! Ain't no hypocrite Man. 🪰

⊙ Preferably away from men

▦ Joined June 2015

3,197 Following   **14.5K** Followers

Misery Lowlife was from Southern California and the loosest canon of the bunch. She was extremely funny, random and much smarter than she let on, and frequently got suspended for forthright views. Staunch Feminist Misery was pretty much the antithesis of straight-laced Philippa who was vehemently anti-Feminist. Both strong women had clashed during a number of major Twitter debates, but were mutual friends with the other guys so agreed on the temporary armistice. Luckily Bubbles the Welsh lass was around to keep the peace. Unfortunately she had recently broken up with a cheater and this somewhat reflected in her attitude:

Bubbles: I only love dogs because they're loyal. Cats are deceitful like men and the world has enough treacherous men in it, so let's move on please.

Approaching the big four O, Bubbles was far from flying bubbles right now. She was very thoughtful and smart, however a negative maudlin mood overshadowed everything she did at the mo'. Relationship break-ups are often like a car crash: a massive shock is followed by a euphoria for having escaped alive! Relationships end up teaching you more than universities do.

Bubbles was too intellectual for most people to relate to, therefore her follower count was miles lower than what it deserved. She used her mind and never her pretty face or tits to communicate, which is a big no-no on Twitter for popularity sake.

Bubbles
@BubbleTrouble

I'd rather have my house burned down than let someone gaslight my mind. 🦄

⊚ Top Secret Ambiguity 🏔️

▦ Joined January 2014

2,262 Following   **5,972** Followers

Misery Lowlife: There's nothing quite like depression to help us move forward. 😬

Bubbles: Better depressed than always undressed, ha.

Misery Lowlife: I'd rather suck dick than get on everyone's wick! 🌀

Bubbles: Rather Netflix than doing tricks. Laugh Out Loud :)

Black Orchid: Calm down now children and focus on the task at hand. We're here to discuss Juliet's serious attack, not call each other hoes. So far all there has been is bickering and silliness. Did any of you even notice I left to take a bath?

Funkin' Dude: No. Who invited mother? Anyway, isn't a hoe a garden implement? 🌑

Misery Lowlife: "Mother." You're going to pay for that dude. 😂🧽😂

Black Orchid: I can rise above a spelling mistake for the sake of Juliet.

Funkin' Dude: Humour is our guiding light. Once you can laugh at yourself, the world seems right again. ✌️

Funkin' Dude

@FunkyDoodling

I'm not a radish I'm rad.

⦿ Twitterverse Bro from future

▦ Joined January 2021

3,694 Following   **60,952** Followers

Funkin' Dude was a mini, up-and-coming internet sensation. He was honest, sharp and most of all hilarious! This guy had funny bones in elephant skeleton size. Juliet needed him in the group for jester laughs and to break through the shittiness of

121

life. But the Dude was much more than just a great jokester: he represented the beta male population, winning daily disputes against the so-called alpha 'beautiful people'. He was the underdog and people's champion rolled into one, and his brand new Twitter account was growing quicker than bamboo!

Different ideas of Twitter romance:
Woman: I want you to love me like a lioness protects her cubs.
Man: I used my erect penis to type this message of love for you.

Poor Black Orchid didn't know how to handle the fast pace of Funkin' Dude, the only man in Juliet's elite detective team. The Orchid was in her 60's and tired of life. She had spent a lifetime being gaslighted by her repeatedly cheating husband, finally summoning the courage to leave him – for the second time. Orchid took full responsibility for having chosen an alpha male and that's often the bad deal you know you will get.

Things weren't going well for the Black Orchid. Not only did she have to return to mother in the wet North of England, having lived in sunny Mediterranean Europe, but she was blissfully unaware her husband's abusive controlling behaviour had rubbed off on her too. Sometimes evil gets tired of its host and needs a fresh horse to trot on. Orchid was well spoken and from a posh background. Unfortunately, like all privileged people, Orchid felt she had some social right to own the poor people and to have them come running at her beck and call. She had recently turned to the dark side and Juliet was unaware that Orchid's blackness was beginning to manipulate her.

If you are experiencing gaslighting then convert to all electric.

Like all the best bullies who adopt their affliction, Black Orchid won Juliet over with a sob story and had adopted Juliet like a pet project to counter her depression and boredom in life. Users always latch on like leeches. Orchid had become twisted by the bad fortunes she made for herself and now spread anxiety and panic like poison ivy everywhere her darkness loomed. And she was in shameless denial. Her profile actually said 'Happily married' whilst she was in the process of getting a divorce. Orchid was also a psychotic serial retweeter, having posted over 161,000 tweets in under 2 years.

Black Orchid
@WhiteBlossom

Happily married mother | Lover of flowers | Don't agree with Feminism but can see how it happened | None of those penis pictures please via DM.

⊚ Happily existing peacefully 🏴

▦ Joined May 2019

8,727 Following   **5,065** Followers

Philippa: We do need some order here people. I'm kinda above this wasting loads of my valuable time banter thing. Juliet asked me to come here to solve a crime, not witness one.

Misery Lowlife: Yu know what is a crime?

Philippa: I'm sure you are about to enlighten me.

Misery Lowlife: Women defending men's rights, especially after Juliet has just been attacked by two dirt bags.

Philippa: So you're saying if one man does wrong, that all men are horrible? 👻

Misery Lowlife: I said two men. TWO!

Philippa: I have a theory about those 2 nasty men, not all the millions of decent men out there who get alienated from seeing their own children because they have no child custody rights.

Funkin' Dude: Spit it out then babe.

Philippa: 'Philippa' please, not babe or dude. Juliet, you said the van's dashboard had a transfer of a walnut on it, and many other similar emblems you can't recall the details of?

Juliet: A walnut or a testicle, not sure, lol. Yes, go on...

Philippa
@Philippa_Fairness

Feminists are a walking contradiction, de-evolving society. Psychology and philosophy exponent. I write because I have to.

⊚ Canada

▦ Joined February 2010

50 Following   **9,923** Followers

Twenty eight year old Philippa was certainly the top brains of this think tank and was on to something. Being such a principled woman made life hard for her, but that's what principles do. She was resilient, strong-willed and had a sense of humour which needed a lot of coffee to wake it up. Philippa was the antithesis of Misery Lowlife. She got a great deal of stimulation from lively, intellectual debate and Misery got most of her stimulation from hard cock.

Philippa: These car logos or emblems seem most pertinent to me to solving this mystery.

Misery Lowlife: Pertinent. Who even talks like that? 😜

Funkin' Dude: Wartime babes?

Black Orchid: Lol.

Juliet: Silence in court please people, it's very late. Continue Philippa, ONLY.

Black Orchid: Sorry Juliet. Yes, people only put images they are comfortable with in their car. Good point.

Philippa: Yes, they are personal and therefore reflect the person.

Misery Lowlife: Therefore, lol. We're not at uni' Phil. I think you're going into too much Satanic detail as per usual. We all like to know the truth, but when it comes knocking it's a bit of a shock like an evil party clown that's gone to the wrong address. Have you considered it's not about the bollocks, but the symbolism in general? Perhaps he's an virulent artist?

Philippa: Satanic? If by evil you mean explicating obfuscatory Feminist agendas to people in direct, understandable terms, then yes, your "what's best for women" Feminism is evil, I agree. Have you considered that a couple of delinquents raping women may not have the resources, willpower or time to paint pretty pictures on a Sunday afternoon?

Black Orchid: This bickering is infantile, maybe not pointless though. I think the friction between you two ladies has created some fire at last.

Funkin' Dude: How so dude?

Black Orchid: Well, maybe both of you are right?

Funkin' Dude: You mean Misery and Philippa agree? That truly is the best joke of the night! .

Juliet:

Black Orchid:

Fuckin' Dude: . Quality spontaneous combustion.

Philippa: I won't believe it! LOL.

Misery Lowlife: L O FUCKING L.

Juliet: Where's the fire at?

127

Misery Lowlife: It's certainly not under Orchid's dress from what I've heard.

Funkin' dude: 😖

Black Orchid: Listen moody misery, my marital status is none of your arrogant and conceited business. I've been married for 42 years; probably the same number as men you've slept with!! I'm not going to stand for these insults. I'm out of this place, pronto! Good luck Juliet. 🍃

Misery Lowlife: 1 down, 4 to go, lol.

Funkin' Dude: You see us like bowling pins then? Probably because we're shaped like your dildos otherwise you won't feel us dude.

Philippa: LMFAO!!!!

Misery Lowlife: Another one bites the dust!

Philippa: You realise you're a bully don't you, misery in your mouth? Feminists love to have everything their own way and when they don't they throw temper tantrums. How's the having your life paid for you by men whilst putting them down thing working out for you?

Misery Lowlife: Just fine thanks. How's the frigid not getting any dick ever thing working out for you?

Philippa: I don't equate penis with 100% of my pleasure in life, unlike you.

Funkin' Dude: I'm sorry to hear that. Was hoping to take you out on a date sometime.

Juliet: Lol. Yes, you two would actually make a good couple. Seriously dude.

Misery Lowlife: Please don't torture our Dude. Going out with Philippa would be like returning to Victorian hanging children times.

Fucking Dude: Actually, I think going out with Philippa would be the best thing that ever happened to me. I should be so lucky. 🐦

Philippa was silent. Beneath all of the hatred Misery and her had for each other, the Dude had developed a major Twitter crush on Philippa and she was warming to his buffoon style hilarity too. From darkness comes light and from humour comes children.

Bubbles: Back from the ladies room, a cup of tea and biscuits in hand. What did I miss?

Juliet: 2 deserters, some flames and a marriage made in heaven.

Philippa: Make it 3 deserters I feel.

129

Funkin' Dude: Don't go Philippa please.

Misery Lowlife: Please go Philippa please do us all a favor.

Fuckin' Dude: Why so much hate Misery? You can't change your abusive past, just accept it and move on.

Misery Lowlife: As much as you can't make Philippa love you loser.

Bubbles: WTF! It seems whilst I've been taking a dump, you've been talking more shit Misery.

Misery Lowlife: Flush yourself down the toilet next time. Count me out Juliet! I don't need this crap!!

Bubbles: You are the only one sinking yourself like a turd, not me. Bye.

Funking Dude: Time for me to take a time out tooo dudes. Adios. Good luck Juliet. 💕

Misery Lowlife: Fuck you all!!! You didn't even stand up for me Juliet, nor the other day when The Art Teacher called me a ho either! I gonna block all your asses!!

Juliet: People are entitled to their opinion Misery. The Art Teacher is totally unique and you're just looking like common hate right now. You've been out of line tonight with the Dude. He's a decent guy. I think you need a few home truths to bring you back to yourself.

Juliet: Anyone there?

Bubbles: I've been blocked by Misery. She's lost the plot tonight. Living up to her Lowlife status, ha! Looks like the Bird Dogs are no more. It's just you and me left sister, haha.

Juliet: Kinda peaceful isn't it. Just checked. Misery has blocked me too. #MeToo

Bubbles: That's so fake after all that time. I've found there's a surprisingly fine line between a soul mate and a shit friend.

Juliet: Wish there were a lot more mature adults around than the hordes of childlike adults you have to deal with daily. The older you get, the less time you waste with morons, even if you are one, lol.

Bubbles: Hahaha! Too true.... Just scanned over the convo'. In the forge of the fire came a sword, not just sparks.

Juliet: Do all you Brits talk like you're in Lord of the Rings, lol?

Bubbles: Ha Haa. No, but I think I found Excalibur for you lady of the lake.

Juliet: ???

Bubbles: Not a Sunday afternoon painter, but a professional artist. And no-one can make a living from painting with oils, but what IS a boom industry these days: drawing on skin, not canvas.

Juliet: A tattoo artist! God, maybe you're right!

Bubbles: It's been known to happen from time to time, bahahaha. Used to be nicknamed Egghead, ha. Maybe this Ryan has got a minor ink rep?

Juliet: By Jove me lady, I believe the butler has served tea with crustless egg sandwiches! 🍵

Bubbles: I'm from Wales, not England, and I believe they don't speak like that anymore, lol. I'm outta here too, ha ha. Only kidding :)

Juliet: I'm the last woman standing, as always, lol.

Bubbles: Night Juliet. 🖤

Juliet: Night Bubbles. Did you know Shakespeare invented the word Bubbles?

Bubbles: Yes. Night again x

Juliet: Are the stars different in Wales? Lol

Bubbles: Goooodnight Juliet! And remember, not everyone is a piece of shit.

Juliet: I know. You remember too, you need quality nighttime sleep to be happy. The planets and stars are the only factors putting us in our miniscule place – as well as our mums and dads too I suppose. I wish dad was here.

Bubbles had drifted into a cloud bubble of dreams and the night wore thin. Thus, the Bird Dogs were totally disbanded after tonight's pitiful display of whatever. But the sleuth detectives had found the truth behind The Romance Rapist's reign of terror, after being nudged by Flynn's suspicions. Furthermore, destiny pulled Funkin' Dude and Philippa together, who eventually hooked up in real life about 9 months later, married the following Spring and had their first child on Christmas Eve. It was one magical Christmas to remember and the Dude had to cut a lot of great pranks out now that his responsibilities had trebled overnight. Philippa was steering the ship, but she always let Funkin' Dude be himself.

Women who don't nag, monitor or manipulate you. Those women. Applause!

133

Deep in the moon of that night, Juliet posted the tattoo artist suspicions on Twitter before sleep and by morning she woke to a bombardment of possible scenarios the criminals were hiding out in. Many tweeps agreed her attackers were probably mobile, not shop based. This seemed to make sense. It's amazing how clever a large group of stupid people can be when they work together. Teamwork using our intuition is what nature intended.

Your intuition is like
a forest sprite moving
faster than light,
so listen to the
knowledge in the trees
and read the wisdom
in your tears.

The two criminals on the loose were A-typical arrogant American tattoo artists living an evil nomadic road trip fuelled by misogyny and loneliness. Pure loneliness is literally a killer. These wretched souls had no anchor to steady their conscience which had died a long time ago. They were completely unloved and couldn't stop ruining people's lives even if they wanted to. Their morality had maggots and chaos is a thug's karma. Evil never lets up, but it can't grab hold of you if you're always positively moving forward. Goodness is your shield and righteousness your sword. These felons were the worst kind of liars and without truth, evil wins.

This is my 1000th tweet! I've got nothing to say. I was just making up the numbers.

11

Got the Runs

Good morning the most aggressive species on the planet! I can't recommend meditation enough to find your inner peace and calm the chimpanzee within you.

Ryan and Caesar were more tigers than chimps. They were always watching Juliet and their other victims – both for pleasure and practicality – before and after the attacks. They really enjoyed the whole victim selection process using Twitter to increase their chances of finding exactly the right type.

Luckily, the foresight of Juliet's bombastic Twitter buddies had rattled these two striped snakes out of their baskets. Nobody had worked out anything about their crimes before. So with hot paranoia attacking their alcoholic brains they assumed it would only be a matter of time before someone had a light bulb moment and fingered them.

Ryan had lost his cool and was panicking. Caesar just felt murderous and all this mental commotion soon produced their second big mistake. They were currently laying low in a large secure garage lock-up in Pawtucket, Rhode Island, paid for using aliases, which acted as their back-up, emergency residence. It looked like a dingy nuclear bunker and had enough food stored to last 3 months. Most importantly, this is where Ryan organised his criminal chaos by faking passports, sorting out his Swiss bank account, fixing up their many vehicles, buying and bagging up weed to sell by the sack load and also occasionally peddling off the radar, guns and bullets. It was quite an impressive set-up and money making operation.

However, the two reprobates agreed to take early retirement and run instead of living with a nihilistic time bomb feeling. Consequently, the Romance Rapists shut up shop and boarded a plane to Liverpool, England that following week. This was a classic mistake because any change of pattern stands out and is what police look for. The crime often doesn't give a criminal away, it's their reactions afterwards.

Flynn was far from happy about Juliet's cavalier attitude to social media which got her in trouble in the first place. At home, he had only just sunken into a comfy sectional sofa when Juliet's wayward internet assumptions caught his tired eyes and he felt angry she had gone back on her word to keep mum. Flynn then fell asleep into the darkness to be woken by the thud of a newspaper hitting his front door. Someday he was going to tell that little rascal off but never did because newspaper boys and girls arc the hard workers of the future.

Things then got serious when Flynn read some media treachery, punching him in the front page face which headed straight for the recycling bin. Misery Lowlife had got all bitter and twisted – turning Judas for a pressed nickel – publically leaking juicy nuggets of undercover info' to the papers. Misery's backstabbing had now twisted the knife deeply into Juliet's consciousness. Why she put faith in a gold-digging woman who once posted a dodgy video of herself using a bidet for the first time, heaven knows.

Juliet had foolishly passed on a few small facts and interpretations from the horse's mouth which only the police held. They weren't that important either, but as far as Flynn was concerned, Juliet had betrayed his confidence and possibly damaged his career too. He texted her in anger – big mistake – later that morning after some damage limitation with his superiors, earning him a verbal warning. Disputes should always be settled in person.

Flynn: Juliet, I feel a little stunned by what I've seen. First you share the case with the entire world on Twitter and then The New York Post publishes 'The Cops are Clueless: Serial Rapists Loose in NY.' I don't know what to say. I just wormed my way out of it with the DI, but I feel profoundly let down by you. I never thought you'd do that to me. I would like to meet tonight.

Juliet didn't see the message until about 4 hours later after delving into all known tattoo artists in New York and was naturally devastated she'd been such a scatterbrained imbecile. Her heart sank and her skin crawled as she felt the bleak vibe of being dumped. Juliet realised in that moment she loved him. Panic set in.

Juliet: Flynn, listen to me please. I didn't think it was anything that bad and was going to tell you tonight anyway. Please don't be mad at me because I love you and I need you. I'm really worried you sound mad :(

And Flynn was mad. He rolled by her mom's house later and broke it all off. Juliet was really devastated and even Shirley had a good cry as she tried to persuade Flynn to change his mind whilst grabbing his belt from behind. Mother and daughter had

139

never been so united when Flynn closed the front door on them as their chance for happiness went out the window.

Bagel and the other pets sort-of felt really bad for Juliet and did their best to comfort her. Bagel was also convinced Hawaiian/Irish Flynn was a racist because he once advised Shirley to not 'let Bagel find chinks in your armour.' Seeing Juliet being physically sick in the toilet and mommy rubbing her back like she used to do reminded Bagel of the nauseous trauma she experienced when torn from Romeo. She empathized as much as undercover narcissists can; not much at all. Life is certainly full of a lot of ups and downs. It's how you stomach the rollercoaster that counts.

True love may only
come to you
once in a lifetime,
so hug it with all
your heart and
don't let go.

Combined female misery waved across the Atlantic Ocean swamping Ryan and Caesar too. Landing at John Lennon Airport, Liverpool, with the idea of staying clear of CCTV by thumbing a lift to live in London so their scent would not be traced, was not going smoothly. The dastardly duo had limited access to their main piggy bank until they got to London, so their patience was limited too. So far nobody was stupid enough to pick them up from a damp roadside, which was causing a great deal of animosity between the rapists. "I would be in London by now if it wasn't for your face putting people off," mocked Ryan, laughing in a nasty way.

Caesar wasn't known for his pianist repartee and seriously got the hump, punching Ryan in the side of the head. Caesar often let his fists do the talking which explained his 46 crimes rap sheet mainly for violent offences. As Ryan picked himself up from the hard shoulder of the M6, he seemed somewhat aggrieved to be paired with such a degenerate.

They were an unlikely team who met by accident in a bar in New Jersey one night: comparing tattoos they got drunk together and were both taken by a knock-out blonde who walked into the bar accompanied with a regulation stallion of a stud. Ryan badly wanted to fuck her but was not that great a charmer he could persuade the boyfriend to let him have sex with his girlfriend in the toilets. So for the first and last time ever, Caesar had an idea.

The two deranged misfits followed the couple back to their house and ambushed them as they entered their property. The jock boyfriend was big, but Caesar was a meathead who pounded the guy into the ground like tenderized meat. Caesar then made the broken soul watch Ryan rape his girlfriend before he too had his fill after. Then, in a mad act of mania, Caesar twisted the man's neck so far back to look at his beaten woman, he accidentally broke the boyfriend's neck, adding homicide to his list of crimes. The first time rapists shit themselves – just like now – and fled the State together because neither one trusted the other.

That original gang rape cemented their partnership in a tribal act of evil and forever since they were bonded in a love/hate relationship. Caesar needed Ryan's wit and charisma to net a victim and escape without detection, and Ryan had no choice but to stick with Caesar to keep him from boasting to the world what a monster he was, getting them both caught. They were a self-inflicted chain gang whose only pleasure and goal in life lasted mere minutes at the expense of innocent and beautiful women.

One way or the other, the universe had to kick some ass and find balance to put these major fuck-ups behind bars. Ironically, that very justice happening to their parents was the very thing which made them turn out as they did, after Caesar experienced the orphan and foster care system that failed him terribly and Ryan had a bad run too. To them, rape was just a nasty present they passed on from their abusers. Your greatest achievement ever will be breaking the chain to a negative family situation.

Develop a calm and silence of your mind which draws people to your haven.

The two villainous men were polar opposites in intellect. Ryan was the Machiavellian leader using dogsbody Caesar to do lots of his dirty work, like regularly selling pounds of weed for extra income or prostituting lost and desperate women along their travels. Ryan was defrauding and misusing Caesar at every expedient opportunity. Caesar was as happy as a bedlamite can be because he'd never had a friend until Ryan spoke to him.

Ryan's background was extremely diverse and unusual, responsible for creating the adaptable and charismatic fruitcake he'd become. For a start, he moved home 11 times in 10 years and his mother never really loved him because she had a slutty weakness for bad men who treated Ryan like shit, making him always feel unwanted.

The worst of his many nasty step-dads was **RALPH**, a part-time handyman and mechanic who rarely made any money fixing cars and mostly used his hands for violence, which he called 'justice.' The young Ryan was his favourite play toy. Once, Ralph lost his temper and whacked 14 year old Ryan in the arm with a kettle full of boiled water, scolding his neck and whole arm with second degree burns. Why is life so easy for some and so hard for others, Ryan often anguished.

In the grand scheme of life, a quality kettle and a decent can opener are very important.

When Ryan received a right royal beating from his drunk stepfather, he would get bent over his mother's bed and belt whipped for no particular reason other than just another screwed-up bully of a man taking out his frustrations on a weaker person. In the long-term, the unfairness and randomness of his punishments hurt more than ten of the best leather strap and buckle imprint sores did.

Most of the time he received the hits very late at night when Ralph the big mouth returned from the bar shitfaced and angry his mother objected to being a sex slave. Teenage Ryan's punishment routine faced him towards a tired magnolia wall with a single painting on it. His mom was really into drugs and escaping life, and part of this avoidance of reality manifested in her love of surrealist painter Salvador Dali who examined the void between dreams and consciousness.

On that lonely wall was a reproduction of one Dali's most famous masterpieces, the Metamorphosis of Narcissus. Ryan had been hurt so many times whilst focusing on that particular painting, to distract from his pain and feelings of unfairness, every last detail was firmly etched into his mind. The great work of art became his salvation after the first few sessions of abuse and he dreamed of seeing the original version in the UK one day.

Ryan's most extreme emotions and persistent memories were experienced whilst looking at Narcissus changing to stone and he felt spiritually bonded to the painting's mystery. He wished he was the stone figure, dead but growing new life somewhere else. In a fucked-up way, Ryan actually believed he was giving his rape victims some kind of new life, which is why they all sickly received flowers weeks after the crime.

Ryan saw himself as the lone rock figure standing before Satan's cave on the left, waiting to be judged. And Caesar was the dog eating death on the bottom right and out of the main picture. As Ryan's warped intelligence grew in adulthood, he very oddly tried to recreate his feelings for this magnificent Dali painting. He thought he was the man on the chessboard, moving people pawns around. This made him feel at home. All anyone wants to do is feel calm and happy at home. We search for home throughout our whole lives. Home is where you feel most loved and if home is hell you'll have to battle the devil's demons to win your freedom.

If you can't listen to your heart then the world won't listen to you.

Ryan was astute and knew his reign of raping tyranny could not last forever. All he wanted was to find a narcissus flower as elegant and undeveloped as the one Dali envisaged. Juliet was the most beautiful of their victims. She was the narcissus flower Ryan had been looking for, which is why he lay out the red carpet so far for her.

Caesar didn't know it but that botched-up evening was supposed to be their last rape together before disbanding. Ryan had big drug trafficking plans with the jewels and money he'd stolen from victims and partner Caesar's cut, and had absolutely no plans to go to jail for life. He was bitterly adamant about that and wanted to make up for his ruined childhood. In Ryan's mind, that was his human right.

You know what real bitterness is? Making a spelling mistake in a viral tweet.

It was drizzling in real life England as well as in their minds. The children were back at school and even though it was still very hot, everyone was just waiting to moan about catching the first chill illnesses of the year. Kids spread colds like rats on Haribo's. Moaning brings us together so you know what moaners to avoid.

Ryan and Caesar were both tired and hungry and in need of a drink. After walking seven miles down a motorway with heavy sore boots, a lorry driver eventually picked them up and really wished he hadn't. He dropped them off at a large motorway services pretending he needed some supplies and then drove off without them. Caesar and Ryan were the perfect example of why no-one should pick up hitchhikers.

Britain had completely changed in only the last 20 years since global companies, who ran the country, let millions of immigrants in to deliberately upset the balance – halving everyone's wages and doubling rents on properties they owned. Even existing working foreigners were saying *no* to more people flooding in. Britain was suffocating as basic services like hospitals and schooling were stretched to their limits.

The workers had taken a real beating and if any one of the original English citizens complained about the drastic downturn in living standards as a direct result of the mass foreign invasion, they were unfairly called racists, not sensible economists. Few people trusted strangers now because crime had soared and industry was dead. Things had got very unfriendly and so bad in good old England – this formerly magnificent sceptred isle – that millions of Poles and Romanians went back to their own countries where they were now really needed.

The West was experiencing a genocide on decent behaviour and friendly manners as more and more couples split, wages were frozen in time, mental illness rife and different cultures not mixing. Consumerism means isolated children lose hope and become ill or turn to drugs, and little old Britain was getting the brunt of globalist dictatorships. So many UK residents felt lost and lonely in cities because Materialism taught us all to see money and possessions as the bench mark for success. However, real success and achievement is having principles and love in your heart, overcoming your weaknesses and being happy.

A lust for money makes people lonely, mean-spirited, unkind, selfish, negative and narrow minded. Where's the heart these days? Many people have got into a frenzy about money and lost the whole meaning and purpose to life. Your family and your love are of the highest value.

In the main food hall of the service station, the couple of cunts drank some watered down piss, barely passing as beer and then accidentally spotted their next potential victim. The brunette in question was shapely and beautiful, yet had three children with her. None of their other attacks ever involved children, more through practicality than morality and Ryan strongly advised against it.

"Small Britain isn't it? Everything's small, even the large coffee cups are small," said Ryan with a long pause. "There're fucking cameras everywhere. Bet they've even got them in the toilets, perverts!"

"I want this one. I gave you that other one and now you're gonna work this out for me," insisted Caesar.

"And what the fuck am I supposed to do with the kids? Drown their heads down the toilet like hamsters?" stressed Ryan.

"If *you* wanted her this badly, you'd make it happen, so make it happen for me. We're gonna see your painting in London, so I want to paint this slut with my cum," spat out Caesar with his homicidal look thinking how clever he'd been to make an art analogy.

The pair of nutcases were not doing very well on security terms and were already being checked out by a 59 year old CCTV surveillance operative called **SARAH** who was reading an excellent murder mystery called Buttercup Socks in between catching mainly petty shop thieves. Ryan and Caesar readily stood out to her, not only because they both looked like menacing trouble and were drinking alcohol, but mainly because they were American and therefore much, much louder than meek English people.

Ryan's mind was in overdrive. The woman had taken her children to the baby changing room toilets and he loitered around outside waiting for her to emerge. After 10 boring minutes listening to crying, the woman came out and as he approached her a security guard intercepted him.

"Can I help you at all sir?" said the much smaller service station security man called **BRIAN** who deliberately made his point by positioning himself between Ryan and the woman they were hunting.

"No, I'm fine thanks. Just doing my thing," replied Ryan. The beautiful woman called Lindsay looked up and steered her kids back towards the car park, assuming correctly it was just another potential stalker.

"And what *thing's* that then? We've been watching you two on the cameras. You think you're the first guys to try and pick up women here after a drink or two?" said the guard nervously as Caesar's bulk approached.

He called for back-up and a big woman and weedy looking fella showed up in support. Caesar looked ready for murder because they had ruined his chances, but Ryan played it well.

"We're new to England as you can tell. We're sorry to cause any inconvenience to anyone. How about we finish up our drinks quickly and be on our way? Just men being men," said Ryan. The female security guard thought, how many times have men said that to excuse unacceptable behaviour. "No harm done," added Ryan to speed up the process.
"Okay lads, no problem," said main man Brian and they hovered around waiting for the two fugitives to down their beers and get lost. As they walked away the large lady shouted out, "No means NO bitches!" Brian was not happy with her unprofessionalism. The cameras followed the outcasts into the car park and watched them walk, not drive away. Then Sarah called the police to pick Ryan and Caesar up for questioning because she a nice nanny who sensed danger. Life had taught her that the men who first catch your eye are the ones to avoid.

"You fucking fool!" shouted Caesar dragging his meat hook legs along fast, "Fucking smooth! We stand out like a sore thumb here! What happened to in cognition?"

"Incognito. I know, it will be much better in London I promise," replied Ryan. "We've got to get off this motorway just in case they called the cops. Through these fields and onto a B-Road to catch a bus or something."

The fields were small and many, and time ticked away with the sun's rays disappearing. They had no choice but to camp up for the night in a flimsy two man tent which didn't cope well with penetrating English rain. Both losers got wet through in a few hours and tried to light a fire to warm their black hearts, but the surrounding deadwood was as sodden and rotten as their minds. It didn't matter anyway because they were on a farmer's land and he spotted them whilst getting the dogs in for the night with his trusty shotgun in hand. Approaching the trespassers with stealth and caution, the owner used his instincts on ground he knew well.

"Hello gentleman! You can't camp here obviously, it's farmer's land; my land!" said the farmer with a high class voice delivered with volume and authority. "Where you from lads?"
"America sir!" said Ryan trying to butter him up.
"I see. Do they not have hotels in America?" chuckled the farmer.
"Yes sir, but we dreamed of camping in the beautiful English countryside as much as possible. We've got money. Perhaps we could stay the night for a fee?" negotiated Ryan.

151

"I love this countryside too. I was born and bred on this farm – know every last inch like the back of my hand. Listen, I'm happy for you chaps to stay the night free of charge if it will help cement Anglo-American relations, ha ha!" laughed the farmer.

"That's kind of you sir," said Ryan.

"There a spot there by that oak tree which is much flatter with good drainage. Camp up there and I'll get you some petrol to start a fire," said farmer Brown looking at both of them now. "What's up son? Cat got your tongue?" he mocked the taciturn Caesar who managed to bite his tongue for once.

"Thank you again. Much obliged," cut in Ryan to break the leaf crunching uncomfortableness.

Farmer **MIKE BROWN** came back with the fuel a while later and when he poured it over some nice pieces of knotted oak and chestnut, Caesar randomly struck him on the top the head with a huge club, knocking him out and into the pile of petroleum sticks. He then threw his lit cigar on and blocked Ryan from covering the burning man with his coat. Farmer Brown burned in agony, passed out and died like an exhausted and dehydrated, sundried husk of a bee. This was not part of their escape plan. His flesh oddly smelt like burgers and rancid yellowing milk combined with a dressing of death.

Caesar felt like he'd got revenge for the farmer's supercilious rudeness and had also brought balance to his oval mind. Accompanying his relief was a fucked-up feeling he was now technically a serial killer in two different countries. What a great achievement, his darkness gloated.

"Are. You. Out. Of. Your. Fucking. Mind!!!" shouted Ryan.

"He's out of his skin," said sociopathic Caesar pointing at the crispy farmer – even managing to summon up a smile.

"FUCK! FUCK! You fucking moron… ruining everything!!" complained Ryan. Caesar just sat down and put his hands on his knees like a child waiting for campsite instructions. Whenever he got stressed he returned to childhood.

"I don't want anyone to ever put me down again," poignantly said Caesar.

"Was your Twitter training not enough? If you killed everyone who offended you on there, over 100,000 massacres would have taken place!" screamed an incensed Ryan.

"But I couldn't see them, so no," replied Caesar.

"Fuck man. You are unique," sighed Ryan with despair.

Caesar put his head down as emotions poured through his sieve brain. Being called 'unique' was maybe the only and greatest compliment he had ever received. His life had been pure misery until he met Ryan and his childhood was a living nightmare. We can't excuse murder, but we can understand it.

Ryan felt Caesar's mental weakness and oddly felt profoundly sorry for him. Whereas Ryan had some chances and numerous abilities to improve his life since adulthood, Caesar was deeply mentally disturbed and was more an asylum case than mere social misfit. Hope had abandoned him and evil had become a friend of sorts. Caesar had experienced a life of never-ending depression.

Depression is like a deadly car crash spread out over years.

The elderly farmer had four middle-aged children, a loyal wife and three loved sheepdogs. Two sons were autistic and doing well, and his wife had Crohn's Disease.

Luckily for them, Ryan and Caesar fled the scene shortly after dumping the charcoaled body in a ditch under a log, instead of heading to the farmhouse where half of his family resided. They did a good forensic clean up job, but obviously farmer Mike Brown told his wife where they were camping and she found the body in the dead of night with her two torch lit sons of fury and some restless dogs.

Too many people waste far too much time trying to placate nasty people.

As the police lights flashed blue over-and-over farmer Browns' carcass, **MAUREEN**, his wife wailed in purple pain with her dogs licking up the tears. Her faithful sons took off with Zeus' anger in the black of night to track those responsible, with the police plodding not far behind.

The manhunt had begun for two rogue foxes with frenzied minds that needed caging. Ryan and Caesar were lost in cramped English woods and totally lost in life's oblivion too. The felons felt very isolated, just like many lonely men do on Twitter.

Men who join Twitter have two choices:

1. Be vaguely popular and servile by pandering to the narcissistic Feminist clans.

2. Be largely unpopular by being a real man with integrity.

12

Fox and Grouse Hunting

Caesar's despicable and callous murder rapidly printed them a UK press title: 'The American Werewolves.' The horrid hot news spread like wildfire because everyone loves to hate Americans. People always hate the top dog and love the underdog. No-one liked to admit it though, but

Twitter would be shit without the Americans. Undoubtedly, Twitter-time was very peaceful when America slept, but most late morning Europeans tapped their fingers repeatedly waiting for the Americans to wake up.

The greater you become, the more hateful they become.

Freedom is the most beautiful word and philosophy, and the American people, not their leaders, represent freedom. America has given us rock-'n'-roll, McDonalds, Ghostbusters, Coke and Pepsi, Levis jeans, Star Wars and Star Trek, the swivel chair (invented and sat on by Thomas Jefferson whilst drafting the US Declaration of Independence in 1776), dental floss, comic books, Keanu Reeves, The Simpsons, sitcom Friends, Monopoly, Muhammad Ali, the Cobra Mustang, the internet, the great expletive 'shit' and of course the dung pile Twitter too.

You're not over-sensitive. Society is overly shit.

Both Ryan and Caesar were physically fit, but Mike Browns' sons were much fitter and experienced hill runners with gripping anger ploughing their feet through green fields and craggy pitfalls.

The weather was dismal and a foul wind creaked through the woodlands like ghosts waiting to catch up to dead men. As the air of fortune changed badly for the two outsiders, they felt foreign and out of their league as their alien lungs burnt with exhaustion. The American Werewolves' shoes slid through sinking English mud with thorny bramble bushes cutting them down to size. The outlanders felt like nature had always held them back. But Mother Nature loved them like she loves everyone who enters her lands. Nature will always welcome you no matter who you are or what you've done. It's the ultimate forgiver and healer. Love the world and plant a few trees along the way.

Have you ever walked through a forest and felt it come alive?

As the honest Northern countryside attempted to harmonize the two wildcat's eternal sins, hundreds of other aggressive humans were plotting their capture and downfall. It takes people ages to forgive and by then it's often too late. Forgiveness is about understanding and must be total or not at all.

It shows a high level of maturity to rise above someone else's nasty failings when you have been a victim of their moral weaknesses or bad upbringing. Forgiving is the opposite of hate; it's the very last chamber of your complete heart which connects your love to the everlasting world of nature and the universe. Forgiveness means energy can flow without obstruction. How can you not forgive someone who had their childhood stolen from them?

Legs were slashed, morale was very low and a clichéd owl noise triggered by the hunters spooked the lamsters. A blackbird called out its territory and a woodpigeon throated a dull roll in disgust. Frogs were diving out of their frenzied foot slips and the damp air seeped into their dry bones.

Both of the farmer's burly sons had already nearly caught Ryan and Caesar up at hare and hound pace. These woods were their childhood playground. The chestnut tree they just ran past was where dad put up their first rope swing when they were just 5 years old. They really loved their dad. He was a great father who always provided and made it clear they didn't have to take over the farm business. They were free children supported by home baked philosophical values and the sinewy strength of the woods. The trees, birds and woodland animals had taught them to respect their fellow man and woman, and they did. The brothers in arms understood that trees are generally much better to talk to than people.

Bird flight and cracking twigs let Ryan and Caesar sense they were not alone in the dark. They had no choice but to keep on running away until a road presented itself. Both desperate men were unaware they had travelled in a long arc half way back on themselves. However, they had a massive stroke of luck. The nearest high surveillance helicopter with infrared sight had already been deployed half an hour before to track a joy riding incident and was too low on fuel to join the search.

This gave the American Werewolves about 20 minutes of nighttime cover before the police helicopter would be airborne in their location.

The main police force on foot were still organising the crime scene and slowly making their way through difficult terrain with well trained Alsatians. Regardless of the dogs dragging the police along faster and faster, the beating hearts of loving sons were now only just a hundred metres behind their targets whilst loading their shotguns on the move. In the distance, a faint silhouette of Caesar could be seen on a ridge with a moody moon highlighting his evil posture.

"There!" shouted son number one **MICHAEL**, pointing his finger at the hilltop movement. Bang!!! The woodland thundered with wildlife fear and trees shuddered. Youngest son **PETER** fired a shot at Caesar and a few widespread pellets ripped at his arm, skimming a flesh wound.

On the hill, Ryan was very close by and spotted some faint street lights in the distance coming from a small countryside village. The survival instincts and cunning fox in him rapidly took over his mind and he seized the day. Dropping his bag, Ryan rummaged furiously as another shot blasted a nearby tree's bark off. Trees will always outlive Man because they give, not take like us.

"Arrrrgh!" shouted Ryan, pretending he'd been hit. Caesar came running to assist and got a belly full of knife for his pains. Ryan didn't hang around for a farewell speech. Grabbing his bag he threw his whole mind and body into making it to that lit village yonder now he'd laid bait for the shooters.

"Traitor!" shouted Caesar who attempted to run after him with blood pumping out like fuel from a busy gas station. His stab wound was deep through the side of his right kidney, yet he still had lots of fight left in him.

Caesar knelt down behind a large Sycamore tree near a path and waited in ambush for his executors. A few helicopter seeds came down from above, instead of the chopper and Caesar felt a holy calm come over him – like he knew this was the end.

In their haste and anxiety to get revenge, the sons came bounding through too fast with their flashlights beaming the way forward and Peter waded straight into the spider's trap. Caesar launched at him and stabbed Pete in the leg, right through to the bone, bringing him down like a flightless bird.

Despite Caesar's painful injury, both of Browns' sons were an equal match for his bearlike muscle and menace in close combat without weapons. But luckily Michael was armed too with his pride and joy pump-action shotgun. He took rapid aim and blew Caesar's head off like a watermelon on an aiming post.

Caesar's reign of evil was now at an end. The world took from him and he took back from the world. He fell into the next realm and Jesus said, 'Come with me," and he went peacefully. His gruesome quick death simply saved a lot of paperwork and legal fees.

"Uhrg! It hurts really bad! Leave me. The police will find me soon," insisted the badly wounded Peter, panting like a thirsty big cat.

"No, you're in a bad way. Can't leave you," said Michael protecting his younger brother as he always had.

"Go! Go! I'll get help… got my phone. Do it for dad! Don't let the other one get away," persisted Peter, grabbing his older brother by the shirt, ripping a few buttons.

"Fucking hell this is my favourite shirt dude!!" shouted Michael forgetting himself. He once climbed Ben Nevis in that sentimental garment.

Michael shot up, snatched his gun and went steaming forward in pursuit of Ryan. Ryan had made great ground now he had a mission to aim for. He was already approaching the village when an oncoming car highlighted a small country lane ahead. It was like the Gods were with him, giving him a chance to escape. Satan had intervened in the eternal battle between good and evil because every master must have a bane to stay sane.

That great feeling when the fear goes and you're gifted with a euphoria and knowledge all is going to be okay.

Ryan made it to the roadside just in time, jumped through a prickly hedge and leapfrogged straight onto the car's bonnet, cracking the windscreen. He slid off relatively unharmed, just badly winded and flopped to the ground like falling out of bed ungracefully. His desperation and exhaustion made him flexible. It's amazing what you can achieve when you're really up against it.

The lone woman driver in her thirties returning from a local pub, panicked big time because she was slightly over the limit and thought she'd killed him. Her conscience could not drive off in shame, but later wished it had. As she knelt down to help Ryan up, he pulled and shoved her to the ground hitting her head on the tarmac, hobbled into the driver's seat, turned the engine over and actually run the woman over as he sped off, further cracking the screen and making it hard to see. "Inconsiderate bitch!" he joked to himself.

However, his chuckles were short lived when Michael, who was only a minute behind, saw the car speed away and fired a close range shot through the passenger window, travelling back out through the windscreen. Ryan swerved the car and was surely doomed as he ploughed into a flood ditch and hedgerow. But Ryan was a clever man and where there's a brain there's a train of thought to escape anything! He thought of himself as a hero, had a lot of megalomaniacal determination and was a spontaneous thinker by nature. You can't progress without self belief and determination.

Ryan popped the fuel cap, grabbed his bag of essentials, climbed through the shattered passenger window with the car at a 45 degree angle, pulled out his lighter, lit some tissue and set the tank on fire. Whoosh!! The car went up as fast as Marilyn Monroe's skirt over a hot air vent, with as much heat too. For a moment Ryan saw the real beauty in fire as the flames flamenco strutted to his power-crazed tune. Then a totally arbitrary imagination whooshed into the air as Ryan recalled seeing a nice Twitter ballet performance by a sunny coffee day girl dancing her emotions away. Nice people make life worth living.

Meanwhile, despite his extreme keenness to get even, Michael had run back to help the screaming woman in agony. He consoled her on the floor for a couple of minutes feeling reassured Ryan was either dead, on fire, or would be picked up by the police in no time whatsoever.

The police were particularly shit tonight though. Many had been celebrating their Chief Inspector's retirement and some corrupt others in the station were plotting the downfall of a whistleblower who was complicating their dishonesty. The honest whistleblower eventually won her court case a year and a half later, but lost her career after some pigs kept making fun of her recent miscarriage and weight gain caused by the depression they created.

As Michael stood there like a lost lemon calling for an ambulance on his mobile, then calling the police, then calling his injured brother, then checking in with his grieving mother, Ryan had sneaked up on him, picked up the gun and offloaded the last cartridge into Michael's good natured torso. He then coldly walked over to the disembowelled man, searched his pockets for more ammunition, reloaded and callously shot the hysterical woman with two broken legs who wasn't going anywhere anyway.

You know that famous inspirational line, "That which does not kill me makes me stronger." We all know in our hearts that's rubbish, don't we.

Flashing lights came around the bend roughly 5 minutes later and screeched to a halt after careering into the sprawled out version of Michael. Two unarmed officers shot out and both got immediately shot by Ryan from the ditch 6 feet away.

Ryan was now a cop killer and somehow the wrongness and fear brought out the best in him. His mind raced at a level of selfish intelligence never quite experienced before. He paused for 7 seconds with the smell of burning petrol fuelling his thoughts. Ryan knew this was make or break time. If he couldn't buy himself at least 9-10 hours decent getaway time, his life was over. His subconscious believed it was over anyway.

Acting with purpose, Ryan dragged Michael's body all the way to the burning car and pushed it into the flames for a premature cremation. The inferno was roaring away now and the hedgerow caught fire too. A small sparrow bird's nest boiled three chick eggs inside, making a nice breakfast for a badger the next morning. Michael burnt like marshmallows on a twig spine of bones, but didn't smell so sweet.

Ryan then hightailed it back to the other three bodies and chucked the male and female police officers unceremoniously into the ditch on top of each other – stacked like a contorted bag of bones. He then snapped a couple of massive branches off a nearby tree and covered the real life lovers as best he could in the limited time available. **PC JANET BLACKWOOD** and **PC CARTER COX** were due to announce their engagement to everyone the following weekend. Now they would have to marry in the daylight of heaven.

Being with nature makes your soul feel more at home than home does.

The black of night was working in tandem with Ryan's black soul. Swiping his trusty bag and the gun, he launched into the police car with the keys stupidly still in the ignition and pulled up beside the burning car to throw the shotgun at toasted

Michael. The ammunition popped in the heat like Michael's organs did when they fried alive.

Stalling for a minute longer to work out how to turn the emergency lights off, Ryan headed straight for the airport. Just a dozen minutes later the police helicopter circled above and guided over fifty police officers with muddy feet and ten squad cars to the scene of Beelzebub's inferno. But they were too late and confused, like most crimes they attend. Ryan's subterfuge had worked a treat. He was a smug son-of-a-bitch.

Someone today said I don't know everything. He's right. I don't understand what he means.

Five people had now been killed in just the last few hours. It was safe to say things had somewhat escalated from serial rapist to serial killer hunt. This wasn't a healthy social promotion. And to think that everything started with Ryan feeling super horny in a bar one night.

The master-plan to live a life of tattooing Reilly in London was completely destroyed. Thick necked Caesar had ruined his life by murdering farmer Brown, but no doubt saved lots more women from being brutally raped with blind rage. Ryan was currently feeling mentally distraught, yet was generally a cool customer. A few miles down the winding country lane he joined onto a main road and hit the police lights and siren, taking him all the way to the airport in no time at all.

Calmly parking up right outside the entrance, he threw on some clean clothes in the back, bought the first flight available to anywhere leaving in a few minutes and was three quarters on the way to Southern Ireland before the police dogs uncovered the pile of bodies down that fateful dark lane. Sometimes speed of action is everything. Pontificating is the shopping basket full of failure.

Bully your comfort zone at least once a week because it's good for you.

The police initially only saw the female driver lying in the road and rapidly came to the wrong conclusion that Ryan had hijacked her car and crashed it in a panic, burning alive. When they realised what had really gone down, the air and ferry ports were alerted, but Ryan had already landed in Ireland and boarded a flight to New York using an emergency false passport both him and Caesar made a few years back for insurance because raping is risky business.

It took a further 9 hours in total to search through all CCTV footage at John Lennon Airport and liaising with a reluctant Cork Airport in Ireland to spot his clothes and name changes. Ryan had escaped with the luck of the Irish in him and was already on a train back to his hideout in Pawtucket to find an old family member; mommy. Boys always return to mum when they feel scared.

The truth comes out when you're tired and you know who you really love.

13

Love Adventures

Back in Brooklyn's mayhem, Juliet had spent the last few days weeping her loses until she saw the national news with Ryan's pixelated CCTV face plastered on most news channels. One minute she was trying to practice mindfulness meditation listening to birdsong, the next she was choked with chronic anxiety and panic, feeling fat and ugly.

If you don't believe you're beautiful, you probably are.

Ryan was now an internationally wanted cop and serial killer, and even though his face wasn't too easily recognisable on the clearest airport images, it seemed he and Caesar may have raped more women than originally estimated. Wild accusations were flying in on TV like homing pigeons when Shirley's landline rang and she answered, spinning her hand around frantically towards Juliet from across her gaudy living room and Juliet hopped to the beat. It was Flynn. He had good and bad news. Juliet gripped the phone like it was Flynn's arm.

"Hi Flynn, I knew you would call. I'm really sorry for everything. I completely fucked up. Please give me a chance to explain..." ranted Juliet, desperate to get him back. She'd lost all self-respect and just wanted him back in her messed up life.

"Slow down Juliet. I'm calling on *official* police business at the request of Deputy Inspector Maddox," explained Flynn trying to sound all professional but melting a bit inside when he heard her sultry voice.

"Oh, I hoped we could just talk," said a depressed sounding girl who threw her pained voiced down the phone just hoping the boy would hear her cries.

"I think we had *that* talk didn't we? You know, the one where you stabbed me in the back?" said Flynn with a bitterness which surprised himself.

He really liked Juliet and was beginning to fall in love before she broke his trust. Trust was a big family theme in Flynn's mostly American Irish family. They believed in honour and never betraying the family code. But perhaps his Hawaiian mother's doting love had made him follow her homeschooled philosophy too rigidly? Maybe Flynn needed Juliet's randomness to counter his precision.

"I'm sorry," was all Juliet could muster to his accusation of betrayal and then she started to whimper. Crying always works. It's a surprise many more men don't do it.

"Okay, don't cry please…" requested Flynn.

"…I just don't think you gave me a fair chance after an honest mistake. My heart never betrayed you," sobbed Juliet, continuing, "It's not like I don't love you because I do."

"If you loved me you wouldn't have risked my career and the trust between us," explained Flynn calmly, sticking to his guns. Juliet immediately struggled for words and thought, shit, that's two very good points in a row. She fell silent. "Are you still there?" checked Flynn.

"Yes," she replied.

"Listen, *I care* which is why I'm calling. Have you seen the news about your attackers?"

"Yes and I'm very scared."

"You'll be fine. DI Maddox is assigning you and your mother 24-hour police protection until this Ryan is caught. He's asked me to assist with a rotation of officers stationed outside throughout night and day, so don't panic," he explained, slightly lying because he knew there was a lot to worry about with a murdering sociopath on the run, in psychological custody of an evil agenda.

"Don't panic!! There's a lunatic out there who might cut my head off and you say, 'don't panic!' For fuck's sake Flynn, I'm worried sick!" blurted out Juliet as the doorbell rang. "Oh fuck, that's the door. Maybe that's him now with a machete?" worried a typically melodramatic Juliet.

"Relax, that's officer **GABBY GONZALEZ** to begin the watch. She's very good and very vigilant and has top marksmanship ability."

"Has she actually shot anyone though?" questioned Juliet as Shirley opened the door to a NYPD officer who looked about twelve. "Christ Flynn, she's like a teenager. I'm fucked!" wailed Juliet and unfortunately Miss González heard.

"She won't let you down. Give her some respect. I'll be there soon," said Flynn feeling a little guilty Maddox has assigned a first week rookie who'd only shot at a piece of paper before.

"Fine," snapped Juliet and hung the phone up. Mother was already in the kitchen making coffee for Gabby. Juliet turned to the very nubile looking 21 year old and apologized. She did have a lot to worry about after all.

Admitting your mistakes takes character, but don't let people rub your face in them.

173

Bagel and Emmental looked at each other with a sense of wry comedy. Yet, they stuck to their newly conceived mission to return Bagel to her original home by stealing the car keys from any visitor and driving to Rhode Island themselves. Who needs humans when you have friends?

The idea was that Tony the tortoise would push the pedals whilst Bagel the cat steered and Emmental the cockatoo changed gear. The fact that not one of them had the physical power to do any of those three tasks had been conveniently overlooked in favour of their newfound confidence and belief in themselves. Also, apparently the car would mysteriously transform into a boat when they needed to make it to Block Island.

All the pets were delusional Transformers fans who believed in saving humanity from the evil Decepticons, or as they called them, Trump supporters. Anyway, Emmental broke free from his cage and caused the distraction needed for Bagel to snatch officer González's car keys from the table and hide them under the sofa before anyone noticed. Phase one was a total success!

The irony is you find what you're looking for when you stop searching in desperation.

Flynn eventually turned up a staggering 5 hours later. He'd joined a briefing by the FBI who had been brought in to head the investigation and then he went to get some diabetes medication for his mom. Flynn had always been a good and reliable son.

Early reports from sketchy public information identified Ryan's most likely original location in Toms River, New Jersey and a few other Ocean County places. That's where he spent much time causing noticeable trouble with Caesar before he got professional about their crimes. After doing a little research, Flynn returned to the meeting and helpfully noted that Toms River was where a woman was raped and her boyfriend killed a few years back by two men who matched their description. It made the national news but the media coverage unearthed nothing with no leads.

Flynn's mind had now taken a detour. Part of him didn't want to face Juliet and another part saw a distinct rise in ambition. The FBI, assisted by detective Flynn O'Connell, did every known background check on tattoo artists in that specific New Jersey area and came up with a staggering 926 names, one of which was Ryan's real name, ARTHUR KOONS, but they didn't know it yet.

A lot of man-hours were needed first to sift through mountains of data because tattoos are kinda hot right now. Arthur was a strange name for a cop killer and rapist, thought many detectives on reflection the following year. Regardless, Flynn being a determined chap was already pumping away on his phone trying to track down all of the suspects' addresses and backgrounds to find the most likely criminal candidate.

Deputy Inspector Maddox was determined that the NYPD would nab their man, not the stuff shirt FBI agents sweeping in to take the glory as always on high profile cases. He lay down the mantle to detective Flynn and his team to research the killer's whereabouts whilst at Juliet's, hoping his most capable detective would pull a rabbit out of the hat. Flynn was most definitely heading this investigation for the NYPD, which was a real vote of confidence from his superiors.

After a further 5 hours around Shirley's gaff, it was past midnight when Ryan had a major intuitive breakthrough despite Juliet doing lots of coffee creeping and bending over near him, which was successfully working away at soothing his mind to her presence. In fact, Flynn's subconscious had already capitulated to Juliet's beauty and grace. He just wanted to wrap this case and promotion up, and then move on with his life, with Juliet by his side because he'd been won over by her genuine remorse and guilt. She promised him she would never use Twitter again as well. The app had already been deleted. This show of commitment to change made Flynn very happy. He was now caught between his job and Juliet. Being assigned to protect her and also finding the cop killer and multiple rapist was a mind splitting paradox which didn't sit well. Flynn was a man of action, not a Field Marshall director of other people's safety. If there was danger to face, Flynn would always be in the front lines whether he felt like it or not.

If you are truly loved, you are a real winner.

Since he first met Juliet, Flynn had been juggling lots of fragments of evidence simultaneously and his subconscious was beginning to get an understanding of Arthur's mind and motivations.

Flynn guessed correctly that Arthur was a frustrated artist at heart and that art and fantasy played a big part in his corrupted behaviour. In the large staff meeting earlier, two FBI criminal psychologists disagreed with Flynn's hypothesis and patronised his honest hunch in front of everyone saying, "What we are dealing with here is *not* a man who cradles artistic endeavours; rather a sociopath in the third and final chaotic phase of the 'stressed animal' condition. To simplify, our most wanted criminal is a totally out of control and dangerous individual whom we colloquially refer to as possessing 'Wild Dog Syndrome'." The psychologists even concluded their educated and inaccurate waffle with a smug smile, akin to the smirking Twitter emoji. 😏

Psychologists really know how to state the absolute armchair obvious in a pompous way. Anyway, they were wrong and Flynn had the confidence to know his instincts were right, so he pursued his line of enquiry with DI Maddox on the fence.

There's not much worse than being a victim of your own idiocy and then refusing to change through fear of looking stupid.

In reality, beyond outmoded academic gibberish, all psycho Arthur Koons (AKA Ryan) ever wanted to do since childhood was express himself. When his unfulfilled creative ambitions were not communicated and satiated, his frustrations finally hit peak, snapping and raping.

Flynn was working away on solving the root cause of the crimes in Shirley's ornate dining room, on her obsessively polished walnut table, when he made the heinous mistake of putting his gun on it. Shirley complained nicely and tried to draw him into a gun law conversation after embarrassing herself by asking, "Could you put your gun under the table please Flynn, with the other big gun? Guns make my legs go wobbly."

"Mother, you're not helping my cause," said Juliet quietly, but firmly.

"Your 'cause.' You're not on one of your misguided political rallies now you know," snarked Shirley. Juliet politely guided mother out of the room as Flynn tucked his piece away.

At last he had some peace and quiet to focus on the case in hand; 'hand' being the operative word. Shirley could be very annoying and calling herself an empathic animal lover didn't stop her from being known by locals as the crazy cat lady. However, her unwanted distraction had done Flynn a favour. Whilst under time pressure in the world's media spotlight, Flynn had the confidence to sit back and relax. He liked to get to the bottom of things – to understand the kernel and core motivations of every problem he faced. Having a good think, he lay out all of the investigation photos and couldn't shake the sketch artist's finger and thumb tattoo images out of his mind because his intuition had dismissed most other irrelevant evidence. The truth is often so clear it becomes see-through.

Flynn used blind faith to dismiss all evidence photos, leaving just the sort of peach or avocado seed car transfer image and Arthur's hand tattoo. What was this object wondered Flynn; a walnut, a dehydrated nectarine or its seed, or perhaps a cracked egg? He cut out the car sticker oval and placed it over the drawing of Arthur's hand. Flynn soon had a moment of inspiration sparked by Juliet's gorgeous cleavage when she handed him a smooth coffee and a smile before leaving him be.

Sliding the oval off, Flynn picked up the hand and cut out the fingers, lining them next to each other revealing a complete image. The half moons and disjointed blocks of ink, puzzle-pieced together into a perfect looking egg shape, wrinkled by skin folds. The crinkly looking oval shape was bugging him and was the key to the crimes, so he simply typed into Google Search the words 'hand and seed artist.' He got nothing and changed the words to 'hand and egg artist.' Nothing again. He was just about to give up on his fanciful, offbeat curiosity, then thought, perhaps an out of control man with no morals needs a steadying force to prevent insanity. Maybe Arthur worships God or idolises a great artist as something to aspire to. So he changed his Google search to 'hand and egg famous artist' and this triumphed!

After flicking through a few ludicrously expensive and sickly Carl Faberge eggs, *there* was the image in a painting which had been unknowingly plaguing his dreams for the last few days. Centrepiece to Salvador Dali's the Metamorphosis of Narcissus were two hands; one holding a walnut looking head and the other an egg with the narcissus flower cracking out of it.

Flynn was now inside Arthur's criminal mind for the first time which would prove critical in days to come. He immediately informed his competitive team back at the station, asking them to search for all tattoo artists in New York and neighbouring Eastern States who specialized in Dali or Dali style tattoos, Surrealism per se, or even egg and metamorphosis symbolism. Flynn was rightly convinced his man, Arthur, had a Salvador obsession.

Shirley popped in again to give him an inappropriate pile of Madeleine cookies to accompany another fine java black coffee and to flirt a little too. She was competing with her daughter again without even realising it.

"I've come up trumps Shirley! Success!" announced Flynn with real enthusiasm.

"That's good, but we'll have no talk of Trump though in my home please mister," explained Shirley, actually being serious and totally getting the wrong end of the stick; the poo end. It must be noted that despite all of Shirley's vehement anti-Trump liberal talk to her friends, she voted for Trump in secret.

"Just ignore her Flynn," whispered Juliet who trailed behind mother to prevent more relationship failure.

"Easily done," replied Flynn and they both smiled at each other. The spark was still there.

"I know when I'm not wanted," said a moody looking Shirley walking out holding tight shoulders.

"That's good," whispered Juliet under her breath.

Whilst all of this was going on, the land and sky pets had escaped outside, realised they couldn't open the police car door with the stolen keys, had a stress attack and then regrouped inside for further brainwaves. Bagel felt trapped like Arthur Koons did. The pet's failure and everyone's uncertainty led to a sullen and pensive atmosphere. Something needed to positively change the mood. And that winner was Juliet who just slipped into a seductive red negligee. It would be a full moon tonight and the oceans prepared for love. Juliet approached Flynn like a cat looking to lap up some warm milk.

181

"You've been working at that for hours on end. Perhaps a quick break would be more productive," suggested Juliet standing close behind Flynn.

"Thanks, but I just ate some of your mom's lovely cookies and feel quite refreshed," said a very focused man, not noticing the overt sexual display. Shirley was eavesdropping and silently put her fist up in triumph because Flynn mentioned her cookies, not Juliet's coffee. Bagel was observing Shirley from the end of the hallway and actually shook her little cat head in embarrassment.

Juliet rolled her eyes and directly said, "It's good to have you back in the house Flynn. I feel safe." Flynn turned around and saw the face of a woman offering herself to a trusted man. He was taken by her beauty like never before and stood up. "Don't say anything. Just kiss me," Juliet ordered in her best bedroom voice.

Needless to say, they fucked like rabbits, yet for much longer. At first, Flynn took Juliet into his arms and just held her. Time seemed to stop. He kissed her passionately and all their tension waned. She then gently shoved him back, walked over to the head of the table, pushed her mother's favourite chair aside and bent right over whilst pulling her gown up over her back, maintaining eye contact the whole time. Flynn's dick nearly exploded. He felt like a teenage boy who just bought the very coolest brand new Nike trainers and couldn't wait to try them on for size.

Eagerly pulling his trousers and boxers down before actually getting behind her, Flynn amusingly had to do a penguin shuffle to reach his mark, which slightly bummed the mood. Mounting her and bonking with baboon passion, Juliet moaned with pleasure and Shirley was still outside the room listening, finally gaining enough self-respect and dignity to walk away from none of her business.

Juliet then pulled off and gave Flynn the best blow job he'd had since his sexy high school history teacher lost the plot and her professionalism one day during break because her husband preferred campanology to clitorisology. Juliet certainly was in charge of this sex show tonight. She stood up, wiped dribble away from her mouth wearing a cheeky grin and sat on the table, spreading her legs. Fuck, thought Flynn, this really is the best paid police research ever!!! As he fucked her brains out after fully removing his pants, Juliet launched backwards and splayed her arms fully out like she was creating a rainbow shape. This satisfied manoeuvre swiped all of Flynn's paperwork and pictures onto the floor but he didn't care about anything now apart from focusing on her beautiful bouncing tits!

A little moan could be heard outside the door too. Would you fucking well believe it! It was Shirley loitering outside the door again, who'd returned with a warmed in the microwave cucumber, pleasuring herself to the beat of Flynn's thrusts. It had been such a long time since a man had ravished

Shirley, she really had completely lost all her inhibitions until Emmental the cockatoo squawked to let her know she was being watched by her pets. Shirley crapped herself, dropped the vegetable and genuinely pretended she was off to make a salad as she walked past her cat and parrot with head held high. It was like the walk of shame in Game of Thrones but with clothes on.

Meanwhile, the lovers were reaching a curtain finish applause. Juliet was in seventh heaven and Flynn had an amazing moment after filling her fallopian tubes to the max. He saw the low lit reflection of his own face in the shiny table's surface, which appeared more like a skull than him. It felt like being inside Dali's Metamorphosis painting – looking into the pool of water. He had experienced the place of the skull; Golgotha. It was beautiful. Juliet was beautiful.

There is a undulating energy in water which is almost unexplainable like a ripple in time.

Flynn was exhausted and fell asleep on the sofa without noticing his phone was full up of messages. It had been an arduous 20-hour working day and even cops need to sleep sometimes. Sleep deprivation should be a crime.

He was regretfully woken about 3 hours later by Shirley. A better description of 'woken' would be 'sexually molested' before Flynn's natural defence mechanisms activated his eyes to discover Shirley with her hands all over his manly chest. She hastily explained the police were on the phone and it was urgent so she needed to wake him, omitting the touching his dick part in front of Bagel who literally couldn't wait to escape now. Keeping Shirley in line had been hard work since handsome Flynn entered her mind. She had no shame left to lose after last night.

Flynn grabbed the phone and echoed the officer's words as he wrote them down, "Hope Valley. Rhode Island. Brilliant job **KATHLEEN**! Thank the team for me please… okay great… yes text address… me right now. Great work! I'm on my way!"

Flynn's handpicked NYPD team had uncovered just one address to investigate of a possible suspect location. Their enquiries started and finished in New York. A unique tattoo artist had gained a great reputation for tattooing all different kinds of melting clocks on people, inspired by Salvador Dali's equally famous painting to Narcissus, The Persistence of Memory.

Clients absolutely loved his take on Dali, even melting mobile phones into elaborate Daliesque tattoos with philosophical messages imprinted. He travelled across NY State focusing mainly on the city after getting a series of lucrative commissions and went by the name Antonio Kravelli alluding to undertones of Mafioso – which was total bullshit.

Getting cocky by using his real initials was a costly mistake because further guesswork investigations indentified his real name, Arthur Koons, albeit no trace of his whereabouts, yet with a great lead on his mother's address in Rhode Island.

Flynn got dressed quicker than a star pop performance change as he prepared for rapid deployment in under 10 minutes. He would not miss his chance to catch Arthur Koons behind the arrogant FBI's back. The CIA were now sniffing around too. He had something to prove to those grandiloquent psychologists and other doubters as well.

Never stop defending yourself from haters and critiques. Always keep your guard up. Don't get pulled into their fake kindness on a random day. It's as simple as that.

Emmental was back in her cage overhearing Flynn's brief journey outline. He knew this was his chance to get rid of Bagel at last! He meant to think, *to help* Bagel out. Poor Bagel was in the conservatory feeling down in the dumps underneath a huge showpiece umbrella plant, so Emmental asked the three wise fish to splash some sense into her. Things were bad. Bagel got wet and didn't even react. She had lost all hope of returning to her lovely Mexican family on Block Island. Depression was setting in like concrete.

If anyone suggests depression is not real, put a black bin bag over their head for the day.

Bagel was switching off from life. All she could hear were faint echoes of reality. It felt like being underwater and short of air. Then, quite miraculously the three lesbian fish managed to lift the fake Treasure Island from the bottom of their tank and tail flip it onto the floor in front of Bagel.

Bagel's tired eyes slowly opened and saw a mirage. It was a casting of her home town island right before her very eyes! She felt a touch of happiness shiver through her spine, yet also wondered if she was going bonkers. The fish had now made an arrow shape pointing towards the sitting room. A cat following fish's instructions is about as low as it can get, but Bagel was desperate to be called Suzie one last time so she sauntered into the lounge to await a screaming cockatoo.

"This is it Bagel! Your chance to escape has arrived! The cop is going to Rhode Island. You've got just 5 mins to pack!" croaked Emmental. Asking a female to get ready for a journey in 5 minutes flat is like asking the Clintons to be honest.
"I'll never make it!" winced Bagel.
"All you need is yourself," advised Tony Curtis who'd been given free range since Arthur's dangerous acts were broadcast across the news.
"Have faith and believe you can do it Bagel," reinforced Emmental.

"Yes, I *can* do it!" pronounced Bagel with some assertion. "Thank you. I'm really going to miss you guys, it's been great," meowed Bagel with tears. Emmental and Tony just looked at each other pensively. "Oh come on! I was a benign dictator for the good of all!" justified Bagel.

"Have a safe journey. Sorry to see you go," said Tony, crawling back into his shell.

Bagel said nothing and just walked towards the cat flap with stiff dignity as Emmental waved his wings in celebration so enthusiastically, feathers flying everywhere. Bagel didn't care anyway. She was going home after years of imprisonment! She thought this is probably like how Nelson Mandela once felt. Bagel hid under the cop car and waited for her opportunity to slink in, which went as smooth as clockwork.

The pace of the room was fast. Juliet barely had a chance to shower, change and talk to her mother for over 2 hours. Shirley was still feeling deep shame and was sad. Juliet wasn't overly pleased with Flynn's fast exit either.

"I thought you were supposed to stay here to protect me?" quizzed Juliet.
"You'll be fine. Officer González is going to hold the fort. I'll just be gone for no more than half a day," answered Flynn, feeling a touch guilty he'd just fucked her and was now clearing off. He also really fancied a hamburger on the way.

"The fort. He's not a Red Indian, he's a rapist," put Juliet sarcastically.

"Sorry princess, what can I say? A man's gotta do what a man's got to do," replied Flynn. It felt like he'd waited his whole life to use that cliché his dad often said and believed in.

"Did you just say that? It's not the 50's you know," said Juliet shrugging her shoulders in frustration.

Flynn smiled and said, "Men haven't changed since then, only women have. Let us be men."

"Are we actually going to have a gender rights debate now, before you go gallivanting around the country looking for a man who might murder me?"

"Gallivanting? Looks like you've got some old fashioned in you too," teased Flynn.

"Seriously though, men can't just do what they want any more," stated Juliet with a political tone.

"Most men have always done what most women say anyway," guessed Flynn.

"Oh, like what you are doing now, just going off on a whim without your Inspector's express permission or my approval?" judged Juliet.

That was a very good comeback which Flynn had no good answer for, so he just put the record on again, like when his dad was outsmarted by Flynn's mum, but delivered the line in a conciliatory tone, "A maaan's gotta do what a maan's gotta do."

"Christ! This is just like Twitter. You make a really good point and someone just ignores you. Maybe Twitter is more for you Flynn than me," joked Juliet. They both laughed at the sarcasm and irony.

189

She hadn't laughed properly for a while. They were good for each other. "Okay, if you're going to do your *man* thing then please be careful. I can't take anymore shocks in my life. I'm serious Flynn." Flynn didn't say a word, he just held her in his arms and kissed her before heading out to catch his man. Juliet had already caught hers.

Every time I chat with you it feels like standing in a beautiful ray of sunshine.

14

Mama, Just Killed a Man

That feeling when you know you can trust someone and they don't let you down. That.

Juliet was happy, despite being under temporary house arrest for her own safety.

Flynn had the bit between his teeth and knew offence is the best defence. He believed the best way to protect Juliet was to eliminate the threat, not sit there like a fish in a barrel waiting for trouble. He had gone hunting and was now happy too.

Arthur Koons, the wanted killer and serial rapist, was unsurprisingly an unhappy man in general. However, he felt a strange sense of childhood happiness as he approached his mother's house after an arduous CCTV dodging journey.

Life is good if you can rely on yourself.

Salvador Dali missed his mother and secretly Arthur did too. For this reason, whilst the FBI were raiding all known suspect's residences and hideouts in New Jersey, detective Flynn O'Connell got his team searching county clerk registrars and police databases for Arthur's mother's current name and location which got him driving at breakneck speed towards Hope Valley. This was a time consuming risk and potential embarrassment to his department.

Positive change doesn't just happen. You have to want it badly and completely embrace the idea of changing for the better with daily motivation.

Arthur's biological mom, Elizabeth, had since changed her name to **GLADYS CRANE** and was successfully *finding herself* after a lifetime of deliberately picking abusive alpha males. Aggressive men excited her until excitement became restriction, violence and mental imprisonment. Gladys now did a spot of oil painting to expand her horizons. She loved the way thick paint merged together to form such beautifully random swipes of colour. She found impasto painting stimulating and fun.

Anyone can be a brilliant artist. It's a question of wanting it badly enough to seek perfection.

Gladys lived in a nice countryside village with lots of room and great vistas. Her neighbours were friendly too. For a previously silly and deeply ignorant woman, Gladys had been careful, almost meticulous in trying to cover up her whereabouts to prevent her fourth son Arthur from catching up one day.

Her cosy retirement home was her little dream which took three divorces, getting raped and a broken jaw to financially secure. Gladys had earned her piece of American pie yet never felt really bad for letting Arthur get physically abused by hubby number three because she was too afraid to stand up to him or call the police. Guilt was not in Gladys' emotional vocabulary because she'd been mentally numbed by a series of shit men doing as they pleased. Gladys was alone and hated men of all persuasions. She was now an avid #MeToo advocate and had a trusty Alsatian bitch to protect her.

Unfortunately, Arthur did not see things in the blameless way Gladys did and he wasn't sure if he found her out of revenge, to find motherly love or just for answers to questions. Being a quasi Predacon by nature, it didn't take Arthur long to track down his mother's new name and address. He knew she would never move out of State because of her best friend and previously close elderly neighbour, Tracey.

Arthur simply paid an internet company just $12.99 to access name change records and new addresses. All personal and private information about you is held for a modest price on the internet: the bastards even listen to your personal conversations for 'sales' purposes. Anyway, the day of reckoning had arrived and Arthur never thought it would be on Titty Tuesday.

Some girls on Twitter think they're auditioning for a strip club. The smart women who leave it to the imagination are the best and gain men's loyalty.

Gladys half expected Arthur to turn up unannounced one day and had psychologically prepared herself for this unwanted and tragic event. Her not so lucky day eventually arrived, when two and a half days previously Arthur made his way up her driveway feeling unexpectedly anxious. He blamed his mom for everything, but she was still his mom.

Her white painted wooden house was surprisingly large and ornate. Financially, Gladys had done well, but she was a 73 year old bag of nerves these days. Arthur hadn't seen or heard from her, or his elder step brothers since he left home in Hope Valley, Rhode Island at 19, where he found little hope. He wasn't sure what to expect but had the courage to fulfil his destiny.

It was a pleasant afternoon's weather, perfect for appreciating the joys of nature. Nobody answered the bell, so Arthur jumped over the garden gate and saw a lonely looking figure painting on an easel from a distance. The beautiful green grass day was about to get red and shocking.

Each step Arthur took towards the woman who he felt betrayed and sold him out, he felt less and less brave. After all, this female human gave birth to him and that has a powerful hold even on a household trained sociopath. Arthur was returning to the beginning of his life and he felt as nauseous as he did in those uncomfortable old days. There's only a certain amount of times a child can get beaten up for fun before all of their emotions are stolen and lost forever.

There's no point bothering with nasty family members just because they're blood.

The grass felt soft and well groomed. Arthur childishly mumbled to himself, "She looks after her grass better than she did me," as he stalked towards her. Gladys heard him but was so engrossed in her landscape painting, she carried on furiously dabbing the brush from palette to canvas, assuming it was a delivery guy or a friendly neighbour.

"How about I help you mother?" announced Arthur as he grabbed the colour palette from her hand and pressed it onto the painting with a grin. He wiped some rainbow coloured paint on his pants and stood facing Gladys.

"Well done! You've ruined everything like before!" said mother who instantly recognised her youngest child in the forty seven year old confused man glaring at her.

"You mean you messed it up because you don't take responsibility for your actions. What was it anyway? A spaceship?" mocked Arthur.

"A tree," said Gladys trying to fake being calm. She obviously knew the situation could become deadly. "But I guess you didn't come here to discuss art?"

"No, let's talk about art Liz! Sorry, Gladys these days isn't it. Bet you still see Ben though?" Ben was her eldest and favourite son. "Why would a woman who treated her kids like shit and who drank herself into a daily coma now be doing landscape painting? God or nature will never forgive you and neither will I," exclaimed Arthur looking upset. Gladys looked a bit stunned. The shock was setting in. She wasn't sure what to say, so got defensive and dug a grave for herself.

"I'm not looking for your forgiveness. After you burned the kitchen out before you left and threw all his clothes away, I got a good month's beating from Ralph," explained Gladys.

"Seriously, why did you go for a man like that?" asked Arthur with some sincerity. Gladys had no real answer.

"I just happens okay. That's life. Life's never perfect. Things happen you don't want to happen," lamely answered mom.

" *Things happen.*' Yes I know. A lot of things happened to me and you didn't care. You even thought he was marvellous for a while. You're just pig ignorant and don't care about your kids one little bit; heartless!" said an angry Arthur.

"I see Henry now-and-then too," said Gladys talking about her second son who didn't particularly like her but felt a sense of duty or something.

"Good for you. Never liked him, the suck-up."

"At least he wasn't a vicious bastard like you. You know what you did to me," said Gladys fighting back.

"And you know what you did to me," replied Arthur.

"Then we're even," twisted Gladys, hoping it would get her off the hook. Some of noxious Ralph's poker mates had a go at the juvenile Arthur when they went to the bathroom for a length of time.

The easel then blew over in the wind into Arthur's face which distracted him, so the elderly lady made a run for the house. Boy could she run for a woman in her early seventies. And she nearly made it just before Arthur caught up and pushed her head through a patio glass window. Gladys was knocked out and had blood streaming down her face. Arthur had wet paint running down his face and looked like something comical from a low budget horror flick. He wasn't quite sure what to do now.

Arthur realised all he really wanted from mom was a sincere and genuine apology, and perhaps forgiveness too. He wanted to be loved, not fobbed-off with lies and pushed away like before. Rejection had become his nemesis. It was too late for love now. Arthur was unlikely to ever get the answers he wanted, one of which was the whereabouts of abuser Ralph. His subconscious had planned to torture his mother and murder Ralph. That plan was sharply ruined when Gladys went floppy and stopped breathing. Arthur then tried hard to resuscitate her with mouth to mouth but failed. She died in his arms and he said, "You loved me really didn't you mother," and then actually nodded her head when she didn't answer.

At the end of the day you just want to be loved and treated right, and that's too much to ask for.

Shortly after Elizabeth passing to the afterlife, Arthur made himself a cheese sandwich and rifled through her address books to try and locate Ralph.

He wanted to kill Ralph before the cops found him. Ralph really had it coming.

The whole time Arthur thought about his new mission in life, Gladys lay on the hearthrug bleeding out and this didn't seem to bother Arthur one little bit. Instead, he felt a sense of accomplishment and closure, and also remembered how much he liked cheese and tomato sauce sandwiches, squirting Ketchup everywhere like a kid. Sitting down he saw one of his late mother's paintings over the fireside. It was a strange portrait of a woman he had no idea existed. She was Arthur's daughter he knew nothing about and his sick mind fantasised about it being Juliet.

Arthur felt in ruins because he had ruined everything. The best case scenario he could hope for now would be getting revenge on Ralph, but despite looking high and low, Gladys had removed every last trace of men from her surprisingly contemporary looking house. Arthur took a deep breath in and thought, shit I would have liked living here. "Too late for that now," he sighed with a deliberate sense of dark comedy and fell asleep in emotional pain, all rigid like mother's anatomy. His killer's mind was as cold as her crisp silk sheets.

Don't Google your symptoms because it will say you should've been dead 5 minutes ago.

Arthur's rigor mortis mind was woken around 7am by a fucking loud lawnmower just after detective

199

Flynn had set off from Hope Valley to apprehend him. Still very hungry, Arthur thought he'd enjoy one last meal before the gallows, so tried to order 6 large pizzas because money was no object now, but everywhere was closed that early. "Fuck you!" he shouted in frustration, half at the pizza places and half at the fucking annoying noise pollution coming from next door.

His willpower was falling into a depression and for a good 10 minutes Arthur lost all sense of perspective or care about being caught. Being stressed and hungry made things seem polysemous. Arthur then took the portrait of his abandoned daughter off the wall and weirdly put it on the coffee table, using it as a food tray for some unhealthy morning snacks. He was bloody hungry and whilst he stuffed his face full of crisps and chocolate, his sly eyes connected with the female subject of the painting. However, instead of seeing the family resemblance, his monotone mind only saw the eyes of Juliet again: that woman who had destroyed everything for him. Yet another woman that is. Blaming women everywhere he went for his nastiness. Arthur then had a surge of anger and flipped the painting off the coffee table, landing on stone cold Gladys. Juliet had to pay! She was now his target of anger and hatred, not Ralph. If it wasn't for her fighting back in that van and enlisting her Twitter pals, he would be free to sell Class A drugs across the world. Juliet most definitely had to die!

The whole time Arthur's delusional mind was plotting whoever's revenge, the belligerent mowing sound kept cutting in and out of his mind, and it was driving him schizo'. He'd had enough of that too! It would be fair to say Arthur was suffering from Post Traumatic Stress Disorder. He put his coffee down – spilling it everywhere – and decided to shut that nasty racket up to work out how to dig himself out of a hole – more like wishing well. "That fucking racket!" he shouted in the living room heading for the back yard.

Striding just a few yards outside he saw a father and son team fine tuning their microlight/ultralight aircraft, not lawnmower. When we say light aircraft, we mean a really quality hairdryer engine with wings. The son was very keen to go on his maiden voyage without dad. They missed the murder yesterday after going out to buy some parts and tools.

Strangely, Arthur had a fit of jealousy when he saw how attentive and loving the dad was being towards his son and shouted out, "Could you stop making that fucking noise! I can't hear myself thinking!"

The dad, **LARRY**, ushered his teenage son inside and then foolishly stood up to Arthur, "Who on Earth are you to holler at us like that? This is my garden. I do as I please. Get back over your side and off my land! Who are you anyway? And where's Gladys?... I'm calling the cops!"

Arthur started to run at the father who stood his ground, picking up a wrench for defence. They had a good fight after Larry slugged Arthur very hard in the arm to begin the violent proceedings. However, the taller, younger and much fitter Arthur won the day, smashing Larry around the head a few times with his own wrench. The son watched the whole thing in horror from his kitchen window as he called the police. Arthur then ran back to dead Liz's house, packed his bag again like a lunatic and hopped back over to his best escape route; the ultralight aircraft.

The poor son who was consoling his dad on the floor whilst waiting for the police and ambulance didn't hear Arthur come up behind saying, "He'll be alright son. It's just a cracked skull probably. They'll sort him out at the hospital."

Arthur then grabbed the boy, made him refuel the aircraft, get it ready for flight and show him how to work it under pain of death. Luckily for Arthur, even a monkey could fly one, so after dumping some weight he was off, off and away towards the sunrise stuffing his face with croissants whilst using Google compass to make a heading straight for Manhattan to kill Juliet! Arthur had got his murderous mojo back.

When life feels like everything is stacking up in your mind, got to nature and watch your troubles unpack into a beautiful landscape.

Most frustratingly, as Arthur soared into the sky like a morally starved seagull, detective Flynn was trailing belatedly behind. After discovering only an hour or so ago at Hope Valley that Arthur's mother had sold up and moved, the new owner was kind enough to direct him towards Elizabeth's old best friend and neighbour who offered to collect misdirected post; the antithesis of what Liz asked her to do to remain untraceable. Anyway, when Flynn finally made it to Liz's new abode, all he could do was comfort a deeply upset boy watching his dad Larry being wheeled into an ambulance. Yet another victim of Arthur's the NYPD didn't prevent, pictured Flynn in tomorrow's headlines.

You've made it if you can turn anger into passion and passion into love.

Flynn kicked a car tyre in pure frustration. He was really hopping mad with himself. If Flynn hadn't fallen asleep at Shirley's he would have caught Arthur whilst sleeping just six feet away from his own dead mother. Thus far, Arthur had been a few steps ahead of Flynn who now had an approximate emergency 1.5 to 2-hour drive back to Brooklyn after calling Juliet and the FBI to explain everything. Flynn had failed for now and his promotion was looking as mysterious as the shadow of Narcissus.

The only good news of the day, unbeknown to any human, was Bagel successfully arriving in Hope

Valley to begin an epic journey of bravery and love. But Shirley was all over the shop wondering where her feline master had disappeared to.

Have women who say Taken in their bio not seen the Liam Neeson film?

15

As the Crow Flies

Eventually the police arrived and got a helicopter up in the vast American sky, but Arthur was way below the radar and long gone. In fact, he got so low at one point he managed to kick a large bird's nest off the top of a tree. That was his idea of fun. Sparrows rustled into bramble bushes and all kinds of chirps were heard from trees set in blue. Nature sure does take it on the chin from us humans.

Arthur didn't feel comfortable learning any lessons from nature. He couldn't trust its 'kill or be killed' environment, therefore only ever relied on himself to make life happen. The morning sun was soon in full bloom and was Arthur's only friend. He felt its heat and healing power through divine osmosis. The sun's sublime presence hanging above made Arthur regretful and mournful about his life. He simply wished it to be something else and to just disappear. Was his life misfortune, a choice or destiny, wondered Arthur. He imagined what it would have been like if his mother had loved him, or if he'd been born into money. He was certainly feeling very angry about everything and still determined to blame Juliet for all his wrongdoing. Madly, Arthur even felt a sense of jealousy towards Salvador Dali because Dali's mother loved and worshipped her son. Blaming others doesn't ever help.

The biggest, most obvious problems with Arthur were being both a narcissist and a cunt who wasn't stupid by any means. He'd immediately got a hang of the ultralight's controls thanks to good instructions from a weeping boy and had downloaded a navigational app which also charted the weather and his steady 75mph progress. Up high in the air, Arthur felt free from his devilish vices, free from the authorities and free to think alone and be himself. He had roughly 2 hours to kill, only enough water to sip at and 2 bouncy chocolate donuts left to devour. It was warm and pleasant and dare he say it but Arthur felt relatively comfortable. He knew these would likely be his last hours of fake freedom before getting the electric chair so he just sat back in his comfy stolen chair and started to tweet to the world how bad his life had really been:

Not a great morning for me. Woke up and felt suicidal. I've fucked everything up. Thinking of just crashing my vehicle into a brick wall. I literally have no-one to help me. SOS. All alone. Fuck you world!

When you've got nothing but pain inside what's the point of carrying on? Maybe I'd be better off dead than carry on with this fucking comedy called life? There are too many question marks without answers. Too many uncertainties and betrayals. My mind is in chaos.

I feel anger and rage I've trapped myself like this!! I'm better than this!!! Least I thought I was. But now the evil black cloak of depression is suffocating me. I can't breathe and just want out. #notasthma

Poignant tweet after tweet started to pour from his conscience like some kind of purgatory. As he felt the long arm of the law reaching out to feather his collar, Arthur had never felt so free or been so sincere for years. It was simply uplifting! He unblocked everyone with a newfound sense of optimism and hoped the people would hear his pain. And they really connected when one suicidal tweet went viral:

I never thought I'd watch myself write these words, especially as I'm as high as a kite, but I've just decided to crash and burn my life away. This is the end for me. I'm not going to jail. I'd rather die or kill the city that made me feel this living nightmare of an abhorrent life.

Arthur personally couldn't quite work out if he was performing self-mockery or telling the truth. He just let his subconscious fly to see what it had to say. Regardless, a total liar and scumbag who lived his life as a self-satisfied misanthrope, suddenly received so many genuine messages of love and support from strangers he couldn't type TY replies quick enough. And yes, the high stress of recent events had drastically lowered his mental defences and Arthur was saying thanks, starting to feel genuinely grateful. People could hear the words of a desperate man and felt extreme pity and empathy for him. He neglected to mention all the rapes and murders, not just because he felt that wouldn't be deemed socially acceptable, but because on his final voyage Arthur chose to wear his heart on his sleeve for once, bleeding out emotions like a throat slit sheep.

All of his previous criminal premeditations were restricting, negative and deceiving. The crimes themselves took him so far removed from his soul they had eclipsed any hope of forgiveness, meeting God or feeling the healing power of kindness. A while back, Arthur even turned his back on Mother Nature, believing that experiencing landscapes or watching wild animals was a waste of his valuable time. He actually thought trees were idiots. Arthur was a pathological liar who now – when it was all too late – was discovering the beauty of creative catharsis whilst flying in the lightest breeze blowing forgiveness across his tired eyes. His phone was no longer the only entertainment around as Arthur the atheist felt the light of God and the crack of thunder.

Is Twitter a secret American government experiment to gather all the world's most random people? If so, it's worked. What are they going to do with us now?

Unfortunately, as he finally approached Manhattan in good time, it was not God that shone upon Arthur when he accidentally rose higher towards the heavens whilst tweeting. The concept of Faith deserted Arthur immediately as two roaring F-35 jet fighters descended upon him like poison darts, deployed as anti-terrorist measures after his little microlight popped up on the radar as a potential NYC missile attack.

"For fuck's sake!!" he shouted out in shock when they soared past to survey the UFO bogey. He hadn't been paying full attention to his altitude and military camouflage had disappeared. Arthur felt like a flapping chicken trying to out-fly two sparrow hawks.

He twisted his neck around in horror to see the sun shimmer on two lightning fast planes lining up to intercept and target him. Arthur's aircraft was way too slow for the pilots to ascertain the likelihood of it being a terrorist bomb drop so they began firing 25mm bullets at his flimsy flying trolley of an aircraft anyway. It was like something from Star Wars as tracer rounds whistled by, yet missing their tiny target. Arthur naturally panicked and dropped like a stone from the sky to lose as much altitude as possible as the war planes bulleted past to circle around for a guided missile attack.

"Fox two, target locked and firing," calmly said the lead pilot over the radio to base.

"Jesus fucking Christ!" hollered Arthur when he saw the burn of two Sidewinder missiles heading his way.

We know Arthur was an excellent spontaneous thinker. He'd been in lots of tight scrapes where he'd had to think fast on his feet. But this was on a whole new level: the warplane's speed was nearly 2,000km/h. In a moment of extreme madness, Arthur actually wasted 2 seconds reaching for a lighter in his top pocket with the idea of using it as chaff to throw the missiles off target. After his brain re-engaged, realising how truly mental a thought that was, he dropped the lighter, totally cut the engine and fell like a peregrine falcon towards the Hans Christian Andersen Monument in Central Park. Fucking great, thought Arthur, I'm going to die and be remembered as a fucking fairy tale.

The rogue missiles completely sailed past him and an electronic guidance malfunction on one of the notoriously troubled F-35's lost control of the Sidewinder which was now headed straight for central Manhattan.

Arthur had since restarted the engine and regained control just seconds before nearly crash landing into folklore. By now the cigarette lighter he dropped had started a fire below his feet so he frantically steered towards the nearest pond available. Most coincidentally and ironically, by some weird twist of fate he was headed straight for the Boatman Restaurant Lake in Central Park where he first met Juliet on their fateful date.

Dive-bombing into the lake with diners watching, Arthur swam across to the restaurant and pulled himself out announcing to the upper crust eaters, "I'll go to any lengths to get my wife back!" and everyone laughed. "I recommend the lobster madam," continued his comedy routine looking at a beautiful lady close by as he pulled out his rescued lighter and lit her cigarette.

Everyone clapped so he juggled three bread rolls like a performing monkey before bowing and exiting with, "I'm on a roll!" The fabulously wealthy gentleman with the highly entertained smoker couldn't have Arthur stealing the show and could see he'd had a shit soaked day, so he stood up and tucked 10 one hundred dollar bills into Arthur's lighter pocket and social order was restored as the new maître d' escorted Arthur out after donating him a dry dinner jacket to match the generosity displayed. It was all so fake and funny.

Meanwhile, the errant missile had circled back on itself towards the malfunctioned fighter struggling to escape the heat seeking stalker. The brave pilot tried to lead the Sidewinder out of New York City but just as it caught up to his jet he went supersonic and the bomb careered into the world famous MOMA (Museum of Modern Art).

The rogue missile knocked a small corner off the building causing middle-class chaos inside. Amazingly, thanks to the grace of God, no-one was killed because that section of the gallery housed Andy Warhol paintings that everyone was always profoundly underwhelmed by and walked straight past onto the real art from Cezanne, Van Gogh and Edvard Munch. It was like a ghost town in Warhol's spaces where the wool had not been pulled over the people's eyes for once. Even Andy himself said he wasn't a real artist; he was merely a shop window display designer who mingled enthusiastically with the people in charge. Art is who you know, not what you can do, like most professions.

Luckily, nobody was even injured either, apart from a disgruntled member of staff who used the furore to try and steal valuable sensitive documents from the director's office and was caught and beaten off-camera by security guards. However, the impact's explosion sparked a fire big enough to even challenge the MoMA's outstanding air conditioning, which ironically was designed by the same firm who made the F-35. The blaze burnt the whole building down and everyone just went about their lives. Art changes nothing. It's just a flagship for the rich. As a great philosopher once said, 'Finance turns art into fart.'

I like art more than people because it has always been there for me.

The US government had no choice but to cover up their catastrophic technical error, blaming Iran for developing small weapons of mass destruction. This paved the way for a future invasion and the American arms dealers were most delighted. More importantly though, the explosion caused mass panic and chaos in New York City. This was just what Arthur needed to stay undetected and get at Juliet. Flynn was a good 1-hour behind him, weaving in-and-out of rush-hour traffic jams delaying him enormously.

A yellow cabby got out of his car to see what the commotion was about. Arthur stole his vehicle and hightailed it to Juliet's former hairdressing salon booming Bohemian Rhapsody on the radio. Everyone had stopped working, listening to the emergency news and embracing the mass hysteria about terrorist attacks. People were reporting explosions everywhere across the city, but it turns out it was just popcorn fantasies and absolutely nothing but propaganda lies. The billionaires were rubbing their hands with glee.

Arthur pulled up beside the salon he had stalked so much on the internet and saw the staff all worried-looking outside. He got chatting to a few of them to ask what was going on whilst discovering they were former friends of Juliet's. Arthur then offered to give the two girls a free lift home before the streets were jammed with confusion. They jumped at the chance to escape the panic with a mysterious tall man. He charmed them, dropped one off close by and then pumped the other one for information on Juliet's whereabouts.

"Come on, I'm an old friend of Juliet's. She used to work at the salon and I stopped by to see if she was okay after the terrorist attack was all over the radio. I was nearby and worried…" he drivelled on.
"Oh I don't know, I shouldn't really say. See she had a horrible episode a while back and went to her mother's to rest," said a suspicious and naive hairdresser.
"So you do know where her mom lives but are a bit worried about telling a stranger?" said Arthur with a trained look of honesty in his eye.
"Well yes, but…" hesitated the girl.

Arthur then pulled out the $1000 dollars and she told him everything she knew, including why men don't like her. The disloyal employee and rubbish friend was thrown out of the cab and Arthur sped to Shirley's street. He didn't have her house number and it could have been any one of over four hundred houses to locate. Fortunately the police were stupid enough to post an officer outside the front door and leave their black and white directly outside too. Arthur pulled up behind the patrol car, waited for inspiration and composed himself before implementing a classic ruse.

You've only got one life, so if you don't explore people you connect with because of social convention, you are going against nature.

16

Road Trip in Flames

Flynn was a great detective, but he had made a mistake in not listening to other people's instincts as well as his own gut feelings. By attempting to be mister brave he'd got caught with his pants down. Flynn was stuck in early morning slug slow traffic. Only his blue lights were rolling. Never *ever* leave your loved one in times of need, especially in danger. The heart must always be protected because what else is there.

I don't think I could get any happier until I met you. You are my light, my moon and stars, and every breath I take.

Arthur hadn't monopolized all of God's luck though. He was just metres away, a kindergarten cop and a few walls from facing the good woman who had destroyed his evil ways when his fake engine trouble plan was partially ruined by an escaped cockatoo.

Emmental naturally had keen eyesight – being a bird – and had spotted trouble through the window. As soon as Arthur pulled up the elaborate bird recognised the wanted fugitive and unlocked his cage with a hairclip. Just as officer Gabby González made her way down some stone steps towards the trap to see what the trouble was, Emmental shot through the cat flap and through Gabby's legs with Shirley following not far behind shouting, "Come back my little prince! Mommy's got you some fresh passionfruit," said in the most irritating baby voice ever.

Emmental wasn't particularly partial to passionfruit and he thought Shirley should have realised by now strawberries were his thing. Shirley had a fixed idea of what every pet should like and do, just like she did with her daughters. All of Shirley's pets got the same Shirley care package whether they liked it or not. Emmental was feeling the pinch, but Tony the tortoise was serious, deciding to abscond for good. He asked Emmental to create a lengthy diversion for him to escape North to Canada where he'd been told the people were loved worldwide.

Shirley's controlling ways had gone neurotic and flabby since Bagel's unexplained disappearance. She was a bag of nerves and was so mad at the police for not allowing her to pin up missing posters around the neighbourhood; 'For her own safety' they said. She'd just about had enough of Juliet's problems restricting her life by now and the thought of Emmental wanting to desert her as well was all too much.

Anyway, Emmental's feather flapping commotion ruined Arthur's simple plan to spanner officer Gabby around the head as she checked out the supposedly broken engine. His chance had gone and officer González was looking sharp while calling for a police tow truck to remove his cab from obstructing police business. At the same time, Shirley was nagging Arthur for a ride, who had now shaved his head as a new disguise using the hairdresser's clippers left behind when he booted the bigmouth girl out.

"I'm sure with a little jiggery-pokery you could get your cab going again my good man!" Shirley mocked with a sense of urgency before Gabby said,

"The orders were to keep you safe inside ma'am. I can't let you go I'm afraid," she insisted.

"I simply want to have my hair trimmed and my nails done, is that too much to ask?" said a frustrated housebound Shirley. She was lying. Her friends had a dodgy card game and swingers event planned.

"Yes, it is," replied Gabby with a cold, sarcastic look in her eye.

During their stand-off, Arthur put the bonnet back down and started up the cab for fear of being recognised. He had to think quickly. If he couldn't get to Juliet now, then perhaps he could torture her mother instead: better still, maybe ransom her life for enough getaway money to escape justice in somewhere exotic like the Caribbean or Thailand? Whilst his mind was whirring around like clock cogs on crack, Shirley had taken the initiative and jumped into the cab without Gabby's permission and locked the door. This was now getting serious. Officer Gabby pulled out her gun and gave out firm instructions, "Get OUT of the vehicle ma'am or I will shoot!"

Shirley was incensed by the rookie and screamed, "You're going to shoot a retired lady are you, after years of service and tax paying to this great country of ours!!" Even her own mind began questioning what years of service and there had been many accountant tax dodges too.

Inside the house, Juliet heard the shrill of her mother's irritating voice and opened the front door to investigate. Immediately she felt the bad vibe of rotten intentions and headed straight for the cab whilst looking directly at Arthur.

Arthur knew the game was up and had to act fast. He put his foot down on the accelerator straight into the back right side of the cop car, spinning it into the road at a ninety degree angle as he made a speedy wheel spin exit.

Officer González shouted, "Stop or I'll shoot!!!" taking aim at Shirley, not Arthur, for reasons unknown. Her subconscious took over.

Juliet ran at Gabby, pulled her arm down and the gun fired a hole in the ghetto bird's gas tank. Gabby ran to her cop car, started her up, reversed into a few parked cars opposite and went in hot pursuit whilst gabbling on the radio for back-up.

Fuel poured out all the way down the street and two naughty teenagers threw their cigarettes at its tail to pure astonishment as chariots of horse drawn flames raced to catch the police car up.

"It was only a joke," said one very worried looking boy with his mouth wide open.

Officer Gabby was riding the first corner at speed when she heard the crackling flames peeling paint off the boot. She looked in the mirror to see her car engulfed in the chaos of fire, throwing herself out the door just in time before one mother of an explosion took the street's attention.

Gabby was knocked out on impact but survived with nasty scrapes and a massively dented pride. All she had to do was stay by the front door as ordered and let nobody in or out. Arthur and Shirley were miles away now and the cops had no idea where they were. It was a disaster to say the least.

"Well done young man! We showed her who's boss. I'll give you a $20 tip for the damage to your car, if that's fair," praised Shirley who clearly had no clue how much cars cost.

Arthur admired her style and bravado for a few seconds until he regained focus and centrally locked all of the doors before taking a major detour back to his secret garage lock up in Rhode Island.

"I think you just took the wrong turn my handsome driver," Shirley said, literally still just thinking about her gambling and whatnot.

"No mistake madam, we're just going on a little road trip," answered Arthur with a flirtatious smile.

"Oh, got something big planned for me sailor?" flirted back Shirley. Fuck she's dumb, thought Arthur, trying to figure out the seafaring analogy. "Anchor's away!" laughed Shirley who had no idea what she was going on about, she just wanted to get away from all the bickering with Juliet and her pets. Yes, I need a holiday, thought Shirley, I need an adventure!

The only way to believe in what you're saying is to listen to your enemy before you metaphorically decapitate them.

This time Flynn had only improved his late arrivals to catch a serial killer by 4 minutes. Juliet was furious with him and the world. Cops were everywhere and neighbours were really gossiping with intent.

Shirley's neighbourhood watch reputation was being destroyed minute-by-minute. "I wonder if her wayward daughter is into drugs?" said one pointless waste of retirement time.

"You can never trust a woman who has a parrot," laughed the back-stabbing next door neighbour, who herself was sleeping with Scott from number 248 down the street behind her husband's back. Shirley liked Scott too and once gave him a blowjob behind some garbage bins nearly 10 years ago which caused the animosity and jealousy between her and neighbour Jasmine.

"You should never have left us Flynn," barked Juliet.

"I know! I know, I'm sorry," said a contrite looking boyfriend who just held her and reassured Juliet he wouldn't leave her side again in troubled times.

"They've got mom," she said despite knowing he knew Arthur had mom.

"I know. We're doing everything possible to get her back. I promise you. I'm sorry, I nearly got him as well," said an angry looking Flynn.

222

"But you didn't and now mom's gone," chastised Juliet, which kind of ended the conversation. A tiny little part of Juliet's pragmatic side thought, wow, me and sis have got two New York residences now; that's so cool!

Juliet's emotions were as mixed and bitter as a kale smoothie. Her heart started to pound, erupting a full blown panic attack which pierced adrenaline through her veins at volcanic pace. She couldn't feel anything. Objects and people seemed distant – untouchable. Her confidence plummeted into the deep occult ocean of mental illness. A raven entered her mind and ripped flesh from her arm, pecking at her unconscious remains. Darkness loomed and she'd never felt so alone and miserable.

Juliet was understandably in mental pieces, again. Her mom had been kidnapped by America's current no.1 wanted fugitive. The media were demanding his capture and Feminists were up in arms after the number of estimated rapes was likely over 35. No-one could tell what was real or fiction; just like Twitter really. This savage monster had to be caught!

Arthur was a really manipulative and sagacious guy though. They had ditched the cab at a service station and hired a new vehicle using Shirley's license details. The silly old mare still believed she was going to get laid by the fountain of youth in her eyes and thought she was on the road trip of a lifetime.

223

God was Arthur charming when he needed to be and he'd now worked out his escape strategy too.

The mark of a good person is leaving others wanting more of what you do.

About three quarters of Arthur's and Caesar's attacks were in the victim's homes. This was so they could rob as much jewellery and assets as possible as part of their escape from justice fund in Switzerland, where most of the world's illegal money is.

Whilst Shirley was looking all happy for herself eating pasta in a tacky and sticky seated diner, Arthur popped outside to call the FBI to arrange a payment of 5 million dollars into his foreign account or the woman gets it in 3 days kind of thing.

As soon as they verified it was Shirley's number and they knew the call was kosher, Juliet was informed of the bad news and Flynn was given orders by Deputy Inspector Maddox to track down Arthur Koons and use all force necessary. To clarify, he told Flynn to kill Arthur to save the tax payer millions and to stop him becoming a serial killer celebrity in jail, and persistent embarrassment to the NYPD. Flynn now had no choice but to leave Juliet again, or lose his job just minutes after promising not to leave her.

I've rarely had a pedestal, but seem to nearly always own a dog house.

Juliet was really up against it now. Her boyfriend was breaking his promises and her belligerent mother had been kidnapped by a man who tried to rape her. She'd lost the support of most of her family after frequently supporting Palestine and now Juliet was going to have to grovel and kiss some big feet to get them to maybe pay the extortionate ransom. Suddenly, a horrible clouded thought entered her confused mind: maybe I should just let mommy go. But as truly frustrating as her mom was, it was her mom and she obviously wouldn't exist without her. The old bat and battleaxe had to be saved!

Flynn had not yet proven himself, especially with his job. Yet Juliet believed in him and wanted Shirley back. "Do whatever it takes to bring mom home safely please Flynn. She's my mother and despite everything I still love her very much," cried Juliet. Flynn went to hug her again, but she pushed him away saying, "Go on, don't hang around this time. Go and get my mom for me!" Flynn felt rejected because he was, but understood her pain. The pressure was on again and he was bloody tired. Life never seems to let up.

Your greatest enemy is often just plain and simple tiredness.

Anyway, Flynn had a job to do and he was going to do it! Surprisingly, he requested and was granted permission for officer Gabby González to assist him. DI Maddox believed in instant justice and

225

giving his officers chances to make amends. Flynn believed in Gabby's policing abilities and potential and also believed – despite some very sore ribs – this would be the perfect opportunity for her to rectify her serious mistake and to also regain pride and honour. Gabby had shown courage to accept the task immediately after being cleared for active duty from hospital and Maddox was very proud of her, secretly saying a prayer to God to give them a safe and successful mission.

Flynn already felt like a Yo-yo going from NYC to RI every 5 minutes, but a trace on Shirley's mobile suggested they were travelling back that way. Frustratingly, Flynn's police instincts had been right all along. He felt like a talented football striker who had yet to put a goal in the new season's net. And Juliet felt like a soccer player who just scored an own goal.

There is lots of beauty in you. Make sure people see it.

Now Juliet possibly had the worst job of all: calling her wealthy extended, partially estranged family for financial help. She correctly assumed it would be a humiliating and sizeable climb-down. Juliet opened the door to depression and a black widow crept into her mind. She downloaded the Twitter app and immediately – within a few psychotic seconds – Juliet's secret nemesis The Black Orchid pinged her spider's web. Evil has a bad habit of turning up when you feel weak.

Those people who try and make you feel bad for doing the thing you love because they haven't found themselves yet. Fuck those people.

17

Tarantino Time Wasters

By the time the police eventually located the roadside diner where Shirley enjoyed a romantic sausage brunch with Arthur (now calling himself Troy, not Ryan), the odd couple had already got cosy inside Arthur's garage den. He was very happy to go along with Shirley's romantic expectations because it made kidnapping the old crow very easy.

You waste a lot of time and energy just sifting out the shit people in life. The best friend to have is yourself.

This was a man who had now killed a number of people and possibly raped dozens of women. I.e. he'd learnt how to keep his cool in many different, deeply insane situations. However, Shirley was a unique lady who managed to get under everyone's skin. She just had this thing about her where you really wanted to tell her to get fucked, but never did. By now Shirley was really beginning to fuck Arthur off like a bad case of eczema. He got a bit stressed and started to tie her up in frustration hoping she'd stop talking.

"Ooo, you like it rough then do you captain?" said Shirley making strange pouting lip movements like Benny Hill used to.
"I just need a second to think. Wait there, I'll be back for you in a while," lied Arthur.
"Don't leave a girl waiting too long you plundering pirate!" called out Shirley as Ryan walked into his office just to get some fucking breathing space. He really wanted to kill her, primarily to stop the nauseating chitchat, but Arthur needed Shirley alive and co-operative. The weird milieu was just a bonus.

The greatest thing about Twitter is realising that someone
you've never met before really cares about your well-being.

Another very bored retiree and ex wife in her
seventies, the Black Orchid on Twitter, was revelling
in Juliet's demise for all those times Juliet had
outsmarted, teased and run rings around the crabby
old English bird. Black Orchid knew this was the
perfect moment of weakness to *carpe diem* and get
revenge. She formerly named herself the Black
Widow until filing for a divorce and didn't like the
acupuncture irony.

The Orchid previously leeched off Juliet's very
popular Twitter account to suck some much needed
popularity into hers. She used to be on fake family
friendly Facebook, pumping away on her keypad for
nearly a year without ever making one friend. Then
a Facefuck/Twatter hybrid user told her Twitter is
where the real action is at, so Orchid joined in hope
of friendship but was just too old to keep up with
the frenetic pace of abuse and jokes. She resented
Juliet's help and phenomenal charisma. The long
and the short of it was that Orchid was yet another
bitter senior citizen who wanted to prove to the
younger generation her life had not been wasted and
she could teach them a thing or two – which it was
and she couldn't.

The ominous time had finally arrived to kick
Juliet when she was down and Orchid – real name
Justine – looked around her spiderwebbed infested
mind for the most apt psychological weapon to use

against Juliet. It was like an imaginary version of a Tarantino film going on inside Justine's brain. She saw basic Manipulation serving drinks, good old-fashioned Bullying playing poker, Harassment and Intimidation readying for a fast draw and even tried and tested Blackmail in the corner of the dark saloon. But as a tingle went down Justine's spine she turned to face the ultimate contemporary and versatile psychological tool to destroy anyone from stupid to smart: GASLIGHTING. Justine had already laid the ground for infiltrating Juliet's mind by being sickly sweet and faking nice on every occasion. Now with Juliet's mother out of the picture, Justine could take the part by offering Juliet some *motherly* advice, otherwise known as nihilistic revenge!

Juliet really needed a friend right now and stupidly let old Justine the Trojan Horse into her DMs for support. After establishing the basic facts of Juliet's trauma, Justine knew it would be difficult to get anyone to top themselves through messaging alone. Therefore she realistically had to choose between breaking up Juliet's relationship with Flynn or buggering things up with her family so they don't give her the ransom money. If successful, Shirley could walk the plank.

Juliet and jealous Justine messaged each other back and forth throughout the day in between Juliet informing the family of the bad news. Once Justine discovered Juliet's important family fundraising meeting was tomorrow at 4pm, her poisonous plan was to make Juliet miss the event.

Juliet: I really appreciate you taking time out of your life to help me through this Orchid.

Justine: Oh please, call me Justine. Just one J girl helping another J girl out, lol.

That last reply summed up why Justine was no longer hip and never had been dookie fresh or even gravy locomotive. Justine was as cool as a plodding dinosaur and not the cool T-Rex type ones.

Juliet: Just finished calling everyone I need to pass on the message to my extended family. Hopefully most people will answer the bat call, lol? I have no idea what I'm going to say tomorrow, whether I should approach people directly or make a speech/appeal??? 🌚

Justine: That's great! No need to worry your pretty little head. I've got lots of experience in speech writing and delivery. Let me help you win them over and write something really great for you. I know you must be so tired after everything and I'm happy to take the weight off your shoulders.

Juliet: Really? That would save me a lot of time. How will you know what to say?

Justine: I used to be a lawyer before moving into finance. Don't mention it because it's boring, lol. I know how to write a generic fundraising speech and you can read it and edit it into place to suit. Deal?

Juliet: Deal! I need it by 2pm at the latest tomorrow please. Thank you sooo much Justine I really owe you one. 🖤

Justine: I've got a few small family errands to run tomorrow morning and then I'll deliver, I promise. 🖤

On seeing those two Juliet emoji hearts, Justine knew her small-minded and nasty plan was going to work a treat. Juliet was very grateful and feeling fortunate. She had a stomach ache which was probably nerves and felt totally exhausted. To put the anxiety icing on the cake, Bagel was nowhere to be found either – seemed gone for good. It felt like life was just taking and giving nothing in return. Things were going very wrong and Juliet's subconscious did think it was a bit convenient Justine was a lawyer, into finance and also a dab hand at organising similar charity type events. In life and in crime, coincidences don't exist. Tiredness gave Justine the benefit of the doubt because Juliet needed her, but when you are desperate that's precisely when you get conned.

Many people on Twitter are self-absorbed and don't understand what being nice is about. I love it when you discover a decent person who does.

A night full of doubts and insomnia left Juliet withered and drawn looking. She fell back asleep in the morning when she should have been getting up and then woke dreadfully late, around 11:30am. Time is a bastard son who outshines the biological one. After a shower and this and that, time was pushing on to 1pm and Juliet still hadn't decided what to wear for the big occasion.

Juliet: Hi Justine, sorry it's so late, I've got a bit of a headache. I wondered if you've got that speech for me to amend please? Thanks.

Responding quicker than a snake strike, Justine had been laying in wait to implement petty retribution, justified as emotional balance. Just because someone is better than you doesn't give you the right to throw daggers at their tree of life.

Justine: Yes, just give me 20 minutes to finalise things and I've got you a perfect set of short speeches to choose from. Just your cup of tea!

Juliet: Wow! That's great. Thank you so much again Justine. I owe you one even though I drink coffee, lol. That gives me time to choose my dress now.

Justine: Take your time and choose wisely. Appearance is everything at these functions.

The minutes were rolling on while Juliet picked a beautiful new outfit designed by Diane Von Furstenberg: a chic little number with shades of Audrey Hepburn sophistication, complimented with a cute box purse, recherché pearl jewellery and studded light pink heels by Valentino. Juliet looked very much the Park Avenue princess with avant-garde class for the prestigious occasion. She was just starting to feel good about herself after seeing how well she scrubbed up, only to have her self-appreciation utterly ruined by Justine sending her what can only be described as a load of acidic gobbledegook. Juliet trusted Justine who seemed relatively smart. The speech was disjointed and geriatric at best. Things were not adding up with just a quarter of an hour before she had to leave for Madison Avenue.

Juliet: Justine, I'm not being funny or ungrateful but it's not what I was hoping for. It's not really even complete :(

… said Juliet really thinking, FFS I'm completely fucked now!

Justine: Oh I'm very sorry if my standards don't meet your expectations! I worked hard on that and all for nothing. Maybe I'm just too old to be any use these days?

…typed Justine trying to play Juliet's heart strings like evil Miss Havisham. The phrase 'too old' stuck in Juliet's mind, remembering she once teased Justine live on Twitter about how people don't refer to dating as courting these days. This dig and public humiliation really cut into Justine who didn't appreciate banter is a regular part of social media. Part of surviving Twitter is to be able to take a joke and eat a shit sandwich. Juliet recalled Justine said those same two words as her reply before. The penny dropped Justine had deliberately fucked up to get her back for what was just a good natured joke. Many old people have a nasty habit of being vindictive.

Juliet: I know what you've done in my hour of need when I don't feel well. Why betray me Justine? I've been nothing but respectful to you.

Justine was on the keypad again quicker than a fly on shit. Her deception was nearly over and time was becoming precious, so plan B was implemented.

Justine: I'm very hurt you would accuse me of that. I did my very best for a decrepit and clearly useless old women nowadays. I instantly feel very ill now too.

Juliet: I'm sorry. I don't believe you.

Justine: Juliet please I've got a pain in my heart and I'm lying on the floor scared and confused I need an ambulance please help

Justine had summoned the courage to miss out full stops to give the DM an emergency vibe. Although every word was spelt correctly, which faking Justine couldn't in all good conscience prevent, being a stickler for correct punctuation. Juliet knew it was a scam but couldn't take the chance of it being real. She would never forgive herself if Justine was telling the truth.

It was now pretty much time to leave when she took down a false address and called the ambulance service in England. Justine had become so dotty and bitter about her divorce she simply needed to take out her bad karma on an innocent person. She wasn't remotely worried about potential police involvement for wasting the emergency services valuable time. Justine just wanted to spit hate like many unhappy people do. It was now 2:20pm (scheduled to leave at 2) when Juliet received the landslide of horribleness Justine had stuffed up inside of her.

Juliet: The ambulance is on its way. Just try and stay calm, okay?

Justine: No I'm not OK you silly girl. After having a husband whom I gave my heart and soul to cheat on me many times throughout my loyalty and devotion to our family, I am not OK!! Then to feel so lonely and lost and have a self-obsessed woman nearly half my age humiliate me in front of thousands of twits (**she meant tweeps**) was not what I deserve in life. Your posts are stupid! You're a silly little insignificant unmarried girl who's had no children and expects everyone to pander to every anxious and fake depressed post you ever make. "Oh look at me everyone, I've got troubles." Attention seeking extraordinaire! That's all you are Juliet with her daddy's apartment in Manhattan! I bet you never even got attacked you LIAR.

Juliet was pretty shocked. This shit was unbelievable! She should've just dropped her phone and started driving immediately. However, pride got Juliet to fall into the Black Orchid's plan C bile. More time was being sucked into hyperventilating air, but her anger had to respond now, in the moment!

Juliet: The only LIAR here is you Justine. Lying about our friendship. Lying about your so-called happy marriage. Lying about helping me when I needed it. Lying to yourself about what life is about. No wonder you have become a bitter and twisted old Medusa if you gain satisfaction from bringing people down. There is no Christ in you, just an empty carcass where wisdom could have thrived. And fuck you and everything you stand for! You're a witch bitch.

They both battled out their differences for a further 10 minutes until Juliet's anger subsided and she realized Justine was fiddling with her mind again. It was like watching Mrs. Danvers at work. Justine even surprised herself how efficient at being nasty she could be when she put her mind to it. Being nasty felt good because she had chosen the easy path of evil from whence few souls return. She even tried a plan D, 'I'm sorry, what was I thinking' routine, but Juliet was already speeding towards auntie Pauline's when a jam sandwich pulled her over for a drink driving test and a healthy fine. Fuck, was all Juliet could think. Justine had potentially botched Juliet's chances of saving her own mother and her stress levels were going through the roof whilst calling Justine a Gorgon cunt at traffic lights and deleting the Twitter app, yet again.

Evil stains your soul like acidic red wine.

18

Nobody's Purrfect

It would be fair to say right now Shirley was the centre of many people's personal and work related stress. In fact, if Shirley had not been so annoying, Juliet would not have left home when she did which was the loneliness trigger for joining Twitter and core reason for all her present troubles.

Anyone else block people solely using your intuition?

In some kind of numb way Juliet did miss mom though and had a duty of care to save her from being murdered. However, not all her family were playing ball. After some tense phone conversations, copious amounts of apologies and dropping the words 'police emergency' in as much as she could, Juliet had arranged a collective family meet around auntie Pauline's house; Shirley's eldest and very, very wealthy sister who owned a $98 million luxurious penthouse apartment in Madison Avenue.

Believe it or not, **PAULINE COHEN** was one of the poorer residents in the neighbourhood. However, her place was a real-life palace and she had personally made a fortune from mental health pharmaceuticals. Unfortunately, Juliet had many times at family events criticized Big Pharma' for controlling illnesses and delaying or killing cures, so naturally Pauline was not a big fan of hers. This would be a tricky challenge to say the least.

The problem with nowadays is everyone has a loud opinion but very few people know what the fuck they are talking about.

The whole family of 91 American members had mainly come from New York and Boston, and a handful flew in from Connecticut and Pennsylvania after Pauline Cohen asked them to. People tended to obey divorced Mrs. Cohen because nearly everyone follows money, so it only took a day to gather everyone at very short notice and they spent

241

a couple of hours mingling in the garden before the main family fundraiser. And would you believe it, because of the Orchid's treachery, Juliet was one painful hour late for her own charity mommy saving event. It was a disastrous start and everyone had already congregated into an impressive banquet room designed by Marcel Wanders, none the less. Juliet wandered in all flustered and 76 year old auntie Pauline began proceedings.

"Glad you could join us my dear. Your mother would be so proud of you," announced Pauline who was determined to make her wayward niece tow the family line once and for all.

It was either eat dirt or lose her mother. The crowd cackled and a handful of Juliet's cousins who liked her cringed with embarrassment. It was clearly going to be a long afternoon, but truth be told, Juliet had been supported her whole life by many members of her family and had undermined their politics and beliefs in an unappreciative way. Now it was payback.

The worst part was that auntie Pauline had already done the necessary deals with her family before Juliet even arrived. Mrs. Cohen was never going to see her own bothersome sister slaughtered at the hands of a madman. For a start, not paying the ransom would be a professional disaster for Pauline, leaving her wealthy investors thinking she hadn't the funds. The money had already been transferred to the police and half of it came from the twisted arms of many family members anyway, who were too scared to lose Pauline's always loyal support.

Pauline simply wanted to watch Juliet squirm, be held accountable for the embarrassment she'd caused sister Shirley, but mainly the embarrassment she'd caused Pauline mouthing off about how Big Pharma are making everyone dependent on mind altering drugs. Pauline decided it was time for Juliet to grow up by making her stand in front of the family and literally beg.

"I very much appreciate everyone coming here today under such upsetting circumstances. My mother Shirley has had her critics and I know she has upset a few people during her divorce and…" began Juliet before being interrupted by uncle Frank on dad's side.

"We are all fully aware of your mother's personality dear and are quite frankly more concerned with how you've upset everyone over the years with your extremist views and scant regard for how much pressure this put on your mother. And now you ask for our help," said **FRANK**, Eric's younger brother with a sting in his eye as well as words. Then his wife interrupted him knowing how long-winded Frank could be.

"We're saying you bite the hand that feeds you," stated **MIRIAM** coldly.

The atmosphere in the dauntingly large room was bitterly cold for Juliet, but great to watch and the crowds were looking forward to her psychological lynching. This was top entertainment most families can only get at Christmas. Juliet was already looking and feeling a bit small. Her winning smile and looks had little currency here.

"Nobody's perfect," was Juliet's very lame response, feeling the nerves set in.
"Quoting 'Some Like it Hot' seems a little inappropriate don't you think?" sarcastically said Miriam. "A little more Pinter than Pinterest wouldn't go amiss," she continued and the gathering chuckled.

A series of other family members with petty grievances had their say too until Juliet felt like a little school girl who'd been locked in a cupboard without lights because she'd sworn. Unfortunately this brought out the defensive side of her and Juliet started to fuck things up with style.

"Maybe nobody is perfect? Maybe no-one in this room is without guilt or blame. Perhaps the least blamed are the best actors," philosophised Juliet trying to wrangle and bullshit her way out of past errors.

The mob wanted to see her take it on the chin, not fight back with intelligence. Suggesting everyone might be a liar simply wouldn't do. Nearly everyone thought Juliet needed to be put in her place, apart from Pauline's grandson and heir to a fortune, **EZRA**, who had always fancied Juliet and defended her, just because. He'd had a few drinks too.

"Perhaps Juliet has a point nanny? Does it even matter what she's done wrong anyway? We're here to save aunt Shirley, not Juliet's soul," said a confident chap stepping way beyond acceptable limits.

"Thank you Ezra," appreciated Juliet feeling attacked.

Uncle Frank had to step in before Pauline's deft financial negotiations were ruined by a niece who'd never even had her own business and also eccentrically laid precisely 11,211 dimes on her kitchen floor (set in clear resin) because they looked pretty.

Self-righteous Frank made his way over to Ezra and faked chronic indigestion, requiring the strapping lad's arm support all the way to the west wing. Juliet had minimal to zero support now. This public flogging had taken a funny turn. Queen Pauline was bored with Juliet's insolence and wanted to wrap things up her way. She hobbled across to Juliet with a priceless walking stick which cost more than most people's homes and whispered some home truths.

"Listen to me very carefully young lady. I rather admire your fighting spirit, but today is a day for humility. Do you want to save your mother?" Juliet nodded. She felt the golden aura of a woman who could crush her life with the snap of her fingers. "Good. We'll pay the whopping ransom if you give me your word to never go on your protests again and I want you to write a personal letter of apology to any family member I ask you to contact, otherwise your future will *not* be in New York. Nobody here hates you, we just ask for some loyalty and due appreciation. Who do you think paid for your hairdressing school and your expensive apartment in Manhattan? Yes, it was me. Your mother hasn't got two dimes to rub together in her bank; it's all show. Now buck your ideas up and say something profound now, to show me how intelligent I know you are," finalised Pauline.

Juliet paused to take it all in whilst the room muttered and mingled. It all made sense now. Her father worked for Pauline and had a gambling problem. She always wondered how he managed to pass on his lush apartment to her and also supply ex Shirley with new plush house furniture to say sorry for cheating on her. The answer is he didn't. He womanised, drank and pissed it all away, and auntie Pauline took pity on her sister, bailing them all out. Juliet felt like a spoilt brat. A lump built up in her throat as she faced auntie Pauline saying, "I'm really sorry auntie, I've been an ungrateful fool. Why didn't anyone tell me the truth?"

"Because I believe you have much leadership potential and the world needs to be discovered at one's own pace. Besides, nobody hears the truth when they're not ready to listen. Time is ticking away," wisely responded Pauline with a smile, tapping her watch, who actually meant, get a move on I want some tea.

Juliet picked up her brimmed to the edge wine glass received on entering the penthouse, tapped it loudly with a fork and delivered an adroit speech to make everyone happy. The deal was honoured and honesty was her best policy. When auntie Pauline pays you a compliment, not only did she always mean it, but it was a secret promise to guide you through life. You need as much help in life as you can get, so take what you can:

"I want to say I've not been as clever as I thought I was – far from it. And without my mother and auntie Pauline I wouldn't even be educated enough to hold different views, which are just ideas to me. I like to express myself that's all. I'm the creative type and know this can rub people's backs up sometimes. And the more I didn't reach my expectations, I suppose the more isolated and desperate my expression has become." The hairs on Juliet's neck rose thinking of her mother possibly being tortured as she continued, "I love my mom… from the

247

bottom of my heart. I just want her back moaning about her crazy cat again…" she started to cry real tears with no sign of crocodiles anywhere, "I'm thanking you all for all the good times you've had with mom and all the opportunities you've given me, which other less fortunate people never have."

Juliet then faced lots of family members with sincere eye contact and gave them the praise they deserved and needed to hear. All anyone wants is to feel appreciated. "Uncle Frank, thanks for fixing mom's faucet last month. Auntie Miriam, mother never stops saying how kind you are to her, especially when dad left. Auntie Pauline, I *do* very much appreciate the support…" and her reality check bootlicking went on a further ten or so minutes with a good joke about buttered asparagus tucked in there somewhere too.

The day was won. Everyone, bar a few miserable old bastards never content with anything, went home happy and they all saved Shirley who was presently polishing Arthur's dick because he couldn't curb her desperate sexual enthusiasm. Oh why not, thought Arthur, at least it will stop her speaking.

There's no age limit for receiving praise. Everyone welcomes daily encouragement.

Fancy free Bagel was also feeling more focused since parting ways with Shirley's internal chatter. Hanging out with Shirley was like hearing an avalanche coming your way and freezing still for no sane reason. Bagel the crafty cat had been made crazy by circumstance. However, Shirley's head may have been a log cabin of pandemonium, yet at least she had a roof over her head. Bagel was now in a strange part of the world which didn't even know why it named itself Rhode Island. She was headed for Judith Point to stowaway on the ferry to Block Island to find her beloved real home, when the fear of loneliness took over her currently jittery sixth sense.

Bagel thought she saw a ghost; obviously a cat ghost because the laws of nature say we can only see apparitions of our own species. The closer she got it became obvious the ghost was just a large watering can.

"Get a fucking grip," whispered Bagel to herself. Self talk had negatively taken over. There was no lion tamer around for her loneliness. "When does a cat's tail *ever* get that stiff you moron?" she chastised herself. Ironically, talking to one's self is a great way to stay calm.

Throughout the day Bagel felt a homecoming parade vibe as she waltzed past MAGA American flags standing proud outside many homes. Bagel didn't care for politics. She thought all politicians were cunts who never did anything for animals, especially cats. She was less than just 20 miles from her early morning ferry connection when the dark night drew in a spooky, unexplained mist and Bagel felt vulnerable. Behind every great change you need in your life will be pure courage.

The greatest inspiration is found looking at the night's stars.

Back home at Shirley's Brooklyn pad, the remaining pets were feeling guilty about everything. Word on the street was that Tony Curtis got flattened like a pancake because he just couldn't compete with the speed of human vehicles. Who would have thought it.

Emmental let himself out again and after a long night's search found what he had been dreading. "I'm gonna miss you buddy," he wept whilst scraping his best friend Tony off the tarmac and accidentally dropping his flattened body down a drain. "You would have wanted a burial at sea anyway," cried Emmental, knowing Tony wanted to be cremated in a forest fire. He dreamed of returning to nature.

Nature bonds people together, calms our emotions and connects your mind to the universe. It gives you all the balance you'll ever need. I'd rather spend time with nature than most people any day.

That sombre night, Shirley's remaining pets felt the pressure of humanity rip at their tiny souls. The three wise fish and the cockatoo agreed it was wrong to send Bagel into the wild because she could get whored out. So they called in some big favours to their bird and fish friends to send protection Bagel's way. Most brilliantly, a double-crested cormorant who once received life saving directions from Emmental agreed to fly all the way to Block Island to tell Romeo that Suzie was returning to her treasured pussy magnet.

Have you ever tweeted whilst having sex?

19

Muddy Puddles

As soon as Arthur received the $5,000,000 transfer from the police, his future looked rose tinted and paved with gold. Bingo, he thought with smug glee. He'd untied Shirley ages ago and spent a gruelling 13 minutes kissing her with tongues because his plans had radically changed. Why have half of life's tough mutton fortunes when you can have everything with lamb and mint sauce, reasoned

Arthur. The very second he heard the ransom money sweetly ka-ching into his Swiss stash, his confidence grew to astronomically schizophrenic levels again. Arthur could have his revenge cake without eating the pussy.

When money becomes your driving force, your soul can't grow.

His ambitious plans were changing by the minute. Big money has a sure-fire way of making anyone go plum crazy and Arthur was no different. He wanted a fresh start and respect from others, and money would buy all his unreasonable demands. Arthur also wanted to remain a criminal, but leaned towards being a respectable criminal like many Senators, State Attorneys and American arms dealers. The drug dream had altered. Arthur now had a much more elaborate scheme in mind. Nonetheless, before recreating himself as an international art thief and money launderer, the past had to be firmly put behind him and he still felt extreme antipathy towards Juliet who nearly transformed him into a jailbird. Be an underdog not an underachiever.

Believing in yourself isn't about telling yourself loads of motivational bullshit. It's about making sure you reward yourself for every last thing you do well.

Despite his newfound wealth and bravado, Arthur didn't fancy his chances assassinating Juliet under much heavier house arrest. The easiest option to hurt Juliet was to murder Shirley in some kind of manic sacrifice to Narcissus, purging the past. The general idea was that her life will bring the stone figure in him back to life. Perfectly logical, he concluded. Mad minds can make anything work.

Let's not be ashamed of who I am, thought Arthur. I shall drown Shirley in broad daylight like a catfish. And what more fitting a place to do so than where he first met Juliet and crashed landed his microlight; the Boathouse Lake in Central Park. But first he would need a grand escape vehicle to do the dirty deed and implement his new career.

It was surprisingly easy to buy a fucking massive ocean-going boat from Newport in online cash. As they say, there are only two great days when you buy a boat; the day you buy it and the day you sell it. Boats haemorrhage money and when some inexperienced mug turns up willing to pay 30% more than the going rate for no questions asked, Mr. Thorne who owned the expediently named Deliverance, nearly had a heart attack he'd finally sold the thorn in his side to pay for his trophy wife.

WILLIAM THORNE was more than happy to spend a day showing Arthur the ropes too. Unfortunately for him, Will also brought along his gorgeous hourglass wife, **CHERYL**, who was very interested in the new handsome hotshot in town. It didn't take long for Arthur to fuck her hard on the hard floor of the cockpit when William went below deck for the lav' and lunch.

Cheryl was desperately bored with boring William and wanted to travel the world forever, and now was her big chance. When she discovered Arthur traded in paintings worth millions, her clit went as wet as the slippery fish below. She was certainly onboard with Arthur's plans after sailing up and down on his varnished mast. It was lollipop hot and so was she.

She floats in with unparalleled grace,
An enchanting look with exquisite taste.
The happy ho has style that's free
To open-minded folk like you and me.

Yes, sex is great, if you've ever had it. Things were on the up! But the first voyage would be executing Shirley out of her delusional misery. After the sea-going training day with wet minded Will, Cheryl hung around to be filled in again with the world cruise plans. She was a friendly and entertaining gal who meant no harm. The following day Cheryl fuelled and prepared the ship for 80 days of fun in the sun playing Captain before picking up Arthur and Shirley to dock late that night in the Hudson River.

The river was calm, yet the Deliverance was choppy inside. It was an uncomfortable night spent with two jealous women who both had no idea of

Arthur's real plans. He told Cheryl he'd be ditching Shirley tomorrow in NY, but forgot to mention she'd be castaway at the earliest convenient opportunity. And Arthur told Shirley the Deliverance and Cheryl were leaving tomorrow for them to spend a passionate night together in The Knickerbocker Hotel. Shirley was smitten and Cheryl was his new kitten. Dinner was a clammed up affair though.

"Did you know the lower half of the Hudson River is actually a tidal estuary?" stated Cheryl to break the ice with a common touch.

"Well obviously," lied Shirley. "Do you know who starred in the pants film Hudson Hawk?"

"Bruce Willis. Oh, the Hudson game, how special. What country did the fur trading Hudson Bay Company operate in?" quizzed Cheryl with an easy one that might catch Shirley out.

"Oh I don't know, who cares? Mexico?" answered Shirley and Cheryl sniggered. Arthur ignored the pair of them and enjoyed the soufflés Shirley whipped up in the galley earlier.

"More wine Shirley?" asked Cheryl.

"Yes thank you," said Shirley showing Arthur she could keep her cool.

"Did you know cheap wines don't improve with age, they just cork?" teased Cheryl. Shirley did not know and just cut into her main course with steak knife aggression.

Throughout the night, Arthur was on dick duty: one minute scrubbing Shirley's decks, the next anchoring into Cheryl. Both women knew what was going on and let it slide – back and forth – because they thought he'd be all theirs tomorrow. Plus despite being anti-Feminist, Arthur satisfied them equally, so they didn't really care he was mopping them both out.

The next morning's breakfast was equally awkward as the previous evening's tense dining experience and as Shirley and Arthur went ashore for her fateful day out, Shirley gave Cheryl the finger like a schoolgirl who got her boy. Cheryl returned the favour thinking she had her man towed in line.

We are little but a combination of positive acts performed.

Things had been very uncomfortable in Shirley's home too. Last night, around midnight, Flynn was back studying on the walnut table trying to second guess Arthur's movements by going inside the mind of the artist.

Juliet deliberately left him alone for hours so as not to break his concentration and she also thought a little friendly cold-shouldering would motivate him more. A constant coffee supply was her only encouraging contact. Flynn loved Juliet and wracked his brains to impress her. Now he was going to throw caution to the wind and let his police hunches do the talking. The FBI, CIA and other senior NYDP members had nothing definitive pinned to the board. After the Liverpool murders, Scotland Yard and MI5 started to investigate as well. It was now down to Flynn alone to logically guess Arthur's most likely next chess move. His head felt heavy like it was under water – pressured by salty worries.

Sometimes all you need in life is a radiant sun, an optimistic blue sky, a few imaginary clouds, sparkling water, glistening ochre sand and just let your mind drift towards a pleasant land.

Is it even possible to guess the future, wondered Flynn. Many people predicted the Twin Tower's disaster and some similar clairvoyants even suggested the American government orchestrated the whole terrorist attack for financial gain. Who had JFK assassinated after he tried to take over the central bank of America to prevent a private bank charging the taxpayer millions in interest through government loans? Are the Bilderberg Group driving everyone into poverty just to show off to each other who has the most billions? Was the Loch Ness Monster just a Russian nuclear submarine? Was Sasquatch really just Disney's Baloo? Many irrelevances spun through Flynn's pressure cooker mind to get into the spirit of the unknown until he had no choice but to sleep through sheer exhaustion. It was like a carbon copy of before, but Juliet herself couldn't see him doing anything productive at all when exhausted.

In Flynn's dreams he was always climbing a church spire, unsuccessfully trying to get in through stained glass windows smeared with blood. Heavy dark clouds open up above him and a godly beam of light shines through his soul conveniently opening the window latches. Standing on solid oak beams inside with gaps big enough to fall through, he looks up to the rooftop and feels his energy being magnetised away. His perception of life leaves his body, replaced with foreign eyes from the future. The roof tiles all slide off and kill lots of flocking sheep below, slicing them into lamb chops. Flynn looks up and sees heavenly clouds puff into new sheep, cascading down to the stone bottom of the building to see a rose reflection in the flint. "Is that you mom?" he asks and momma says it time to fly the nest and make your own chicks.

Flynn woke up around 7am refreshed, yet feeling like a partial failure, so Juliet decided to add some normalcy to his thoughts by agreeing to forget the world for half an hour and enjoy pancakes together. This was just the revival and syrupy inspiration the doctor ordered. With a fresh pancake flipped mindset and new determination to impress Juliet by saving her mother from a fate identical to death, Flynn went back to the drawing board and rolled out a life-sized poster of Dali's Metamorphosis of Narcissus, analysing it in finite detail. He stood hovering over the glossy picture trying not to be a detective for once, rather an enthusiastic amateur observer. If Flynn was to save Shirley then he had to see the painting through the eyes of an abused child to work out the riddle of the crimes.

When the yellow sun reflects on still water, time stands still long enough to find out who you really are and see truth in your reveries.

Arthur Koons had a very unconventional, profound interpretation of the Metamorphosis of Narcissus which was far superior to the stale, fuddy-duddy art critics who can't paint to save their own lives. His abusive experiences warped his mind, yet opened up a deeper understanding of the world and people's motivations. This is what made Arthur such a good manipulator.

Arthur understood that art critics always underestimate how badly every artist wants to put secret, private ideas into their work. He had uncovered a number of significant finds just by feeling each brush stroke and sometimes literally looking from different angles. Therefore, Arthur's analysis of the Metamorphosis painting was profound and real, rather than an elitist, pond scum reflection. One cornflakes morning he explored random thoughts on some light gray card from a cereal box, but ended up drawing a skull.

On the face of this great work of art we see Narcissus falling in love with his reflection in a pool and turning to stone because he couldn't posses the liquid image. This overt display only scratches the varnished surface of its real unconscious meaning.

Salvador Dali painted his chaotic dream worlds in a very deliberate and premeditated way, and was heavily criticized for trapping himself in a paint style which allowed little room for his subconscious to paint away freely. However, the truth always has a way of escaping any restraints imposed.

Arthur's sexual ordeals kind of gave him the emotional language needed to understand this unusual painting his mother obsessed over too because the same thing happened to her which is why she hung the framed reproduction on the wall in the first place – to escape and learn about life.

As the buckle spike pricked into his arse during a foul thrashing in the early hours on one dark night, the young Arthur's eyes noticed multiple unseen figures in the background. After his tormentor left, he often lay down on the bed and psycho-analysed the painting. He saw a small man in a pile of rocks standing in front of the cave on the left guarded by the face of his biological father in the large lit boulder on his right and his mother seen in the crack in the cliff on his left. A cracked rock heart just in front of him symbolised his mother's death. The black cave was Dali's unknown fears.

To hide from the fear, Dali imprisoned himself on a plinth in the middle of a chessboard with only 21 squares: one for each year he'd been properly doing art and also the year his mother died (1921). It shows the untimely separation from his mother who died of cancer and an attempt to lock himself away from his demons who were already eating away at his conscience seen in the foreground greyhound chewing on bloodied raw ribs.

Eventually, the same figure travelling throughout the painting in many disguises decides to face his fears and literally grows with confidence into a giant fiery statue full of volcanic creativity. The eternal party of eight behind Dali celebrate his magnificence as the pool of water tries to cool his ambition without success.

Life returns Dali back to nature in the form of rock to remind him that no-one is above God by picturing the little home and background he grew up in, seen through the finger's window. The sky and mountains on the right, echoed his mother's wish for him to get married and settle down with a beautiful flower, but Dali defies this by making his worshipers – fans and family – turn into ants, gnawing holes in his ideals and cracking his fingertip creativity.

What age do you start shitting yourself about death?

Arthur's former raping run was really about searching for a woman he could worship more than himself – believing if he destroyed her soul this would set him free from his demons. Crazy, yes. He planned to be even more ambitious than Dali by recreating the backbone of Metamorphosis in real life, sacrificing many souls until he found a woman worth dying for. The plan in the fateful white van was to kidnap Juliet and keep her for good, but it obviously all went wrong luckily for Juliet who was earmarked for basement sex slavery.

Flynn was still totally absorbed in the work of art after 9am. The house was silent and cold with worry. However, he was getting warmer and warmer with every thought. He begun to work out that, for Arthur, the painting was more about water than stone. Arthur's crime wave was like riding a canoe in heavy rapids around rocks, instead of looking down from the Daliesque mountains and Godly sky like previously believed. Flynn also correctly guessed the echo egg in the mountainous background was a representation of Dali's mother who he felt an eternity away from – just like Arthur did. Dali was a magnificent artist, therefore he could recreate his pain for catharsis and finally have his beloved mother by his side.

With these grand assumptions floating around in Flynn's head, by the grace of God or the forgiveness of the universe, he then had a Eureka moment after looking for a motherly image lost in the shadowy, murky reflection on Narcissus in the water. At first nothing transpired. Then Flynn went to get his magnifying glass from his bag on the other side of the room and briefly looked at the painting upside-down. And there it was, a skull, as clear as daylight (half in the water and half on land above the eight upside-down dancing figures which represent an eternity in the afterlife of his mother). This was about laying his mother to rest in between the two statue versions of Dali.

Flynn's later described his spontaneous conclusion as 'death in water' for mother Shirley somewhere with lots of people around: The Lake in Central Park was the obvious conclusion. Flynn knew that serial killers often return to the scene of their crime for sexual gratification and believed Arthur would easily be bold enough to tempt fate. Flynn's conclusion was final. It was now make or break time.

Everything you do in life is a risk worth taking.

Detective Inspector Maddox couldn't sleep he was under so much media, political and police pressure. He'd been utterly dry of ideas and just lay in his office nervously waiting for detective Flynn and his team to make their call. Failure would mean the end of his fat pension and hard earned reputation.

It was now 9:36am as Arthur and Shirley hired a rowing boat for a romantic row around, but in her case a voyage to the bottom of the lake. At roughly the same time, Flynn took a deep breath in, like a heavy gambling man pushing all of his roulette chips onto one black number and called Maddox with his conclusion, more like guesswork. "Let's hope you're right lad," is all Maddox had to say with a depressed

264

sounding voice, agreeing to sanction the full might of the NYPD to descend upon Central Park, disrupting many important businesses and upsetting a handful of VIP movers-and-shakers. No-one wants to be a laughing stock, but if you don't take risks you don't get any rewards.

When even their shadow is negative, stay in the light of truth and they can't harm you.

The only person who didn't feel remotely cornered now was Arthur who could see vast continents and fortunes ahead of him. 'I'll conquer Europe first,' he told Cheryl last night before falling asleep on her mountainous mammary glands. Bad boys always get the best sleep and sass.

The most important thing in life is to believe you are worth something to this world.

20

Sunken Hearts

After a delicate breakfast of smoked salmon at the Loeb Boathouse, Central Park was witness to a very strange homage to Salvador Dali indeed. Arthur, still calling himself Troy, disrobed to reveal his birthday suit in front of a procession of glorious morning walkers and then changed into a scuba diving outfit before hiring a rowing boat.

There was a funny moment when Shirley got all excited and very embarrassed at his eccentric behaviour, so just pointed both her fingers and thumbs like guns at Troy's penis when a few people objected. Dali, who once turned up to a prestigious art preview cocktail evening wearing a wetsuit and snorkel, would've been proud of Arthur, omitting the Twitter stalking and rapes.

What path would you most like to spend half an hour with?

A psychopath	18%
A nature path	55%
An empath	21%
A pathologist	6%
264 votes · Final results	

"If that's your thing it's gonna cost you twofold to row me in circles son," said the cranky old boat hire owner who'd seen all kinds of weird shit happen on his cherished rowing boats over the years, including deep sea diving gear.

Old seadog **RANDOPLH** actually handmade some of the boats. They were like his little water babies, so naturally he made anyone suspected of wanting to cum in them pay double. Spunk and marriage proposals were always double priced; people with pierced noses too. Arthur paid up and respected the scam and definite bigotry, while

Shirley excitedly imagined she was going to be proposed to.

A congratulatory crowd gathered to gawk like seagulls at the exciting forthcoming proposal, but Arthur just rowed away with Shirley looking nervous and thinking about giving the crowd the bird. She was having a renaissance on water, ironically just before getting drowned.

If you don't listen to your instincts, life will be difficult for you. Trust your gut feelings.

Comfortably far away from shore, Arthur asked Shirley to stand up in the wobbly boat which she was hesitant to do but believed Troy was just about to propose to her, not nudge her in and drown her.

The whole morning Shirley felt like something was up because her lover Troy seemed slightly on edge, yet he'd gone to so much trouble and thought in preparing some kind of ceremonious homage to Dali and her, she remained open-minded. Quite obviously wealthy and handsome Troy was going to ask her hand in marriage – she now believed – because Shirley was only 20 years older with flabby arm wings. She was clearly a real catch for any fisherman and was already planning the pre-nuptial agreement in her mind.

Arthur unusually felt a little guilty he was just about to sink Shirley, despite her being deeply annoying, because for an old vessel she put maximum effort into stoking his boiler. However, just as Arthur pulled down his goggles and put the snorkel in his mouth, his peripheral vision caught sight of some major commotion on the lake's banks a hundred or so metres away. It was an army of police starting to run in both directions to encircle the lake.

The cops obviously didn't know Arthur was on the lake and had been fully briefed with pictures to look out for Arthur and Shirley together. Arthur acted immediately saying, "I'll be back, just getting the ring!" as he dropped backwards into the lake leaving Shirley stranded and very bewildered.

Was this just another charismatic stunt and joke to woo her, she hoped. Poor ship abandoned Shirley thought he was going to pop up any minute with a pearl ring or something. Love had made Shirley blind. People may not appreciate you, but if you don't appreciate yourself, you are failing the world in return.

If they don't make you feel good they're not worth knowing.

Meantime, Arthur had already made it to the lake's edge and dragged himself out like a diamondback terrapin. Police were running around in every direction past him, yet not one single officer batted an eyelid because many eccentrics float about Central Park; some who lost a fortune and went mad. Arthur casually walked all the way to the West perimeter of the park with his flippers and goggles on and only received a few funny looks and laughs from bewildered tourists.

When he approached police entrapment barrier two near 73rd Street, which was flooded with hundreds more cops lining the park's borders, he nonchalantly walked straight up to the largest group of officers, announced he was a frogman from 24th Precinct and was in shock after just pulling the bloated drowned body of an old woman from the lake. Arthur was escorted to an ambulance who just put a blanket around him and said he'd be OK: hundreds of years of medical advancements went into that treatment.

To cause further police confusion, he asked to borrow the ambulance driver's phone to call his concerned family, but instead texted the hidden whereabouts of his RI hideout, guaranteeing Shirley was in a basement there. Swat and squat thrust teams were already on their way to burst into an empty borrow!

Back to the lake, half of the cops ran towards the area Arthur described where Shirley's dead body supposedly lay covered in wet leaves and the others radioed frantically for back-up and new orders. By that time, Arthur had returned the phone politely, removed his diving gear, wrapped the blanket around him like a sarong and then paid for a leisurely horse drawn NY tour nearby, ironically picking up the same horse that shat near him after dinner with Juliet, who now did a massive piss splash on his bare feet. They say elephants never forget. The same applies to horses.

Maddox and Flynn were controlling operation Narcissus Flower from the superb Boathouse Restaurant end and their hearts sank on hearing news of a body. Nevertheless, all the cops found by the water's edge were 14 plastic bags, a car tyre and most oddly a mud encased laptop which had been discarded in fear by a paedophile wanting to drown indecent images. Unfortunately for the 39 year old single waste management consultant, the high profile nature of Arthur's manhunt led them to examining the recoverable hard drive weeks later and he was sentenced the following winter where inmates ironically drowned him in a shitty toilet.

With millions of people around it's hard to accept that when your life falls apart only a few decent people will help you if you're lucky. Be grateful for genuine support.

Shirley was soon discovered and recovered meandering on the lake in a melancholy tenor, muttering lost sweet nothings. She was in a chronic state of emotional denial and refused to tell the police what happened for a further 3 hours. By then, Captain Arthur Koons and saucy Cheryl were bouncing off optimistic ocean waves way into their Atlantic voyage.

Shirley was bitterly upset the cops had totally ruined her perfect day out and her happiness. At first, intense police pressure and threats of aiding and abetting a high-priority fugitive had absolutely no effect on her, especially when she answered, "I'm not a gambler, how dare you!" to DI Maddox who just slapped his forehead in disbelief.

The poor woman refused to leave Central Park and was suffering from nervous shock. She dreamed of returning home with Troy to flaunt his handsomeness to Juliet and Flynn, and hoped a relationship would force Juliet to move out so she could have her lounge and mind space back again. Shirley was still on cloud nine in love with Arthur and now didn't know what to think, refusing to co-operate. Eventually, Juliet was fast tracked to the park and managed to get the information out of her mother after enduring a tirade of silence, then mad bitterness.

"Typical of you to ruin my happiness. I suppose you're jealous, aren't you?" said Shirley to her daughter. Juliet was incredulous.
"No mother…"
"For the first time in ages I felt alive in the arms of a wonderful man!" continued a stubborn Shirley.
"Mom, he's a multiple rapist and killer," pointed out Juliet with a perplexed expression.
"Oh you would say that because you're going out with a policeman. You're corrupted already!" Shit, thought Juliet, there's no winning with her *ever*. Shirley then looked Juliet dead in the eyes and said,

"Troy and I were lovers. Old people can love too you know."

"I know mom," said a despondent Juliet, now hugging her mother.

"You know, you want to listen to your mother a bit more often and you wouldn't get me into all this trouble," said Shirley as the penny was beginning to drop that Troy might have been a player. "At least I've still got my adorable and loyal pets, and you," Shirley said lovingly.

Juliet didn't have the heart to tell her Bagel was missing, presumed dead. There had been enough talk of death recently. Maddox was in the background and interrupted with a polite cough. "Okay, okay mister high pressure! Troy the supposed 'killer' with a wonderful way about him… brought me here on a big motorboat on the Hudson estuary. Satisfied!? Are you satisfied now you've torn my whole life apart with your meddling in other people's affairs!!!?" said Shirley eyeballing Maddox like a crazed snapping turtle.

"Pier number please madam," pushed Maddox with professional politeness.

"11. The number of God!" concluded Shirley before bursting into crocodile tears.

"Ooargh, fucking hell, she's un-be-lievable," whispered Maddox loudly as he walked away to tell detective Flynn.

Life is a simple equation: the more you excel, the more people want to see you fail. It's about developing the strength to fight

off jealous haters and becoming friends with nice people who
are happy for you to succeed.

Flynn was awarded a medal of commendation by
the Mayor of New York City a month later for
saving Shirley's life. This appreciation of his first-
rate efforts meant a great deal to him. He was also
nicknamed 'Sixth Sense' by fellow officers, who
frequently mocked 'I see dead people' to him for
years to come. The joke never died with the act.
However, for now the bad guy had escaped again
and that just didn't sit right with Flynn because he
had integrity. So he put his thinking cap on nice and
tight to get his brain cells churning out elastic leads.

An hour later his crack police team relayed news of
the raid on Arthur's hideaway, uncovering a lot of
fucked-up shit and crazy plans. Arthur was kind of a
mind artist and screwed-up crook combined, always
on the look-out for new exciting and profitable
enterprises.

Many walls in the lockup had multicoloured
marker pen notes written straight onto them,
insanely capturing the core moments before his
crimes – like an evidential dairy of his rapes, drug
deals and even plans to hack banks which he didn't
yet possess the computer knowledge to do. If
Arthur could think it, he would have a go at doing
it.

Arthur's subconscious mind was like a rabbit
warren of worry, so he sometimes used famous

artists to help him rethink a problem. For example, he found looking at Braque's morbid Cubism therapeutic because it was like seeing a sculpture flattened onto canvas as a mind map. He always tried to make sense of his life because it was so haphazard at times. The older Arthur became, the more diverse, extreme and outlandish this problem solving thought-process became until he no longer had any social perspective. To him The American Dream was a lie to get mugs to pay taxes their whole lives for fuck all.

Arthur's pokey office space was his inner sanctum where his loose wall thoughts found conclusions. For comedic effect, he also drew one of Dali's melting clocks using a thick black marker on the wall with the time pointing towards 3pm. Flynn received photo images later that afternoon and began to further understand the unzipped mind of this most bizarre killer.

The big hand pointed towards an obstacle course of clues revealing his ultimate ambitions. This fucked-up fresco covering every inch of the walls looked like the scribblings of a turbid psychopath in full flow. But to Arthur it made perfect aesthetic and logical sense. Who's to say what's normal anyway?

What was immediately obvious from the cacophony of black lined drawings and madman wall hieroglyphics is that Arthur was obsessed with two similar shapes: **eggs** which represent new life and

skulls representing death. Scanning one's eyes around the four walls was like looking at oval and round stepping stones hopping across the globe. Arthur had even drawn a Fabergé egg and a diamond studied skull on his psychological doodling travels.

It's a well-known fact that all crazy people worship eggs and passionate souls idolize skulls. Flynn looked into the deep psychological connotations of skulls and eggs, highlighting something very interesting from an eccentric doctor of psychology:

'The only mammals (monotremes) which lay eggs are the weird looking echidna and the equally odd duckbilled platypus, yet people have always possessed a strange fascination for eggs beyond their nutritional value. The oval egg shape is a decorative and celebrated marvel of nature; total symmetrical perfection symbolising the beginning of life.

Some cuckoo astronaut theorists even believe that aliens implanted the thalamus (an egg-shaped central part of the brain) into people to awaken our consciousness. However, the most likely and logical explanation for egg apotheosis is we naturally think in the same way we grow.

Humans are obsessed with birth and death; the conception and bony end of a unique universe which is you. It takes half a lifetime to understand that living in the moment is the elixir of happiness to achieve cosmic balance because our unconscious remembers every last moment in time and is unwilling to let the most significant traumas go. It is illogical to fear death because it's inevitable and unknown.

A cracked egg becomes like an empty skull with its life yolk drained out. The psychological relationship between eggs and skulls is centuries old. Skulls are a gruesome reminder of our evolution and mortality; a symbol of danger to ward off evil. The third eye of life is replaced with two eye socket cavities looking into an empty shell of memories.

Observing a skull increases the imagination like a blank canvas can; we wonder everything about the person's life. Who were they? What did they do and were they ever loved? How did their life end? Skulls are such a powerful and morbid mystery they are fashionable in hard times. A skull is the cranial protection of history and they also look really cool too.'

(Dr. Hoffingboffin, *Psychology Now*, 2019)

After some productive pondering and reasoning, Flynn fully appreciated how obsessed Arthur was with Dali's artwork and figured out he would at some point want to see some of the original paintings in the flesh – so to speak. However, the world is full of time and Dali masterpieces. Predicting when and where Arthur would resurface was a major detective conundrum.

Detective Flynn's new insight was right again though. He guessed correctly Arthur probably had the Metamorphosis currently closest to his heart – to absorb its theatrical power before disappearing into a dark criminal world. Arthur had to touch everything he desired. Flynn had seen firsthand Arthur's 'get it done now' impetuous and equally productive mind in action. Arthur's frequent impatience was both his strength and weakness.

Flynn was going to relay his deductions to all authorities investigating, suggesting they alert relevant galleries and gain access to their CCTV, but then Gabby emailed him more garage evidence: a set of Arthur's childlike drawings found on long rolled-up sheets of baking paper.

The pencil drawings looked unprofessional and haphazard, and certainly not what they were; architectural plans of national art galleries with illegible notes of execution. Arthur had meticulously planned-out two robberies of Dali's greatest, most priceless works: The Persistence of Memory in the

MoMA and Metamorphosis of Narcissus in the Tate Modern. He'd also secured an eccentric Middle Eastern buyer from Jordan with a few billion to spare.

Neither Flynn or the FBI could interpret Arthur's scribbled notes, yet Flynn and Gabby persisted with the elongated landscape of lines until they indentified the two correct buildings. Despite Arthur being the master of double and triple bluffs, there was no way in the realms of applied psychology that Arthur would be doubling back on himself again for a third major crime in New York City, so naturally Flynn put all of his gambling chips on London.

Furthermore, after all the unfair doubt and shit Flynn and his loyal team had taken from the FBI and other major US and even UK law enforcement organizations, Gabby agreed to seal her lips, giving Flynn and the NYPD another chance for glory. He believed in her and now she agreed to believe in him. That's how life should work.

Therefore, after being told he'd done excellently and the case was in international military hands way above their station, Flynn asked for immediate leave to take Juliet to central London for a holiday. He simply had to know if his latest hot hunch was right. The worst thing that could happen, figured Flynn, was they'd have a great vacation if he was wrong, so it was a win-win situation. But he was wrong about that. Flynn had connected with Arthur's intense mind and that could only mean danger.

Naturally Juliet was happy to run away from all her responsibilities and go on a spontaneous romantic trip with Flynn because mother Shirley would have mentally tortured her to death going on about her lost love Troy. Yet she was a bit suspicious of why Flynn chose to leave behind a case he cared so much about. Plus Juliet wanted to go to the romantic Eiffel Tower, not the pigeon grey London Dungeons.

Whilst the couple were already on their first-class flight to London Heathrow, Arthur had begun mulling over his new occupation as an international art thief and was feeling very happy with his career change.

Life is like a box of chocolates and I advise you to eat every last one.

Later that day, the stressed-out FBI accessed satellite imagery to scan the Atlantic Ocean. It was like searching for a thumb sized toy boat in Central Park's Onassis Reservoir, with no luck. They focused their main search over the Bermuda Triangle and Caribbean Sea areas because Arthur cleverly lied to former boat owner Willy, saying he planned to live in Panama in peace. This became a fatal error for more innocent victims.

Three sweet cruising days over a serene ocean went by for Arthur and Cheryl taking shifts to captain in between copious sex sessions. The waves bonked them into near exhaustion and both silly sods felt so happy away from technology and the world. The ocean seemed to speak to Arthur, saying how it forgave his mortal sins, so he cracked open a bottle of ten year matured Dom Perignon bubbly to celebrate his spiritual renaissance.

However, Arthur's jubilant celebration was drastically short lived when a buoyant country sized ship armed to the teeth, headed their way. The big guns had finally been called in and radar from the aircraft carrier USS George H.W. Bush, diverted from the Middle East, eventually located the Deliverance.

Arthur could see the finishing line in sight and almost smell the English fish and chips just as the humongous warship descended upon the relatively little boat like a blue whale in a bath, only 12 miles before Arthur approached the mouth of the Thames River.

The warship's motto was 'Freedom at Work'. It didn't feel at all liberating to Arthur though. He felt instantly defeated seeing the extraordinarily large steel bulk channelling through the English Channel on a collision course. The devil himself prayed to God for guidance. Arthur looked like an abused child in the corner of a room, praying to Father Christmas to make it stop.

The mighty aircraft carrier was just about to launch a fighter plane to blast the Deliverance out of the water, when a French Battleship intercepted her, setting in motion an international disaster!

The UK naturally gave the US permission to seek and destroy, but European directives vehemently objected to such a powerfully armed vessel being so close to mainland Europe in French waters, they claimed. It was Brexit all over again. America no longer had a special relationship with Britain anyway because half of Britain isn't British anymore. Consequently a political standoff ensued until two slightly antiquated looking British Frigates steamed towards the hot zone, firing on the French craft and sinking her.

"That will definitely secure a No Deal Brexit!" shouted the British Captain of HMS Lancaster on his very last operation. His repeated Admiralty orders were to *only* fire a warning shot across their bow, but Captain **HENRY VILLIERS** Fortescue-Hamilton absolutely hated the frog leg eating French and literally wanted his career to go out with a bang! He blamed the accidentally-on-purpose direct hit on a technical fault and kept his pension.

Everyone was quite happy with the result though, including Arthur, now speeding towards the Thames Barrier which had been promptly alerted about the outrageous sea war developing. They began to close the giant gates as Arthur rammed into them at full speed. Bang! Crash! Wallop!

The Deliverance got trapped at first like a toddler trying to run through a parent's squeezing monster legs. But then she broke free, squashed like a cigarette boat and carried on down the Thames slowly sinking with pride. There was an urgency to abandon ship as a fleet of police patrol boats nearby pushed the water towards the floundering Deliverance.

Arthur kissed Cheryl goodbye before cuffing her hands to the steering and jumping into his motorised escape pod. The very cool dolphin boat (a one person jet ski and speedy submarine highbred) was way too high-tech and stealthy for UK river cops all scratching their heads stupidly like they had lice. Arthur splashed past them waving and then did a stylish 180° underwater flip, slipping back through the Thames Barrier's now broken doors without even being spotted. It was like something rad from Top Gun, yet underwater. Arthur had unbelievably escaped once again. The worldwide press now named him 'The Houdini of Horrors.' In a former life, the universe must have owed him some good karma. Arthur was all alone again in this big bad world, but he was free! Age had taught him the importance of enjoying his own company. You had to hand it to Arthur; no matter how much he vomited in society's face he still believed the world was lucky to have him. Confidence was his winning hand.

People who say you're lucky to have them really need dumping.

21

A Pain in the Neck

Poor Monday. Everyone seems to have it in for Mondays. It's just another day which needs caring for and loving like the other six. All the colours of the rainbow work together beautifully and Monday is blue.

It was the boring start of the working week for most economic commodities, but the blithe beginning of a much needed holiday for Juliet. For the first time in ages she could grab Monday by the reins and ride that bitch into the ground! Unfortunately, Juliet was really looking forward to riding on the London Eye tonight, but it was temporarily closed due to potential flooding caused by a Syrian terrorist attack on the Thames Barrier, according to the number one corrupt news channel which has the same initials as a pornographic term. Nevertheless, Juliet was in a good mood, in a magnificent city she'd never visited before and was going to make the very most of her leisure time by exploring as much as possible!

Time had just creaked into a cooling October. Flynn splashed out on the renowned Hotel 41; a hidden gem tucked behind Buckingham Palace. He wanted a traditional English hotel look and service to romantically and emotionally connect with Juliet. She was well worth a mere £412 a night, sort of thought Flynn.

London was a great city to explore because the absence of architectural master plans in its history created an ant build mentality full of lots of skew-whiff angles and creepy alleyways ensconced here-and-there by Victorian doom. Plus England's ancient capital once housed Jack the Ripper and a whole host of famous Tower of London ghosts such as Guy Fawkes, Lady Jane Grey and Henry VIII's beheaded wife, Anne Boleyn, whose tortured spirit still reputedly walks with her head tucked beneath her arm. London blooms with daytime beauty as much as it being nighttime spooky.

Juliet believed in ghosts but first she had some Bond Street shopping to attend to before afternoon tea at a ritzy establishment with Flynn. The adorable American couple were just loving the history and etiquette of everything. Flynn even commented on the traditional English napkins which were identical to traditional American napkins. "Do they say napkin or serviette here?" he asked Juliet, tongue and cheek like, unaware that most British folk eat with their fingers in front of the TV. Juliet rolled her eyes and Flynn laughed. After so much anxiety back home, both of them were happy to be a bit boring for a week or so. You're only bored with life if you're boring anyway.

"Do you reckon English people are better in bed than Americans? You know what they say about the quiet ones," quizzed Flynn slightly putting his foot in it because Juliet was an extrovert, yet quietly confident.

"I think as long as people's souls connect when they make love, that's all that counts really," she teased. "Only shitting, I love American cop's hard cocks!" said in a salacious voice with a sexy slow wink imitating cockney dialect.

"Ahkem!" fake coughed the unimpressed looking serving girl who appeared to magic from nowhere, trying to diffuse Juliet's foul language. "Would handsome sir like some clotted cream cake to go with that cock?"

Flynn was somewhat shocked but just found himself replying, "Yes please. Cake with oodles of cream please," while laughing.

Juliet gave Flynn the look and felt a touch jealous the pretty young waitress made a clear move on her man's stomach and dick, responding with, "Perhaps madam could shove a couple of éclairs in her gob and bring me some cake whilst you're there *please*."

"Are you sure you would like a second helping of cake at your age lady?" said a cocky girl on her last day at work.

This was turning into a cat fight so Flynn just sat back, relaxed and enjoyed the women fighting over him. What self-respecting man wouldn't love to see two hot women in an éclair mud wrestling match?

"Yes dear, when your zits burst and you start having sex you'll know cake is the next best thing. Anyway, shouldn't you be at school?" bitched Juliet.

"I've got a boyfriend and he sticks his chocolate éclair up my asshole whenever I tell him."

"And I've got a man who knows the value of class and kindness. Would yours be what they term chav?"

"He's not a chav, he's just unemployed because the system sucks."

"The system always sucks around you I bet," retorted Juliet with spunk.

"Better than gorging on cakes and talking funny. You know you stole our language," said a waitress getting confused with her history.

"The only thing I'm stealing from you is your tip." Flynn was quite impressed with that comeback and nearly clapped before he remembered this was England where the losing underdog is always the winner.

"Do you know how little I earn?"

"Don't know. Don't care. Just want cake," calmly stated Juliet.

"Typical greedy American."

"Typical rude waitress."

"Typical dumb blonde."

"But you're blonde too." Flynn was just about to say they could be sisters, when he thought better of it and giggled. They both stared at him and he drank his dainty cup of tea with a mugged expression.

"These are just highlights. You're naturally stupid," continued arguing the most obnoxious waitress ever.

"The only highlight about you is bringing the cakes, which you still haven't done. Perhaps the manager could help?" asked Juliet, stepping up her authority.

"It's my last day so I don't care if I get fired if you want to be spiteful."

"Listen, you can't go around telling everyone to fuck off. Life doesn't work that way," explained Juliet.

"My boyfriend cheated on me last night so I don't give a fuck about anything. I suppose you want my tears to glaze your sponge cake now and my wrist blood for jam sponge?" sarcastically teased an upset girl.

"Just the sugary glaze please," joked Juliet and they both laughed before **DANNI** the waitress burst into tears, sat down and Juliet got her a slice of cake and some tea instead. This was the shittiest service ever so they knew they were definitely in England.

After some comforting words in her ear from both Flynn and Juliet, Danni stole Flynn's wallet as planned when she hugged him and promptly left to give the proceeds to her sister's drug addiction, which she felt was a worthy cause. Danni had been stealing from many customers over the last week because it was her last probationary day and being patronised by people spending their inheritance money wasn't her thing.

Losing all of his credit and debit cards, plus lots of cash drawn out that morning wasn't the greatest first full day to a holiday. On the plus side though, Juliet insisted on paying for the hotel and everything without knowing the concept of English value for money. Welcome to London, voted best destination in the world, 2019 by TripAdvisor, beating Paris, Rome, the Crete islands and Bali.

Sometimes the most beautiful thing in the world is just having a good day.

That little slice of bad luck reminded Flynn of his mission to stake out the Tate Modern and keep his ear to the ground listening for whispers of Arthur Koons. He also wanted to check out Dali's work in real life too, so later that afternoon they both stood in front of the glossy oil in awe.

Flynn left the gallery very contentedly and Juliet was finding London costly. But at least she had some money to spend, whereas way back in America 4 days ago at the beginning of Arthur's sea voyage, homeless cat Bagel didn't have a penny to her name despite owning a fur coat.

Bagel was a frightened female cat in a strange land with lots of sex trafficking cat clans around. Dropping her guard on a very long day's walk could cost Bagel her dignity and freedom. She'd heard a terrible story once of a cat forced into eating pounds of coffee beans for sick humans to drink her poo. Those humans really were a fucked-up bunch of animals, believed Bagel, guilty of bestiality and extreme cruelty to donkeys. Humans will fuck anything!

Bagel made her silent way through Rhode Island post haste, trying to avoid seedy alleyways and rows of potential trashcan ambushing from dodgy dogs. However, it wasn't long before some black rats had a go at her first. She fought them off with anti-racist gusto only to have the local pimp cat **ROMAN** alerted to her screams and howls. Bagel fought hard again, but was soon scratched up and rounded up with the other bitches destined to become Puerto Rican sex slaves or cat fur market products.

"All this way only to be skinned alive," jittered Bagel, shaking in fear in a chain gang.
"Keep your fucking commie cat flap shut bitch unless you want the hedgehog to spike ya ass!" aggressively shouted leader Roman.

Roman's street name evolved because he trained his gang to fight like organised Roman soldiers. But his home name was embarrassingly Fidel Catstro and he despised Communists. There is no community anyway, was Roman's top complaint and excuse for being a community pimp.

Bagel had no idea what being hedgehoged meant, yet correctly guessed it wouldn't be a pleasant spa session. She whimpered as she walked, just like the other girls who had lost all hope of freedom.

It's well known that people who hurt others have been hurt themselves. Be the hero that breaks any negative chain.

The previous day, **DAPHNE** the dilettante cormorant sent by Emmental had finally found Romeo's hotel to tell him to find Bagel. Luckily so because she unknowingly ate the sea bass messengers on the way to Block Island to refuel and ponder on life.

"Why does life have to be so competitive?" complained Daphne after a seagull stole one of her catches.

"Survival of the fittest!" shouted out the herring gull flying away, laughing his head off. Daphne regurgitated a little sick on the fish before it was stolen from her beak, which was some consolation. The seagull gagged.

In between some surfing on wind currents with maudlin thoughts, Daphne eventually glided inland to speak to the Block Island hotel manager, but was offensively waved away because she was a seabird who are still openly discriminated against even in this day and age.

Tapping away at a little girl's bedroom window a few doors down, Daphne felt hawks shadowing above the menacing clouds masking a picturesque half moon. Her instincts were half right. The danger was not hawks but much worse; a flock of Twitter birds were murmuring away waiting for her to take off. Twitter blue birds assume many characteristics of cute blue tits, but they are known as the piranhas of the sky. Anyway, the seven year old sleeping girl was dreaming of umbrellas and was a bit perturbed she'd been woken, so drew the curtains back in anger.

"What do you want stupid bird?" **AVA** whispered with her lips to the window.

"Open the fucking window you little twat!" yawped Daphne.

Luckily she was speaking in bird language which Ava hadn't learnt at school as of yet due to a limited curriculum. She was learning Mandarin instead, to prepare for when the Chinese take over. Ava opened the window quietly so as not to wake her mother who had moodiness issues.

"I was having a really cool dream blackbird," explained Ava with zeal.

"Screw your dream! I'm gonna be spit roasted soon if I'm not sharpish. Listen I've something important…" blabbered Daphne, flapping her wings, desperately trying to convey her message and gtfo of there.

"Calm down blackbird," said Ava, copying her mom's words when she gets in a fluster.

"I'm not a blackbird. You're just a pip of a kid. Stop fucking around with my actual life! This is the wild out here, not playschool!" sounded-off Daphne with persistent anxiety.

"I'm not listening to you until you listen to my brilliant dream," parried Ava.

"Jesus fucking Christ! I've a got a message of life and death to attend to. And it could be my life!" wailed Daphne.

"I don't care about your problems blackbird," explained Ava beginning to comprehend the desperate language through flapping actions. "My mommy says children never care about anything but themselves. Are you going to sit quietly and listen to my dream or am I going to close the window on your silly giraffe neck?" negotiated Ava.

This clever kid was clearly persistent and not going to take no for an answer. Daphne's feathers secreted oil in fear of some hungry looking cats congregating below, hoping for a fresh meal.

"Good boy," said Ava, seeing the bird folding its wings in with resignation and patting it patronisingly on the bonce.

Daphne was going to have to listen to the bullshit boring dream while death approached her; just like Ava had to listen to elementary school teacher mommy going on about her 'poor choices' and 'unhelpful behaviour.' Ava then took a deep breath in and began her sermon imagining that her picayune shrimp of a dream was an allegorical masterpiece or something apocryphal, which *would* change lives:

"I was on a blue submarine shaped like a coconut and bumped into a lost country called Lost Foundland where umbrellas are more important to people than pets because it rains a lot there," began Ava.
"That's wonderful!" announced Daphne trying to speed up proceedings.

"I've only just started! Please don't interrupt me again," said the massively over confident, spoilt child.

"Sorry."

"Good. Now, in the Capital of Lost Foundland, called Loserville, everyone was sad because they kept losing things. Because it rained all of the time it made people's brains soaked like bath sponges and they couldn't remember anything. That's why the country is not on the map," Ava elucidated.

"That's actually quite funny," complimented Daphne, beginning to forget her fears and messenger mission.

"It's not a joke. It's real!" explained Ava. "This is a joke: why did Shakespeare not like The Tempest? Because windstorms shake his beer." Daphne pretended to caw with laughter, but was not amused. "In Lost Foundland everyone lived in boats because nobody has a castle anymore," continued Ava.

"You mean just like Block Island Boat Basin?" questioned Daphne.

"It's not the New Harbour Boat Basin! It's a secret lost world that only I know about because it's not on my Disney globe!" defended Ava.

"I see. I've probably fished there," digressed Daphne.

"There was a disaster one day because boats started to disappear…"

"You mean like in the Bermuda Triangle?" quizzed Daphne again with her adult knowledge ruining everything.

"It's not the Bearmuuda Angels stupid bird! But there are bears and angels in my dream. Bears are everyone's favourite pets because they float well and can catch fish. And also they are warm and cuddly at night," said Ava, making it up as she went along. "Angels protect the bears and people with rays of light."

"Protect them from what?" asked Daphne, now curious.

"The giant sea monster that takes children away who play on their tablet too much."

"Is the behemoth your mom perchance?" asked the curious cormorant.

Ava didn't know what those words meant, but didn't want to look like a child, so played along saying, "Yes, giant moths drown in daddy's beer and he swallows them pooing out beautiful brown butterflies who stick together like angels."

Even Ava realised she'd reached her child cuteness limits, so totally changed the story onto something more adult-like.

"My dad says global warming is not caused by people," said Ava.

Now Daphne was really interested in this and was fuming! "People are the scourge of the Earth!! The 1970's graph between commercial aircraft flights taking off and global warming starting is too big a coincidence to ignore. Your daddy's a moron!" kicked off Daphne.

"I love my daddy, but he does say some funny things. The other day I caught him talking to himself waiting for the kettle, saying he was going to kill someone if they said it again. I asked him what they said and he said nothing. 'How can you kill nothing dad?', I asked and he said there's no such thing as nothing. I think he's having a mental breakdown. Want me to give you a breakdown blackbird?" toed Ava into Daphne's deep waters.

"You're just a kid. Kids are small like their talk. Nothing you say can upset me. I once survived an oil slick. Got cleaned up in a rescue centre, only to be sent out into this monstrous Wild West again. I'm a survivor, so hit me with it shrimp cake," goaded Daphne.

"OK. The talk of pollution in the sea is made up says my dad," swung Ava with a home run.

"WTF!!!! Have you seen the mountains of plastic in the Pacific! Over a quarter of the world's ocean surfaces are covered in floating plastic made by guess who; HUMANS; the most pernicious force on the planet!

"Plus the oil, the aluminium air clouds and toxic pesticides! It's like you've gone out of your way to destroy bird populations. You even eat some of us! You're such a fucked-up, emotionally confused species you even spray chemicals on your own food to kill naturally occurring cancer curing agents so that loads of people get cancer and a few people can make money from the super expensive treatment. It's like the blind leading the blind!" vented Daphne the cormorant, so angry she'd lost so many family members to immoral global companies.

Ava was a little flustered by Daphne's clear passion and getting so worked up. She kindly handed the hothead bird some fresh water, unfortunately in a plastic bottle. Daphne then went berserk and in her rage slipped off the windowsill and plummeted into the baying clowder of greedy cats before her wings could straighten out and lift her above danger.

Feathers flew everywhere and stuck in jabbing claws until Daphne, on her last legs, screamed, "Suzie! Suzie! Suzie!" and suddenly a scary lion's roar echoed all the way down from the end of the street – dispersing the salivating cats with tremors.

Daphne couldn't fly away because her wings were so damaged. She felt like Luke Skywalker when Jabba the Hutt opened the trap door, falling into a pit to face the terrifying Rancor beast. Daphne previously pictured herself quietly passing to the next life in the relaxed and warm Caribbean on a red sunset day, not being left alone for a wild monster to devour. It didn't help that Ava up above was clapping as the lion's shadow stretched closer to her.

"Go on Romeo! There's some kitty fish fingers for you there," giggled Ava whilst blowing a kiss to Daphne. Giving children a voice has gone too far these days, thought Daphne coughing up a fur ball in fright. She could see the muscular cat beast lurching forward in hunting mode before he got fed up with the posing and just walked normally.

Towering above the poor, defenceless bird, Romeo spoke calmly to reassure her, "I'm sorry my friends tried to eat you, it's not our usual way – to shoot the messenger of good tidings. Did you say Suzie?"

"Yes sir I did," acquiesced Daphne.

"I've only ever known one Suzie. It was a long time ago before Trump, when the economy was far worse under Obama…"

"Sorry sir, I have to just stop you there," interrupted Daphne, who was a massive resistor, proving she would actually lay down her life to see Trump out of office. "What you're saying isn't true sir, you see…"

"All I see is a half bald bird talking statistical nonsense," growled a slightly peeved Romeo.

He had to keep her alive though to hear about Suzie, so Daphne and Romeo chatted about politics for over half an hour until both of them agreed to disagree with honour. They did however both agree that nationalism and proud patriotism was essential to stopping globalization defrauding hard working people.

Daphne told him that newly named Bagel was heading for Block Island and then felt pressured to hear Romeo's past tales about Suzie, as an olive branch gesture. The hope was that Romeo would keep the other cats off her until her wings could heal. The other storyteller, Ava, had gone back to bed and was dreaming of her game console this time.

"Suzie was like no other filly I have ever known: such beauty and wits to rival Vivien Leigh," said Romeo with a smiling nostalgia.

"Did you love her? Obvious answer really, sorry," wondered Daphne, a little taken by his caddish charm, but mostly faking interest for damn survival purposes.

"Love! Oh no, ha haa, haaa, meow, purr! I don't love any of my hoes, I simply admire their wiles and graces. Forget decade, what fucking century are you in, thought Daphne, holding her tongue. "Anyway, I owe that dame so it's time to move out. You better come with me to the ferry or those pussies will pluck you bare like a chicken dinner without the winner."

"Thanks," said Daphne with genuine appreciation. It turns out Romeo slightly believed queens should change the litter tray, not tomcats. Regardless, he did have some great virtues; honour and action in the face of adversity being his top ones.

People will just keep taking and taking from you until you project a defiant aura called self-respect.

The two rescuers lost valuable time waiting for the morning ferry. This worked in Daphne's favour

300

because Romeo had spare time to secure her a pigeon coop nearby to recuperate until ready to fly. About 6 weeks of just seed should keep her political opinions in check, figured Romeo. But at least she was safe. Romeo was a gentleman at heart, just very rough around the edges. In fact, the only reason that Block Island was free from all pet tyranny was because Romeo's fighting prowess preceded him. The evil Roman himself made the call not to invade the carefree island because of legends he'd heard about Romeo beating the notorious CFT smuggling mob into submission in one battle alone against 23 big cats. Times were tough and Roman couldn't afford those kind of severe losses.

A day later, Bagel was currently travelling West towards Connecticut's straight as a die border. Soon Suzie would be lost forever. Yesterday, she planned to make a run for it until she saw Romeo set one of the slaves on fire over a gas stove whilst the elderly resident napped in front of the television. The frazzled cat looked like a string of beef jerky and each cat was made to lick the stiff burnt carcass to maintain fear. Bagel rapidly changed her mind about escaping when the salt hit home. Atheist Suzie looked up to the heavens and asked for help. No harm in trying, she supposed.

Without warning the heavens opened and thundered Romeo towards her! He had managed to hitch a ride under a lorry after questioning the black rats on Suzie's whereabouts. At first the recalcitrant rats refused to talk; he then ate one of them alive and they all talked rapidly.

Romeo wasn't a great thinker, he had no plan, but excessive violence usually wins the day anyway. He had already picked off the trailing cat guards and set some of the pussy slaves free. Unfortunately, the best looking queens were up front, close by Roman. Romeo V's Roman was on!

When the one you love seems out of reach, let go and you will find the love you seek.

The battle of battles was over surprisingly fast. It was like one of those Madison Square Gardens heavyweight fights everyone pays out a fortune for a prime ringside seat and then it's all over in round one.

As the rains descended, Romeo scampered up ahead and adroitly stretched himself out on a car to look like moving windscreen wipers. His clever purring engine sounds totally fooled Roman who was expecting the car to pull away from the curb, not having a flying ninja cat slashing his throat before even landing.

Roman didn't even have a chance to look tough. Blood gushed out and was washed away down the road on pavement grey. The pink hue looked pretty. The other gang cats jumped ship immediately after Romeo slashed open Roman's guts gushing away down into the gutter like worms. The violent prophylactic symbolism worked better than hoped

302

for. Romeo let them go and wasted no time at all by shagging one of the prettiest cats while talking to Suzie.

"I want you next baby, just getting warmed up for the most beautiful feline in the State!" lied Romeo.

This wasn't the romantic reunion his name promised or what Suzie hoped for, but the grateful to be alive cat assumed doggy-style position ready for being mounted next. It felt great to be saved, especially when he put his rolling pin dick in for sharpening.

Two days later, after having swum the remaining kilometre to Block Island because they got caught shagging on the ferry and were thrown overboard, Romeo and Suzie finally made it back to his hotel and her old house too.

Ava was playing hopscotch outside, wearing a panda costume. Hopefully this reunion would go more according to script, wished Suzie. She saw her old playmate Ava from years ago looking so grown up and tall now. A tear of total happiness dropped when her best human friend stopped skipping and spotted Suzie.

"Meoooow!" said Suzie, approaching in the friendliest of ways with her tail erect in anticipation.

Ava was only 3 years old when Suzie was taken from her and children don't even remember their own dad if they don't see him at least every fortnight, but Suzie left such a cuddly lasting impression on Ava, all the right senses were alerted in her growing brain. Ava didn't recognise her, but *knew* she knew her from somewhere.

The old best friends ran to each other with joyous, childlike enthusiasm as Ava hugged a very grateful cat loving the attention. She carried Suzie to an open front door and took her upstairs to bounce on the bed like the good old days. Ava had a big bed now and Suzie was overcome with emotion as mommy walked in to find out what all the celebrating was about.

"Mommy, I've got a new best friend, can we keep her please?" begged Ava.

Mom recognized Suzie straight away and felt faint. Suzie had returned from the dead and as strange as it sounds, they were all very happy with that, especially Suzie who had never felt so loved and appreciated. It was a beautiful moment full of happy smiles and upbeat violin whiskers. The kind of cheerful moment you live for.

Sometimes a simple smile is the greatest reward you'll ever need.

Bagel had finally become Suzie again and reached her happy destiny. She was a happy cat now being stroked by Ava. Romeo was loitering outside, waiting to stroke her too. However, Juliet, Flynn and Arthur had not yet met their fates. Who had the strongest mind to face what was coming and become last man or woman standing? There can only be one!!!

We're all amazing. You just have to learn how to feel it.

22

Drugs and Bugbears

Within just 20 minutes of drying his mind and soaked clothes out in a spruced up modern city, Arthur Koons the maniac was already incognito as a homeless man. Police CCTV is no different from city bankers; neither help nor notice homeless folk struggling to survive.

The world of psychology has made mental illness worse, not better.

When you slow the pace of your eyes from the hubbub of London's busy bus, car and pedestrian traffic, you immediately notice hundreds of homeless people moved on and pushed along by security in a never-ending cycle of social shame. Some kind-hearted people care, but the vast majority view vagrants as a daily reminder of what happens if you don't cower down to the corrupt financial system. Ironically, homeless pain via enforced austerity becomes a symbol of fear to follow the order.

When you find out the truth it's frightening how many people will try and prevent you from telling it.

Arthur really cared about London's street living population for as long as he needed to use them; about a week. Obviously his target painting to steal was Salvador's Metamorphosis on permanent display in the Tate with the chimneys. He planned on using destitute people's discontent to flood the building with chaos and confusion. This was an excellent plan with little defence.

It was immediately obvious to Arthur that most of the transient unfortunates were men and a large portion were Eastern Europeans promised a vastly superior life in Britain, only to discover tens of thousands of other people fighting for a handful of low paid jobs too. These foreign vagabonds with no foothold or friends anywhere, were fucking desperate, living cold nights right near Britain's uber wealthy scum responsible for the financial subjugation of millions worldwide.

Luckily for Arthur though they could all speak English really well so he began using his newly found financial clout to employ hundreds of protestors and helpers to fight back against a system which treats human beings so appallingly. For a snip at only £500 cash a day, Arthur had secured himself a top cardboard box property near Waterloo Bridge and now had his own private, anarchist army just a few days later.

These genuinely homeless men and women were also alcoholics; the odd ex cracked English stock broker; small business owners who lost everything to globalisation; drug abusers and mostly serious mental health abandoned patients; abused women running from domestic violence; sad people who lost loved ones; Romanian and Albanian criminals on the run; and a surprisingly wide variety of all types of people from different backgrounds. The problem with Western society is it doesn't take much to lose everything and end up down-and-out.

We live in an age if it doesn't have fame or money attached to it, it must be worthless, therefore nearly everyone ends up feeling unappreciated. Know your true worth and don't let anyone or society tell you otherwise.

Obviously, word on the streets spreads fast when someone is dishing money out, so Arthur decided after two very tired undercover days to make his strike on the art gallery tomorrow at noon, then wished he hadn't used the word 'noon' because half of the foreigners didn't know it meant 12 o'clock pm.

Regardless, the planned rally and commotion was set: if anyone living on the streets objects to the greedy political system and wants free money, meet outside the Tate Modern during the day at twelve and follow some crazy instructions. The £100 each protestors were the bulk crowd noise. Arthur's compact elite army of Albanian helpers would get a personal windfall of £1000 cash each for causing violent mayhem inside the gallery.

Arthur was throwing his money around like a lunatic lottery winner determined to lose it all. He had gone a bit funny in the head and in his madness began to believe that Salvador Dali was ultimately responsible for his previous downfall. Losers always blame someone else when things go wrong. First it was Caesar's fault, then Juliet's and now it was a dead artist to blame for exercising creative powers beyond the grave.

After waving loads of wonga around, naturally the press caught minty wind and advertised it on Capital FM radio an hour before the event, which Flynn and Juliet heard whilst lying on their luxurious hotel bed, post filthy coitus. The mood turned from relaxing to rambunctious in seconds as the penny dropped.

"Why are you getting dressed?" asked Juliet.
"I just feel like some fresh air, maybe looking at that Dali painting again. It was great wasn't it?" replied Flynn, bending the truth.
"Oh I see," said a suspicious Juliet.
"See what?"
"There's a strange man handing out free money on the South Bank and you want to get some of it to pay me back. Ahhh, that's so sweet of you Flynn."
"Okay you got me. Just thought it would be nice to buy you some flowers and chocolates because you're so beautiful," said Flynn with a lying child vibe.

Juliet turned her smile from warm to Mona Lisa in a split second and Flynn looked uneasy as he put on his coat.

"You must think I was born yesterday! So this is why you brought me to London all along. It's him isn't it, on the radio? The crazy killer and rapist. I thought it was odd how 'Macho Flynn' dropped his case so easily for me. This whole romantic holiday was simply a ruse to catch Mr. Fucked-up Koons, wasn't it!!?" said one very angry woman.
"No. That's not the case Juliet. I just thought we could take our relationship to the next level, that's all... And if by good fortune I could get closure on

310

the man who caused you so much personal distress, then it would be a double bonus and you'd be happy with that," explained one top bullshitting man.

"OOOOOOOOOOH, did you realllly!? If there's no trust Flynn then I'm gone for good! I mean it," said Juliet packing her things in anger.

"Wait, wait, wait, wait, wait, please listen. I fucked up I know, but as God is my witness I love you Juliet Jessica Green!" exclaimed Flynn.

Then, unbelievably, at the most totally inappropriate of moments, he bent down on one knee in desperation to recover the situation, "Juliet, I *do* love you and want to spend the rest of my life with the most amazingly clever and beautiful woman I've *ever* known."

Before Flynn had the chance to ask her to marry him, Juliet, still very angry, interrupted asking, "Does that include your mother, mommy's boy who always gets what he wants?"

Flynn didn't want a mommy versus fiancé fight right now and just replied with, "Will you marry me?" presenting a modest engagement ring.

Juliet sat down on the bed and started crying; a little bit because the ring was so unimpressive. "You deceive me and then ask me to marry you. Are you crazy Irishman?"

"You love me. I know it," said a sorry looking cop. "I'll protect you forever. I promise."

"I don't know Flynn, I just need space to think," said Juliet wiping tears from her eyes.

She felt a little manipulated but also it was true, she did feel a deep love for yet another man not as emotionally mature as her. It seems all men are childish at heart, but some mean well and she felt his good intentions.

Juliet looked Flynn square in the eyes and said, "If you're going to catch him you better go now and if you do catch him I'll marry you." Juliet stood up and pushed him out of the door. Flynn was on his last journey to meet his destiny. If your heart's not in it, keep changing direction until you find your natural compass. Love is often the magnet.

Be honest with people and they will love you for it.

Arthur's rally against the system was going great. Over a thousand people showed up. He opened his suitcase full of cash and threw it at the caterwauling crowds like a benevolent king whilst laughing like a hyena. Chaos ensued. It was perfect. However, just as Arthur nodded to his elite soldiers to implement the art gallery siege, six paddy wagons full of baton wielding riot police rolled up to arrest him for social unrest.

Nevertheless, Arthur had the crowd well and truly on his side, pointed at the bacon and shouted, "They're the ones responsible for keeping you down! They work for the rich, not you! Charge!"

The massive group of homeless protesters ran at the officers in a cattle stampede, knocking them over like skittles. Then Arthur, playing peasant revolt Watt Tyler shouted, "To the art gallery!!!!" and they all stormed the pristine building before staff had a chance to close it down. Arthur immediately made a beeline for the Dali painting.

Just because it's what we're used to, doesn't make our society normal or healthy.

Before the riot, Juliet felt very guilty she'd sent Flynn on a dangerous mission without backup. She wasn't thinking straight, so she called the emergency police who sent the carriers full of over forty shielded officers currently being trampled. Plus, MI5 had been alerted and a handful were in plain clothes with the protestors, yet made powerless by crowd motion and people power.

Juliet should have stayed in the hotel, but Juliet being Juliet loved a good protest! She got in a black cab, arriving just as everyone rushed the Tate Modern and was swept in with the mobbing wave, looking for Flynn. The funniest part of the day was over 700 illegal immigrants turning up at 12 midnight to find themselves arrested for terrorism questioning.

Virtually all the art gallery staff and guards had deserted their posts. That kind of extreme public disorder was well out of their hands, comprehension and job description. More police cavalry arrived, yet literally had to queue up to try and fight through the ever growing crowds. No-one seemed to know what was going on.

When people say just be yourself what they really mean is don't be yourself. Think about it.

Arthur was now in a white gallery space upstairs facing his philosophical nemesis; Dali's masterpiece which stopped him dead. Being Arthur he couldn't just look at it like a normal person, no. He *had* to possess it with his soul and hands.

Overwhelmed with its conceptual resonance, Arthur began crowbarring it off the wall. The alarms all sounded when he levered the plaster and painting away from the wall into his thieving arms. He then paused for a strange moment looking at it murmuring, "All I ever do is steal people's souls. This will be the last one."

Arthur felt really pleased with himself in the middle of all the rabble's pandemonium. Most people were destroying the art, not appreciating it like him. Art doesn't mean anything when you're hungry. One starving man even sat down chewing on a funny looking bowl of Cubist fruit. It looked and tasted like shit.

Anyhow, Arthur Koons scooped up his booty with a smirk and headed for his planned escape route, but one strong looking man stood in his way. Finally Flynn had caught up with his bête noire, his bane. The rival men eyeballed each other before

Arthur carefully lay the painting down like it was a wailing baby. Another big fight was on!

A few protesters darted too close to Arthur and he knocked them both out as a show of force to scare Flynn. It worked. Flynn knew this would be the fight of the century for him and gave it everything he'd got!

Flynn ran at Arthur like a charging Picasso bull but got tripped over by a manic crying employee running across him, trying to save the masterpieces from ruination. Arthur waded in with violent kicks while the man was down, breaking two of Flynn's ribs before his foot was caught by Flynn who stood up rapidly to pull Arthur down, returning the rib pounding favour.

Flynn backed off for a few seconds to catch his breath and because Arthur looked beaten. Big mistake. Arthur was up and in martial arts mode, jabbing out kung fu kicks and punches like a praying mantis on steroids. Flynn couldn't sustain the rally of insanity and went down again after a temple blow.

Arthur had met his match and thought he'd prevailed as he ran back to get his prized painting, only to find himself yanked back from behind and tossed to the floor again by Flynn. The painting was upside-down but undamaged. Flynn was much more badly bruised and hurt, yet his Irish grit and determination was growing to the surface like never before. He was NOT going to let Arthur escape!

They both hammered at each other in a frantic fashion with heavy slugs and painful bollock kicks for over a minute until Arthur's nose exploded and impaired his vision. He was half blinded and howling in agony with a badly broken snout when Flynn went Rocky style and worked Arthur's body like hanging meat.

Equally covered in blood, Flynn was on the cusp of victory when Juliet ran in directly behind Arthur and shouted, "Flynn, be careful!" This gave the Houdini of Horrors the motivation he needed to escape by scraping himself off the floor and running at Juliet, catching and holding her firmly around the neck, threatening to break it.

She was taken by surprise because Juliet loved Flynn and all she saw were his crystal blue eyes and that he was alive, albeit spattered in the blood of his enemy. It was looking like a hostage situation, yet life rarely goes according to plan. Assumptions are for fools.

"Let her go Arthur! You've hurt her enough already!" demanded Flynn.

"I'll let her go when you let us go!" shouted back Arthur.

"Don't hurt her!" pleaded Flynn.

"I won't if you leave now!" bargained Arthur.

"Yes!" hollered Juliet. Neither one of the men had any idea what Juliet was going on about and the large gallery space seemed to stop time. "Yes, Flynn Liam O'Connell, I will marry you!"

Flynn was torn apart. He felt like if he left Juliet in Arthur's vicious arms he would never see her again. But if he didn't she might have her neck snapped. All he could see was her, which was his downfall.

A menacing gang of roughly a dozen thugs came up behind Flynn and smashed him over the head with a hammer. He was out for good, lying on the floor like a loose pile of bricks. In quieter times he could have passed as an exhibition piece. One of the thugs even laughed and took everyone back to the nineties by joking, "Hammertime!" It was tragic, made worse when they surrounded Arthur and Juliet, punching Arthur in the head and knocking him out too, and the same short smartass guy said, "U can't touch this, oh-oh oh oh oh-oh oh," when he squeezed Juliet's tits before picking up the painting.

Juliet was bagged up and dragged away kicking and screaming, along with the painting and Arthur slung over the biggest guy's shoulder. The gang violently pushed, kicked and punched their way through the huge Turbine Hall crowds and exited without any police resistance. The gallery was in tatters but who cares because most modern art is a money laundering scam that needs burning.

With a heavy hood over her head and moving along in a Ford Transit van, Juliet wondered what the hell had just happened. She couldn't breathe very well and was afraid.

Arthur's homeless Albanian helpers grassed him up on day one to the infamous Albanian drug lords running the main UK drug trade. They came over to Britain in the late nineties exploiting the Kosovan refugee crisis and quickly set up sex trafficking rackets in London, needlessly brutalising many women in a show of power. Once established, they took over the drug market and became hugely financially successful. One gang member even posted a photo of nearly a quarter of a million pounds in cash on Twitter to show off how confident they were of escaping justice, just before he was jailed for 11 years.

Splashing his stolen dough about like Robin Hood got Arthur and Juliet kidnapped after the Metropolitan Police high-ups did a secret deal with the Albanians: if they caught the most wanted criminal in the world, they could keep the 5 million on the condition they returned his dead body in one piece. Everyone would be a winner then. The Met and MI5 would be heroes for apprehending the notorious American fugitive and the Albanian crime wave gets to torture Arthur until his hidden Swiss bank account details are revealed. Only it didn't go that way.

The enormously dangerous Albanian gang located Arthur in a day, but after hearing of his grand art theft plans decided to let him continue so they could clean up and sell a painting worth far more than his $5 million ransom. Everyone was seriously afraid of one of the largest criminal organisations in the world who did deals with the Mafia and bought pure cocaine directly from Columbia. And so they should be because any opposition usually ended up as hacksaw pieces of flesh for seagulls and crabs. Kindness and crime are what humans do best.

Who would have thought that being genuinely nice makes your life better too.

23

Fresh Meat

In a small bleached room in Central London, a few regular electronic beeps were the only sounds Flynn was making. His plan to be a brave super-cop going it alone was stupid. He was in a deep coma. The doctors said his condition was stable but had no idea how long he'd be comatose, or whether he'd sustained any permanent brain damage. His world was underground and full of unknowns.

Is it normal on Twitter to write a tweet and get zero likes? I'm just asking if I'm normal.

Naturally, Shirley had been informed about her daughter's kidnapping and the brutal attack on Flynn. She was lucky to get a flight because tensions between France and Britain were sky high and there was talk of war, especially after a British diplomat in France sent to smooth over the naval crisis, accidentally on purpose drowned a pack of biscuits in his tea during the meeting whilst making tiny shell whistling sounds on each biscuit dunk. Also, some terrorists let off a bomb in the Channel Tunnel which caved it in, flooding Folkestone and Calais, killing hundreds of European hedgehogs and millions of English fish. Rumour had it that Conservative Prime Minister Boris Johnson sanctioned the SAS to blow the tunnel in a desperate bid to secure a No-Deal Brexit. These false allegations were never substantiated and the fact Boris went on to sell democracy down the river, proved his apathy for the people's wishes.

Many cars also washed away down the Channel Tunnel, including a Mini called Maxi who reportedly plugged up the explosion hole, saving many lives. The brave red, white and blue car was deemed a heroine and martyr to the Brexit cause. Five years later a bronze statue of Maxi controversially replaced Nelson's Column in Trafalgar Square and many said the colour design looked more French than British.

People who name their car must be fucking lonely.

The powerful Albanian gangs were so organised and profitable that some factions even started to copycat middleclass English lifestyles by commuting to London from the classy green suburbs of Surrey and Sussex. Obviously they weren't mixing with the posh knobs, just emulating their exorbitant lifestyles.

Approximately 19 miles from the Albanian's heart of crime in Soho Central London, Juliet and Arthur were being held hostage in a quintessentially English Grade 1 listed building in Esher, Wayneflete Tower, dating back to the 15th century. The magnificent stately looking manor with four castle turrets was transformed into a Gothic mansion house in the 18th century for Prime Minister Henry Pelham of the Whigs.

This opulent slice of rented English history was a very beautiful and private base for the gang to put their feet up, shoot some fucking pheasants nearby and fuck high-class escorts (an oxymoron if ever there was one). The neighbours didn't mind the Albanian's criminal antics because there weren't any. It was the perfect place to let loose and also torture people, unluckily so for arrogant Arthur who had already been slapped about and rammed a fair amount. Juliet was next for sex; the down side of being a beautiful blonde.

Most of the gang had travelled back to London for a major shipment of cocaine coming in and only left behind four men to keep its treasures and guests shipshape. When they return about midnight, Juliet was going to be the cherry on the top centrepiece of a party full of whores.

Things were looking distinctly grim for both prisoners and there was no man around with a particular set of skills to save them. Or was there? Arthur was a master bullshitter, fighter and thinker. Surely he could worm his way out of this little scrape? Karma fucked him up the arse last night though and he wasn't feeling very charismatic right now.

It was breakfast time and the two prisoners had under 10 hours to escape before it was game over. Juliet courageously recognised the need to work as a team, but Arthur looked deadbeat and whipped. Regardless, he didn't have much choice but to co-operate because his left hand was handcuffed to Juliet's right.

The two sorry looking captives were on the second floor in a very small room with no windows and two heavily bolted, locked doors. Juliet thought the claustrophobic room was kind of cosy and clean apart from sharing it with a man who once tried to rape her. *Tense* didn't really do the blade cutting atmosphere justice. And with some irony, the

Albanian gang who were more partial to assholes than art, nailed Dali's painting to a blank wall in their room last night saying, 'Keep it, that's the last view you will ever see again.' Charming, thought Juliet, although she did admire the painting with its two majestical figures reflecting their imbroglio.

Bluntly put, the Albanian crooks made it patently obvious to Juliet and Arthur they were to be fucked for weeks on end and then cut into lobster pot meat. This was *serious* real life, not pissing about on Twitter. Worse than that, Juliet felt she could die without her mobile or any Wi-Fi. The bandits didn't even have the decency to give the hostages any hope whatsoever. There's no need to lie when your organisation is virtually untouchable.

If you don't consort with the enemy you won't ever change their minds.

Juliet felt psychologically trapped by her predicament but there was no way around it. She had to escape from certain doom whilst chained to a mass rapist who had temporarily lost the will to live. Arthur was very sore all over and for the first time in yonks, felt very defeated and deflated. Juliet needed to snap him out of his bad humour fast before she became the laughing stock of the party.

A woman usually has to step in and finish what a man started and now it was Juliet's turn to help out good over evil. She was good at a wide variety of pragmatic tasks: wallpapering; proficient at sewing and upholstering chairs; handled her own tax accounts; could wire a plug and mix cement; had superb twerking skills; cooked wonders on a shoestring budget; successfully ironed clothes with hair straighteners and picked things up with her toes. Juliet even once taught herself to solder different low temperature metals together to fix an antique brass chandelier and a few other decorative nick-nacks. She was a very versatile and capable woman, but escaping from seasoned body beaters was not her field of expertise; it was Arthur's.

"For fuck's sake!" said an annoyed Juliet, whacking Arthur around the head with a stained cushion which acted as their mattress too. "Whatever they did to you isn't going to get any easier unless you get your thumb out of your ass and start helping."

Considering what actually did happen throughout the night, Juliet's analogy was somewhat crass.

Arthur looked up from his crouched position and said, "They made me pretend I was a teapot, but instead of pouring tea I had to…" he whimpered a little, mumbled incoherently and finished off with, "Up my spout."

Juliet was not an insensitive lady, priding herself on being an empath, yet really struggled not to laugh for a second or two biting her lips. She was also thinking, serves you right for being a rapist piece of shit, but just said, "No point stewing on it is there?"

325

"Very good. That's the kind of joke my step father would crack before his pals sodomised me as a child," said Arthur playing the sympathy and guilt cards together.

"You honestly don't think I'm going to feel sorry for you do you? You took me on a date before trying to gang rape me, leaving me with a broken arm after stalking me on Twitter," said a huffed and puffed looking lady.

"I know it doesn't sound good, but there are reasons for everything," explained Arthur.

"No means NO!" said Juliet in a crystal clear way.

"Oh fuck, you're not on Twitter now bitch. This is real life where boundaries of good and evil merge until you no longer know what side you're supposed to be on," justified Arthur, starting to warm up his bullshitting ways.

Juliet was doing a good job. He was coming back to life. She needed him and his devious mind.

"To me dumbass, good has always been good, and evil looks like death and you. I know in my heart what is right and wrong. You say it's someone else's fault don't you. You're wrong and an evil piece of shit!" shouted judge Juliet warming her anger up too. The venting felt good.

"Shhhhh! They'll hear you," said Arthur in fear. And they did. Thudding footsteps elevated up the stairs, the door opened, a big man walked over to Arthur, punched him really hard in the head twice and calmly walked out.

"Sorry about that. My bad. Are you okay?" asked Juliet, feeling kind of good on seeing her tormentor receive some punishment.

Arthur spat out a tooth and said, "Never felt better thanks." They both laughed very quietly. "That's the one they called the English tea cosy because he likes to smoother his victims." They both laughed again, this time covering their mouths to muffle the sound of ecstatic comedy. "I'm not partial to anymore tea bagging so let's escape!" announced a revived Arthur.

Juliet forgot and laughed out loud this time, and as the footsteps returned, she pushed her luck saying, "This is a fun game. I laugh and you get lumped. L O L."

Unfortunately the tea cosy man wasn't a moron and knew a woman's laugh so Juliet got a massive slap across the face which sent her flying in a circle around Arthur, chain linked to her.

When the pleasant Albanian chap left, Arthur's spirits had risen considerably and he joked, "That was like that swing ball tennis garden game, but you were the tennis ball. I liked it. Perhaps we could play again?" mocked Arthur.

"If I start crying, he's going to punch you lots next time. Let's play the crying game instead," threatened Juliet.

"Hopefully not like the film?" replied Arthur.

"Imagine if you found out I was transgender. I'm not, but just imagine what a misogynist and bigot like you would do," replied Juliet, getting all snarky.

"I'm not a misogynist. I just hate nearly 100% of women," answered Arthur.

"Oh well that's okay then. A male rapist saying they are not a woman hater is like Trump embracing his King of Israel title," said Juliet, not really hitting the analogy on the head.

Neither one of them knew what the other was talking about, so they stared at Dali's painting for a good minute or two, which inspired Arthur's escape plan.

The painting is about temporal duality and escaping one's mind into the cave to explore your real self.

If it's all in the mind then how comes your body and soul feels it so much? Mental illness is more real than reality because it speaks more languages than we use. The same goes for art.

Arthur pulled Juliet closer to him and whispered in her ear, "This is a very small room for such a large estate and doesn't follow the layout downstairs. It must be a divided cell, explaining the lack of windows too. When I was downstairs, they made me get the sugar and inside the kitchen was a big old-fashioned chimney shaft easily big enough to fit a person in."

"You are hilarious! A walking innuendo. Sugar. Big shafts. And did the cat get the full-cream milk too? And?" quipped Juliet.

"Fuck you. Listen. I would guess the room behind that door has the kitchen chimney in it which I can drop down, hopefully undetected," he said pointing at the interior wall with the Dali painting on it.

"A solo mission aye? Don't you mean WE? This isn't fucking Star Wars Han. How are WE going to undo these handcuffs and break through that wall first, let alone escape without detection?" asked an untrusting Juliet.

"One step at a time Chewie. Ever heard that?" said Arthur checking out the door's lock.

"Like your one rape at a time philosophy?" retorted Juliet.

"Identical," said Arthur giving Juliet the finger. "How about I suffocate you and squeeze your arm through these handcuffs to give me more elbow room?" he threatened.

"How about I resist, scream and tell them about your plans to escape? Couldn't see them liking that," defended Juliet.

"Hmm. This is a quandary," said Arthur making the thinking emoji face.

Juliet responded with the finger emoji followed by the smug smile one and dubiously said, "Looks like we need to escape together. Agreed?"

"Agreed," lied Arthur. "We'll never get through this lock without a tool but this wall seems like plasterboard," he said whilst tapping it lightly with his fingers and running his hand across the surface like it was a woman's skin.

"You know, you couldn't look more creepy if you tried," teased Juliet.

"Hey bitch, you met your cop boyfriend because of me. You owe me," Arthur genuinely said with a straight face wondering why Juliet seemed so ungrateful.

"I owe you at least a broken arm and a hard kick in the nuts. Deal?" she replied. Arthur didn't even respond because he was beginning to get his confidence back and taste escape.

The wall they needed to get through was just a double plasterboard divider. It would be easy to punch a hole through it, but not so easy without making a noise. Arthur took the painting off the wall carefully and tried to slowly push a hole through with all his weight and might so no impact sound would be heard. But it needed too much power and there was nothing in the room that could be used to lever onto the wall as a press. The wall needed at least one good punch to get a hole started on both sides and that would create a shuddering noise.

After a little confab, Arthur punched the wall hard. Together they efficiently picked up and swept away the plaster, hiding it under the cushion which was the only object in the room apart from them. They just about managed to get the painting back on the wall again with great teamwork before the same guy with a woollen sweater burst in looking reasonably angry. At first he said nothing and looked around. All seemed normal.

"What the noise?" he demanded to know in broken English just off the boat. Arthur started to speak and just got a punch for his trouble. Then, the strong-arm called **CLIRIM** grabbed Juliet by her hair and repeated his enquiry.
"It was him! He tried to knock me out so he could fuck me in the ass and ruin your merchandise for later. He's evil, unlike you," explained Juliet, really pushing sarcasm to its limits.

Luckily Clirim was unlike his bosses and very stupid. He hit and kicked Arthur a lot of times before he was convinced his message was thoroughly understood and then said with a pernicious tone, "Tonight at 6 we watch football! You make noise, I cut," pointing his finger at Arthur then doing the obligatory index finger across throat gesture all gangsters make. Clirim really liked the beautiful game. For him it was a matter of life and death.

When an abuser has you in an uncomfortable place, trapped in financial or psychological restrictions, that's the exact time to leave no matter how scared you feel.

About an hour went by of carefully prizing and peeling away plaster from the wall after Juliet scored a line around the painting with her fingernails. The hole was big enough to squeeze through later and revealed a dragon's den of riches. The much larger room was stacked with piles of money, boxes full of stolen watches and jewellery, bags of drugs and there was even a Jenga style stack of gold bullion bars in a corner glistening next to a barred window. Arthur's eyes glowed with greed. Most importantly though, their escape chimney was on the far wall. Arthur was right and that was their best way out. This was a one-shot deal though, so they agreed to stick to the original plan of waiting until the gang were distracted by the football.

The dominant species dominates. That's just the way it is. Our dominant strains are bullying and greed. We must break this or face extinction.

Many hours passed as Juliet and Arthur waited in anticipation, which gave ample time for both prisoners to plan different things. Arthur planned on using a kitchen knife to slit Juliet's throat and cut her hand off once they'd safely climbed down. Juliet had other ideas. She talked to Arthur a little bit more during their time together and got the feeling his blackness would never go away. Both of them rested with the top of their heads on half a cushion each and their souls were like repelling magnets.

At 5:33pm Clirim bounded upstairs and gave them a bowl of gruel each to scoff. He delicately spat in Arthur's food before warning him, "Game starts soon. You make noise, you die," pointing his finger at Arthur. He was a man of few words. Then he ran his fingers through Juliet's lovely hair and said, "We have fun with you tonight huh?" Juliet smiled and nodded to keep the whipped prisoner illusion going, but his creepiness strengthened her resolve to do whatever it takes to get out alive!

Twenty five tense minutes went by until they heard the gang shouting and laughing in a corridor as they made their way to the games room far from the kitchen. The double door-sized TV was jammed right up to shuddering wall and vibrating glass sound levels. They heard football crowds cheering and anthems playing. It was clearly the signal to escape!

Would Juliet ever see Flynn again, she wondered? Was Flynn even alive? Many other heartfelt thoughts were going through her mind while Arthur was as placid as a poker player and focused on living his mad existence. However, love is a powerful emotion which gave Juliet the spirit to fight back.

They helped each other clamber through the hole. Both of them were momentarily stunned by the landscape of wealth. It was impossible not to touch the gold. Juliet stroked the bars like a pet sphinx as Arthur filled his pockets with jewels. She quickly picked out a few handfuls of diamond studded necklaces too; a girl's gotta live!

Both of them wanted to stab each other in the back and their escape was further confused when Arthur whispered, "This way. We're not leaving the painting," dragging Juliet back to the hole.

"Fuck the painting!" she said a bit too loud. The guys downstairs were so drunk already and into the game, Juliet could have used a battering ram on the door and they probably wouldn't have heard.

"No. I'm not leaving it! It's what I came here for. Plus it's worth millions," justified Arthur.

"Our lives aren't worth risking for money," insisted Juliet.

"Easy for you to say. They stole your mom's ransom money. I've got nothing now," complained Arthur.

"Oh, I'm sorry you lost money that you stole for threatening to kill my mother. How terrible for you. Fuck the painting! It's only art," insisted Juliet.

"ONLY ART! There's art and there is art. This IS art," said Arthur getting all deep and possessive.

"For fuck's sake Koons. It's great, but it's just oil on canvas. You know, it hasn't got a beating heart like me," Juliet said sarcastically.

"It's what it does to your heart that counts," replied Arthur philosophically.

"It's going to stop mine beating if we don't leave it," stressed Juliet.

"This isn't a democracy. I'm taking it with us."

"I get the feeling your whole life has been a dictatorship," judged Juliet correctly. Arthur pulled the painting through the hole and took a second to

admire it. "How the fuck did you escape so many times with this lax attitude?" asked Juliet with genuine curiosity.
"When you're relaxed more doors open for you," explained Arthur with a knowing smirk.

Arthur was full of answers, but to be content with a happy soul you have to see life as more than a game.

He fitted himself into the chimney first and climbed down a few feet as far as their arms could stretch before Juliet got her legs in.

"That is one sweet looking pussy baby," perved Arthur looking up her skirt. Whilst admiring her pert arse he simultaneously smelled boiling cabbage and fish coming from the Aga below whispering, "The oven's on. Be careful and take it slow."

His plan was to get Juliet's help to carry the painting down safely and then send her to the afterlife. Arthur's plans always went well because he was clever. However, Arthur never expected Juliet to be brave enough to go it alone, like many men don't anticipate nowadays, especially during this challenging part of the escape.

Juliet was on top of him, had gravity on her side and sensed danger. She pulled the painting through the gap, made out she was passing it to him and just as the frame was balanced on his shoulder, Juliet let go and jumped on the top of the frame, putting all of her weight on Arthur whose grip gave way immediately.

They plummeted all the way to the bottom with Juliet's force being taken by the picture frame which simultaneously cushioned her fall and punched all of her weight into Arthur's neck and head. His vile contempt for women over the years was his literal downfall. Arthur never expected to be betrayed by a woman whom he erroneously presumed was psychologically dominated.

Making his kismet recipe much worse, Arthur was totally knocked out cold on hitting the solid cast iron cooker, despite the boiling pan of cabbage going flying. He was breathing funnily because of many cracked ribs. Luckily, the gang didn't hear the pan catapult into a cupboard door because they were so engrossed in their team currently winning.

Now was Juliet's chance. She was lying on him with the painting in between like a Dali sandwich. Carefully sliding off onto the kitchen floor, Juliet looked at Arthur with the Narcissus on top like a coffin lid and thought he actually looked at peace for once. She wanted just to leave him to the slaughter but was still handcuffed to his menace. The painting frame fell to bits as Juliet lifted it carefully away. She got burnt a little by the boiling water on the fall and felt very angry, yet also a sense of relief which confused her.

On a work surface nearby was a wooden block full of knives and even better a used meat clever slightly closer with human blood on it. Juliet pulled

Arthur's chained arm towards the knives for extra reach, but his floppy body was heavy as fuck. She was just one frustrating foot away from her finger tips getting hold of the big knife, so put her foot against the oven and heaved away pulling Arthur right across the boiling stove plate waking him in screeching agony.

Half of his face was burnt blood red like a raw steak but much stranger tortures had happened in that kitchen. Last week a rival gang member had his penis guillotined and served to him in a sesame bun with mustard. Before they killed him, the brave soul actually said, 'You forgot the tomato sauce.'

As Arthur tried to flip himself off the oven, Juliet had already grabbed the meat clever and swung it at his handcuffed wrist. It must have taken over ten heavy hacks before the bone severed.

Juliet had never vented her lifestyle frustrations so much before. It was almost cathartic and legally classed as self-defence, yet very messy. She got a face full of pumping blood though before he passed out with one arm sizzling like bacon on the hot plate. Arthur's subconscious started to dream of Beethoven's 9th in his mind as his life drifted away.

Lying down in a dark room listening to music which plays your emotions. That vibe.

Arthur had led a profoundly unique life up until the chimney tomb ejected him into a world of darkness.

His whole life had been soot black with salty evil rubbed into his skin from an early age.

What more could the world expect from him? If you've had super-shit parents you will receive very few good finds in amongst heaps of trash talk putting you down. However, Arthur had seen some high life via crime and raped some women who showed him compassion, forgiveness and mercy in the eyes of their God. It's all too easy to blame our parents for our mistakes. Once you've left home you have a chance to panel beat their faults out to a smooth running lifestyle. Life is what you make of it.

Juliet didn't hang around to see if he was totally dead. Even if Arthur survived the blood loss he would certainly end up as crab and fish bait anyway. She uncomfortably eased out Arthur's chopped-off hand from the handcuffs and it dropped on the floor with a finger twitch like a nervous squid.

In her adrenaline fuelled emotional state, Juliet found herself briefly waving at the wriggling hand as some kind of warped respect for the dead. Killing does weird things to people, but not the Albanian gangs who really enjoyed it. She was then sick.

During his previous tea time, Arthur overheard a few gang members talking about a speedboat which Juliet and Arthur previously assumed must be outside. She looked out of the kitchen window, could see the River Mole but no cool boat to escape.

What she was alert enough to spot though was a very organised set of hooks with keys on them in the kitchen, one of which looked like the speedboat ignition key because it had a boat name on it; *veni vidi vici*. She took all of the keys anyway to double check and to slow the gang down once they discover her missing. A smart move from a temporarily unzipped mind.

The moronic sound of football hooligans upset they were now losing, resonated throughout the English manor. After Juliet rolled up Dali's painting, which now felt worth saving, all she had to do was walk out of the house near an annexed room full of murderous drunken men without them noticing, to win her freedom! And that's precisely what Juliet did. She simply took a deep breath in and decided to let fate choose the outcome. As cool as a cucumber sandwich, Juliet simply walked along the garden like a cricket player changing ends and found some skimming stones to launch into sun flooded water.

You swam through 2019. Some of you near drowned. Surf 2020 with style!

24

Courage Island

Way down the bottom of the beautifully mowed garden with English oak trees and pruned bushes, Juliet found a quad of colourful streamlined kayaks. The speedboat she hoped to escape in was 7 miles away in Kingston-upon-Thames where the Mole and Ember rivers meet the Thames.

To avoid police detection and stay in physical shape, this sub branch gang of Albanians couriered drugs and guns up and down rivers, which was the natural way to transport goods and gunpowder in days of old.

I'd rather admire gardens full of flowers than hang out with people because they make you feel good and don't argue back.

Juliet was covered in blood and very thirsty. Despite the impeding dangers behind her she took a few minutes to compose herself and connect with nature. Washing the congealing blood off her skin, Juliet heard some house sparrows chirping nearby and a wagtail landed on one of the kayaks. She drank handfuls of fresh running water which cleansed her soul. Juliet was surprised she didn't feel bad about killing Arthur because he deserved everything he got. Mad dogs need to be put down.

She was just about to go running for help when nature talked some sense into her vexed mind. If she walked down the lonely road nearby, the gang would easily pick her up then or further down the line in town. Even going to the police was ill advised because Juliet had no idea how well connected these Albanians were. Their gangster business model was perfect, controlling eyes on every suburban street. Juliet doubted how far she could make it into a tech obsessed city with more security cameras than any other city in the world. Big Brother was no longer a fictional concept, instead a fully working operation designed to wheedle-out and destroy any objectors of corporate tyranny. Philosophy used to be about exploring the world. Now it's about wondering why humans fucked-up the balance.

It can be very frustrating living in a human created zoo with rules and regulations everywhere from the day you're born. We were designed to live amongst nature. Nevertheless, here we are, so be determined that you'll put your happiness and family way before this money matrix.

A beautiful barn owl swooped by and Juliet watched until it flew out of sight down the river. The water was calming. Her thoughts were becoming real again. What she needed to do was reach the American Embassy in London. There, she would be safe and could find out what happened to Flynn. Plus she knew that the alien, Borg-like embassy building was situated right near the Thames approaching Vauxhall.

Juliet had the muscle and fitness required to make it in a kayak, perhaps before nightfall. At least on the river, figured Juliet, it would be hard to catch her even if they found her. She took action, removing a few hand stashed pistols in the other kayaks before sinking them with rocks. Juliet was no expert yet had done kayaking over a dozen times before with a friend and knew how to forward paddle quite well, and recover from capsizing. She tucked the painting and guns into her yellow kayak, peeled over the spray deck and began her epic journey into the unknown!

As Juliet began paddling she felt a great sense of euphoria on each paddle stroke gliding her towards freedom and Flynn. However, only a few miles down the river she was feeling drained and very much doubting being able to make it the whole way, famished and stressed. Negative thoughts started to creep into her mind as Juliet wondered why so many shopping trolleys had been dumped into the serene shallow river runs. Some people have no respect.

When the cheerful sun dips its hot head, the first chill of the night rises from Prussian blue, and we only have a duvet family to protect our personality hue.

The sun was beginning to drop and even its beautiful orange glow couldn't take away Juliet's hunger, but it helped. She even asked a dog walker how far it was to reach the Thames and the dad joker said, "Just a couple of miles love. Going to take you a while to row across the Atlantic, ha haa," in an odd English way, wondering what the hell an American woman was doing in that neck of the woods.

"I'm not rowing, I'm paddling,' replied Juliet and that was the end of that stale meeting of minds.

A bullfinch settled on a willow branch up ahead. Its beautiful pink breast caught the sun's orange rays and felt like a beacon of hope to Juliet, which doubled her paddling pace. And a jolly good job too because the football game had ended in dismal

343

defeat and the main Albanian mafia had returned with their leader, **LUAN BARBANEAGRA**, for the sex party with Juliet as lead singer. Their cocks were to be the microphones.

Nevertheless, things had taken a sour turn in Little Albania and nobody was in a party mood after Luan stabbed Clirim to death 31 times. The guy had passive-aggressive issues, yet was mainly aggressive.

Arthur had somehow managed to revive and escape on his hand and knees, and the other three soldiers responsible for losing him and Juliet knew their lives were over too if they didn't get them back. They had already emptied the kayaks and made excellent ground on catching Juliet up – just a mile away – but no trace of Arthur.

Meantime, nearly 100 men were circling the leafy Surrey streets in cars looking and asking around for traces of their fresh meat and the painting which had already been sold for $88 million to a private dealer in China. Not delivering Dali's most sought after masterpiece to one of China's wealthiest collectors would bring the Chinese triads of Soho knocking their doors down. Even the fearless and powerful Albanians couldn't risk double dealing with billionaire backed, violent triads. Sociopathic Luan had to recover the painting and torture Juliet or he was *not* going to be a happy man.

The happier you become the less you listen to a single word anyone says.

At last Juliet made it to the Thames and was dreaming of plain sailing all the way on elated adrenaline when she looked behind on hearing some shouts. It was the Albanian kayakers – much faster and stronger than her – only about 500 yards behind!

Juliet paddled in panic like a duck taking off and then pulled off the spray deck to jettison a load of heavy cocaine packages she was hauling as proof of crimes for the Embassy. A whitewash of coke filled the Thames with high fish as the gang ploughed through the cloudy water. Approaching Kingston-Upon-Thames bridge Juliet spotted some further gang members under streetlights waiting to drop bricks on her. It was kinda like Pooh sticks for them, but with people.

Surely Juliet's days were numbered unless she got very brave, lucky, or a miracle befell on her. A couple of half bricks thrown landed just a few feet away and soaked her lovely wavy hair. The closer she got, the closer their aim was until one brick hit home, cracking the kayak and capsizing her. The shock of cold water froze her fearful mind until a lack of oxygen kicked in a capsize recovery roll. Juliet bobbed back up and parried another brick descending with her paddle. She looked like a drowned cat and was beginning to feel like one. The men behind were only 75 yards away now and closing rapidly.

Fearing death, Juliet pulled out one of the pistols, took aim and shot one of the men on the bridge who flipped over the barrier, splashing into the Thames like an ungainly seal. She then turned the kayak around and off-loaded an entire magazine into the oncoming kayaks, sinking two and killing another man. Juliet was in the zone. It was fucking impressive to watch! The third kayaker headed for land. Christ that was effective, thought Juliet! Guns really are the great leveller. A couple eating a romantic kebab by the waterside called the police and clapped at the same time.

However, the crack in her kayak was seeping water through and she didn't know what to do. Juliet would be killed if she docked up because even more Albanians were turning up by the minute. She closed her eyes and asked for help. Then things got a lot worse when she cleared the bridge to the other side where a gang member on a boat far ahead started firing a machine-gun at Juliet, missing repeatedly. She was very well camouflaged in the looming darkness and had the upper hand because the shooter was flooded by streetlights. Grabbing the other loaded piece, Juliet took careful aim at his distinct silhouette and on her fifth shot he slopped into the water like shark bait.

Her brain was now working ten-to-the-dozen. Why didn't the guy on the boat just pull up next to her and blow her out of the water? It was the *veni vidi vici* speedboat and Juliet had the keys! God was surely on her side. With water now a few inches deep inside her kayak, she paddled like a maniac on speed to her best escape option. Most Albanians couldn't see her so went up ahead in ambush for firing round two.

Finally, Juliet reached the river bank exhausted, got out with the painting and jumped on the boat. Three gang members with guns spotted her and came running up to the boat as she jingled around her pockets for the keys. One fired a shot and missed and Juliet fired back, but they were already upon her about to leap aboard when she shot one directly in the forehead, then cleverly unrolled the painting and used it as a shield in a moment of pure inspiration!

Neither scumbag could shoot because any damage to the art would mean their lives – one limb at a time. She shot them both in the leg just because and then turned the key to the most beautiful engine sounds she'd ever heard; powerful twin racing outboards purring away like Bagel used to but a fuck of a lot louder!

Chucking the docking rope ashore, Juliet opened up the engine and roared away with supreme style. It was the fastest boat on the River Thames and nothing could stop Juliet now! Sheer grit and determination had won the day. Her survival instincts took over. Juliet was a winner gliding through water as a divine woman.

It's excellent when you're pleasantly surprised how brilliant someone is.

Arthur was a survivor too. Shortly after Juliet launched into her destiny, Arthur came alive again when the hotplate painfully heated his bone. Despite being in a ghastly state with melted skin everywhere, he managed to stem the flow of blood with tea towels and stanch his horrific wounds with vodka, teabags, ice and salt.

Limping away in agony and feeling faint, Arthur swam across the River Mole like a mole and disappeared into a vanishing landscape. His mind was as a slippery as an eel and ghostly in tormented times. Arthur's only ambition now was to not die and escape this godforsaken country with no identity. Juliet had been victorious over the world's most dangerous man and should feel very proud of her courage in the face of adversity. She had crushed Arthur's baneful spirit for the good of womankind.

When they give you hate, don't pass it on.

25

Occult Members

Juliet sped down the Thames in triumph with her blonde hair blowing like she was on a Hollywood film set. Her fresh thoughts were like rainbows showering fatigued citizens with positivity and love! However, something very unsavoury was happening in another part of London where Shirley really took umbrage to being criticised.

Those who refuse to be judged, sure know how to judge others.

Flynn was still unconscious and his dreams were becoming angry and choppy. Most oddly, he was imagining himself riding the waves on Arthur's boat days ago. One minute he was talking reasonably to Mr. Koons and the next they were embroiled in fisticuffs. This was his mind simultaneously trying to understand and empathize with the killer, and also stop Arthur's reign of evil. The men chatted for a while before the cabin was trashed with flying fists and saucepan swings:

"What did you want from life?" asked Flynn.

"I just wanted to be happy."

"Do you care about who you've hurt?"

"No because they hurt me."

"How so if you've never met them?"

"They embody the time spirit of all female hatred."

"So you're saying they're not a person, but rather an energy force?"

"Not so much energy, more souls and light."

"You realise you're deeply mentally ill don't you?"

"I do but also understand that normal people create the venom I share."

"You're not seriously saying you're a vessel for truth?"

"More an amalgamation and symbol for the fear of others."

"The wolf has a choice to not kill. Whereas the sheep must follow. Am I right?"

"When you present choices to people, is it not in our nature to try all options?"

"Only if you think you can get away with it."

"Precisely. And I can."

"You can so you do?"

"Are we not bigger than this?"

"No my friend. Not enough of us are. We are a collective consciousness."

"The individual thinker is dead."

"Only a dying mind thinks that way," concluded Flynn's deep ocean thoughts.

Flynn was in a strange dream world where you can't hide your thoughts from the truth. There's no need to lie in dreams because there are no consequences. Flynn's unconscious mind dreamed of being woken by a beautiful princess named Juliet. However, yesterday Juliet was otherwise indisposed.

On receiving the tragic news about her daughter and detective Flynn, Shirley got the first flight available and had been stuck by Flynn's hospital bedside ever since late last night. She had an anxious 5-hour delay at the airport because of the oncoming war between Britain and France which was eventually solved with some nice cupcakes and the UK giving the European Commission billions of pounds to line their pockets; so just like before then.

Shirley was wracked with nervous tension. Her daughter was missing, possibly murdered and the only man she trusted to save Juliet was in a sorry looking state with tubes and whatnot coming out of him. I must revive Flynn, thought Shirley's racing mind. Flynn was her psychological link to Juliet and she had a great deal of love for him too because he made her daughter happy, plus he was very handsome.

Despite Shirley's total lack of medical expertise, she took on the mantle and full responsibility for bringing Flynn back to life using her clairvoyant powers. Shirley was very much secretly into the occult, reading palms, tarot cards and all that kind of stuff. She started by holding Flynn's manly hands and rubbing her fingers up and down his life line, then the overly attentive nurse walked in.

"Patients in a coma can often respond best to talk, rather than touch my dear," said the fat white nurse who enjoyed giving Flynn a bed bath last night.
"We are making a spiritual connection," pointed out Shirley.
"Oh I don't believe in all that mumbo jumbo spirit world crap, but if it makes you feel better…"
"It's not crap! There's a science behind it nurse," explained Shirley feeling defensive.
"Sister please, I'm a Sister in charge," explained the senior nurse.
"You're not my sister!" blurted out socially awkward Shirley. But it was fine. She was in Britain now and

everyone is rude to each other as routine. It's more peaceful that way.

"Okay, I'm just going to take his temperature…"

"And break our spiritual connection?" complained Shirley interrupting, who felt she was beginning to get through.

"Yes, science breaks a lot of beliefs."

"The spiritual world is not a *belief*; it's an unexplained fenomona far more powerful than your drugs which haven't brought him back alive," defended Shirley, saying phenomena all wrong and getting smiled at.

"Experience has taught me that medical advancements are much better than talking someone's illness better, ha!" laughed atheist **SISTER COOMBES**.

"You wanna bet?! I once brought a cat back to life using mindfulness meditation," justified Shirley, totally lying to herself.

"Ha ha! You Americans are a real hoot. How did that happen?" questioned a very doubtful sister.

"My beautiful Bagel…"

"Bagel! You named your cat Bagel, like a morning roll? Haaa ha!" teased the belligerent Mrs. Coombes.

"Yes, one morning she was curled up all cosy like and I thought she looked like an unbaked bagel. It's my cat and my choice. Why do you have to mock everything I believe in?" asked Shirley.

"OK madam, his temperature is stable. I'll be back in 45 minutes to check on your 'spiritual' progress," said the rude, black and white thinking sister who only believed in results. Then she walked out with a smug grin after laying down the gauntlet.

"Good riddance!" said Shirley after the belligerent woman left.

Shirley felt very upset by the sister's attitude and went outside to complain and explain everything to another nurse who just said, "She virtually runs the place single-handedly for 5 days a week whilst only getting paid for 3. Still want to complain to a privatised management who won't care?"

"No... I err. Oh nevermind," pontificated Shirley.

"Listen, why don't you prove her wrong and use your spirit world to bring him back? It can't hurt anyone," suggested a junior nurse.

"Yes! Yes I will! I'll show her the power of the afterlife," said a satisfied looking Shirley. "Thank you nurse and don't underestimate the power of the underworld."

"I'll bear that in mind whilst I administer 300 patients medications today and change two dozen catheters," sarcastically said nurse **FIONA**, but Shirley had already returned to Flynn's room to perform her magic.

When you're really good at something you have to waste half your creative energy stopping jealous people trying to sink you behind your back.

Shirley sat down right next to Flynn and closed her eyes. Nothing seemed to happen for 5 whole minutes and she felt like a failure. Step two was to try summoning the dead using her newspaper as a Ouija board but all it spelt was the word 'cat'. Shirley simply had to show that fat bitch Sister Coombes a thing or two about life so she slapped Flynn around the face in frustration saying, "Wake up you fucking lazy bastard!" failing to sound motherly.

Sitting down and feeling like a fraud, Shirley had a brainwave thinking of one of her neighbours, John, who once said to her, "Oh God, you're sucking the life out of me Shirley," whilst cumming all over her alley cat face. Shirley was a bit of a floozy for a while after her divorce and now all that hard work was paying off.

Checking that no-one was around, Shirley started to manhandle Flynn's balls after lubricating with anti-bacterial gel first hoping it would refresh his spirits. No joy though. Then her head went under the sheets and Shirley began licking and sucking his member in what can only be described as a serious act of sin. Flynn's flaccid cock at first didn't react and Shirley was just about to give up her shameful head when the heart monitor started to increase its beeps.

She came up for air and to check his vitals, then went down under again and after a further 10 minutes of hardcore sucking her daughter's boyfriend's penis off for her daughter's sake, Flynn's dick had risen from the dead! It was big and looked like a pink courgette with a purple hat on.

"Wow!" shouted Shirley, who was wanking his dick off with a maniacal look on her face. "For Juliet!" she said with panting breath.

Her carnal actions were so deeply wrong on so many levels Shirley genuinely considered stopping, but then Flynn's legs opened a little at the knees and she felt him beginning to pull out of the lost planet he'd been orbiting. Then his hands twitched and Shirley got very excited seeing the movement. "Just one final flourish and the old Shirley swirl should do it," she whispered to herself, going to work on Flynn's knob for the last time.

Flynn's whole body started to shake like he was having an epileptic fit and Shirley panicked. She couldn't rush to the get help because his penis was erect and her lipstick was all around it, so she just finished him off gagging on it. Bang! Flynn not only shot out mountains of cum, he also shot up like Frankenstein's monster to catch Shirley with a face full of jizz.

"What the fuck's going on!" shouted a delirious and confused patient coming out of his coma.
"It's perfectly fine Flynn, it's me Shirley and you're in good hands," said the red faced mother-in-law to be.
"I can see that. Why am I naked. What the fuck were you doing to me?" vexed Flynn.

"I was doing some yoga and it worked and here you are! It's a miracle!" announced Shirley, feeling guilty and horny wiping semen off her face.

"Jesus Christ Shirley! What's Juliet going to say if I tell her this?"

"Now don't blaspheme Flynn. Your mother wouldn't like that would she?" answered Shirley with a question.

"Were you actually…"

"Calm down Flynn!" shouted Shirley slapping his delirium around the face. "You've had a traumatic experience and you don't know what you're talking about, do you? Lie down and let me take care of you," said an embarrassed motherly voice.

"I think you just did," joked Flynn lying down in shock.

"Don't be a silly boy and just rest. That's it. Be calm and get your strength back so we can save Juliet," cleverly digressed Shirley.

"Juliet!" said a pained Flynn, sitting up again but feeling giddy, "They took her."

"I know, I know. Lie down and pull these sheets over you," insisted Shirley covering her shameless act.

Just at that moment Sister Coombes returned earlier than planned, concerned about leaving Flynn with a batty old lady. She saw Flynn and ran outside the room calling out, "Doctor, doctor! Mr. O'Connell is conscious!"

The doctor immediately walked in with that irritating, pretentious authority most doctors have, then carried out a series of tests and walked out to inform the police and press.

"It seems like the spirit world needs an apology Sister," sardonically said Shirley. Sister Coombes had a good look around for ghosts or something before examining Flynn and didn't say a word until she noticed his medical gown had been removed, passing it to a suspicious looking Shirley who said, "He was very hot nurse."

"Oh yes, he is very hot isn't he madam. And it's Sister by the way as I said before," she said in a huff, grabbing the gown out of Shirley's hands and walking out to examine the wet stains.

Shirley was feeling the need to escape and her spirits called for Juliet to be alive and save the day. She may have committed a sinful act, but Shirley did whatever it took to bring her family back together again and that makes her a great mom!

In life, be your own judge and jury because no-one else knows what you've been through as much as you.

With time nearly synchronized back to reality, about 3 hours before Shirley's prayer for her daughter, Juliet had made it to Battersea Power Station along the Thames and was only a bloody long stones throw away from the American Embassy.

As her pace slowed to a gentle wave whilst approaching Vauxhall, the scenery was no longer blurred by exciting speed and she could clearly make out a long string of undercover Albanian crooks lining up either side of the river to end her journey with guns clearly in hand.

Juliet only had a cannonball shot of a few hundred yards to land in the weird looking sci-fi embassy, but bullets and knives kill. After everything she'd gone through to escape this could be her final curtain. Juliet felt lonely and afraid but was not prepared to pull the plug on righteousness.

You're not lonely, you're in the process finding yourself and once you do you'll never feel lonely again.

26

Heroes and Villains

FUCK IT SEND, thought Juliet, I'm going down with all guns blazing! She opened fire on the gang who returned the favour by spraying her boat with hundreds of bullets. The vessel began to sink immediately and oil leaked out as well. A few more rogue bullets and Juliet could be engulfed in flames. She felt timorous and couldn't decide what to do, but the rising water was rapidly forcing her hand. It all happened so quickly. Perhaps bravery is for fools she thought and it's not over until the fat lady sings, weirdly entered her mind too.

You're going to live a long time with yourself so it's best you learn how your mind works.

The criminals were shooting from both sides of the river, accidentally maiming a few tourists and their own people in the crossfire. London was on red alert! Juliet lay down in the flooding river water to avoid hull penetrating bullets and looked like Ophelia. She felt desperate and doomed. Where the hell were London's anti-terrorist units, fretted Juliet. A constricting pain went across her chest in panic as Juliet honestly thought she was going to die just as the cavalry finally arrived in the nick of time!

A few hundred armed US troops totally surrounded their embassy in routine defence protocol and a whole platoon headed straight towards the shooting with WW2 bravery. The Albanian gangsters were swamped by professional soldiers and marksmen on buildings already picking off the shooters the other side of the Thames. It was one hell of a standoff!

Hundreds of guns cracked into chilling air like the London Eye New Year's Eve fireworks and in just over 4 minutes, forty nine Albanian men were shot dead or mortally wounded. Despite heavy injuries, thankfully not one American lost their life.

The Albanian godfather Luan was on the other side in Pimlico Gardens and mortally bitter with his loses. As Juliet dived into the water holding Dali's painting and swam towards her fellow Americans cheering her on, Luan fired a bazooka missile at the boat and an oil fire spread across the river forcing her underwater.

A few brave soldiers immediately dived in to save Juliet as Luan reloaded, but he was too bold standing exposed on the river's edge and got a infrared marksman's bullet in the head for his troubles. The rest of his gang dispersed without a second thought.

Juliet passed out and started to sink, but the super fit swimmers were very eager to win a medal for bravery in the line of fire. Both soldiers dived down and pulled her to the surface still holding the art, crawling into military floodlights. The youngest soldier didn't care what was in her hand because life is more important than anything, so he pulled the art away and let the timeless masterpiece slowly sink like forgotten dreams.

They swam Juliet to safety where a handful of GI's lifted the unconscious woman up onto dry land. Her chief rescuer with medical training pushed everyone aside and started to give Juliet mouth-to-mouth. She eventually revived by vomiting in his mouth and bizarrely he seemed very happy about that. Their eyes met and god was he handsome thought Juliet – like James Dean.

"Take me to your leader," she joked to the dude and he carried her all the way to the US Embassy medical room before she was re-clothed and arrested on suspicion of terrorism.

Once the American's got Juliet's story and realised it was all a silly misunderstanding, they informed the UK Government what happened, who went straight into default mode and informed the public it was another terrorist attack, but from Iran this time.

No-one believed their lies anyway after the Weapons of Mass Destruction bullshit. They also forgot to mention Juliet's attackers were helped by some corrupt police in tracking her down the Thames. What they did focus on though were the efficient police divers who thankfully recovered Dali's oil painting from the riverbed. There was a peewee bit of damage, but nothing a hairdryer, a paint roller and a few spray cans couldn't restore. That saved the UK specialist unit's mass embarrassment of being beaten up by US forces when they tried to break through the Embassy perimeter.

You're probably not aware of it but somewhere out there lots of total strangers are inspired by your good deeds and achievements, so don't give up.

Anyway, the long and short of it was that Juliet was a massive hero who had not only stood up to a huge violent drug syndicate, but most impressively killed

America's number one fugitive (wrongly assumed) as well as saving the Metamorphosis of Narcissus. A very productive day's work thought Juliet, akin to spending a full day listening to momma screeching out opera like a knife and fork rubbing each other up the wrong way.

The American papers were already writing up her exceptional escapades of how America saved Britain again for the morning papers. To rub it in, the English Prime Minister had to attend a photo shoot the next day receiving the stolen painting outside the American Embassy where UK anti-terrorists squads embarrassingly turned up 20 minutes after the battle because they knew there was no active terrorism anywhere. It's just a hoax to scare people into doing what they are told and to pass unfair laws behind the scenes.

People and organizations who claim victimization are usually the same ones trying to take you over.

Juliet's newfound stardom pretty much gave her a free pass to recover Flynn and make safe distance from crime riddled London. Cities slowly kill people with loneliness and fear.

The great news that Flynn was alive felt euphoric, only to be told he's in a coma was deflating to say the least. After some legal loose ends were quickly tied-up, an Embassy driver escorted Juliet with two armed guards to the hospital. America looks after its bona fide citizens abroad. One of the soldiers was the handsome hero who saved her, called **MASON**. She thanked him with a lip kiss and a wink before getting out of the vehicle, but her heart lay with Flynn who was presently being blown by her own mother back in real time. Juliet eventually located her mother's ward and asked a passing nurse for directions who was storming towards the exit holding a gown for evidence.

"Could you direct me towards Mr. O'Connell's bed please? The American detective in a coma," asked Juliet depressingly.

"He's not in a coma anymore madam. Wide awake and resting. Some strange goings on with that woman for definite," said Sister Coombes looking huffed and puffed.

Juliet instantly saw the face of someone who'd just met her mother and walked towards his room with urgency, forgetting to say thanks. "Bloody Americans, think they own the world," she said to the soldiers guarding the ward exit staring them right out with penetrating toxicity.

"We do," said GI Mason casually and the sister walked away in a very angry strop.

At the main desk, nurses were running around frantically and Juliet asked what was wrong before asking for her needs. She was nice like that.

"Everyone's looking for an escaped mental patient who's threatened to kill herself. Apparently she's been here, saying she's gonna jump off the roof or something," explained the receptionist. "It's probably just one of the cleaners complaining about low pay again, ha." On seeing Juliet's disapproving expression she added with monotone expression, "Suicide is a serious business though and this hospital will do everything within its legal powers to prevent the loss of life. Can I help you at all?"

"I once felt suicidal after a boyfriend dumped me," said Juliet.

"Yeah, same here. Men are bastards," she explained.

"Not all men. Some are kind and handsome as hell," expressed Juliet with va-va-voom.

"Too true, there's a dashing American chap in that room there. Shame he's awake now because we loved having a sneak peek at his…" Juliet gave her another look and then the receptionist twigged she was the wife or girlfriend. "Sorry, it's that room there madam," she said pointing.

"Thanks for your help," said Juliet sarcastically.

On the way up in the lift, Juliet and the soldiers shared the claustrophobic space with a distressed looking young woman. She asked her if she was okay but got no reply and had bigger fish to fry.

Juliet guessed that was the patient they were all looking for. As desperately as she wanted to hold Flynn forever, she was an empath and couldn't in all good conscience leave a disturbed woman's life to the jaws of fate. Sometimes you have to just pull fate out of the way and say, I'm the fucking boss not you! So Juliet stormed into Flynn's room with urgency and Shirley panicked thinking perhaps the nurse had divulged how Flynn was revived. Rushing up to her lover who tried to get up but was too weak, Juliet hugged and kissed Flynn lots and lots until he just wanted some breathing space. You can't rush love. Kisses were bouncing off the ceiling and Shirley got a bit jealous, wishing she had such love with a handsome soul mate.

Juliet finally came up for air and said, "Hello mother!"
"Juliet! Why didn't you call to say you were alive! My goodness, I was worried sick! Didn't know what to do with myself," frantically wailed Shirley. Flynn just gave her a funny look.
"Listen guys, this is going to sound a little rude but I need to do something urgently!" announced Juliet who then grabbed Shirley's phone, started to walk out and turned to say, "Yes Flynn I will marry you. I'll be back!"
"Juliet! Don't be so rude!" shouted Shirley, but Juliet was long gone.

Juliet flew out of the hospital wing like a seagull who'd spotted food, keen as mustard to save the young suicidal woman. It was now past midnight and she was obviously exhausted, but this was Juliet's calling. She was once suicidal herself at a similar age and somebody talked her out of taking her own life for which Juliet was eternally grateful. Sometimes all you need is just to talk to someone who genuinely cares.

The soldiers ran after her in support, making a split decision to go with the flow and not question the hero of the day. They had her back. Bounding up the emergency escape stairs to the top, Juliet came face-to-face with five hospital security guards, blocking the roof exit and setting up uncomfortably bright roof lighting. There's nothing quite like shining powerful lights in a petrified person's face to prevent them from killing themselves.

"Sorry madam, no access to the roof. There's an emergency situation. We're waiting for the psychiatric team…" explained the security manager.

"Yes, yes I know," interrupted Juliet, "I'm here to talk her down. I'm the doctor."

"Oh okay, she's over there on the ledge. Good luck. Rather you than me. Do you want to take this Mars Bar with you?" asked the obese staff member offering a mini bar of chocolate to Juliet from the large stash of gluttony in his pocket.

Juliet just sighed and said, "No, I think I'll just get on with helping the suicidal woman over there as soon as possible please."

"It's just they say chocolate is good for depression," continued **TOMMY**.

"I think she needs more than a small chocolate treat dude," said Juliet losing her cool a bit.

"Get out the fucking way you fat cunt!" said Tommy's mate and the other lads laughed out loud.

Mental illness frequently goes up and down, so when people see you're having a good day they tend to discredit your illness, which ironically can encourage further mental suffering.

As Juliet stepped onto the flat roof, the real doctor team responsible for the woman's fragile mental health came wheezing up the stairs. Chief Psychologist **DOCTOR JULIAN SHEINK** was absolutely useless at his job. He'd gone through the middleclass academic essay writing degree conveyor belt, costing his mommy and daddy big money, and knew absolutely nothing about practical psychology when he walked into the top position through nepotism.

Sheink's answer to mental health was to drug people who didn't respond well to a mainstream therapy that doesn't work, therefore making people more ill than when admitted. He didn't care because he had a big house and a big bank balance, and rarely even apathetically asked his patients how they were feeling. But now that his reputation and career was at stake, he suddenly cared enormously.

None of the greatest minds I've ever encountered have any qualifications at all. Some of the weakest, most unoriginal thinkers I've ever met have degrees or PhDs. Academia doesn't make you smart. Fact. It means you're privileged, that's all.

Coming up behind Juliet on the nighttime floodlit roof, Dr. Sheink insensitively shouted to Juliet, "Who on Earth are you!? You're not on my team!"

The suicidal woman was standing right on the corner ledge of the flat roof many stories up and seemed desperately alarmed by his grandiloquent shouting. Juliet could see her recoil from his presence and spotted the mark of evil straight away. The girl glared at Juliet with a look which, please save me from him. All kinds of thoughts were rushing through Juliet's mind. Maybe he was sexually abusing her, wondered Juliet.

What was obvious though was that the suicidal girl in her early twenties, **ABIGAIL**, definitely felt trapped and really wanted Dr. Sheink and his team to go. Juliet made a snap decision to fuck the rules and save a hurt soul in danger.

As the hospital security took Juliet by the arm and began wrenching her away on Sheink's instructions, she pulled herself towards Mason and said, "Stop them. I can save her. Please."

Mason and his army buddy looked at each other believing it could cost them their career, and then threw the men off Juliet and aimed their guns at everyone.

"What are you going to do, shoot a well respected doctor!!" screamed Sheink like a little girl, not even thinking of the others.

"Yes, precisely, right between those beady eyes if you don't get off this roof now," said Mason with calm determination.

Sheink could tell he meant it and as him and his team made their way back to the roof exit door he pathetically shouted, "You'll hang for this!"

"Sir, they don't do hanging anymore," explained Sheink's lickspittle assistant, for which she received a right royal stare.

Mason turned around to his army bud and said in a team building voice, "Where we stand, this is American soil," and they both hi-fived each other just like in the well used Top Gun gif.

During the squabbling, Juliet told Abigail she was going to get her out of here and it would all be okay. She really had a good way with people. Abigail believed her because Juliet had dragon integrity in her eyes. She was still on a high from escaping the Albanians and also for being told she will be gifted a key to the City of London for recovering the treasured painting, so naturally Juliet felt invisible.

Multiple floors below, crowds were gathering as fast as flashing emergency lights. Dark sky was filled with shadows of days to come. The media had turned up and Juliet had already been working on a plan using Shirley's phone to call for any of her Twitter Superman or Batman followers around London to assist. Juliet thought she'd have to download the app, but unbeknown Shirley had already opened a Twitter account 2 months ago. It

371

seems mom Shirley had been flirting with loads of caddish young men on Twitter using pictures of herself 30 years ago. Some of the sexual DMs Juliet later unveiled were way too traumatic for her eyes. She never knew mom could be such a goer. Shirley had even hooked up with her local handyman's son and his friends for a gangbang. However, when they saw how old she was in real life they laughed her out of the park after all getting sucked-off first. Shirley had such a cheeky grin on her face for the rest of the day she felt thirty years younger anyway. Whatever works for you works.

Anyway, Juliet begged her Twitter pals to find anyone in London who owned a bouncy castle business to go to the hospital and rig it up under the jumper by the large crowds. 'Twitter, do you thing!' were her final words and it wasn't long before a good bloke named **ROB** a few miles away headed their way with his inflatable novelty castle.

Just before this major result, in the middle of all the commotion and extremely helpful tweepz doing their best to save a suicidal lady, it was Twitter, so obviously some stupid reply guy popped up at the most inappropriate of moments, said he'd DMed Juliet some useful info', but messaged a picture of his mushroom shaped cock instead. Say it with flowers, not a dic pic.

With her plan in momentum, Juliet now faced a suicidal girl on the corner of a high building. All she knew for sure about her condition is that the woman desperately wanted to escape the mental health wing and possibly end her life.

Abigail looked fragile, innocent, intelligent and most of all tired as hell. She had dark insomnia rings around her eyes and a defeated tone to her voice. Juliet could tell she was not ever going to get her down those stairs again unless rhino darted. That was obviously set in Abigail's concrete mind. When the mind disintegrates on itself, it focuses more and more on detail until death seems like the only way out of mental tyranny.

Suicide has to be the saddest of events ever. Someone was gifted a life and they found society so awful they didn't want to live anymore. So many failed suicide victims regret their attempt to end their life and now live happy lives. If you ever feel suicidal, call for an ambulance.

"Don't come any closer or I'll jump!" warned Abigail as Juliet tried to slowly edge her way forward. She told her soldiers to go away and stop anyone from coming up the stairs. Armed police anti-terrorism units were only 3 minutes away, determined not to fuck-up with lateness this time.
"You don't want to do this. What do you want?" asked Juliet.
"I want to fucking end this… this shit, this pain, all the bullshit this world has become! It stinks like garbage in my mind!" cried out a frustrated young

woman wondering why the world is full of cunts and scum running everything.

"You're right, the world is full of shit people doing shit things all day long. Nasty humans are destroying the world, but some of us are trying to save the beautiful lakes, the trees and birds singing a different song of eternity," replied Juliet. This seriously resonated with Abigail who wanted to hear more hope and happiness. Juliet was connecting. "I'm Juliet. What's your name?" she said moving a few slow steps closer.

"Abigail, my name is Abigail not that they care down there you're just a number in their money making game," she said with speedy bitterness.

"We are all just units to the billionaire's crazy ambitions," explained Juliet trying to echo the woman's words. It was working. Abigail hadn't had anyone agree with her philosophy for what felt like eons. Juliet was a smart cookie and so was Abigail who just wanted to be understood.

"Then why do they do it knowing everyone doesn't have to be an economic slave; its relentless, unforgiving, fucked-up?" stressed Abigail.

"Because they don't care and because they are unloved sociopaths who crave power above kindness," answered Juliet, now really resonating with Abigail. Then Juliet said a cool tweet she posted before her troubles began: "The best superpower you can exercise is kindness." Abigail was very impressed and edging towards Juliet's light.

Juliet was talking Abigail's clever language. Lots of people are mentally ill simply because society won't recognize their talents and special abilities. Abigail carefully shuffled around to face Juliet as Juliet bravely stepped up onto the two foot wide paving stone ledge to hold her hand.

"Oh God, I really don't like heights," gasped Juliet as she looked down to hundreds of waving mobile phone torches. She noticed that Twitter hero Rob 'the knob' had made it on time and had fully inflated his novelty cock castle below as the police gained control of the crowds.

"It's OK. I've been up here many times before without them even noticing I was missing," reassured Abigail wondering why Juliet would risk her life for her. "Why do you care? Why are you here?" asked Abigail.

"I don't know really. I just knew I had to come," said Juliet looking unsteady and anxious, and exuding the perfume of truth. One very strong puff of wind and they'd both go over the edge.

"You don't have to help me."

"I know," replied Juliet.

"I'm not going back to my room," Abigail insisted.

"Then don't. Stay with me," reassured Juliet.

Why not give out kindness everywhere you go just because.
You may even receive a gift of love back just when you need it.

375

Just as Juliet worked wonders on a heavily vexed mind, most inconveniently, shooting began on the stairwell. Armed police were steadily working their way up the stairs with bulletproof shields and gasmasks after firing tear gas at the American soldiers. The special transatlantic Anglo-American relationship was having yet another blip.

Mason's mate **BENICIO** took a bullet in his leg as they exited onto the roof for fresh air. Mason had only fired a few warning shots and the UK cops retaliated with a shoot-to-kill policy. The duo were heavily outnumbered and out-gunned, yet unprepared to surrender! It was Pearl Harbour odds all over again but in Britain and this time with the advantage of being in a hospital. Their orders were to protect Juliet from terrorists (aka drug dealers) and neither one expected it to be trigger happy UK swat teams.

"We're on the same side you dumb fucks!" shouted down Mason who was answered with some more friendly fire. He barricaded the door with his gun now out of ammo and dragged his buddy over to Juliet apologising and taking life way too seriously, "We can't hold out any longer!"
"Let's chill the fuck out! This isn't worth dying over is it!?" shouted Juliet with a real sense of urgency. "Look down there."
"What the fuck's that!" asked Mason.
"It's obviously an evil witches castle with an inflatable dick as the drawbridge," clarified Juliet.

"Fucking hell!" exclaimed Mason who then picked up his injured team member and threw him over the edge without consultation. They all watched Benicio scream his way to the bottom with an elongated FUUUCK YOOOOU sound, landing safely. Mason then stepped up and said, "Women and children first," holding his hand out to chuck Juliet off first.

Juliet was kinda tiring of his antiquated chivalry, so pushed him off. He landed a bit funny like, but was okay bouncing into the arms of arresting police. "At least we know it works now," joked Juliet to Abigail as the police up top blew the door off with explosives.

The fake news later said that three foreign terrorists from Lebanon took a mental patient hostage, then fired upon authorities before jumping off a roof in a failed suicide bomb attack on British civilians.

"Put the girl down and step away from the edge!" shouted the hostage negotiation team leader.

WTF thought Juliet; Abigail isn't a gun. These guys were so pumped up they didn't have a fucking clue what they were going on about. "Come on, let's jump onto the massive dick down below," said Juliet to Abigail with a smile.

Abigail laughed and said, "Let's." It was the first real laugh she'd had in how many months, she couldn't remember. They dived down holding hands and landed straight onto the bell end of the inflatable knob. It was a perfect landing. Juliet even found time for a performers bow to a cheering audience. Empaths never give up.

Don't ever feel guilty if people don't get your keen insight into others. Being empathetic, sympathetic, insightful, even clairvoyant at times is full credit to your intelligence and understanding of the world which you've put a lot of thought into achieving. Don't hide; own it.

27

Empaths in Psychiatry

Both Juliet and Abigail were immediately handcuffed and incarcerated. The stars were alight now and it looked like a sky full of sheriff's badges. Juliet was now all alone again and waiting for a lawyer in the early hours.

On the way to the police station she had a brief few minutes with Abigail in the back of a police carrier where Abigail begged Juliet to save her from Dr. Sheink's madness:

"Please Juliet there's no time to say everything. That spurious doctor on the roof Sheink is insane!" blurted out Abigail at hummingbird pace.

Juliet was a very open-minded person and had witnessed how controlling doctor Sheink tried to be on the roof, but it was hard to accept he could be insane, especially coming from a suicidal woman who'd rather jump off a roof than just walk down the stairs.

The test of you being open-minded is listening to diametrical opinions without feeling any hate.

"You've got to believe me Juliet… at least listen," begged Abigail seeing some reticence in Juliet's green cloud eyes.
"I'm listening. Tell me everything," reassured Juliet, thinking that listening couldn't hurt a thing. Plus sometimes, crazy people are the most sane ones out there.
Abigail spoke at high speed more like she'd been released from her shackles than a crazed, overthinking mind – which she possessed too, explaining without pause, "Sheink is part of an underground organisation to control the masses'

minds. He's using patients like lab rats or monsters like the Angel of Death did in the war. We're free to experiment on and have no rights and as soon as we escape we're dragged back in for punishment, or 'conditioning' as he calls it. Some of the women have even been raped, I've been tortured and drugged more times than you've had boyfriends…

"I don't know, I've had quite a few," interjected Juliet trying to lighten the mood.

Abigail ignored her and carried on her rant explaining, "Sheink works for the government as part of a master-plan for one sub-culture to dominate the entire world's electronic devices, media coverage, advertising, computer systems and most of all people! He's basically the star head of the Nine's propaganda machine advising the billionaires how to control the masses with plans to exterminate us all in the bleak future using robots and facial recognition."

"You mean he's like a Terminator?" asked Juliet, just going along with the madness.

"Yes exactly, no not like the machine, more like the hard drive. Sheink is just the pawn; the facilitator of evil. This is what drones are all about, they want to be able to take over opposing countries with the press of a few buttons and then when they've brought us to our knees in poverty we will slowly be starved to death whilst robots do their bidding from the least flooded parts of the world. Climate change gives them excuses to blame their global destruction of nature on natural forces and all of us instead of them. We've got no power, no democrazy..." pumped out Abigail like a loquacious Uzi.

Saying demoCRAZY and not democracy got an automatic interruption from Juliet. She was beginning to think perhaps Abigail was dangerous and needed major psychological attention.

"Why are you in the hospital in the first place? Are you saying they just dragged you off the street and started using you for their plan?" questioned Juliet.

"I got admitted when my elder sister died last year and I couldn't cope with the trauma; had PTSD and a breakdown. I know this doesn't sound..."

"Good?"

"You don't believe me?" asked Abigail.

"I want to... it's a lot to take in. Have you got any proof of these allegations?"

"I've got loads of stories to tell but there isn't time..."

"Any solid proof or evidence against Sheink though?"

"No, but if I had a little help from you I could get it."

"How?" wondered Juliet.

"If somehow you could get into his office he's got a filing cabinet on the right where he keeps a record of his psychological experiments. He does everything by hand because the resistance keep trying to hack him," explained a far-fetched Abigail.

"The resistance?"

"Yes. A group of freedom fighters from Japan who aim to expose the Nine's nasty work and bring down the global masters."

"Shit Abigail. The Nine; The Resistance; Global Masters?," said a pensive Juliet trying to be open-minded. "Okay, let's just say by some miracle I could scoop up some of his patient files, then what good would that do? If they control the media then no-one will ever hear about it," continued Juliet with logic.

"If you get me in that room and out of the hospital I can contact the V Resistance and they know what to do. We can win this war!"

"What war?" fathomed Juliet.

"The cybernetic war coming… it's already started! It's here to destroy our emotions and crush your feelings."

"You mean like automated checkouts and mechanical car washes?"

"Yes, they are the soldiers of the wealthy, soon to be programmed with the Extirpation System leaving only the heartless," continued Abigail who could clearly talk about her fantasy world all day long with real zeal just as the police wagon came to a halt and they were both parted.

As Abigail was escorted down a different gloomy grey corridor, she shouted out, "Juliet, you must save me, please!!! For the sake of humanity and freedom!!"

One of the officers holding her said to his mate, "Juliet, what light through yonder window breaks?"

and they both chuckled. "It's your skull if you keep on shouting" he jokingly threatened Abigail.

"What, like Yorick's head?" his partner jested.

"Good one Steve," said PC plod feeling really chuffed with himself.

One of the worst feelings is being lonely while surrounded by people who don't understand you.

While sitting in her cell after questioning, Juliet couldn't get the horror in Abigail's eyes out of her mind. She had plenty of time to kill waiting for the American Embassy to complete sensitive negotiations with her lawyer Shirley got and the British authorities.

Giving Abigail the benefit of the doubt, Juliet thought, what if she was actually telling the truth? What if Abigail was a prisoner in the hospital with no way to escape and had uncovered some hidden darkness? If Abigail had brought to light something really sinister going on, she would remain locked up to keep her silenced. Or perhaps Abigail was suffering from something like schizophrenia or chronic bouts of manic phantasmagoria?

All that Juliet did know for sure is that an empath can't just let it go. Empaths feel compelled to help often at detriment to themselves. They become targets for narcissists because empaths always want to make the world a better place by not choosing sides.

If you find it hard to make decent friends you're likely a good person who struggles to come to terms with a money orientated, superficial society. Enjoy your own company and appreciate yourself more.

Juliet was exhausted after stuffing her face with about four Ginsters Vegan Moroccan Vegetable Pasties the police provided her starving stomach. She was annoyed they wouldn't get her some bananas. Apparently the police don't believe in fresh fruit preventing crime.

Anyhow, Juliet was released forthwith and the Police Commissioner got a ticking-off from the Mayor of London for putting Britain's hero of the day behind bars. Juliet's heroism was all over the papers and media. They were going bananas for her to give an interview. Agents were even harassing Shirley who had already appeared on TV at the hospital explaining why her good parenting was primarily responsible for her daughter's bravery in murdering America's most wanted fugitive (unconfirmed), rescuing Dali's masterpiece and now saving a suicidal woman from certain death. Shirley calmly explained that she modelled herself on a hybrid of Jane Fonda and Wonder Woman, and some of that must have rubbed off onto Juliet. The hand over forehead emoji was used a lot by every journalist who interviewed Shirley in weeks to come.

Humility is the biggest turnon, especially if the person is truly great.

After a delightful reuniting with mother and cuddling Flynn, Juliet slept in the hospital like a hibernating bumblebee. However, when she woke up her willpower had other ideas to resting. Juliet's inquisitive mind just couldn't forget about Abigail. Had God sent Abigail to her? Was it her duty to at least see that Abigail was in good hands? Was she prepared to break her empathic link to Abigail to give herself a chance to recover? Of course not was the plain and simple answer. Juliet had been brought up by Shirley to always defend women against vindictive men.

Men who only think about women in sexual terms are missing out on a world of creativity and the chance to feel the power of a woman's mature appreciation.

Flynn was up on his feet now and Shirley had big TV plans to show all of her New York socialites how marvellous she was. Mommy couldn't wait to ride off the media wave of Juliet's phenomenal success. Juliet even received a phone call from Prime Minister Boris the backtracking buffoon, congratulating her and offering any assistance she may need, leaving his contact number. He liked attractive blondes.

Juliet was certainly the global woman of the hour. Agents, photographers and all sorts of leeches were lining the streets waiting to sign her up. And mommy too was being sickly sweet and attentive to her superstar daughter – now apparently her favourite daughter according to the papers. Juliet liked the idea of fame for a while, but not at the expense of her feelings, so first there would be a big wedding.

Yeah sex is sex, but have you ever looked deep into their eyes and felt at one with the universe?

28

The Big Day

Mother Shirley was absolutely delighted on the great matrimonial news. Everyone loves a good wedding apart from grumpy sods and bitter loners. The greatest news for many was the wedding was to be streamed live on Twitter. Juliet didn't want her favourite Twitter nuggets to miss out on the grand show, plus $1 million from a huge news network for exclusive broadcasting rights helped secure her mind.

Twitter is one big audition show for a low budget film that will never be made.

Divorced from the wedding, Juliet's conscience had one final mission to accomplish before leaving London. In her deep sleep last night a vision of an angel came to her, awakening a compunction and obligation to use her special day to save Abigail. Despite the gobbledegook coming out of Abigail's mouth, something untoward was clearly happening to her and Juliet couldn't leave an abused woman defenceless. Empaths never abandon their feelings.

Dr. Sheink's outrageous rooftop behaviour made Juliet very suspicious and angry. He needed salt rubbed in somewhere sore. Therefore, upon Juliet's request, the wedding was to held in the mental health hospital's psychiatric wing in just 2 days to get to the bottom of this newfound mystery.

The worst evil is always found in the most innocent of places and vulnerable situations.

'I'll be the laughing stock of the world if you get married in a loony bin,' stressed Shirley earlier in the morning with inadequate political correctness. Flynn also objected until he heard about Juliet's Christian motivation. He was so overwhelmed with her force and goodwill he couldn't be more in love. In fact, what Flynn didn't love about Juliet could be written on a small matchbox with a thick black marker. Consequently, he was also very much up for saving Abigail and giving the patients a real psychological lift too.

The prestigious wedding would be on the Friday and the Prime Minister saw to it that Juliet got her wish despite Dr. Sheink's vehement objections. PM Boris won the UK general election just last week in a landslide victory despite giving no guarantees the Conservatives would honour the referendum result with what democracy called for. The PM was desperate to get in America's good books because he had big privatisation plans. Selling your country's public assets off can be hard and hungry work.

Doctor Julian Sheink was livid he'd been overruled, but had no choice to obey the hospital administrator and board members way above his pay grade. Juliet now had friends in high places and Sheink was just a minion in the Sand People's clan Abigail spoke about.

Flynn was discharged from hospital that afternoon and Juliet's family were offered the stunning Dome Suite at the Hotel Café Royal with compliments of the American Embassy who'd also arranged the whole wedding for them both at extremely short notice. Juliet didn't even have to leave the hotel to shop for a dress or shoes because top designers like Vera Wang and Jenny Packham took over the foyer downstairs desperately hoping she would pick their design for worldwide publicity.

Turning the mental health wing of a hospital into a beautiful wedding location at extremely short notice was not so easily accomplished however, but was being arranged at considerable cost by over 300 embassy staff and roped in UK civil servants. More pertinently, Juliet expressly asked that the patients be an integral part of the ceremony so as not to feel left out. The correct attire needed to be arranged for them too which was not so easy because they had a mind of their own.

The biggest news though was that Abigail no longer had to be rescued because Juliet called in all the special political favours offered which got Abigail her release papers sorted out for after the wedding on the condition she stays with her elder sister in London with frequent assessments. Sheink was worried sick as he should be because the secondary mission now was to expose his malpractice.

After that privilege bestowed, it was strongly suggested to Juliet her *favours* had reached their political limits which was fine because all Juliet, Flynn and Abigail had to do now was steal Sheink's medical files to find out the whole truth and nothing but the truth so help them God.

Since joining Twitter, random people have married and divorced you without you even realising.

Anyhow, the big day was tomorrow and Juliet was duly excited. Juliet and Flynn agreed to defy tradition by sharing a bed the night before the ceremony. Most of their love making took place outside on the majestic copper dome balcony. Post passion the happy couple cuddled for hours sipping at fine wines in warm woollen blankets and soaking up London's finest nighttime views.

From Lower Regent Street they could see a luminous Big Ben and the light of St. Paul's Cathedral. And inside Flynn couldn't stop pissing about with the super cool multicoloured interior party light settings which was the only thing not perfect about the evening. London's rooftops are made for stories and adventures tap-dancing colourful ideas across slate grey tiles. As midnight chimed, the tulip lovers drew their petal sheets across into a faithful Friday.

Juliet never lived a fast life but was always in the fast lane. Before she even had time to sip a smooth coffee it was afternoon and a chauffeur driven Vintage Rolls Royce was picking her up with Shirley inside to make her more nervous.

Flynn left 4 hours earlier with a special mission to buy a ring. He spent 1-hour finding the perfect rock in Hatton Garden, then a further 2 hours locating and persuading Shirley to lend him the exorbitant sum of money to pay for it. Eventually, Shirley agreed to pay for the iceberg diamond outright on the condition no-one ever found out about how he awoke from a coma.

Feeling a little bitter she was made to feel embarrassed for saving Flynn's life, Shirley even made him write a quick note and sign it for legal reasons. Shirley had become fed-up getting blackmailed for her blowjob exploits over the years and was quite the little litigator on the quiet.

Anyway, by the time Flynn finally bought the blockbuster diamond and got dressed, he only barely made it to the church setting (mental health hospital) before Juliet arrived looking as holy and beautiful as any angel, wearing a Reem Acra princess bridal gown. Flynn was knocked out and his last minute best woman, Abigail, steadied his metal.

"You really love Juliet don't you?" told Abigail.
"I do, from the first time I ever met her. She's a phenomenal woman," replied Flynn. Abigail's eyes watered, wishing somebody would once love her like that.

The hospital layout was surprisingly beautiful and the wedding planners were justifiably proud receiving much pre-emptive praise. All the way to the entrance of the psychiatric wing, the patients in fine attire scattered thousands of pink and white rose petals over Juliet and Shirley holding her hand. A couple of them went a bit crazy with the flora throwing and Shirley got a right mouthful, but the greatest surprise were deft piano keys echoing down the corridors, played by a former renowned concert pianist who became too creative and snapped one ugly day. Life is full of unpleasant and pleasant surprises, and all you can do is make sure you're ready for the good times.

Most of Flynn's family made it to the wedding which meant a great deal to him, especially seeing lots of long lost distant relative's faces from Ireland – some of whom he'd never met before. This was truly a special occasion for him. Juliet had a good showing too. There was no way auntie Pauline and all of her NY family would miss this celebrity bash talked about for years to come. Later in the day sister Pauline ended up paying for the painfully expensive ring after asking Shirley why so strained looking.

The vicar was well respected for sounding and being boring, so he was perfect. The ceremony and vows went smoothly apart from the odd person being removed for antisocial behaviour and as always the highlight was the kiss at the end which Flynn delivered with passion to rapturous applause.

All of the family guests now congregated outside for wedding photos before heading towards location two, the glamorous Kimpton Fitzroy Hotel, for speeches, a banquet and lots of charged reception drinks. But first the newlyweds had to sign their marriage certificate and with no disrespect to her new husband or eternal love, this was the moment Juliet had been waiting for to frisk Sheink's office for incriminating evidence. Juliet asked Julian Sheink personally if she could take a 10 minute breather in his office to freshen up before the photoshoot. He seemed so calm and smug about her using his private office, Juliet knew something was off.

Inside the clammy affair, Sheink's room echoed of cream walled suspicion. The filing cabinets were unlocked and mostly empty. He'd cleaned everything out 2 days ago in the early hours and took it home. However, Juliet saw this as good news. Not only did Abigail know where Sheink lived – having rifled through his desk many times – but the blatant removal of information was proof enough to her that something major was awry.

Sheink was no good at psychology. One minute he was hopping mad his shrink world was being compromised and the next he seemed relaxed about having his personal office open for inspection. The treatment did not fit the disorder. Sheink was *definitely* up to no good. He was a toxic cocktail of vitriolic drives.

It's hard to repel toxic people who are determined to give you a dose of their negativity. They look for sympathy and to spread hate. The very best defence against toxicity is to entirely focus on your positive goals and to not get drawn into their unhappy world.

Nevertheless, the wedding ceremony was a raging success despite the massive fracas at the end when Juliet threw the bouquet of flowers at a mixed group of patients suffering from abandonment and domestic abuse issues.

The guests moved on and finally it was speech time in the Kimpton Fitzroy ballroom. Many famous faces had delivered speeches in the luxuriant ballroom; part of a new renovation costing a mere $113 million and now it was Flynn and best woman Abigail's turn to impress prestigious guests!

Abigail had gained her freedom at last after enduring many months of Dr. Julian Sheink playing god with her life until the real God reversed his fortunes. That's what her sister **NATASHA** believed anyway. Abigail was as equally ecstatic as vengeful and in mental disarray with the excitement of the day. Therefore she wasn't in a great frame of mind to make a speech; feeling anxious and somewhat discombobulated. In spite of this Abigail was a survivor who wouldn't let a great opportunity to speak the truth to the world go unsung.

After an edgy start to her speech calling everyone, "My lords, ladies, gentlemen and other posh tarts with more money than sense," which Juliet found hilarious, things went from bad to worse when Abigail caught a beam of light in her eye, triggering a flashback to Sheink's interviews – more like interrogations.

She mumbled on for approximately 3 minutes about clandestine world orders, ending with, "I just don't know anymore, thank you Juliet for everything I will never forget," until Juliet put an arm around her, sat her down and poured Abigail some water after passing the microphone to Flynn with the look.

Flynn was still feeling bad about not saving Juliet at the art gallery, despite heroic efforts, but this was one situation he could and must save, delivering a humble and loving toast to life and his wife:

"Before I tell you why I truly love Juliet," announced Flynn with clarity and confidence, looking directly at the guests and then Juliet, "I would first like to say a few words about my best woman Abigail who's had a very tough time recently."

This was the Flynn that Juliet loved: a decent man with film star looks who was reliable. She nodded to him to continue. For all her fantasy, Juliet loved realism best.

Flynn continued, "It's not easy facing your fears, but Abigail here has done so and much more than you know." Abigail smiled. "I learned through my job at least 1 in 4 of us suffer from mental illness, yet for some crazy reason it's often kept hidden from our society we all make up.

"Many people live with daily emotional pain in total secret because they're afraid of being judged and this isn't good enough." A number of people clapped. "The irony being many of us are hiding an illness from other people with a similar illness! That's the real madness.

"It's time to end the stigma surrounding mental illness and bring it out into the open so people can find the support and kindred friendships they need to help them through difficult times. Stigma is just a lack of knowledge and ignorance combined. Hands up who has mental health issues," Flynn asked everyone in a no bullshit cop's way.

His sole intention was to make Abigail feel worth something after her traumatic calvary and it worked brilliantly. Flynn put his hand up first, followed by Abigail, then Juliet and to their astonishment nearly half of the 206 guests raised their hands like bidders at a charity auction for kids with cancer.

Flynn then turn to Abigail and said, "See, you are among friends." Abigail started to cry she was so happy and Juliet hugged her again. Juliet was so impressed with Flynn's impromptu digression, she knew she'd made the right choice picking a man who will support her beliefs with action, not cheap talk or false promises. The audience loved his sincerity too, empathising with similar problems they once had, or experienced now, on all different scales, levels and spectrums.

The most important factor for mental health sufferers is to believe you can get better once you find the knowledge to recover and rebuild your mind.

Dreadful experiences and common nightmares unite people. Flynn continued to wow people with an edited version of how he crossed paths with Juliet and fell in love. The events and aftermath of their fortuitous meeting was too good material to skip. He had the crowd in the palm of his hands, especially after saying, 'The only winners in life are people who are loved,' so it was the perfect moment to high-five everyone with another poem he'd spent ages writing to woo Juliet since they first met. Flynn wasn't a natural wordsmith, rather a grafting amateur, but he wrote for relaxation and from the heart:

Pretty little button-sized fairy,
Wings open to a prevailing wind,
Umbrellas full out, exposing love's fear,
Parachuting into my lonely beer.

A loving pool of hops,
Echoing talk to clear rooftops,
I hear hummingbird lemon zest,
Flying absurd words and fizzy jest.

Clouds absorb your distilling love,
Raining happiness in my heart,
Pitter-patter Mozart from heavens above,

Key tapped air feelings to jump-start.

With you I can be myself ale free,
The greatest gift ever infused on me.
Even when you are beyond touch,
My stout mind desires you very much.

"Someone needs a beer then," joked Juliet, partially
disappointed Flynn's love for her had been
fermented in beer metaphors, but God loves a trier.

The most beautiful scene to see is a sweet old couple whose
marriage lasted forever on love.

29

Farewell Sociopaths and Sinners

It's too easy to go from love to hate and hate to love when the orchestra is evil. Abigail was a lover who got hurt badly and ended up as a pawn in some crazy psychological game. She was as mad as March hare with sly Sheink!

Basically, Abigail volunteered admittance into hospital under the Mental Health Act (1983) and soon discovered this meant being stripped of all her civil rights and dignity. Sheink's psychiatric wing was a dangerous place to be. Sociopaths and sinners could do whatever they wanted to anyone without repercussions. Women became the overwhelming statistical victims.

Don't ever tell a woman who's having a bad day to cheer up. It's like telling an active volcano to keep the noise down.

Apart from a few incidents of male cleaners brushing up against Abigail and a security man grabbing her left breast when she was restrained for complaining about the perverts, Abigail's entire anger focused on Dr. Sheink. The buck stopped with Sheink who routinely ignored many female patients being sexually assaulted, which he officially termed, 'difficulties working with staff and figures of authority.'

Sheink was not a popular man even with his own team, not only because of the unprofessional conduct, but mainly for the same objections Abigail had too; his deceitful nature hiding a sinister work agenda. Dr. Sheink's staff were sick to the teeth having no independent authority to take responsibility for a patient's future. He was a classic control freak who made people's lives worse, not better. Sheink had zero empathy and gave patients no hope, nor optimism. Sufferers came to him for help in all kinds of desperate, vulnerable and disturbed emotional states, only to end up confronting the numb hand of injustice.

Only from experiencing emotional darkness can you truly appreciate the light of days to come.

It was now 9:18pm and as the white wedding party rocketed, Abigail and sister Natasha were dressed in guerrilla black, not to mourn, but to burgle. The two vengeful sisters in arms sat in a car opposite Sheink's imposing Knightsbridge residency until watching him and his family go out for dinner. It was obviously way too late for children to eat but everything revolved around Sheink's schedule, so the kids had to sleep awhile before he returned from work to look lively and hungry for daddy's grand return. Psychos, intellectual narcissists and professional clowns always think their lives and time are more important than anyone else's.

The rebellious sisters had never burgled a property before and were immediately baffled by how to break through a solid oak front door. Natasha put a screwdriver in the lock and pulled really hard. It snapped and stuck in the lock. Buggered. "This doesn't happen in the movies," joked Abigail.

Eventually they managed to scramble over a number of high fences into Sheink's back garden and used a spade in his shed to prize out a window from its frame by leaning both their bodies on it.

The double glazing unit levered out and popped like a broken light bulb when the air vacuum cracked open. An elderly neighbour heard the snap but was too engrossed in a rerun of Inspector Morse dying on TV to bother moving. "What a great series of detective dramas. I shall never forget you John Thaw 'til the day I die," said 76 year old Miriam with a tear in her eye and a lemon cupcake she forgot about stuck to her cashmere cardigan.

Inside Sheink's pseudo palace things were pretty much what one would expect: published psychiatrist with expensive rip-off contemporary leather furniture and enough weird ornaments around to counter his lack of interest in anything but himself.

The original paintings were by named artists too, yet lifeless abstract confusions. The décor was all about show and status, not being comfy in one's home. How could anyone relax on the settee with a real monkey skull on the sideboard nearby and the same monkey's brain in a jar of Formaldehyde in a recessed bookshelf. Difficult not to be creeped out. No surprise Julian Sheink didn't have any real friends. He never texted anyone for a casual chat. The haughty house was a just a business showpiece for trumped-up fake acquaintances.

Friends who never ever message you first. They're not friends really are they?

Rummaging through drawers, untouched bookshelves and cupboards, the two investigators found nothing of interest until they bashed through the inside garage door. Unfortunately it was alarmed, but most serendipitously the files were actually still stacked up on a trolley. Sheink was meticulous, yet lazy.

As the housebreaking sisters opened the garage door and wheeled their treasure to the car, they could hear Sheink shouting out to them from the burglar alarm using his mobile, "I can hear you! Drop everything you have now!! The police are on their way!!!"

The next-door neighbours came out to investigate just as Abigail and Natasha drove away. Sheink was so furious his wife forgot to set the house alarm yet again, he threatened her with a clenched fist gesture in front of some prestigious diners, adding fool to his list of personal attributes.

In defence of his mum, Sheink's rebellious teenage son also added salt to the wound by saying in the most eloquent of voices, "Mother would probably beat your arse in a fight anyway father. Just eat your poached prawns and stop being a dweeb." Mother **HANNAH** laughed and Sheink rubbed his forehead with stress before driving off without his family to check on his precious files. On the frantic drive home, Sheink had the added psychological conflict of believing his kickboxing wife would probably make mincemeat out of him in a real fight. He felt weak and compromised.

Back in Natasha's home, Abigail was sifting through the ghost files like a card dealer on ice. Things soon became better than a big scratch card win. Nearly everything she suspected was happening, was.

There were two sets of files for each patient, like cooked account books. One set held basic information for the public eye and the other much larger files contained details of numerous psychological and chemical tests – all clearly off the record with personal notes jotted down in margins by Sheink.

Throughout an enthusiastic night's reading, Abigail, Natasha and her boyfriend Chillipuss (aka **CHARLES**) fitted the puzzle pieces together using an old fashioned thought process called common sense. Evidence suggested that Sheink worked for an undercover organization called Hiberg who were conducting lab rat experiments on real people throughout the West to perfect the art of mass manipulation, all just for money.

Sheink was simply a small cog in a large unscrupulous machine designed to cattle millions of people's minds into believing any lie they were told, with the express idea of total, unconditional subjugation to global elites. Once this psychological conditioning – blinding you from the truth – had been accomplished, these moguls planned to keep freezing wages until inflation made 99% of society riddled with debt and, in effect, bonded slaves.

The Hiberg Consortium's predominantly male psychologists who publicly ridiculed the Myers Briggs personality profiling (MBTI), privately used the genius test designed by a very inventive American mom and daughter team, as the catalyst and mainframe for categorising and governing us populace, who they offensively referred to as 'the sheep'.

After using his patients to experiment with psychological algorithms, Sheink's little part in the underground world takeover was using Twitter and other social media networks to test his conclusions on a grand scale. That's what some bots and catfish are doing; like a persistent mother-in-law probing your mind.

In brief, this global network of evil psychologists and scientists were tasked with working out effective ways to brainwash, suppress, cajole and coerce all types of people into any form which suited their insatiable, narrow-minded, greedy needs. It was all very frightening, sinister stuff led by a mad scientist called **PROFESSOR ZINKEL**, known for liking young boys with autism.

Hiberg already owned everything in the world apart from one huge obstacle towering above them: CHINA. China was more a giant sequoia lance than a toothpick thorn in their side. The Chinese billionaires and rulers were very savvy. Predicting the inevitable collapse of the Capitalist monetary system which relies on monopolising free trade and running off debt, they began buying up thousands of tons of gold, backing a new cryptocurrency to replace unlimited paper money which has no promissory backup. Therefore, a significant part of Professor Zinkel's iniquitous research was also directed towards eventually using millions of people to overthrow the entire Chinese regime!

In these debt ridden times, what the world could use more than anything else right now is a little bit of kindness from everyone.

There was absolutely no question in Abigail's mind that the Hiberg Consortium needed to chill the fuck out and smoke a nuclear-sized joint. After placing the final corner pieces down, confident she'd made a true picture of Sheink's insidiousness, Abigail immediately called Juliet 19 times to tell her the good news, but selfishly Juliet was enjoying her wedding reception.

The highlight of the wedding party was watching wealthy auntie Pauline being unexpectedly slung over a drunken Irishman's shoulder and spun around on the dance floor. Her private security pinned the idiot down before he could perform an Irish jig on her bum. The different families were not bonding as hoped. Who cares, thought Juliet, this was *her* day and all the love and attention made her feel truly magical.

Anyway, you can have too much of a good thing as they say, so Juliet went to powder her nose for a quiet break. Her face was stiff with laughter and excessive smiling. She sat down on a bog in her beautiful dress, closed the door to the world and became reflective, almost melancholy.

Juliet's thoughts rippled like sand dunes. Isn't life funny, she pondered; the strange sequence of events which led to this day. What is life actually about? Why are we here? Had beauty brought her misery? Juliet did not know the answers but thought it was the continuous wondering and dreaming that really counted. If you don't explore life you won't know anything. What Juliet did know for sure though was that she was lucky to be alive and for that thanked the heavens above.

Her mind drifted towards the clouds as she shed a few tears. She felt her consciousness fly away to see new lands. A baby turtle popped out of pink sand and Juliet coaxed it to the sea with love. Swaying palm trees sheltered the private beech where her thoughts felt free to be themselves. A tropical bird flew by full of colour and life.

Feeling around for her mojo, Juliet found a clump of turtle eggs. She encouraged the little wonders out and they changed into baby crocodiles. One nipped her finger. She didn't care. It was only blood.

Looking out to a light green sea Juliet saw her destiny behind her in the shape of a rainbow tortoiseshell. She felt a sense of belonging, like she'd been there before in a previous life. A coconut fell and cracked open the milk of human kindness as her reverie floated away.

A toilet flushed in the adjacent cubicle and that was the end of her peace and quiet. Juliet quickly fixed her makeup and returned to the celebrations with song and dance until her legs and liver could take no more.

The newlywed's romantic wedding night was far from a blast though. Both Juliet and Flynn passed out shitfaced and were moved into recovery position by Shirley. Scraping themselves out of bed like fried eggs into a meringue clouded morning, the lovers packed up, stole as many towels as possible and then thankfully made Pauline's private jet on time for all the family to return to New York City! Juliet missed home. London had been terrible and terrific rolled into one jam-packed tourist package.

Juliet slept most of the flight and dreamed more of a surreal tropical paradise. By the time they finally made it back to Shirley's house in Brooklyn, the zonked-out and madly in love couple were too preoccupied with each other to notice Arthur Koons' far too subtle conundrum of death threats made with wet leaves on the lawn. He was alive, yet infected and in great pain, vowing vengeance on his nemesis Juliet one day!

Overnight the wind blew Arthur's leafy malice away and the one-handed man couldn't be bothered to honour his hatred anymore. He was a tough devil's spawn with bags full of stolen jewellery and diamonds from the Albanian's safe house. Packing up his evil intentions, Arthur decided to start a new life far away from Western Civilization, which by his reckoning was the root cause of all his malevolence.

Don't be honest with the world because society will punish you. But always make sure you're honest with yourself.

30

The Calling

Mrs. Juliet J. O'Connell-Green woke up at the crack of dawn, drove to her New York, Manhattan apartment and started to box everything up. Mother generously agreed to swap residencies, hoping a large garden would encourage more grandchildren. Plus even more relevantly, now Shirley had tasted fame, her new talent agent suggested a strategic move to Manhattan to develop a TV celebrity career.

Shirley was loving her personal renaissance and regretted every second of getting upset with the divorce which nearly destroyed her. Things just happen. People struggle and don't do their best, failing others. You have to move on slowly until you find a passion for life.

Juliet was happy to see mom with some self-purpose again, but didn't really give a fuck about fame herself. Fame is desired by nearly everyone and cursed by many who have it. You don't become famous unless the people who run the show want you to be anyway. Besides, she had already made a packet from her fifteen minutes and the generous finders fee for saving Dali's masterpiece. All Juliet wanted was a chance to be happy and she was until making the mistake of turning her phone on. An armada of messages needed answering. No they didn't. What they needed is putting in their place. Twitter can wait, thought Juliet, I'm going to spend some quality time reconnecting with nature instead.

Our society has become so mentally unhealthy it makes you forget how truly beautiful nature is.

She opened a window to free her thoughts from the insidious complexion of technology. It was bright and cheerful outside, and New York City seemed quieter than ever before.

Adversity had changed Juliet. She was calmer and more optimistic for sure, seeing a world of possibilities ahead. Peering out across Greenwich Village's green horizon, Juliet tried to fathom the depths of her recent traumas.

Passing clouds distracted her maudlin reflections and she could have sworn one looked just like a white Persian cat that Bagel used to lick anuses with. Anyhow, Juliet was bored packing boxes and dusting. Too much of life is spent moving objects from A to B and then smoking C.

A ghostly swirl of wind caught her attention and static currents ran down Juliet's spine. Shivering, she felt the dark power of her android calling like a slab of chocolate melting neurotransmitters. Her fingers twitched like sausages frying in lard as they reached out to pull the phone towards her orbit.

Briefly catching her reflection in the blank screen, Juliet thought she looked kinda hot and took a spontaneous selfie. A mischievous pause froze time as her mind prepared for an obsessive universe. "Fuck it!" said Juliet with Vodka punch, "Let's see what my favourite Twitter lovelies are up to."

What a crazy world we live in where your social media family can be more supportive than your real-life family.

After half an hour of sorting out Bubbles' emotional misanthropic issues whilst juggling well-wishers, routine death threats and stacks of unsolicited dic pics, Juliet decided to switch off from the matrix and take a relaxing breather outside where sanity is often found. She even left her phone at home.

Oh look, lovely trees, thought Juliet, I'd forgotten about them and birds making nice bird sounds. And a family of grey squirrels performing high wire acts from tree to tree for free. Juliet even spotted retired Mr. Winkleman from a few doors down leaning against ornate railings *actually* talking to real people rather than spying on them from his 'astronomy' telescope. Life felt positive and hopeful.

She strolled down the leaf scattered street with no purpose whatsoever, for once. Juliet had nowhere to go and the time to saunter along anywhere her ballet feet wished. She even winked at Winkleman passing by to give his shrivelled-up old dick some pep. "You look amazing my dear!" he called out to her posterior. Juliet didn't turn around, she just smiled to herself and waved backwards nonchalantly.

What insouciant mischief could I get up to now, wondered Juliet. She was feeling frisky and up for a mini adventure, so veered off the usual, well-trodden blocks to explore new streets and angles.

Her neighbourhood was quite bohemian and artsy. A statue man painted in silver on a street corner waved at Juliet robotically. She saluted him in a friendly way and went in the opposite direction towards more golden times. Some people just don't magnetize well, especially those desperate for attention.

Juliet was really feeling good about herself. She didn't even feel suspicious about feeling great. It was actually happening; her subconscious had no ulterior motive. She was living in the moment without having intelligence trip her up or overthinking impeding her happiness. A striding feel-good factor stretched Juliet's ass-kicking legs out into a modelled walk and the whole world looked at her with admiration!

Being fabulous is thirsty business, so Juliet popped into her local coffee house for an Americano. Urban Pearls used to be her regular caffeine pit stop until mother caused a massive scene about 5 months ago and Juliet had avoided it ever since. Rather than a claustrophobic, chesty vibe like many coffee shops, there was an atmospheric and alive busyness which was welcoming.

"Hi, could I have a regular Americano please?" asked Juliet with a dry tongue. The cakes looked mouth-wateringly scrummy too.
"Wow! Oh sorry, ermm, are you Juliet Jessica Green by any chance?" interrupted an enthusiastic looking barista, pouring no coffee for now, with the manager fixing a beady eye on Juliet.
"Whoops, I take it you remember my ex elderly friend then? Sorry about the other month when she caused that embarrassing scene over what I agreed was an ample whipped cream serving. There absolutely no need for her to smear custard tart all

over your employee's crotch. I fully understand the serious implications and once again apolo…" explained Juliet jumbling away as the manager came to ask her to leave for the second time.

"…I have no idea about that but I bought this earlier today," said the young woman with a big grin, pulling out a copy of Time Magazine with Juliet's picture on the front from when she was dragged out of the Thames. **MANAGER MARGOLA** did a double take from picture to real-life face, smiled at Juliet and then started making her coffee on the house with a free chocolate cookie too.

The headline read 'Brought Back to Life to Save the World of Men!' "Is this you? There's more pictures inside which look just like you. You're the 2019 Person of the Year after Greta Thunberg received millions of complaints for saying if anyone doesn't agree with her they should be put up against a wall and shot. Anyhow, it's you isn't it? Could you sign it please? I would love that thank you Juliet. Can I call you Juliet?" asked an awestruck barista handing the mag to Juliet who took it and couldn't believe her eyes. Some of the customers were eavesdropping and Juliet's name was being passed around like sachets of white sugar.

Juliet had given her agent complete carte blanche to make money from her ordeal with the express condition she doesn't bother her in between their agreed monthly meeting. Juliet genuinely didn't seek fame, but money is always helpful so why not cash in on your courage.

Her cover photo was totally sensational, black and white, and dramatic. One of the soldiers took it from his iPhone and it had become a worldwide symbol of female empowerment.

Juliet was deeply moved, shocked and speechless. She wanted to cry but now had an audience behind her all queuing up for a chat and autograph. All she wanted was a quick coffee and now fame had encircled her. Some people are born great, some people have greatness thrust upon them and others just want to be left the fuck alone to drink their coffee! It was all too much, so Juliet grabbed her takeaway coffee and bolted out across the road into thin air before signing one single autograph.

"What a fucking bitch!!" said the waitress.

"Fame's gone to her head quite clearly," agreed the first customer in line.

"Did she even pay for the coffee?" questioned another.

"No she didn't," answered Margola despite giving it to her for free.

"Bloody thief," said the customer's daughter, "One taste of fame and they think they can do what they like to the ordinary people." She had a common tone to her voice.

"Ordinary! Speak for yourself!" shouted out a comedian and everyone laughed.

"She's trouble. I banned her from coming back here after my son got sexually assaulted..." began Margola and over an hour's worth of malicious gossiping continued. Dirt was already being dug up so everyone could have their pound of flesh.

Meantime, Juliet had partially recovered, bought three copies of Time Magazine and strode the streets reading about how magnificent she was. "I had absolutely no idea how truly fucking brilliant I am!" she maniacally uttered to a passing couple, somewhat flummoxed by the randomness. She gave them a copy and a wink, and walked off chuckling.

"She's a mover and shaker that's for sure," said the man blatantly staring at Juliet's lovely arse moving in perfect equilibrium.

"Yes, a real hero with extraordinary bravery," said his wife looking at the magazine, then looking up and punching her husband in the arm for being a disloyal pervert.

Juliet got carried away. Fame wasn't what she wanted and didn't need the claustrophobia it brings. She dumped the magazines and moved forward with her life, sipping at coffee and dreaming of all the great things she could do with Flynn. Egypt was somewhere she'd never gone which really took her fancy. Or perhaps Croatia, or Sweden, planned Juliet's travelling mind and feet.

By now, she had walked so fast and far, Juliet didn't know exactly where she was and that's what she wanted from her day and life in general. Her inner mind was relaxed, proud of herself and on an alternative dimension. Do we ever know why we do anything? Are we primarily led by thoughts or energies? Similar metaphysical thoughts eclipsed her mind until an annoying barking dog broke the focus.

Inside Juliet's dynamic mind, a realignment of chakras had taken place. She paused to figure out which way to go. Home was behind her, but her brain said keep walking for reasons unknown. She felt weird. Walking without a purpose often can. Her legs were perambulating on intuition and Juliet's senses felt on full alert. A casual walk now became about the curiosity of self-learning and discovery. It was a little scary as most new phenomena is. Try and let things happen naturally.

You don't search for love, you find it by accident like all beautiful things.

A short while into the voyage of her mind, nothing transpired as obviously mystical or untoward, so Juliet decided it was nothing and probably just her imagination. The supernatural feeling wasn't pretend though as the universe called Juliet using an unfamiliar language. Subsequently, the obvious tapping on her mind's shoulder had naturally been replaced by doubt and confusion. It's hard to see the invisible, but if you open your mind to anything, then anything can happen.

Her previously pleasant walk now dragged along. Juliet just wanted to go home now and finish packing, so found a main street and hailed a cab. The cabby was annoying too. He drove slowly and kept looking at her in the rear-view mirror hoping their eyes would meet. What the fuck did he actually think was going to happen; that she would suck him off for a free ride?

Turns out married and faithful for 32 years Richard (known as **DICK**) only kept looking because he'd just bought a Time Magazine resting on the passenger seat, but was too respectful to intrude.

An uncomfortable silence slanted Juliet's head towards the window. She saw a dog walker tripping over their pet's lead which made her laugh at lot inside. The owner didn't seem hurt, just mortally embarrassed. The cabby saw too and burst out laughing, "Sorry lady, I just couldn't help laughing at that guy. Did you see him?"

"Yes," replied Juliet.

"It was funny," said Dick.

"Yes, it was," confirmed Juliet, thinking *here we go*.

"I once had a really friendly mongrel called Tiger we got from a rescue centre who used to get so excited he'd run the lead around you in circles and tie your legs up! Did it once when I was at a cash machine and the money came out and some little shit grabbed it and ran away. I miss that dog though. Been 2 years 3 months since he got the cancer and had to be put down. Worse day of my life. I'd honestly rather it was me than him," explained Dick in a monologue fashion.

"I'm very sorry to hear that. Can't be easy losing a member of your family," sympathized Juliet.

"No it really wasn't. Worst day of my life," Dick said with a long sigh and deep breath.

You already fucking said that literally 10 seconds ago, thought Juliet, who instead said, "Sorry, I don't know what to say."

"Nothing to say. Just miss the little rascal terribly." A long pause followed an upbeat change of mood and Dick said, "Still, life goes on! Onwards and upwards as they say. No point going barking mad over a dog. Ha haaa! Do ya get it?"

"Yes, I get it," replied a dull sounding Juliet.

"What's up miss? I mean I hope you don't mind me asking but I've had a house full of daughters fly the nest and I can spot unresolved problems a kilometre away. My eldest Emma once got caught up with this nasty guy and I gave him a right good thumping."

"What did he do?" asked Juliet.

"Cheated on her while she was pregnant. Got rid of him for good I'm pleased to say. She got over it in the end thankfully. Picked a much nicer man. We're happy with him. Anyway, like I was saying I've become known for being a bit of an agony aunt on wheels, haa! The other cabbies call me Dick Tracy. People know they're unlikely to see me again so spill their heart out and sometimes guts too, ha! I've heard and seen everything under the sun, you belieeeve me. What's your poison as they say?"

"Isn't that about drinks?" questioned Juliet sarcastically.

"Oh yeah, I get muddled up sometimes because of an early Alzheimers condition. Still OK to drive though, so don't worry. Won't suddenly forget where the brakes are, ha ha!" Dick had reached an age where he had to prepare his mind to move his body.

Oh *fucking-hell* thought Juliet, wishing she'd never gone for a walk now. She was just about to ask him to pull over for health and safety reasons, but mainly not to listen to his drivel anymore, when she figured fuck it, perhaps this was some ironic destiny she was meant to experience so let's give Dick a chance – but not in *that* way.

"Actually, I do have a problem maybe you could help me with?" prospected Juliet.

"Oh really? That's great news, I mean bad news, ha, but happy to help," joked Dick as his eyes lit up. He loved helping a damsel in distress and full credit to him, in all his driving years never once got sleazy.

"Fantastic. You ready?" asked Juliet with an open mind.

"Fire away!"

"I went for a walk because I was looking for a higher purpose. I know, sounds stupid right?" said Juliet relying on never seeing Dick again.

"No, no, give yourself a chance to breathe. Carry on please; you mean like God?" encouraged Dick in a fatherly way. Juliet really missed her dad so started to warm towards his steady approach.

"More like the meaning of my life than God and it felt like I was searching for something," continued Juliet.

"Sounds like me and my damn glasses case, ha! But you didn't find it obviously. I think I get what you're saying. My guess is it was there because you felt it but you couldn't see it or understand how to find it. Am I right?"

"Exactly! Yes you are," for once thought Juliet.

"Sounds like my wife's man in the boat, haa haaa ha!" Juliet was not impressed. She'd had enough of boats for the time being. "Sorry. Give me a sec' to think… So you just walked around the streets and nothing stood out to you?"

"Not really," replied Juliet.

"This is because you're looking for something that can't be seen," said mystical Dick.

"Maybe?"

"So don't think through your eyes then. Hold on, let me pull over so I don't crash," said Dick beeping his horn at oncoming traffic so he could park.

"Good idea," agreed Juliet.

"I used to play this game with my youngest for fun so we could connect and learn about each other on a, erm… 'a higher level' I suppose you would say. Close your eyes and answer my questions straight away with only one or two words, without any thought whatsoever!" told Dick in an unusually sharp manner.

"Okay."

"No thinking. Clear your mind," double-checked Dick.

"Clear," confirmed Juliet.

"What did you see?"

"Yellow cab."

"What did you smell?"

"Coffee."

"What did you taste?"

"Fear."

"What did you touch?"

"Flower."

"What did you hear?"

"God."

"What did you feel?"

"Hunger."

"That's it. Now open your eyes. Those undercover answers should give the game away. Let me just get my trusted $1 fountain pen and write it down," said Dick going through a process of elimination: "Yellow cab; no you're in one. Coffee; way too obvious. Fear, we all have that. Flowers, maybe baby? Dog barking, an echo perhaps? Hunger, you're probably just hungry. Are you hungry?"

"Yes," Juliet said politely but was thinking, yes, hungry for the flipping answer please Cryptic Dick!

"I'm sorry, shall we take a break and get you some food and drink?" he asked.

"I'm fine thanks, in need of another coffee but really want you to do your truth finding thing please."

"Right you are, where was I then?"

"Hunger, at fucking hunger!" stressed-out Juliet.

Now there's one thing Dick didn't like to hear from his daughters was swearing. It grated on him and he explained with feeling, "I don't really like swearing from a lady if I was to be honest with you…"

"It's Juliet. I'm very sorry Dick, it's been a long day," apologised Juliet, thinking, you could use a dose of Twitter buddy to get into this century.

"It's only just gone 9am," laughed Dick.

Juliet just gave him a blank expression and said, "Lack of coffee. We were at *hunger*."

Dick mouthed out the words again to himself written on his newspaper and said, "So that leaves Flower and God."

"Great, so what does that mean?" Juliet asked in hopeful anticipation.

"I don't know." Juliet was feeling very frustrated. Was Dick just taking the piss? He could see she seemed agitated. "Just be patient. All good things come to those who wait. Flower God is what we've got. What could that mean?"

"I have no idea, what that could mean?" asked Juliet very rapidly and sarcastically.

"Patience is a virtue. Let's do a little crossword jiggery-pokery, anagrams and stuff." Dick was a crossword ace, although you wouldn't know it by talking to him. "The God of flowers is Chloris I believe, sounds a touch like… OK skip that. Hold on, I'm getting there…"

"Please get there Dick," pleaded Juliet, not intending a pun.

"What if we do it from behind?" muttered Dick to himself.

"I knew that's what you wanted!" exclaimed Juliet in a muddle.

"No, no, don't be silly. From backwards. Like this, watch." He then tore the written clues section out, turned it the other way round to get the reverse view and held it up against his window. "That's it! I got it. It's a Semordnilhap."

"What's that again when you're at home?" Juliet mocked.

"Palindromes backwards. It means when a word spells a different word backwards, like desserts and stressed," explained Dick.

"Yes I'm stressed and need a dessert," japed Juliet.

"Haa, haaa, ha! Brilliant Juliet, that was funny. Getting to like you now. Didn't before. Right, let's see. So Flower God backwards is Rewolf Dog. Just stick a hyphen in there and *hey presto*, you've got your answer! It's re or *about* the WOLFDOG."

"Wolfdog," repeated Juliet bemused.

"Yes, did you come across any dogs on your walk before you met me?"

"No. I just saw that one who tripped the tall guy over."

"You sure?" questioned Dick.

"Yes! No. I heard a dog barking," recalled Juliet.

"That's your destiny then! We made it in the end. Can you remember where you heard the barking?"

"Yes, but I can't remember how to get there," unhelpfully answered Juliet. "Oh, there was a cherry tree leaning right into the road I recall."

"Aha, I think I know just the road you're talking about. Do pick-ups from around there all the time. None half as petal pretty as you though. Let's go back, investigate and solve this mystery," offered Dick Tracy because the meter was still running.

"Thank you Dick," said Juliet appreciating the genuine, non-creepy compliment. Dad used to say similar inspirited remarks to her all the time.

If you pay a woman a compliment, the first thing they do is research whether you pay other women compliments. When did uplifting women become a crime?

As soon as they found the correct location, low-and-behold the dog started barking again after a minute of Juliet sniffing around. As she got closer to a large black painted iron gate where the barks echoed through, the trapped dog howled for help from behind the house. "I'll be back!" Juliet shouted with Arnold Schwarzenegger persistence.

She ran back to the cab to tell Dick she'd found the dog, but Dick only had time to take her money. The fare was not cheap. His wife called saying her hairdryer was on fire and burning the bed. Plus Dick could now afford a few weeks holiday after securing his biggest payday ever in the bag: hours later, after dumping a mattress with a burn hole in it, Dick called all the papers and described his encounter with Juliet Jessica Green, who he recognised immediately, recording the whole conversation. Sometimes acting stupid can work to your distinct advantage.

Juliet was reported in the media as mentally unstable and when news of her stealing a coffee and running away added to the morning's events, Juliet's global status plummeted right down to where Greta Thunberg's was; half the country hated her and the other half loved her, just like her enemy Trump.

Dick did feel bad but $20,000 US dollars for the hot story to pay for his middle daughter's wedding and Bahamas trip, made him feel less bad. Lovely he thought, that was his destiny! And what a nice man thought Juliet, who'd returned to the gate, climbed over and heard a dog in pain who was locked in a small wooden shed. The owners were clearly not home and the dog whimpered to her words, "Wait there little doggy, I'll be back to get you out, I promise." The dog fell silent so must have understood English.

The door was heavily locked and the tools she needed to break her way in were inside the shed with nothing useful looking anywhere in the garden. She needed help and had no phone. Clambering back over the gate – now adding burglar to her media resume – Juliet remembered a bunch of builders further down the road who gave her some filthy chants and wolf whistles earlier. Let's turn these jerks into something useful, thought Juliet.

The mostly young lads spotted her coming again and repeated the same tiresome routine every woman got, proving how little they understood women and explaining why only one of them had a steady girlfriend. The older boss let them do it because it was good for morale, he justified. Half the women walking by liked the attention and the other half hated the harassment. Juliet was indifferent as she walked up to site manager **AUSTIN** who was making the coffee.

"Could I have one of these bricks please guys," asked Juliet nicely.
"Gonna need more than that to build yourself a house," mocked Austin trying to look all smart in front of the guys.

A short, cocky and stocky young brickie fresh out of high school then stepped forward for a laugh and actually said, "You can have anything you want sweetcheeks! Like 'em hard do ya?" The men jeered, but Austin looked apologetic feeling consequences were coming.

Juliet picked up one the coffees on a stack of bricks ready to be handed out to the group of mugs and commanded, "Hold your hands out boy." He did like a beggar with background laddish murmurs and jibes propping him up.

"Oww, ouchhhh!" screamed the builder bloke like a little girl as Juliet filled his hands up with boiling hot coffee. "What the fuck ja do that for!?" he cried like a mommy's boy who needed a plaster. All his mates laughed their heads off with raucous gaffaw.

Juliet paused until he'd finished whimpering and said, "I like my men hot as well as hard!" and everyone pissed themselves laughing apart from the man turned boy.

Juliet then picked up the brick and walked away shaking her booty and would you believe it, not one man whistled or perved, they just stood there silent and gawped in idolization.

"Ever seen the movie Lost in Translation?" asked Austin.

"No," replied the scolded lad going for some plasters.

"You need to," advised Austin, who secretly had quite a sensitive side.

Back in the unkempt garden, Juliet couldn't smash the lock off with the brick, so instead began shattering the side panels of wood into pieces until eventually the desperate dog could stick his noble head out through the hole to get comforted by Juliet.

Their eyes met along with their souls. He pushed hard and she pulled with all her might and rusty nails broke free. The cute little doggy was a massive wolfdog and Juliet hugged him like a huge soft teddy bear.

She felt his undernourished ribs and checked his teeth. It was a clear case of animal abuse; no question. Forget the ASPCA assessed Juliet because she instantly fell in love with the magnificent creature sent by higher forces.

"I shall call you **APOLLO** because a wine hangover brought you here," announced Juliet getting confused with her Greek Gods. Apollo then licked her and ran over to the shed, scraping at the doormat. "What's that boy? What you trying to tell me?" Lifting up the mat she saw the key to the shed and Apollo put his paw over his eyes in embarrassment. "Mommy makes mistakes okay?"

Using a pair of ladders from the shed, Apollo managed to climb up and jump into Juliet's arms who got squashed like a beanbag under a horse. He licked her face to say thanks and then did a massive poop outside his former owner's front door. Apollo the huge wolfdog was destined to be saved by Juliet and – unawares to her – had a higher purpose in the grand scheme of things.

The newfound best friends walked all the way home to her apartment without any wrong turns because dogs are fucking spooky with shit like that. Juliet sneaked Apollo in because no pets were allowed. After eating 12 hotdogs, 3 bags of chips, a block of cheese and drinking 3 litres of water, Apollo lay down on a rug like he'd been living there for years and comfortably farted. Juliet laughed and sat down at the piano to entertain him in return.

Playing the beautiful first movement of Beethoven's Moonlight Sonata healed Apollo's tortured heart and he fell asleep on the final pillow settling notes. A calm musical silence rested in the air. God was Julie happy. Life is so unbelievably interesting and brilliant sometimes, she fathomed into her soul. Why can't it always be that way? She felt truly at peace looking at Apollo sleeping until the unimaginable happened.

"Oh shit!" she complained loudly, pricking-up Apollo's ears. "I've done exactly what my mother did!!" Rushing over to Apollo now waking, Juliet stroked and cuddled him, and asked repeatedly with humility, "You don't feel kidnapped do you boy?"

She got Apollo some extra tasty treats and it was plain to all and sundry that his honest answer was, no, he did not feel stolen from someone's garden whose lawyer owners left their dog in the trusted care of their cleaner while they were on holiday, who took the opportunity to steal her employees precious belongings, returning to Puerto Rico after locking Apollo in the shed last week.

Juliet was more worried about the flack she'd receive from mother for equally stealing a pet, than the morality or truth. It wasn't like her to shy from the truth but sometimes you have to just do what is best for you.

Besides, Juliet didn't know it but she was now a divine conduit. Apollo's rescue/kidnapping was ordained by celestial influences we will never understand. The next journey in the never-ending war against evil needed Apollo's bravery and backbone. This majestic canine was destined for the enchanting Orient, not as supper, but loyal protector of Abigail in her quest to root-out and destroy Professor Zinkel's plans for worldwide tyranny of innocent people.

I cannot stress enough the importance of always defending yourself throughout life. The second you drop your guard or go quiet with apathy, the wolves will tear you apart.

It's shit to find out you're similar to one or both of your parents because their failures are the perfect excuse for you to give up when times get tough. Juliet looked in a mirror and saw mother Shirley looking back. She eventually calmed down. Regardless, what she'd recently achieved was nothing short of phenomenal. Feeling proud is underrated these days. Juliet felt the kinetic power of success moving her mind forward. Fighting with mom and her extended family over the years had no less given Juliet the fighting spirit of a lioness!

In a quiet moment of confidence – locking her fingers together – Juliet understood that everything in her life had happened for a reason. She was the sum of all the parts of pain and paradise ground in together, seasoning life with her unique experiences.

She knew that everyone is unique. Only those who believe and explore their individuality find more happiness. You look for others to entertain and inspire you when your mere presence should generate inspiration from within! How ironic the main person who can stop you achieving your dreams is you.

Juliet's mind was expanding like it was playing stepping-stones on the night's stars. Whereas before she paralysed any rancour with sharper venom, now Juliet was beginning to get into the idea of giving everyone love, including the people who hate you.

To love yourself is the beginning of kindness.

Front cover illustration: *L'Amour de Pierrot*, The Love of Pierrot, 1920, oils.

Back cover painting: *Metamorphosis of Narcissus*, Salvador Dali, 1937, oil on canvas, 51.2cm x 78.1cm, Tate Modern, London.

Printed in Poland
by Amazon Fulfillment
Poland Sp. z o.o., Wrocław